THE HEAVENLY FUGITIVE

BOOKS BY GILBERT MORRIS

Through a Glass Darkly

THE HOUSE OF WINSLOW SERIES

1. *The Honorable Imposter*
2. *The Captive Bride*
3. *The Indentured Heart*
4. *The Gentle Rebel*
5. *The Saintly Buccaneer*
6. *The Holy Warrior*
7. *The Reluctant Bridegroom*
8. *The Last Confederate*
9. *The Dixie Widow*
10. *The Wounded Yankee*
11. *The Union Belle*
12. *The Final Adversary*
13. *The Crossed Sabres*
14. *The Valiant Gunman*
15. *The Gallant Outlaw*
16. *The Jeweled Spur*
17. *The Yukon Queen*
18. *The Rough Rider*
19. *The Iron Lady*
20. *The Silver Star*
21. *The Shadow Portrait*
22. *The White Hunter*
23. *The Flying Cavalier*
24. *The Glorious Prodigal*
25. *The Amazon Quest*
26. *The Golden Angel*
27. *The Heavenly Fugitive*

THE LIBERTY BELL

1. *Sound the Trumpet*
2. *Song in a Strange Land*
3. *Tread Upon the Lion*
4. *Arrow of the Almighty*
5. *Wind From the Wilderness*
6. *The Right Hand of God*
7. *Command the Sun*

CHENEY DUVALL, M.D.[1]

1. *The Stars for a Light*
2. *Shadow of the Mountains*
3. *A City Not Forsaken*
4. *Toward the Sunrising*
5. *Secret Place of Thunder*
6. *In the Twilight, in the Evening*
7. *Island of the Innocent*
8. *Driven With the Wind*

CHENEY AND SHILOH: THE INHERITANCE[1]

1. *Where Two Seas Met*

THE SPIRIT OF APPALACHIA[2]

1. *Over the Misty Mountains*
2. *Beyond the Quiet Hills*
3. *Among the King's Soldiers*
4. *Beneath the Mockingbird's Wings*
5. *Around the River's Bend*

TIME NAVIGATORS
(for Young Teens)

1. *Dangerous Voyage*

2. *Vanishing Clues*

[1]with Lynn Morris   [2]with Aaron McCarver

THE
HEAVENLY
FUGITIVE

★

GILBERT MORRIS

BETHANYHOUSE
PUBLISHERS
MINNEAPOLIS, MINNESOTA

The Heavenly Fugitive
Copyright © 2002
Gilbert Morris

Cover illustration by Bill Graf
Cover design by Eric Walljasper

Published by Bethany House Publishers
A Ministry of Bethany Fellowship International
11400 Hampshire Avenue South
Bloomington, Minnesota 55438
www.bethanyhouse.com

Printed in the United States of America by
Bethany Press International, Bloomington, Minnesota 55438

Library of Congress Cataloging-in-Publication Data

Morris, Gilbert.
    The heavenly fugitive / by Gilbert Morris.
        p.   cm.
    ISBN 0-7642-2599-5 (pbk.)
    1. Winslow family (Fictitious characters)—Fiction. 2. Brothers and sisters—Fiction. 3. Organized crime—Fiction. 4. New York (N.Y.)—Fiction. I. Title.
    PS3563.O8742   H43   2002
    813'.54—dc21   2001005678

GILBERT MORRIS spent ten years as a pastor before becoming Professor of English at Ouachita Baptist University in Arkansas and earning a Ph.D. at the University of Arkansas. During the summers of 1984 and 1985, he did postgraduate work at the University of London. A prolific writer, he has had over 25 scholarly articles and 200 poems published in various periodicals, and over the past years has had more than 70 novels published. His family includes three grown children, and he and his wife live in Alabama.

CONTENTS

PART FOUR
April–July 1927

THE HOUSE OF WINSLOW

★ ★ ★ ★

THE HOUSE OF WINSLOW

★ ★ ★ ★

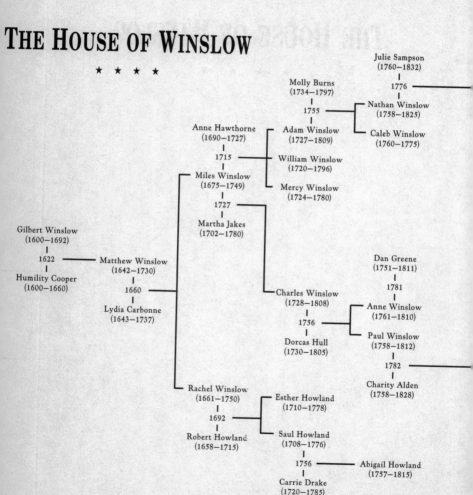

Gilbert Winslow
(1600–1692)
1622
Humility Cooper
(1600–1660)

Matthew Winslow
(1642–1730)
1660
Lydia Carbonne
(1643–1737)

Miles Winslow
(1675–1749)
1727
Martha Jakes
(1702–1780)

Anne Hawthorne
(1690–1727)
1715

Adam Winslow
(1727–1809)
1755

Molly Burns
(1734–1797)

William Winslow
(1720–1796)

Mercy Winslow
(1724–1780)

Julie Sampson
(1760–1832)
1776

Nathan Winslow
(1758–1825)

Caleb Winslow
(1760–1775)

Charles Winslow
(1728–1808)
1756
Dorcas Hull
(1730–1805)

Dan Greene
(1751–1811)
1781

Anne Winslow
(1761–1810)

Paul Winslow
(1758–1812)
1782

Charity Alden
(1758–1828)

Rachel Winslow
(1661–1750)
1692
Robert Howland
(1658–1715)

Esther Howland
(1710–1778)

Saul Howland
(1708–1776)
1756
Carrie Drake
(1720–1785)

Abigail Howland
(1757–1815)

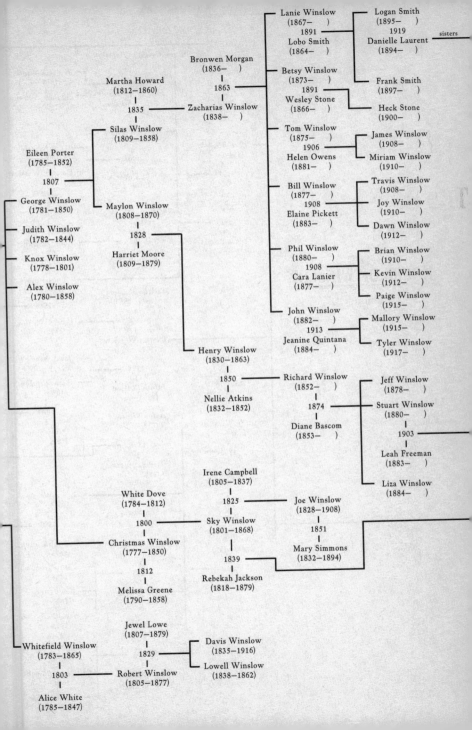

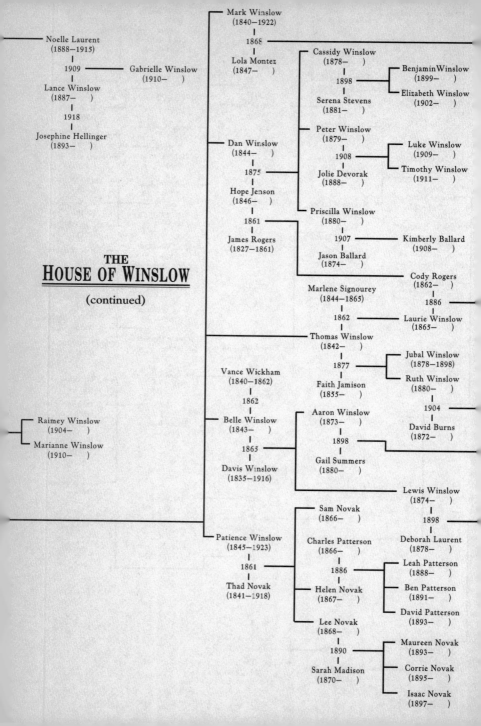

THE
HOUSE OF WINSLOW

(continued)

Noelle Laurent
(1888–1915)
|
1909 —————— Gabrielle Winslow
(1910–)
|
Lance Winslow
(1887–)
|
1918
|
Josephine Hellinger
(1893–)

Raimey Winslow
(1904–)
Marianne Winslow
(1910–)

Mark Winslow
(1840–1922)
|
1868
|
Lola Montez
(1847–)

Dan Winslow
(1844–)
|
1875
|
Hope Jenson
(1846–)

1861
|
James Rogers
(1827–1861)

Marlene Signourey
(1844–1865)
|
1862

Thomas Winslow
(1842–)
|
1877
|
Faith Jamison
(1855–)

Vance Wickham
(1840–1862)
|
1862
|
Belle Winslow
(1843–)
|
1865
|
Davis Winslow
(1835–1916)

Patience Winslow
(1845–1923)
|
1861
|
Thad Novak
(1841–1918)

Cassidy Winslow
(1878–)
|
1898
|
Serena Stevens
(1881–)

Peter Winslow
(1879–)
|
1908
|
Jolie Devorak
(1888–)

Priscilla Winslow
(1880–)
|
1907
|
Jason Ballard
(1874–)

Cody Rogers
(1862–)
|
1886
|
Laurie Winslow
(1865–)

Jubal Winslow
(1878–1898)
Ruth Winslow
(1880–)
|
1904
|
David Burns
(1872–)

Aaron Winslow
(1873–)
|
1898
|
Gail Summers
(1880–)

Lewis Winslow
(1874–)
|
1898
|
Deborah Laurent
(1878–)

Sam Novak
(1866–)

Charles Patterson
(1866–)
|
1886
|
Helen Novak
(1867–)

Lee Novak
(1868–)
|
1890
|
Sarah Madison
(1870–)

BenjaminWinslow
(1899–)
Elizabeth Winslow
(1902–)

Luke Winslow
(1909–)
Timothy Winslow
(1911–)

Kimberly Ballard
(1908–)

Leah Patterson
(1888–)
Ben Patterson
(1891–)
David Patterson
(1893–)

Maureen Novak
(1893–)
Corrie Novak
(1895–)
Isaac Novak
(1897–)

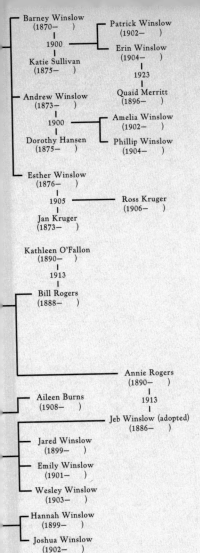

Barney Winslow
(1870—   )

Patrick Winslow
(1902—   )

1900

Erin Winslow
(1904—   )

Katie Sullivan
(1875—   )

1923

Andrew Winslow
(1873—   )

Quaid Merritt
(1896—   )

1900

Amelia Winslow
(1902—   )

Dorothy Hansen
(1875—   )

Phillip Winslow
(1904—   )

Esther Winslow
(1876—   )

1905

Ross Kruger
(1906—   )

Jan Kruger
(1873—   )

Kathleen O'Fallon
(1890—   )

1913

Bill Rogers
(1888—   )

Annie Rogers
(1890—   )

1913

Aileen Burns
(1908—   )

Jeb Winslow (adopted)
(1886—   )

Jared Winslow
(1899—   )

Emily Winslow
(1901—   )

Wesley Winslow
(1903—   )

Hannah Winslow
(1899—   )

Joshua Winslow
(1902—   )

November 1923–June 1924

★ ★ ★

CHAPTER ONE

A SPOILED BEAUTY

★ ★ ★ ★

New York City
November 1923

A series of harsh cries caught Phillip Winslow's attention. He turned to watch four black crows arise from a field with a great flapping of wings, then alight on the branches of a leafless oak tree. Its bare limbs cast long shadows across the frozen ground to where he stood. He shivered in the cold air and went on his way, slapping his hands together and whistling a favorite hymn. The old hymns kept him from getting too homesick for his parents in Africa, where he'd spent his childhood. He wondered how his sister, Amelia, was doing—if she was enjoying life in the States as much as he.

Phillip had quickly adjusted to the faster pace in New York, and after living there for over a year, he had even adopted the American preference for nicknames, gladly answering now to "Phil" and asking everyone to call him that. He had always been a good student and a hard worker, so his college studies were stimulating, and his job at the Thornton Stables provided the physical work his manly young body needed. Except for missing his parents, who now pastored a church in Nairobi, he loved his new life in America. But he worried about Amelia.

When he reached the whitewashed barn of the Thornton

Stables, he made his way inside and down a line of horse stalls. The smell of horses, leather, and feed had become so normal to him he no longer noticed the odor. Stopping before one of the stalls, he looked at a sleek Arabian mare, who stared back at him with cold arrogance.

"Ready for your trip, girl?" The horse gave him a snorting reply. He picked up a bridle and cautiously opened the stall door, waiting to see what the mare would do. When she merely stared at him, he laughed. "You're in a better mood this morning. Yesterday you tried to wipe up the floor with me." He stepped forward, grateful when she accepted the bridle. Slapping her on the neck, he said, "That's a good girl. Come along, now. You're going to your new home."

He led the mare out of the stable to a horse trailer hitched to the back of a truck. He cautiously guided her up the wooden ramp into the open door of the trailer, admiring her sleek coat, which glistened like sunlight on water. To his surprise she entered the trailer without hesitation. He closed the door and stepped back to take one last look at her before delivering her to her new owner. He had longed to put a saddle on her and try her out himself, but his boss, Luke DeSalvo, had refused to let any of the stable hands ride this particular animal. She had been kept for a special customer.

Phil turned and walked over to a small brick building, the downstairs of which housed the office for the stables and the upstairs a small apartment for DeSalvo. The door opened before he reached it, and the manager stepped out to greet him. DeSalvo was a short, stocky man with muscular legs and arms and almost no neck. He wore a pair of faded corduroy trousers, old rubber boots, and a tattered sweater. He thrust a clipboard toward Phil and, chomping on his ever-present cigar, growled at him, "Here, college boy. See you don't let nothin' happen to that mare."

Taking the clipboard, Phil read the order. He smiled and said, "Boadicea, huh? That's a pretty fancy name for a horse."

DeSalvo rolled the cigar around in his mouth with his tongue and studied Winslow. He had not wanted to take on the young man, who had seemed too educated, in his opinion, to work at the stables. He had told the owner, "He won't last. The first time he has to muck out the stalls he'll be outta here." Phil had proved him wrong, however, for he had cheerfully mucked out stalls and never complained about the dozens of other chores DeSalvo heaped on him. Now that he was in college and had to study every day, Phil couldn't come to work until midafternoon, but he willingly worked late into the evening when necessary to get all the chores finished.

For all his gruffness, DeSalvo admired the young Winslow and couldn't figure out what such a bright young man was doing working at the Thornton Stables. He eyed the nineteen-year-old briefly and took in his tall, lean physique and ruddy complexion. Much outdoor living in his years growing up in Africa had made Phil strong. Strands of auburn hair stuck out from under his cap, and he had the most penetrating green eyes DeSalvo had ever seen. He wore a pair of faded blue trousers, a striped shirt without a collar, a gray waistcoat fastened by two buttons, and rubber work boots.

Phil looked up and said, "Ten Oaks. Where's that, Mr. DeSalvo?"

"Just the other side of the Jamison place, where you took the gray stallion last Thursday. Ten Oaks is about a mile beyond that, back off the road, with a big black iron fence around it."

"Yes. I know the place."

DeSalvo removed his cigar, studied it as if it were a valuable jewel, then jammed it back into his mouth. He drew on it until the end glowed a cherry red and nodded. "Keep your mouth shut when you're there, college boy. There's some real tough hairpins in that place."

Startled by this revelation, Phil focused on the stubby manager, waiting for some explanation. When none was forthcoming, he asked, "What do you mean 'tough hairpins'?"

"This mare belongs to Tony Morino," DeSalvo said with a snort. "You ever hear of him?"

"No. Don't think so."

DeSalvo laughed. "Well, you don't know everything, college boy. He's a tough one, but he's managed to stay out of jail."

"You mean he's a criminal?"

"He's never been convicted, but everybody knows he's a big-time bootlegger, and he's got his finger in other pies, too. He runs with a rough crowd, so mind your manners." He paused then and almost turned to go back in the office, but curiosity touched his gray eyes. "What are you doing mucking out stables, anyway? A college boy like you could get a cleaner job."

"I like being around horses. One of the things I miss about my home in Africa."

"What kind of horses they got in Africa?"

"Same as here. Some fine ones like that mare and some not so fine."

DeSalvo grunted. "Well, get on your way. Mind what I told you."

"Okay, Mr. DeSalvo."

The manager watched Winslow climb into the truck and start the engine. As the truck pulled away, a tall, heavyset man with blunt features approached DeSalvo and grinned broadly. "What's Joe College doin' now? He don't look like much man to me."

"What would you know about it, Cotton!" DeSalvo spat. "If you had his brains, you'd be in velvet! Why, I showed that young Winslow the stud book last week, and he just leafed through it and memorized that mare's bloodlines all the way back to Adam. I couldn't believe it. He's got a memory like flypaper!"

Cotton wasn't convinced by the boss's defense of Winslow. "Some kind of foreigner, ain't he?" Cotton grumbled. "Why didn't he stay where he come from?"

"Go feed those horses, Cotton!" DeSalvo grunted and stepped back into the office. Despite his praise of Winslow, he too wondered about the young man. *Funny guy. Smart as a whip but don't mind muckin' out stalls. Not many like that around. . . .*

★　★　★　★

Following DeSalvo's instructions, Phil drove past the Jamison place and a mile farther down the road spotted the black iron fence. The house was set back off the road, and the driveway was lined with large oak trees reaching their naked limbs into the sky—*Like they're praying*, Phil thought. He stopped at the front gate and got out, leaving the engine running. There was no sign with a name on it, but he knew this had to be the Morino estate. He punched a button but heard no bell. He waited, glancing around at the woods that surrounded the property. A blue jay lit above him, proclaiming his presence loudly, his bright colors shining brilliantly against the dead grays and browns of the trees. Hearing footsteps, Phil turned and saw a small man approach the gate. He was bundled up in a heavy plaid coat with a soft cap pulled down over his forehead.

"What'cha want, eh?" The question was shot at Phil like a bullet from a gun.

"I'm delivering a mare for Mr. Morino from the Thornton Stables."

"You got a paper that says so?"

"Right here."

Phil shoved the invoice through the bars and watched as the man scanned it suspiciously. Apparently satisfied, he handed it back and unlocked the gate. Phil had started back to the truck when the guard's gruff command halted him. "Hold it right there, Mac!"

The man walked toward him and said, "I'll have to frisk you."

"Frisk me? What for?"

The guard's cold gray eyes twinkled at Phil's confusion. "Gotta see if you're packin' a gat."

"What's a gat?"

"Don't give me that, kid! I ain't got time for games." The man ran his hands up and down Phil's body.

Remembering DeSalvo's instructions, Phil kept still. When the inspection was over, he smiled and asked, "Am I okay?"

"I'll have to check the truck and trailer."

Phil walked back to the truck and waited while the man checked under the seats and inspected the horse trailer.

"Okay," the guard said, turning. "You can go on in."

"Where are the stables?"

"Take that road up to the house. Bear to the left and circle around. You'll find them out behind in a big field. Ask for O'Connor. He takes care of the horses."

"Thanks."

Getting back into the truck, Phil was amused at being the object of such suspicion, but he had read enough detective novels to recognize the methods of gangsters. Now he was even more curious about Morino, but he knew he'd better be careful. The guard's businesslike attitude and steely eyes warned Phil that he was walking into a potentially dangerous situation.

He chuckled to himself as he made his way to the stables and thought, *Maybe I'll get to see a real live American gangster. I've heard about all the bootleggers but never thought I might meet one!*

★   ★   ★   ★

A white ball rolled across the green felt, struck a red ball sharply, and sent it toward the pocket, where it disappeared with a heavy *plunk!* The girl who had made the shot nodded with satisfaction at her younger brother. Fifteen-year-old Rosa Morino shook her lustrous ebony hair and grinned, a sparkle of mischief in her enormous dark eyes. She moved around the table with the awkward grace of an adolescent and made shot after shot. When she had cleared the table, she racked up the balls for a new game, but the noise of a truck backfiring caught her ear. She slammed the cue down on the table and ran to the window. "Jamie, she's here! My horse is here!"

Leaving her brother and running out of the billiard room, Rosa dashed down the hall but halted at the sound of her father's voice coming from an open door. "Where are you going, Rosa?"

Rosa stepped into her father's study, her eyes flashing, and cried out, "It's my mare! She's here, Daddy! I'm going to ride her right now!"

"Oh no you're not, young lady! Not until O'Connor checks her out."

Rosa's father rose from his desk chair and came toward her. A daunting figure, he was a solid man with heavy legs and arms and massive fists. He had a round face with blunt features and a ragged scar that traced its way down his right cheek and along the jawline. The scar was the result of a run-in with a horse, not a brawl. He had been kicked, but as was typical of him when it came to animals, he had insisted it was his fault, not the horse's.

Big Tony Morino was more understanding of animals than of

human beings. He had come to this country as a child speaking only Italian and had fought his way up through childhood on the tough streets of New York City's Lower East Side. He had managed to stay out of the clutches of the law except for one thirty-day bout behind bars, but after that month of incarceration, the crafty Morino had determined to find a way to get rich without going to jail for it. He now ruled over several organized gangs of bootleggers in New York City, along with five or six other kingpins.

Though Morino was a fearsome man to anyone who crossed him in his business dealings, to Rosa he was simply her father, and she was not afraid to plead with him to let her see the horse right away.

The hardwood floor shook with his weight as he crossed it and stood face-to-face with Rosa. "No riding until O'Connor's checked her out," he bellowed.

Rosa was hardly fazed by his stern demeanor. "Oh, Daddy!"

"You mind what I say, Rosa. O'Connor said that horse is too lively for you."

"I can ride her!"

"Maybe you can, but you're not going to yet. Now, you mind your father." His dark scowl relaxed a bit as he reached out and tenderly tugged a lock of Rosa's black hair. Her skinny, girlish shape had given way to womanly curves, and she looked stunning in a pair of dark blue jodhpurs, a wine-colored jersey, and shiny riding boots. Big Tony took special pride in her beauty, and he often gave in to her pleading expressions, but this time he refused to let her get the better of him completely. "You can look at her—but no riding without O'Connor. And that's final!"

"Oh, all right, Daddy." She suddenly threw herself against him and kissed him on the cheek, her eyes sparkling. "Thank you so much, Daddy. It's the nicest present anyone ever got!"

"Well, go along now," Tony said, pleased at her embrace. She was an affectionate girl, and as she wheeled and ran out of the room, he realized how much of his heart was in this girl on the brink of womanhood. His first wife had given him no children, and after her death Tony had married Maria, who had quickly given him two—Rosa, followed two years later by James. Tony never minded interruptions from his family, and he was especially happy when Rosa was around. Now he moved back to his desk and perused his list of business contacts.

Before long he was interrupted again—this time by his wife. He looked up as she entered the room and smiled at her. "The mare is here, Maria. Rosa's already gone out to look at her."

Maria Morino crossed the large study and stood beside her husband. She was a trim woman of forty—nearly twenty years younger than her husband. She had been raised in a conservative home, and her family had been horrified when she had announced her engagement to Big Tony Morino. Although she had introduced him as Mr. Anthony Morino, they knew who he was and what he did for a living. They had done all they could to prevent her from marrying a gangster but to no avail. Maria could not explain it to herself. She had turned down many more suitable men, and her family feared she would never marry. But then Big Tony had simply swept her off her feet. She was happy in her marriage and proud to have given Tony two fine children. She was grieved at his illegal activities but had never tried to interfere in his work. It was one area of his life she could not touch. She knew the nature of his work when she married him, but she couldn't help loving him for who he was at home. He was always kind to her and loved his family as much as any man could. There was nothing he wouldn't do for them. He was also a patriotic man who loved America with a passion. He proudly carried the American flag in parades and attended Fourth of July speeches, applauding with his ponderous hands and whistling at the oratories extolling the virtues of his adopted country.

"I'm worried about that horse," Maria said. "O'Connor tells me she'll be a handful for Rosa."

"Rosa can handle her," Tony said confidently.

"But she's barely fifteen."

"She's been riding since she was six years old, Maria. She's ridden everything we've ever had on the place with four legs, even that big dog we had when she was a little mite." Tony grinned. He stood up and hugged his wife. "She'll be all right, dear. I won't let her ride the mare until O'Connor says she's ready. You should have seen her just now. She's so happy."

Maria reached up and touched his cheek, and when he kissed her, she said reluctantly, "You're so sweet, Tony, but I worry about Rosa. She's quite spoiled, you know. A spoiled brat, really."

"Why, you shouldn't say that, honey."

"She *is*, Tony! She's had everything she ever wanted. You can never refuse her anything."

"Well, what's money for if not to make you and the kids happy? I only wish you wanted something for yourself. You never ask me for anything."

"I don't need anything, and Rosa has too much. Someday," Maria said quietly, "she's going to want something you can't buy for her."

Tony snorted. "Why, money buys everything!"

Maria shook her head but did not answer. "I hope you'll talk to O'Connor," she said as she turned to leave. "Tell him to be extra careful."

"Okay. I'll give him the straight talk." Morino smiled and sat back down at his desk. He couldn't concentrate on his work, however. His mind was filled with the pleasure of giving his daughter the purebred Arabian. Staring out the window, he daydreamed of seeing his lovely little Rosa bringing home trophies in all the riding shows.

★   ★   ★   ★

As soon as Rosa darted out the door and caught sight of the truck pulling the horse trailer, she ran toward it full speed, her hair flying out behind her. She scarcely glanced at the young man who had gotten out of the truck and now stood beside the trailer. Her eyes were all for the horse, and she peered in through the windows, admiring the mare's sleek coat. She smiled at the large eyes that watched her in return—rather wickedly, Rosa thought.

She cried out, "Oh, you beauty, and you're all mine!" She turned to the man and said impatiently, "Well, don't just stand there! Get my horse out!"

"I'm supposed to see somebody named O'Connor first," Phil said.

"He's not here. I'll sign for it."

She moved to the back of the trailer and snapped her fingers impatiently, but when the driver only looked at her and made no move to open it, she said, "Didn't you hear me? I said open the door and bring my horse out!"

"I'm sorry, miss. I can't do that. I have to have an adult here. Is O'Connor around?"

Rosa's dark eyes flashed. She had little time for hired help, and now she marched over and snatched the clipboard out of the young man's hand. "Look," she said, pointing to the paper with a superior air. "Anthony Morino—that's my father. He ordered this horse for *me*. Now just unload her and be on your way. Give me a pencil. I'll sign for it."

Phil made no attempt to remove the pencil that was behind his ear. He looked down at the attractive young woman whose beauty, he thought, was considerably marred by her spoiled attitude. "I'm sorry, but I can't do it, miss."

"I'm Rosa Morino, and this is my horse!"

"I'm sure that's true, Miss Morino, but—"

"Look, you see the name of this horse? I gave it to her myself. It's Boa-ad-ecah."

Rosa was surprised when the deliveryman laughed. "What are you laughing at?" she snapped.

"Well, I don't think you pronounced it quite right."

"What are you talking about? There it is right there! Boadicea. She's named after a queen from Egypt, and I guess I know how to say my own horse's name!"

Phil found himself enjoying the confrontation with the young woman. She was as pretty as a girl could be and had more spirit than the mare, if that were possible, but he could not help wanting to put her in her place. "Just two things wrong with that, Miss Morino. The name is pronounced Boo-dee-kuh, and she wasn't an Egyptian queen. She was from a tribe in Britain, the Iceni. When the Romans attacked her people and raped her two daughters, she raised an army and led them to battle against them."

Rosa's eyes flashed. "You don't know what you're talking about! I don't care what you say! This is my horse!"

Rosa whirled and moved back to the rear of the trailer. She reached up to unlatch the lock but was suddenly seized from behind. She began to kick and scream. "Let me go! I'm going to get that horse out!"

"I'm sorry, miss. I can't let you do that."

In her fury, Rosa swung around and slapped his face with a sharp crack that carried on the air. When she tried to slap him again, he caught her wrist. She struggled, and since she was a strong young girl, it took a great deal of strength to hold her off. Phil was embarrassed. "Cut it out, Miss Morino," he said with exasperation. She tried to pummel him with her fists, and it was all he could do to hold her without hurting her. She thrashed and kicked, screaming, "You turn me loose!"

While Phil was trying to defend himself without hurting the girl, he did not see the big man lumbering toward them from the house. Dominic Costello, bodyguard for Big Tony and his family, had heard the altercation from inside and came running as fast as his huge frame would allow. He had the blunt face of a pugilist, one ear puffed up, scar tissue around his eyes, and cold light gray eyes. He reached the struggling pair and pulled the girl loose so violently she staggered. Without hesitation he struck out with a tremendous right-hand blow that instantly cut Phil's eyebrow to the bone and drenched his face in blood.

Stunned, Phil fell backward, seeing nothing but swirling lights—yellow, red, and brilliant blue. He felt strong hands yanking him to his feet, and then another blow rocked him on the other side of his face. He tried to get away from the blows, but the powerful fists landed squarely on his face every time.

Rosa caught her balance and stopped dead still as she watched Dominic pound the helpless young man into semiconsciousness. Even as the man was falling toward the ground, Dominic dealt a massive blow to his midsection. Rosa heard his muted cry of pain as he doubled over and fell facedown in a pool of blood.

When Dominic began kicking the man as he lay still, she ran forward and grabbed his arm. "Dom, stop—!"

"I'll kill him," Dom screamed, still kicking. "He was trying to hurt you!"

"No, he wasn't, Dom! I was trying to get the horse out, and he was trying to stop me."

Dom stepped back to catch his breath and looked at her,

puzzled. "You mean he wasn't bothering you?"

"No, Dom. It was my fault," she said, tears streaming down her cheeks at the trouble she had just caused. Rosa knelt and gently rolled the inert body over. She was sickened by the wreck that Dom had made of the man's face, and she whispered, "Oh, Dom, you've hurt him bad!"

"Well, how was I to know he wasn't bothering you!"

Her face pale, Rosa shook her head. "Quick, carry him into the house. I'll have Daddy call a doctor." She whirled and ran inside. Dom knelt down, stared at the bloody face, and shook his head. "You shouldn't've put your hands on her." He scooped Winslow up with barely a grunt and marched toward the house. He felt bad about the misunderstanding, but he knew he would not be in trouble for it. After all, he was there to protect the family of Big Tony Morino. He was just doing his job.

★　★　★　★

"Is he all right, Daddy?"

Morino had stepped into the drawing room to talk to Rosa and Maria. Rosa's face was pale, and her hands were trembling. Tony could not stand to see his child in distress, and he put his hand on her shoulder, saying, "He'll be all right. The doctor's with him and will take good care of him. Now tell me once more what happened." He listened as Rosa went over the story again and shook his head. "I wish you hadn't made such a fuss over that horse, Rosa. We don't need something like this."

Rosa's eyes filled with tears, and she whispered, "I'm sorry, Daddy." She had a tender heart, despite being so spoiled, and now the tears ran down her cheeks. "Dom hurt him so bad. I never saw him act like that before."

Tony had hired Dom for his destructive ability, but Tony had always kept his business out of his home. Rosa had no idea how violent a man her father was, nor how violent were the men with whom he surrounded himself. She had grown up sheltered from all of this. Now Tony met Maria's eyes and winced at the accusing glare in them. "He'll be all right, sweetheart. The doc will fix him up."

The three waited for what seemed like a long time, and finally Dr. Clarkson came striding into the drawing room. Instantly the three converged on him.

Rosa was the first to ask, "Is he all right, Dr. Clarkson?"

"No, he's *not* all right, Rosa." James Clarkson was a tall, rangy man with light blue eyes and reddish hair, whose speech carried the echoes of his boyhood home in the North Carolina hills. He had been Rosa's doctor since she was born, but Clarkson now ignored her and glared at Tony. "You're in trouble here, Tony," the doctor snapped.

"Why, what's wrong with him?"

"He's got a broken nose, and those cuts around his eyes are going to leave scars. Besides that, he's got several broken ribs. What was he trying to do—rob the house?"

"Well, no, he was just delivering a horse."

"Why did Dom beat him up so badly?"

Rosa spoke up timidly. "He . . . he thought the man was bothering me."

"Was he bothering you?" Clarkson demanded.

Rosa dropped her head. "No, sir, he wasn't. I was being awful to him. He was trying to stop me from letting the horse out of the trailer."

"Well, that's not good, Tony. He may go straight to the police—maybe even sue you for this. If there's a trial, I'll have to be a witness against you. I won't have any choice."

"We'll take care of it, Doc," Tony assured him. "He'll be okay."

The doctor eyed Tony pointedly. "But he may *not* be, Tony. He could die—you understand? He needs to be in a hospital for observation. And you ought to get rid of Dom. He's a dangerous man."

Tony did not comment but instead asked the doctor, "Is he awake?"

"Yes, but I've sedated him, so he's groggy. I tell you again, he needs to go to the hospital."

"I'll take care of that, Doc, and all the expenses. Don't you worry."

Clarkson stalked out of the room, indignation in every line of his body. As soon as he was out the front door, Tony said, "I'll go see him."

"I want to go with you, Daddy."

"Better if you didn't, sweetheart."

"But I want to. It was my fault."

Big Tony shrugged, and the two of them, along with Maria, made their way down the hall and into the bedroom where the young man rested.

As Tony walked in the door he was shocked to see the damage Dominic had done. The man's face was puffy beyond recognition and badly discolored under both eyes. A bloody bandage covered his forehead where the doctor had stitched up the most serious wounds over the eyebrows. His lips were swollen, and his eyes stared steadily at Tony through narrow slits.

"I'm sorry about all this," Tony said gruffly. "What's your name?"

"Win . . . slow. Phil Winslow." He could barely pronounce his own name.

"Well, it was all a misunderstanding, Phil," Tony said quickly. "Now, listen, we're going to put you in the hospital—and I'm going to take care of all the doctor bills—"

"No," Phil said, his tone firm this time.

Tony halted and looked at him, surprised. "Look, young man, you need to go to the hospital."

"Gotta . . . take . . . truck back."

"I'll take care of all that. I'll have one of my men drive it back. I'm going to have another one take you to the hospital."

Phil found it difficult to move, but he struggled to his feet. Rosa stepped forward to help him and said, "I'm sorry. It was all my fault."

Phil glared at her. "Forget it," he whispered. "Now . . . I wanna go home."

"Sure," Tony said quickly. He reached into his pocket and pulled out a roll of bills. "Here, you'll be off from work awhile. This will take care of that."

Phil stared at the bills but could not even shake his head he was in such pain. "No . . ." His voice was barely audible. "Just . . . home."

Tony argued briefly, but finally Maria said, "You'll have to let him have his own way. He's going to pass out."

"Okay. We'll get you home. Don't worry about a thing." Tony rushed out quickly and came back almost at once with Dominic behind him. "Dom will take you home. He's sorry about what happened—wants to make it up to you. Anywhere you say, and we'll be in touch. I still think you ought to go to the hospital, though."

Phil did not answer. He didn't want to be anywhere near the man who had beat him senseless, but he was too weak to argue. He shuffled across the floor like a very old man, moving on will-power alone. Dom reached out to steady him, but Phil deliberately pulled his arm back.

When the door closed behind the two, Rosa began to cry. "He's hurt so bad, and it's all my fault. Why wouldn't he go to the hospital?"

Tony's eyes were fastened on the door. "He wouldn't take money, either. Not a very smart kid turning down dough. He'll learn better someday," he murmured. Then he turned to Rosa and put his arms around her. "It's all right, sweetheart. He'll be okay. Don't worry about him."

"But, Daddy, it was all my fault, and he's hurt so bad."

"People get hurt bad, Rosa," Big Tony Morino said. "You'll learn that as you get older."

CHAPTER TWO

"I'LL GIVE IT ALL I'VE GOT!"

★ ★ ★ ★

A can of chicken soup was on the first shelf of the upper kitchen cabinet, but when Phil lifted his arm to pull it down, a blinding pain struck him in his left side. It was like being stabbed with a red-hot knife, and he leaned forward gasping, biting his still-swollen lip to keep from crying out. He rested his palms on the counter and waited for the waves of pain to recede before he straightened up carefully. He had been out of the hospital for four days now, and while his face was healing rapidly, the cracked ribs were more painful than anything he had ever experienced. Although he'd insisted on going straight home that day he was hurt at the Morino estate, Tony had surreptitiously ordered his bodyguard to take Phil to the hospital instead. Phil had tried to resist but had found it was no use. The doctors and nurses at the hospital had given him excellent care, and he had been grateful after all. When they released him he was worried at the prospect of taking care of himself in his lonely apartment. Now, as he drew a ragged breath, he muttered to himself, "If cracked ribs hurt like this, I'd hate to know what broken ribs feel like!"

He looked up at the soup can on the shelf and shuddered at the thought of building a fire to cook a meal. Unable to bend over and feed the coal stove with the large chunks, he had let the fire go out and the room was freezing. He had awakened shivering and had delayed getting out of bed as long as possible. Even putting on his robe was painful, for he had difficulty getting his arms behind him.

I didn't know a few cracked ribs could be this much trouble. I'm like an old man creeping around! Can't do anything for myself—not even tie my shoes.

Simple survival had become a grim matter for Phil. He discovered that once he lay down on the bed, he could not roll over without waves of pain flooding him. And getting out of bed was a nightmare. Lifting himself up and twisting, trying to throw his feet over the edge, brought agonizing pains to his side. He had not shaved since coming home and knew he looked terrible.

He stared at the elusive soup can, wondering how he could possibly build a fire in his condition. He had eaten nothing the day before, and now hunger pangs gnawed at him. "It's cold soup or nothing," he grumbled. Turning, he stepped to the table and slowly pulled a kitchen chair over to the cabinet. Grasping the back of the chair, he put his left foot up on it and then gritted his teeth. "Should I do it slow and easy—or should I do it all in one motion?" He decided on slow and easy, but even that was hard. Finally, standing upright and trembling from the exertion, he reached out, grasped the soup can, and tried to step down. He lost his balance when a searing pain struck him, and he made a wild grab for the back of the chair, which he missed. He fell to the floor and almost passed out. He lay on his back moaning and holding his side, waiting for the pain to pass.

The linoleum was ice-cold, but that was the least of his problems. Getting up from such a position was agony. He would have to roll over on his right side, shove himself upright, get on his knees, then hold on to the cabinet and pull himself to a standing position. He dreaded the thought and wished he were safely back in bed. For a long time he lay there, listening to the ticking of the clock up on the table. He knew it must be some time around ten in the morning, but from where he lay he could not see the clock face. He was summoning up his will to endure the pain when suddenly a knock came from the door. He whispered, "Come in." No answer and then another knock sounded, more insistent this time. He rasped out as loudly as he could, "Come in. The door's open."

The exertion strained his ribs, and he lay panting as he heard the door open and a familiar voice cry out, "Phil, what is it? What's happened?"

Lifting his head, he saw his sister, Amelia, standing framed in the doorway. The sunlight from the kitchen window caught her hair, bringing out the auburn of the rich brown, and her eyes were wide open, her lips parted in shock.

"Hi, sis. Good morning to you."

Amelia Winslow dropped her purse and came flying across the room. She knelt down by her brother's side and put her hands on his cheeks. "What happened? Was it a burglar?"

Phil tried to smile, but the effort hurt his bruised cheekbones. Nonetheless, he was delighted to see a familiar face. "I tripped over a matchstick, sis."

Amelia stared at him. She looked around the kitchen and took in the open cupboard door and the fallen chair. She studied his face. "You've been beaten," she said. "Who did this to you?"

"Just a guy. Help me up, will you, sis? I got some cracked ribs."

She moved behind him and put her hands under his armpits, asking, "You ready? Careful now."

"Ready."

As Amelia straightened up, Phil gasped in pain. Anger flooded through her. She did not know what had happened to him, but she intended to find out. "Come on. Let's get you back to bed," she said, supporting him as he walked painfully into the bedroom.

When he sat down he shook his head. "Lying down's the hardest part. Ribs hurt like blazes."

"Are they broken?"

"No. Just cracked. Help me down, will you, sis?"

Amelia eased the upper part of his body down, noting that his puffy lips were drawn tight, then lifted his legs up onto the bed and stood over him. She studied his face, noting the yellow-and-purple bruises around both eyes and the stitches over his eyebrows. She shook her head. "When did this happen?"

"About a week ago."

"Was it a burglar?"

"No—would you believe it happened while I was delivering a horse? Perils of the job!"

Amelia raised a questioning eyebrow. "I didn't know you were in such a dangerous profession, Phil. Why didn't you call me?"

"Well, I was in the hospital part of that time, and then when I got home I thought I could handle it myself."

"I'd like to take a switch to you! You should have called!"

Phil grinned faintly. "I guess I should've. I'm not as tough as I thought."

"What were you doing on the floor?"

"I was trying to get a can of soup. I can't reach up very high, so I got on a chair, but when I came down I didn't make it."

"You lie there. I'll fix you something better than soup," she said, taking off her coat and flinging it over a chair.

Phil looked up at her with both gratitude and admiration. As she stood with her hands on her hips, he thought she looked stunning in her drop-waisted pink frock of silk and wool. Phil was amazed that Amelia could look so good even in this un-shapely style. The flat-chested straight look was popular with many women, but it was impossible for Amelia to hide her womanly curves in the new styles. She was taller than average and quite strong. Her hair was cut short in the fashionable new bob, and she had curled it with curling tongs.

"Thanks, sis," Phil said, smiling. "You look great."

"So do you. Just peachy!"

"Come on, now. Don't preach at me. I feel bad enough."

Amelia reached out and brushed his hair back from his forehead. A great pity welled up in her as she realized how very much she loved her younger brother. They did not talk about their feelings much and were not given to emotional statements, but now she bit her lip and wanted to cry. "I'll get you something to eat," she said quietly. "You just lie there."

A thought struck her, and she said, "Do you have anything for the pain?"

"Yeah, I had some pills, but I took 'em all."

"You stay right there. I'll go get you something. And don't leave that bed! You hear me?" she said loudly.

Phil smiled. "I think the people next door heard you, sis."

"You lie there. I'll be right back."

Amelia reached for her coat, then paused again, suddenly realizing the fire was out. "It's cold in here."

"Couldn't make a fire. Hurt too much."

Amelia shook her head as she pulled her coat back on and turned to the task of filling the coal stove. She lit it carefully, thankful that there was kindling, and when she got the coals going well, she closed the door with the draft half open. "It'll be warm by the time I get back."

She left the apartment and ran down to the corner drugstore. When she got back with a brown paper bag in hand, she noticed with satisfaction that the room was starting to get warm. She grabbed a tablespoon from the kitchen drawer, opened the large bottle of medicine she had purchased, and took it into the bedroom. "It's too cold in here. I'm going to fix you up on that chair near the stove. But first take a dose of this." When she got him upright, she ordered, "Now swallow it all."

Phil took the dose and made an awful face. "What is that stuff?"

"Same thing Mom and Dad used to give us when we had stomachaches. The druggist said it's the best stuff for pain, even for grown-ups."

"I remember it now. Seems like they could make it taste a little better."

"You wait here until I get your chair made up."

Quickly she fixed the chair with pillows and a blanket covering it, then helped him into it. He sat back with a sigh of ease while she fetched another blanket to drape over him. "You soak up some heat while I fix your breakfast."

Phil relaxed, letting the luxury of the warmer room sink into him. He was comfortable now, and within ten minutes the strong medicine was taking effect. He found himself listening to Amelia hum as she moved around the kitchen making his breakfast. The smell of frying bacon and coffee filled the air, and when she finally brought a tray over, he found he was ravenously hungry. "That smells wonderful," he said.

"Just scrambled eggs, bacon, and soft toast. Is your mouth sore?"

"Better now, but it still hurts to chew. The inside of my lips was cut pretty bad. You should have seen me. I looked like a baboon with my mouth all pooched out."

"Don't talk. Eat."

Amelia watched him eat, and as he winced in pain from the simple act of chewing, the cold fury in her intensified, greater than any emotion she had ever known. They had been close growing up in their isolated home on a mission station in Africa, where they'd been far from neighbors and white faces were rare. As the older sibling, she had always felt protective toward her brother, and even though it was illogical to feel guilty about his present condition, she somehow blamed herself for allowing this to happen to him.

Phil stopped eating long enough to ask, "So what have you been doing lately, sis?"

At first Amelia was disinclined to talk about her life in America. Phil had found everything about life in the States exciting. When they had first arrived in August 1922, Phil had immediately found work at the Thornton Stables and began saving money for college. He had begun classes this fall and had found his niche there, but Amelia was unhappy, dissatisfied with her life. She had always harbored a rebellious streak, which she had managed to cover up for the most part. Being the daughter of missionaries, she had learned to play a role and not embarrass her parents too much, but her gnawing frustration at life had grown since coming to the States. The two siblings had at first lived with their grandmother, Lola Winslow. While Phil had worked and saved, Amelia had worried her grandmother by running around late at night with friends of dubious character. She had shown no inclination to find a job, claiming she was having too much fun to work. Within a short time, Amelia had been unable to bear the restraint of her grandmother's genteel life and had run off without warning to find a place of her own. Phil stayed with his grandmother for several more months, not moving into his own place until he started college. While Phil found a life of hard work and responsibility an exciting challenge, Amelia's initial excitement at being in the States had turned to misery, now that she had to work so hard just to make ends meet.

"I've got a job I hate," Amelia said. "Could you drink some more milk?"

"No. This is fine. What's wrong with your job?"

"I'm a cook at a restaurant, Phil! What kind of a life is that?"

"Doesn't seem so bad to me. I thought you liked helping out in the kitchen at Grandmother's house."

"Nope—I hated it then, and I hate it now," Amelia said flatly. "It's a rotten job, and what's worse, the boss can't keep his hands off me."

"Why don't you quit and find another one?"

Amelia reached out and picked up the jar of blackberry jam. She spread it on a piece of buttered toast and handed it to him. "Eat this. You always liked jam. I *am* going to get away. I'm going to quit soon and try to find a job in show business."

With the toast halfway to his lips, Phil dropped his hand. "Show business?"

"You know I always wanted to do that."

"Oh, I knew you were interested in movie stars and actors and actresses. And you've always been a great singer, but I didn't think you'd want to do it for a living."

"Well, I do. It's what I've always wanted to do, Phil. I'm going to do it too."

Phil took a bite of the toast and chewed it slowly. "That's a pretty hard life, I hear. Hard to get into too, isn't it?"

"Yes, it is. But as soon as I get enough cash saved, maybe another two months, I'll have a stake." Amelia leaned forward, her eyes glowing with her desire for a different kind of life. "I can do it, Phil. You wait and see."

"Mom and Dad will have a fit."

"I expect they will, and I hate to hurt them. But it's what I want to do." She did not want to talk anymore about her plans, for she knew Phil disagreed, although he didn't say so. She said only, "I tried it Mom and Dad's way, and now I've got to do this thing for myself. Now tell me about school. Are you falling behind being in the hospital and all?"

"I've had to miss some classes, but I can catch up on the reading over Thanksgiving vacation."

"What exactly happened to you, Phil? You've got to tell me."

"It was just a fight. I got the worst of it."

Amelia tried to get the story out of him, but he adamantly refused to tell her any more than he already had. He'd always been like this, she remembered, taking his lumps without whining. It was one of the things she admired about him. She took the tray to the sink and began to clean up the kitchen, all the while talking about Africa, old friends there, and family.

A knock on the door interrupted her monologue. "Are you expecting somebody, Phil?"

"No. I can't think who it might be."

"I'll see." Amelia took off her apron and crossed the room to open the door. She quickly took in the big man and dark-haired young woman standing in the hallway, thinking they made a strange pair. "Yes? What is it?"

"I-I'd like to see Mr. Winslow if he's here."

The girl was a beauty, Amelia saw, and she stepped back and glanced over at her brother. "Company, Phil." Turning back to the couple, she said, "Come on in. I'm Phil's sister, Amelia."

"I'm glad to know you, Miss Winslow. My name's Rosa Morino. This is Dom Costello."

Amelia murmured the appropriate phrases and then looked over at Phil again. "Are you up to company, Phil?"

"Yes. Of course."

Amelia sized up the young woman as she stepped over close to Phil's chair. Her well-tailored clothing had to be expensive. She wore a cloche hat over her curly black hair, a woolen plaid jacket and pleated skirt, cashmere sweater, and a decorative silk scarf draped around her neck. Amelia also noted a gold necklace with a diamond as large as the sapphire on the girl's finger. *She comes from money*, Amelia thought, trying to guess her age. No more than sixteen, she reckoned, and then her eyes went to the big man. He stood out of the way with his back almost against the wall. He had a battered countenance with hands as large as hams. Her eyes narrowed as she drew his gaze. They studied each other for a moment. Then Amelia turned as she heard the girl say, "Mr. Winslow, I came to tell you how sorry I am that . . . that all this happened."

"You didn't have to do that," Phil said. "Pull up a seat. Sis, will you find some chairs for our guests?"

But Amelia did not move. Addressing the young woman

directly, she demanded, "You're sorry that *what* happened?"

"That . . . that he got hurt."

"Why are you sorry? You didn't beat him up, did you?"

"Didn't he tell you what happened?"

"No. He won't say a word about it."

At the harsh tone in Amelia's voice, Rosa licked her lips and lowered her eyes. In a faltering voice she explained the incident and then pleaded, "I'm so sorry. I never intended for anybody to get hurt."

Amelia seemed not to have heard her. She turned around and faced Dom, studying him carefully. Then, without a word, she walked over to pick up her purse. Dom's eyes grew alert as she approached him.

"You beat up my brother?"

"I thought he was hurtin' Miss Rosa."

"How much do you weigh?"

"About two-twenty, I guess."

"My brother only weighs about one-sixty! You look like a pug. Am I right?"

Dom shifted his feet and glanced at Rosa, then back to the woman, who held him with her gaze. "Used to be," he muttered.

"You pretty proud of yourself for beating up somebody who didn't do anything?"

"I thought—" He cut off his words, and shock showed in his eyes. "Hey, be careful!"

Amelia had pulled a thirty-eight pistol from her purse. She held it steadily in front of Dominic Costello's face, aimed right between his eyes. "You're quite a man for beating up on people smaller than you. I think I'll shoot your nose off."

"Hey, lady, watch it with that gun!"

Dominic was a tough fellow, but he did not know this woman. Her green eyes were glittering with a ferocity he had never seen in a woman before. He held up his hand as if to ward off the bullet and said, "That thing could go off."

"It *will* go off if I pull the trigger." Her eyes dropped to his waist, and she said, "You're wearing a gun. Why don't you pull it?"

Rosa cried out, "Please don't shoot him! Please!"

Amelia was smiling as if she were enjoying this, but anger

was crisp in her voice. She lowered the gun until it pointed at the floor and said, "Now we're even. See if you can get that gun out before I can put a bullet in your brain."

"Hey, sis, take it easy!" Phil cried out. "It's not that big of a thing."

Rosa flew over to put herself in front of Costello. "He was afraid for me. He just made a mistake."

Costello lifted the girl off to the side, out of harm's way, and said to Amelia, "C'mon, now, lady—you don't want to hurt anyone."

"Yeah, c'mon, sis," Phil pleaded as well, "put that gun away."

Slowly Amelia obeyed. She dropped the gun back into her purse and then stood looking at the big man.

Dom tried to appear nonchalant. "Were you really going to shoot me?" he demanded.

"I shot a leopard once back in Africa. I didn't feel bad about that, and I wouldn't feel bad about shooting a beast like you!"

Dom did not answer, but he relaxed somewhat now that the gun was out of sight. "I have to be careful," he mumbled. "There are people that would like to hurt my boss and his family."

Relief washed through Rosa's face, and she ran across the room to stand beside Phil. "How do you feel, Mr. Winslow?" she asked.

"Fine," he said.

"I don't believe you. I know you're hurting, and I'm so sorry."

"Well, you don't have to think about that."

"I have to think about this, though. I asked about you at the stables. They said you're in college and that you work there to help pay your bills. But you won't be able to work for a while, so won't you please take the money my daddy offered you?"

"What money's that?" Amelia asked, crossing the room to stand beside Rosa.

"My daddy wanted to pay Mr. Winslow. He did pay his hospital bill, but your brother wouldn't take any money."

"Well, *I'll* take it," Amelia said coldly.

Eagerly Rosa's hand darted into her purse, and she drew out some bills. "I'm so sorry. I didn't mean for your brother to be hurt. Please take the money. If it's not enough, I can get more."

"I'll let you know," Amelia said coolly. She stuffed the money into her purse and smiled. "My brother's not very wise about money, but I am."

Rosa stood there helplessly, then said quickly, "I guess we'd better go." She turned to Phil. "Mr. Winslow—"

"Hey, you can call me Phil."

"Well, okay . . . Phil, if you need anything, please ask."

"Sure. Good to see you again, Rosa. How's the mare?"

"Oh, she's wonderful! She's so beautiful."

"She's a handful, though," Phil warned. "Be careful."

"That's what Daddy says." She started to say something more when she caught the expression on Amelia's face. "Well," she added hurriedly, "we'd better go. Good-bye."

"Good-bye, Rosa. Thanks for your help."

Rosa left at once, but Dom turned before leaving and stared at Amelia. "You wouldn't have shot me. You don't have the nerve for it."

"You'll never know, will you, Costello?"

He laughed a little and shook his head. He turned and faced Phil. For a moment he stood still, and then he came over and put out his meaty hand. Surprised, Phil took it. The big man searched for words but could only say, "Sorry . . . like . . ." He dropped Phil's hand, then whirled and left the room.

★ ★ ★ ★

Amelia Winslow had always had difficulty controlling her temper, whereas Phil had always been mild mannered and easygoing. It was not uncommon for Amelia to flare out and let people know exactly how she felt. It had been several weeks since she had found Phil in an almost helpless condition, and every day she'd had to struggle with the anger that rose in her at the sight of his battered features. She had a strong maternal instinct where her brother was concerned. She had been back every day to help him, except when her work schedule did not allow it. Phil had returned to his classes now, limping and still somewhat bruised.

Amelia had been secretly pleased that Rosa had come back twice, bringing generous quantities of food that needed no cooking. The girl was spoiled rotten, but at least she had a healthy conscience, and it pleased Amelia that she was showing it in this way. Dom was the girl's ever-present shadow, but the big man had shown Amelia no animosity. In fact, she got the strong impression that he rather liked her. The first time he saw her again, he winked and said, "Still packin' that gun?"

"Still packin' it, Dom. Still got yours?" He had laughed at this, and she had been able to forgive him, more or less. Realizing that he was not unlike a trained attack dog that responded to stimuli, she'd decided he wasn't entirely to blame for what had happened. He had attacked Phil simply because he thought he was harming his charge.

On Thursdays Amelia worked the late shift at the restaurant, so she would spend the morning cleaning her own apartment before going to Phil's place to clean and cook for him. This particular Thursday they'd had an early supper so she could get to work by six. As they were eating their steaks, baked potatoes, and salad, Phil described his college classes with great gusto.

"Are they hard for you, Phil?" Amelia asked.

"No. They're a lot easier than I thought they would be."

"You were always able to make the top grades."

"I'm going to be able to double up on courses. I think I can finish in two years if I do that," Phil said.

Amelia made no comment, feeling almost jealous that his studies came so easily to him. But then she told herself she had other plans anyway. College was certainly not her ambition in life.

After washing the dishes, Amelia left Phil's apartment and went at once to Paladino's Restaurant. She tried to enter inconspicuously and get to work without Charlie Paladino noticing her. She avoided him as much as possible. He never missed a chance to put his hands on her—usually just a light touch on the arm, but lately he had been getting more and more familiar. Amelia had tried to freeze him out, but he was a thickheaded, insufferable man. It was common knowledge among the workers at the restaurant that he'd had affairs with several waitresses, even getting two of them pregnant and having to pay them off to keep quiet about it. Amelia felt sorry for his wife, a plain woman worn down by long hours in the restaurant and the trials of raising five children. She deserved better than the likes of Charlie Paladino.

"Hey, you don't say hello?" Charlie complained as Amelia hurried toward the kitchen. He cut her off and reached out to squeeze her arm. "You sure look pretty today."

"I'd better get started, Charlie," Amelia said coldly. "I'm a little bit late."

"That's all right. When the boss says it's okay, it's okay."

Amelia wrenched her arm free from his grasp and ran into the kitchen without another word. She smiled at Joe Francis, the day cook. "Hi, Joe," she greeted him as she put her purse and hat away and hung up her coat. Tying on her apron, she listened as he rattled off the things that needed to be done and the orders that were already in. "I'll handle it, Joe. Have a good night."

"See you tomorrow, Amelia."

It turned out to be a busy night, so the hours passed quickly. She hated the slow nights when there was little to do, for it gave Charlie far too much opportunity to harass her. She handled the orders efficiently, shoving them through the window into the dining room for the waitresses to pick up. Charlie came back unnecessarily several times during the evening to speak to her. She always turned to face him, but when he drew close, she'd put out her hand and say, "Stay away, Charlie. Don't touch."

He always laughed at her and backed away, but the gleam in his eyes told her that sooner or later he would step over the line. She was not about to let this self-proclaimed ladies' man have his way with her. Amelia's mind whirled with thoughts of how she was going to escape from this dead-end job and make her big break into show business. She needed to save more money before she made her move, but she wasn't sure she could stand another day of fighting off Charlie.

By nine o'clock the rush was over, and it was only an hour until closing. As she went about cleaning up her work area, she more carefully considered her problem. *If I just had a little more money, I could survive long enough to make the rounds at the producers' offices. Make myself visible.* She thought of her grandmother, Lola. Even though she couldn't stand living at her house under her rules, she did love her grandmother dearly and had visited her twice since moving out to her own apartment. She knew her grandmother was lonely since losing her husband, Mark, a year ago. Amelia had always intended to spend more time with her grandmother, but the time was never there now that she had to work so much to pay for rent and food, as well as trying to save.

Grandmother would give me the money to make my try if I asked for it, Amelia thought. Reaching up, she took an order from the clip where the waitresses fastened them and read it. It included two eggs over easy. Still thinking of going to her grandmother to ask for help, she reached over and picked out two eggs from the wire basket hanging above the counter. She had been so engrossed in her thoughts she had not heard footsteps, and she gasped as two arms came around her and two hands ran across her figure. Anger flooded through her, and twisting around, she glared into Charlie's greedy eyes. Without hesitation, she lifted both hands and brought the eggs down on his balding head. She laughed as the yolks ran down over his pudgy face. "Have some eggs, Charlie." Then planting her hands on his chest, she shoved him backward into a cabinet full of heavy pots and pans.

In the midst of the clattering cookware, he spluttered and cursed, kicking several pans across the room. She stared in disgust at the overweight little man, who was, in her opinion, as pathetic as he was ugly.

Her mind was made up. Stripping off her apron, she plunged her hands under the faucet to wash off the dripping egg yolk, paying no attention to the stream of lurid language still spewing from his mouth. Plucking her coat off the hook and slamming her hat onto her head, she grabbed her purse and said, "Pay me off, Charlie."

"I'll pay you nothing, you vixen!"

"Then I'll go tell your customers exactly what kind of a man you really are!"

Paladino blinked and cursed again. "All right. I'll pay you off. You're a rotten cook anyhow."

Five minutes later Amelia was outside. The air was cold, though winter had not yet fully come. Christmas lights twinkled in the streets and windows. Taking deep gulps of the crisp air, she headed slowly toward the river and, as she often did after work, stood at the waterfront looking out over the water. The river moved like a living thing, and overhead the stars glittered cold and distant.

Amelia was not a fearful person. Indeed, her parents thought she was too aggressive and would tackle anything, even a leopard. But here she was a stranger in a strange land with no help. Looking up, she saw Orion overhead, and the impulse came to her to salute the constellation. She laughed aloud. Her breath made a frosty incense that rose upward as she declared, "I'm not helpless. I've got a little money saved. I can make it last for three months if I don't eat much. I'll give it all I've got!"

The stars did not answer, but she stared at them defiantly and turned and walked away, her footsteps echoing clearly in the darkness.

CHAPTER THREE

A GIFT FROM AFRICA

★　★　★　★

The excitement of the approaching Christmas holiday had meant nothing to Amelia as she spent most of her time visiting the offices of producers, nightclubs, and theaters—anywhere that she might get a start in show business. Now as she walked down Broadway, snow began to fall in large flakes, and Amelia shivered as the cold bit through her thin clothing. She had invested an inordinate amount of her small savings in one outfit she hoped would impress producers and directors. It consisted of a navy blue tailored suit with a lightweight wool jacket and a checkered skirt, a bow tie, and a cloche hat. A red fox fur, complete with head and tail, gave her outfit a smart touch. Her skirt only went down to her knees—a new fashion that many found shocking. She had seen several newspaper articles quoting clergymen around the world who declared the short styles the work of the devil. The archbishop of Naples had even claimed that Italy's last major earthquake was due to God's anger at such indecent exposure. Amelia sniffed at such attitudes. She just enjoyed being stylish.

She weaved her way through the crowds of last-minute holiday shoppers, aware that men and women alike were casting glances at her legs. The cost of her silk stockings had made her gasp, but she'd simply had to have them. Delicate decorations meandered playfully down either side, and it pleased Amelia to see women looking her over with jealousy and men with a smile of approval.

The snow began falling harder, and she leaned into the face-numbing wind. She could not afford a cab, but her new apartment was only a few blocks away. The neighborhood was composed of three-story brownstones, once expensive mansions of the rich but now converted into apartments and boardinghouses. She entered her building and walked down the hall, grateful to get out of the wind. Her fingers were stiff as she fumbled in her purse for her key, then clumsily fit it into the lock. As she stepped inside, the warm air from the radiators felt delightful. The apartment was never warm enough at night, but after coming in out of the cold, it provided a comfortable contrast.

"Is that you, Amelia?"

"Yes, it's me." Amelia took off her hat and tossed it to one side, adding the fox fur with it. She stepped into the bedroom she shared with Blanche Meredith. Amelia considered herself fortunate that Blanche had lost her roommate, opening up the opportunity for Amelia to share the small but clean apartment close to Manhattan's theater district. Sharing rent helped her conserve her small savings, and the location was convenient to the nightclubs and theaters where she hoped to land a job.

Blanche Meredith was a tall woman with bleached blond hair and dark blue eyes. Her face still had a prettiness about it, but the years of struggling to make it big in show business had taken their toll. Fine lines around her eyes were visible when she did not have time to skillfully eliminate them with cosmetics. Amelia thought she must have been beautiful at eighteen, but Blanche was one of those types who did not age well, and she was probably pushing thirty now, Amelia surmised.

Amelia blinked with surprise when she went into the bedroom and saw Blanche filling a suitcase with the rumpled clothing that was scattered on the bed. As Amelia stared, Blanche tossed some underwear in on top.

"Are you going somewhere for the holidays, Blanche?"

"No, I'm going somewhere for good." Blanche fidgeted and lit a cigarette. Her smoking was one habit that irritated Amelia, for the apartment always smelled of tobacco smoke. "I'm giving it up, Amelia."

"Giving up what?"

"The whole thing. I've tried it for eight years now, and I haven't gotten anywhere. I just don't have what it takes for show business."

Amelia was not altogether surprised. Several times during her stay, Blanche had indicated that the strain was too much, but now that she was quitting, Amelia could only say, "Don't give up. It may get better after the first of the year."

"It'll get worse," Blanche said flatly. "Look, I know you've still got stars in your eyes, Amelia, but this is not a good life. A few people make it to the top, and they've got everything. But for every Fanny Brice making it big, there are hundreds like me and you. It's just not worth it. I gave it my best shot, but—" Here Blanche shook her head, grabbed the last of her undergarments from the bureau drawer, threw them into the suitcase, then slammed the bureau drawer shut. "I'd tell you to do the same while you're still young, but you're like I was. You think someday your name's going to be up in lights."

Amelia could not answer. She was already trying to figure out how she could pay the full rent on the apartment. She knew she would have to get another roommate, and the thought of trying to find someone compatible troubled her.

"But what will you do, Blanche? Where will you go?"

"Where I've always known I'd go. Back home to Concord. It's where I grew up. My parents are there, and I've got two brothers and a sister. They never left the place. I'll get some kind of a job," she said bitterly. "At a flower shop or as a waitress maybe. Then I'll marry a mechanic or a store clerk, have half a dozen kids, and that'll be it."

Amelia moved at once to put her arm around Blanche. "I wish you wouldn't go. It may get better."

"You're a sweet kid, Amelia, but I'm facing up to it. I'm thirty-one now. That's old for this business. If you don't make it quick, you don't make it at all. You'd better think about it." Then she laughed suddenly. "But you won't, and I wish you luck."

Amelia hardly knew what to say. "When will you go?"

"The train leaves at six o'clock. I'll be up all night in that club car."

"Will you write to me?"

"There won't be anything to write, Amelia. It'll be dull, dull, dull. But here's my address. Write to me and tell me when you're a star."

Since Blanche had a little time before she had to leave, the two women had coffee and sandwiches, but Blanche only nibbled at hers. Amelia desperately wanted to say something that would bring comfort, but what was there to say? This woman had spent a third of her life trying to break into the glittering world of the theater—and had failed. Amelia had seen such women before in producers' offices as they applied for jobs, the pitiful hope on their faces turning to despair as they heard yet again the hated words *We'll call you.* She had seen them on the streets, those who had risked everything and lost it all in this one bid for fame and immortality on the stage. It was almost a disease, Amelia thought, and she herself was infected with it. It made no sense, for she knew well that the odds for success were terrible.

Finally Blanche rose, and the two women embraced. "I wish I could convince you that this is no life, Amelia, but you're as stubborn as I was at your age. I hope you make it." She turned, picked up her suitcase, and left without looking back. Amelia watched her go, and the apartment suddenly seemed very empty. She gazed out through the window at the vast, teeming city and felt like a tiny ship caught in a great maelstrom, slowly being sucked down into black nothingness. She was not a woman given to fits of depression, yet the defeat of her friend and the utter lack of joy and happiness in her eyes had indeed given her an uneasy feeling. She rubbed her hands together and shook her shoulders, muttering grimly, "I'll make it. I'll stay no matter what!"

★　★　★　★

Unable to stand the silence of the apartment, Amelia changed into a warmer outfit and went out again. When she had first arrived in New York, she had been eager to see all the sights and had exhausted herself doing so. Now, however, there was no eagerness to see anything new. She was simply fleeing from the leaden silence of her apartment. As she moved woodenly along the street, she noted once again that men were watching her. She was accustomed to this, and a part of her still felt pride in her ability to attract their attention. During her stay in the city, however, that pride had gradually changed to wariness. She still carried a gun in her purse, although she had only used it the one time she had threatened Dom. That memory came back to her now, and she thought about the big man and about the girl Rosa. A touch of envy rose in her—envy for the girl's beauty, and also for her family's apparently unlimited money. Rosa could go anywhere she pleased, do what she liked. What that was Amelia had no idea. She had asked Phil once about the girl, and he had shrugged, saying he hadn't seen her again. He had added that he felt sorry for her, and when Amelia had asked why, he'd remarked, "She's got everything . . . and she's got nothing. That's a bad combination, sis."

With Christmas only two days away, the shoppers were out in force. The city exuded a warm holiday spirit that amazed her. She had thought of New York as a soulless place, but now she sensed a happiness in the crowds and a welcome of the season. She passed people of all ages laughing and smiling, listened to the din of cars blowing their horns, and watched trucks muscling their way through the traffic in the street, their engines rumbling. The scene was noisy as always but had a sense of life and gaiety about it. New York might be as hard as a diamond, but at this time of the year the hardness was not so apparent, only the glittering richness.

She passed a well-dressed couple and their two children, a boy and a girl, all of them holding hands and laughing as they swung their arms. Amelia was struck with the thought that perhaps there was such a thing as beautiful simplicity for some people. She, on the other hand, was torn between what her parents had taught her and the contrasting complications of the city and of her own heart. She longed for simplicity but could not fathom how to find it in her present life. A fire burned in her to express herself, to find happiness through her work. Phil had found such contentment in college, happily throwing himself into his studies. But for Amelia nothing was that crystal clear or simple.

As she finally reached Central Park the sun appeared as a white hole in the sky, filtering down antiseptic light. The reds and golds of the trees were long gone, brought down by wind, bruised and discolored by the hammering rains of autumn. Now she stopped by the lake and enjoyed watching the snow fall in long, slanting lines. It covered the ground in strips until all was sheer white, a beauty to behold. There had been nothing like this in Africa, and the splendor of it held her transfixed. The noisy city gradually grew quieter as the carpet of snow muted the cacophony of squealing wheels, blaring horns, and roaring engines.

She thought about Africa then . . . about the heat, the discomfort, the flies, the danger of snakes and leopards . . . but that part of her life was over. She instinctively knew that if she ever saw it again, it would be as a visitor and not as a part of it. Seeing it again would not be living it again. She knew she could always go back and rediscover an old haunt and that she would say, *Oh yes, I remember this.* But she reminded herself that the valley and the river and the path she had once followed in Africa, though she remembered them, no longer remembered her.

The afternoon was growing long now, and gray blades of light sliced through the gathering darkness. She lingered still, hating to go home, hating the thought of spending the night in the quiet of the empty apartment. With Blanche gone there would be nothing but the sound of her own voice or maybe a scratchy Victrola record. But finally the dusky night settled in, and she turned and made her way homeward in the glow of the streetlights. The cold bit at her, and the snowflakes touched her eyes like tiny, seeking fingers. People leaned against the wind, bundled up in their heavy winter clothing, looking for all the world like bears waddling back to the warmth of their caves.

She passed by a church on the way and for a moment almost turned to go inside. She had not been to church since living on her own, but now she felt it might bring her some peace. Her thoughts of God were conflicting. She had grown up listening to sermons and had made a public profession of faith when she was only six years old. Her parents had doubted her sincerity at the time, but her emotions had been stirred by the preaching, and as a child she had insisted she had meant it. But as she grew older, the experience gradually left her until she had known as a young woman that she did not truly intend to follow God.

That childhood experience of God seemed long ago and very far away as she stood staring up at the church spire, a cold mass of blocky stones pointing at the sky like a bony, accusing forefinger, almost invisible now in the darkness. She turned away from the church and made her way home, feeling lonelier and more lost than she had felt in a long time.

She had barely stepped into the apartment and begun taking off her good clothes when the phone rang. Eagerly she ran to pick it up, hoping it might be a job offer, but then she heard Phil's voice. "Hi, sis. How do you like this snow?"

"It's beautiful. I've just been out walking in it."

"Listen, sis. Get ready. I'll be there at noon tomorrow to take you to Grandmother's for Christmas."

"Oh, I don't want to go there, Phil. Maybe we could meet by ourselves on Christmas Day and have our own quiet celebration."

"Nothing doing. Grandmother won't hear of our not spending the holidays at her house."

Amelia wasn't sure she could face her grandmother with the news that she had quit her job at the restaurant. She still felt a shred of guilt over the way she had left Lola's house last spring in anger and frustration. Although Amelia longed to ask for help to accomplish her plans, she wasn't sure her grandmother would even approve of them. Without completely understanding her own conflicting emotions, she decided it best to avoid contact with her grandmother until her circumstances improved. "I'd rather not go, Phil."

"You don't have any choice. Grandmother's sending a car." He laughed then and said, "You're going one way or another. Come under your own power or be dragged."

Amelia sighed. She couldn't think of an adequate argument. After all, it was Christmas. "Well, if you put it that way, I guess I'll have to go."

"Of course you will. It'll be fun. Twelve tomorrow in front of your apartment. I'll see you then, and merry Christmas!"

*　*　*　*

Before returning to his apartment Phil made a quick shopping trip. He had little money, but he easily enough picked out a present for his grandmother. He could not buy her an expensive gift, but he found an old poster advertising the grand meeting of the Union Pacific and Central Pacific Railroads. It pictured the two trains pulled up nose to nose with men standing on the engines and the engineers holding up bottles of champagne. His grandmother had followed the track of the Union Pacific and had met the man there who became her husband, and he knew she would love the poster. At his next stop, a used book store, he found a book of poetry by Walt Whitman that was in excellent condition. He knew Amelia would like it, and he was pleased to be able to purchase it for only two dollars.

He bounded up the stairway to his apartment and found a small package wrapped in red paper with a green bow lying on the floor propped against the door. He picked it up, unlocked the door, turned on the light, and took off his hat and coat. There was no card on the outside of the present, and he thought perhaps his landlady had left it. From time to time he helped her make small repairs, and the two had become friends. He removed the wrapping and found a white box with a gold seal. Opening the box, he pulled out a beautifully designed, rich-looking leather billfold. It glowed with a dull sheen, and when he opened it, he found several pockets for cards.

"Mmm . . . pretty fancy," he murmured, still thinking it had come from his landlady. Then the edge of a white paper caught his eye, and he pulled out a card that read, *I'm sorry! Merry Christmas.* It was signed simply *Rosa.* Rubbing his thumb over the rich texture of the leather, Phil was touched by the thought. He had not seen Rosa for weeks now and had not expected to see her again, but this changed his mind.

"I get a gift—I give a gift," he said aloud. He thought hard for a moment, then smiled. "I'll give her something she couldn't buy in any store in New York." He started whistling "Joy to the World" as he went into the bedroom to get it.

Finding a scrap of Christmas paper and some ribbon, he

quickly wrapped the gift and left the apartment. The snow was coming down hard, so he decided to go first-class. He hailed a cab and told the driver, "I'll tell you how to go. I don't think they have a street address."

"You're the boss," the cabby said, putting up his flag and starting off.

Phil directed the cabbie through the streets of New York to the outskirts of the city. The snow was coming down even faster now, and Phil remarked, "Gonna be hard driving."

"You're tellin' me! Seen a couple of wrecks already."

They made their way slowly through the thickening snow, and when they neared Ten Oaks, Phil said, "It's right over there. You see those big iron gates? Just let me out there."

"Okay, buddy. You want me to wait?"

"No, you might get buried under all this snow. I'll find another way home."

Getting out after they had pulled to a stop, Phil paid the driver and said, "Merry Christmas!"

"Merry Christmas to you too, sir."

The cab made a U-turn and left almost silently in the three-inch layer of snow. Phil pushed the bell and waited. As he did so, he thought of his first visit here to the Morino estate. He had gotten over the beating fairly well, except for a scar on his forehead that he would probably carry to his grave, and occasionally his ribs still gave him a twinge. He tensed suddenly at the memory and started to panic at the thought of what he might encounter this time. He began to wish he hadn't sent the cab away, but at the thought of seeing Rosa's face when she received her gift, he shook off his jitters. The Morinos had gone out of their way to help him during his recovery. They surely meant him no harm now.

He didn't know the man who came to the gate this time, a short fellow in a furry overcoat. "Yes. What is it?"

"I'm here to see Miss Rosa."

"You got an appointment?"

"No, but I think she'll want to see me."

For a moment the man hesitated, then shrugged. "You can go up to the house, but I'll have to stay with you."

The gate swung open, and the man waved him on.

"Don't you want to see if I'm packin' a gat?" Phil teased.

The man had a sharp, foxy face and a mustache. He grinned broadly. "It's almost Christmas. You wouldn't be carrying a gun on Christmas, would you, Mac?"

"No. Just a present for Miss Rosa."

"Come on up to the house. Man, it's cold out here!"

The two walked up the long driveway and to the front door. "Ring the bell. I'll stick around to see if you get in. If not, I'll have to show you out."

"Sure thing." Phil rang the bell, and after a short wait the door opened. A woman Phil recognized stood framed in the doorway, and though he couldn't remember for sure, he thought it might be Rosa's mother. He had caught only one glimpse of her on the day he'd been beaten, and his memory was vague. "Mrs. Morino, isn't it?"

"Why, yes."

"I'm Phil Winslow. You remember me?"

A flush touched Maria Morino's face. "Why, yes, I do remember you."

"I brought Rosa a gift. Do you suppose I could give it to her?"

"Yes—of course. Come in out of the cold. Thank you, Jerry." She nodded to the guard.

"Sure thing, Mrs. Morino."

While the short man took his leave to continue patrolling the premises, Phil stepped in and stamped his feet on the rug. Snow was on his shoulders, and when he pulled off his hat, flakes fell to the floor. "I'm making a mess."

"There's no help for it. Come in by the fire. I'll get Rosa for you." She hesitated, then said, "Do you feel all right, Mr. Winslow?"

"Oh, fine, thank you, Mrs. Morino. Never better."

"My husband's in the study. He'll want to see you too."

Phil followed the woman down the hall and through a door into a large study. A fire blazed in a massive fireplace, and Big Tony himself was seated in a Windsor chair. He turned his head, then got up alertly and came over to shake hands. "Well, it's Winslow, ain't it?" he said guardedly.

"That's right, Mr. Morino. How are you?"

"I'm fine. You're sure lookin' a lot better than the last time I saw you. What brings you way out here? Bad weather to be out in."

"Not too bad. Until last winter, I'd never seen snow before."

"Never?"

"Nope. We didn't get it in Africa."

"Africa?"

"Where I come from, sir."

"Oh, yeah, yeah. I guess you told me that, huh? There must've been plenty of heat, though."

"Yes, sir, plenty of that. You're probably wondering why I came. Rosa sent me a present. I'll be visiting with my family tomorrow, so I thought I'd come by tonight to give her something, if it's all right with you."

"Why—I guess so. Sit down by the fire and thaw out. I'll go get her."

As Tony left the room Phil was aware that Mrs. Morino was standing by nervously. "Are you planning a big Christmas, Mrs. Morino?" he asked pleasantly.

"Oh yes! We always have family in and lots of company. You say you're going to be with your family?"

"Yes, ma'am, I am. My sister and I are spending the holidays with my grandmother."

The door was filled then as Tony entered and Rosa followed right behind. She was wearing a bright aqua jumper that contrasted with the darkness of her eyes and a white blouse underneath with delicate pearl buttons. She looked at him with an odd expression and then smiled. "Merry Christmas, Mr. Winslow."

"It's Phil," he said. "It's good to see you."

"It's good to see you. Are you . . . all right?"

"Sure. I'm fine now. I got your gift." He pulled the billfold out and said, "Nothing much in it yet, but it's a beautiful piece of work. Thanks so much."

"You're welcome."

"I brought you something too—if it's all right, Mr. Morino."

"A present? What is it?" Rosa asked.

"The wrapping's not much, but then, I'm not much of a wrapper either." He handed her the package, and her parents watched as she took off the bow and paper.

"Why, it's a book!"

"A very special book," Phil said. "That cover was made by a Masai war chieftain out of lion skin. He killed the lion himself and made the cover for me."

"Killed it with a spear?"

"That's right. Every Masai warrior has to kill a lion."

Rosa ran the tips of her finger over the book cover. "This was a real lion!" she breathed.

"Sure was. Black mane. They're frightening creatures. I wouldn't want to tackle one with a cannon much less a spear. But my uncle killed one once with his bare hands."

"Oh, come on!" Tony protested.

"It's a fact. His name's Barney Winslow. He's been in Africa for years. They call him the lion killer there, the Masai do."

Rosa opened the book and then lifted her head with a puzzled light in her dark eyes. "It's a Bible."

"Not a new one. It's one my father gave me when I was twelve years old. It's pretty badly marked up. I just got a new one myself. I thought you might like this one."

Maria moved closer and glanced over her daughter's shoulders. The two turned the pages, and together they saw that the margins were indeed filled with tiny notes written in a very clear hand.

"That's just some of my thoughts I had when I was reading through. You may not want to read all of them. I was kind of a drip at times."

Rosa looked up, a smile wreathing her face. "We're Catholic. I've never read the Bible."

"Well, Catholic or not, I thought you might like it. At least the cover." He shifted his feet uncomfortably, for Rosa was looking at him with lips parted and eyes bright. "I guess I'd better get going."

"You say you're going to be with your family?" Maria said.

"Yes. My sister and I will be with my grandmother."

"Is that the pistol-packin' sister Dom told me about?" Tony grinned.

"That's the one."

"Where does your grandmother live?"

"A little ways north of here in a residential area. She lost my grandfather, Mark Winslow, just over a year ago and is rather lonely."

"Wait a minute! Wasn't he that railroad bigwig?"

"He was vice-president of the Union Pacific."

"Hey, I knew him! I met him at least. He was a real straight shooter."

"Yes, he was actually a straight shooter when he was a young man. He had to keep peace on the railroad. He could whip any man with his fists or with a gun, so they say about him. And my grandmother dealt blackjack in the saloons along the right-of-way."

"You don't say," Tony said with interest. "I'd like to meet that lady."

"You'd like her, Mr. Morino. She's right up front, just like my grandfather was. Well, I'd better go."

"Hey, how'd you get out here?"

"I took a cab."

"Well, you can't walk back. I'll have Dom take you back."

"I can call for another cab, sir. You needn't go to any trouble," Phil said.

"Nonsense, my boy," Tony bellowed. "We'll see that you get safely home."

Rosa piped up, "I'll take him out to the garage, Daddy. Maybe I could ride out with him and Dom."

"Sure, sweetheart, you do that. Let me see that gift while you're gone."

Rosa ran to get her coat, and then she led Phil outside to the garage. Dom lived over it, and as they climbed up an outer stairway to his room, she exclaimed, "It was nice of you to give me such a personal gift, Phil."

"Well, it was nice of you to give me a billfold. Someday," he laughed, "I'll have some money to put in it. It is a beautiful billfold, though, and I appreciate it, Rosa."

Dom met them at the door, and Rosa told him her father's instructions. "I'm going along," she said. "Drive through the city so we can see it. It ought to be pretty with all this snow and the Christmas lights."

"Not as pretty as the woods, I'll bet," Phil said. "As Jefferson once said, 'God made the country, and man made the town.'"

"Jefferson who?" Dom asked.

"Why, Thomas Jefferson, the former president." Phil grinned.

As they got into the car Rosa said, "You've got to come back and see Boadicea." She laughed at his expression. "You see, I did learn to pronounce it right."

"You sure did. I'll do that come spring."

They made the trip too quickly for Rosa. She found out a great deal about Africa and was fascinated by it all. When they reached Phil's apartment building, she said, "I'd love to go to Africa someday."

"Get your folks to take you. They can stay with my father and mother there. They love having visitors."

"Will you be going back?"

"Maybe when I finish college. Thanks again, Rosa, and merry Christmas! Merry Christmas to you too, Dom."

Phil climbed out of the car and headed for the front door of the building as Dom drove off slowly. Rosa craned her neck to watch Phil out the window as long as she could, then settled back down, thinking about the handsome young man.

Dom interrupted her thoughts. "I wonder what a smart kid like that's doin' workin' at a stable. From what I hear, his grandmother is loaded. She'd probably help him."

"I think he has too much pride for that," Rosa said softly.

After they arrived back home, she took the Bible up to her room. She lay flat across her bed and opened it to page one and studied the first note: *"I give my heart to Jesus Christ. He will ever be Lord of my life, and I will be obedient to Him no matter what it costs."* For a long time she lay there turning the pages slowly, and somehow she got a sense of the life of Phillip Winslow. The notes were very personal, intimate even, and there were times when he cried out almost in panic. Finally she closed the Bible, sat up, and held it on her lap. She rubbed the cover and murmured, "A real lion-skin cover! I'm going to read it all the way through!"

CHAPTER FOUR

THE WINSLOW CLAN

★ ★ ★ ★

As Lola Winslow's big Oldsmobile moved along the snow-packed streets of New York, Amelia and Phil sat in the roomy backseat staring out the windows at the pristine whiteness of the world. Snow had continued falling all night, leaving a dazzling whiteness on the city and countryside. Ugly brownstone buildings had been converted to fluffy white palaces, their rounded tops pierced only by chimneys that sent clouds of dusky smoke into the air. Long dagger-shaped icicles hung from the eaves, giving the houses a sinister appearance despite their wintry beauty. The soft blanket of snow muffled the city noises, so that the usual clashing of cars and trucks was muted to a gentle humming of the tires.

The driver, whom Lola Winslow had sent to pick up her grandchildren, steered the big car through the downtown area, into the quieter residential streets, and finally out to where buildings and houses gave way to snow-covered hills and trees. Turning onto a dirt road, he said, "Good thing the roads are frozen. When this thaws, the mud's going to be ten inches deep. There won't be any traffic until the sun bakes it out."

"How long have you been driving for my grandmother, Robert?"

"Mr. Mark hired me fifteen years ago. I've been with them ever since. Driving and gardening and everything that needs doing around the place."

"I know you miss my grandfather," Phil said, "but then, we all do."

Robert was a tall, lean man whose black hair was salted with white. "Yes, sir. He was the finest man I ever knew. How your grandmother manages without him is beyond me."

Phil and Amelia fell silent, taking in the beauty of the New York countryside. The trees were all soft now, their outlines smooth and rounded with white crystals. The sun reflected off of the snowy landscape, creating a luminous glow that blinded the eyes.

Lowering her voice so that Robert could not hear over the roar of the powerful engine, Amelia leaned closer to Phil and whispered, "I wish I weren't going."

Phil lifted his eyebrows in surprise. "Why would you say a thing like that? You don't want to sit alone in your room on Christmas, do you?"

Amelia shook her head. The cold had permeated the car, and she kept her hands inside her coat pockets as she leaned against Phil. "I'm afraid I'm going to be uncomfortable because I didn't stay with Grandmother like you did."

Indeed, when Phil and Amelia had arrived at their grandparents' house the summer before last, Amelia had at first been excited. She had felt free to come and go as she pleased, finding friends in the city who loved to party and go to speakeasies, but when her grandparents tried to get her to stay at the estate and live more responsibly, she had rebelled at their restrictions and run away. Not telling them where she was going, she had simply left a note saying she loved them, but she had to try her wings. Her grandmother had only learned that she was still in the New York area when she showed up at her grandfather's funeral in November 1922.

"That was such a stupid note. I had to 'try my wings,' I said. It's going to be very uncomfortable."

"Forget about it, sis." Phil pulled his hand out of his pocket and put it around her shoulder. He drew her closer and turned and whispered, "It's going to be great. You're going to have a fine Christmas."

Amelia leaned closer and let herself enjoy the pressure of his arm. She needed a strong right arm, for her heart told her it had been wrong of her to leave. Now she looked up at Phil and said, "I'm just worried that Grandmother does not approve of me, Phil."

"Well, just stop worrying. Grandmother loves you. It's going to be fine. You'll see."

Amelia shook her head and glanced up. "There's the house." She straightened up and watched as the car pulled into the long, curving driveway. "Why can't I be good like you, Phil?"

"That's nonsense!" Phil snorted. "You're just finding your way, that's all."

The car came to a smooth stop at the front door. Robert hopped out and opened the door for Amelia. She climbed out and said, "Thank you, Robert. You're a fine driver."

"Thank you, Miss Amelia. I do the best I can." He turned to Phil. "It's good to have both of you here for the holidays."

"We're just glad to be able to spend some time with Grandmother, Robert."

The two turned and, leaving Robert to bring the small bags, walked up the steps. "Be careful. Don't slip on the ice," Phil cautioned. He took her arm, and the two slowly made their way up to the front door. It opened before they got there, and much to their surprise, they were greeted by their parents. "Mom! Dad!" Phil exclaimed. "We didn't know you'd be here!"

Smiling and laughing, Andrew and Dorothy came out to meet them. Phil shook his father's hand, then gave him a hug. His mother had embraced Amelia and was holding her tightly. He heard her say, "It's so good to see you, Amelia!"

Amelia let go of her mother and lifted her arms to her father. Andrew put his arms around her, squeezed her, and kissed her on the cheek. "Come in by the fire, daughter," he smiled. "That's a long, cold trip from the city."

As the four of them went inside, Phil and Amelia plied them with questions. They hadn't expected to see their parents again so soon, since they had just been to the States the previous year for their grandfather's funeral. Dorothy explained that their church in Nairobi had taken up a collection to help them make a return trip this year, so they could spend Christmas with Andrew's mother and their children. Another surprise was that their uncle Barney and aunt Katie and their daughter, Erin, and her husband, Quaid, had also made the trip with them while their son, Patrick, stayed in Africa to look after the mission station. The four of them were expected to arrive on Christmas Day.

Now Dorothy said, "Let's go see your grandmother. She's waiting for you."

"How is she, Mom?" Amelia asked quickly.

"Well, she doesn't say much about how she's feeling, but I know she misses your grandfather more than any of the rest of us."

The four of them made their way down the wide hallway and turned left into the big drawing room, which had been Mark Winslow's favorite place to spend time. A freshly laid fire blazed cheerfully in a massive fireplace, showering sparks up the chimney from time to time. The flames licked eagerly at huge logs, releasing a pleasant woodsy odor into the room.

"So, you're here. Come and give your grandmother a kiss, both of you."

Lola Winslow, even at the age of seventy-six, retained traces of her youthful beauty. Her skin was not as smooth as it used to be, but the large dark eyes still dominated her face. She took the kisses of her grandchildren and then said briskly, "Sit down now. I want to hear all about what you've been doing."

There was a peace about her grandmother that amazed Amelia. She had seen firsthand the love that this woman had for her husband, Mark. If ever two people had been inextricably bound together, it was Lola and Mark Winslow. Amelia had seen how they could not get close without touching each other, and she had also seen how Lola's eyes were always fondly fixed on him whenever Mark was in view. After he had died, Amelia had expected her grandmother to be marked by grief, but there remained a sweet serenity about Lola in the midst of her loss.

I hope someday I can be like her, Amelia thought, and then she heard her mother saying, "Now, Lola, let me get our children settled in first. Then you can have all the talk you want."

"All right, but don't take long. I get to see you so seldom." Lola smiled.

"We'll hurry, Grandmother," Phil said. "I'll even let you beat me at a game of blackjack."

"You never beat me at blackjack in your life, Phillip," Lola smiled, and her eyes sparkled with mischief. "I think we'll play for money this time. You need to be humbled."

Phil laughed and moved across the room to lean down and kiss his grandmother on the cheek. "You're right about that, but I'd rather lose to you than to anyone else I know."

"Come along, Amelia, Phillip," Dorothy said. "We'll get you settled in. We've got a lot to talk about."

★　★　★　★

Later in the day, while Lola was napping, Amelia put on some boots and a heavy fur coat of her grandmother's and went out to enjoy the crisp day. Amelia's father and mother were talking with Phil, and Amelia felt a twinge of envy. *They're so proud of Phil. He's doing so well at college and work. He can do anything!* That thought brought another—a sense of shame that she had failed her parents. Although she did not often let it show, there was a sensitive side to Amelia that was softer, gentler, and more easily hurt than most people knew. She kept this carefully hidden, glossed over with an artificial hardness. Phil knew this tender side of her, but even her parents did not discern it as readily.

Trying to dismiss her feelings, she wandered out onto the estate—some fifty acres, most of them covered by untouched first-growth timber. She loved being alone in the thick woods. The big trees towered over her now, their limbs rounded with snow. Her feet made no sound as she broke through the fluffy carpet that lay even underneath the trees. The snow fell gently on her shoulders and from time to time she would hear a *clump* as a dollop of snow fell from a branch. She liked being out alone, although it was different from the aloneness of her apartment. Here there was life. Winter birds called out from the treetops, and furry animals burrowed through the snow looking for food.

She even spotted a six-point buck, which seeing her, leaped away, startled, in the most graceful of flights, making almost no sound on the carpet of snow.

"Go on! I wouldn't shoot you if I could. You're too beautiful for that!" Amelia called out. Her voice disturbed the still air around her, and she turned and walked back toward the house. She went in the back door and stamped the snow off her feet. Stepping into the warmth of the kitchen, she saw her grandmother was up now, wearing a white apron and working alongside their cook. Cora had been with the family for years. She was a huge woman, tall and strong, not fat but just heavy in the way of some women. The cook shook her head as she said, "You gonna freeze yoself and get a pneumonia out there, Miss Amelia."

"No I won't, Cora." Amelia laughed. She took off the fur coat and hung it carefully on a peg beside the door. "That's a beautiful coat, Grandmother. Have you had it long?"

"Mark got it for me ten years ago. It's mink, you know. He paid way too much for it, but I've always loved it." The coat was indeed the softest and most comfortable thing Amelia had ever put on. "I expect it'll be yours one day," Lola said.

Amelia blinked with surprise at this calm reference to Lola's leaving the world.

"That won't be for a long time, Grandmother."

Lola simply smiled. "Maybe not, but in the meantime, I'm helping Cora cook."

"I tried to run her out of this here kitchen," Cora said, "but she won't go. Maybe you can make her mind, Miss Amelia."

Immediately Amelia went over and plucked an apron from a peg on the wall. "You're talking to a professional cook."

"What you mean professional cook?" Cora sniffed.

"I mean I've been cooking for a living at a restaurant. So, Grandmother, why don't you sit on the stool and tell me about your misspent youth while I help Cora."

Lola protested, but Amelia led her to the stool and helped her down. "Now, you sit there."

She turned back to Cora and gave her a big hug. Amelia had spent time in the kitchen with Cora during her brief stay in the Winslow house last year. "You taught me enough about cooking to get me a job. Now, what are we cooking today?"

"We's gonna prepare the turkey so's it's ready for roasting tomorrow and make corn-bread stuffing."

Lola laughed. "You ought to hear Cora's opinion of Yankee cooking."

"They cain't cook *nothin'!*" Cora said vehemently. "Look what they do with dressin'. They put white bread in it! Now ain't that a tragic shame? Ain't nothin' but corn-bread dressin's gonna be any good!"

"What can I do, Cora?"

"Here, you work on this celery whilst I makes the corn bread."

Making the dressing was an exacting task under Cora's tutelage. The celery had to be split first with a sharp knife and then cut into tiny fragments. Amelia obediently began cutting the stalks into small cubes, all the time listening as her grandmother spoke about the rest of the family. Cora went about mixing up the corn-bread batter, then scooped it into a pan and shoved it in the oven to bake. After this she measured out the remaining ingredients, which included butter, chicken broth, crumbled bacon, salt, pepper, and bacon drippings, and put them into a large bowl. The corn bread came out of the oven and was ready to be crumbled into the bowl at the same time Amelia had finished chopping an onion.

When the corn-bread stuffing was finished, Cora said, "I gots to leave for a minute. You be sure you don't mess up none of the cookin', Miss Amelia."

"I won't," Amelia promised. She waited until Cora had left the room and then shook her head. "She's an amazing woman."

"I don't know what we would have done without her. She idolized your grandfather, and he was so fond of her."

Amelia moved over to the stove and picked up the kettle to fill it. "I think I'd like some hot tea."

"That would be good."

Amelia made the tea as she listened to her grandmother, then brought the teapot to the low counter, where she poured two small cups and sat down with her grandmother. The two sipped it gratefully.

"Nothing like hot tea on a cold day," Lola said. She looked out the window and saw the snow falling. For a time she sat there silently, and then she turned and put her dark eyes on Amelia. "Every time it snows like this, I think of the time your grandfather and I got snowed in, in a big blizzard down in Texas."

"Tell me about how you met Grandfather."

"But I've already told you."

"I know, but you always think of something different. Please tell me again."

Then Lola began speaking of how she had been raised in a saloon by her mother and felt helpless to escape her circumstances. When her brother-in-law forced his attentions on her, a young railroadman named Mark Winslow stopped her attacker. Lola later learned that Mark had been arrested for a shooting and was sentenced to a long term in a Texas prison. Grateful to him for saving her, she had helped him break jail, disguising herself as a young Mexican man and Mark as an old Mexican. The two had fled together, only to be trapped by a blizzard.

Lola's voice grew soft as she continued. "Mark was sick when we got him out of jail, and when we got shut in by that blizzard, the fever took him. I thought he would die. It was so cold, I couldn't believe it. It was all I could do to keep a small fire going and keep us both alive."

"When did you fall in love with him, Grandmother?"

"I think it was there in that little deserted cabin. I took care of him like he was a baby." She smiled suddenly and said, "That's a good way to fall in love. Baby a man."

"You've had such an exciting life, Grandmother."

"Too exciting at times, I'm afraid."

For a moment Amelia hesitated, then said, "It must be terrible for you to have lost Grandfather."

Lola did not seem to hear for a moment. She sat very still, her fine old hands cradling the teacup. She took a sip and then put the cup down. Turning to Amelia, she said gently, "We lose things a little bit at a time, I think. I haven't really lost Mark. Something's lost when you don't know where it is, but I know where Mark is. He loved Jesus so fervently, and now he's with Him. And soon I'll be with them. I'll see him very soon."

"No, not for a long time, Grandmother!" Amelia protested.

"I can't help feeling it won't be long. You're young and don't want to think about such things, but I've got more to look forward to on the other side of death than I have on this side." She reached out and took Amelia's hand and said, "It would be hard to leave, though, not being around to help you."

Tears came to Amelia's eyes. "I've made such a mess of my life, Grandmother, and I'm so unhappy. I know I've broken Mom's and Dad's hearts. I don't know what's wrong with me. I've disappointed every one of you and done awful things."

Lola took both of Amelia's hands in between hers. "You haven't dealt blackjack in a saloon like I did."

Amelia bowed her head so that her grandmother would not see the tears, but Lola knew what was in her heart. She stood up and pulled Amelia's head over against her. "You don't know, Granddaughter, how often Mark and I prayed for you. Especially during his last days. He loved you so very much."

Amelia threw her arms around her grandmother. She felt so helpless and alone and confused. Two things pulled at her. She wanted to give up all ideas of being independent and just be what her parents and what everyone else seemed to want her to be. But there was a side of her that would not give in, and as she clung to her grandmother, she thought, *What's wrong with me? Why can't I be like Phil?*

★　★　★　★

Very early on Christmas morning Andrew and Dorothy rose, dressed, and went downstairs. They found Barney and Katie had arrived early and had let themselves in. After exchanging greetings, the women had made a quick breakfast while the rest of the house slept. Katie explained that Erin and Quaid were visiting old friends and planned to come in time for Christmas dinner. As the four sat around the table eating lightly—knowing that the big dinner was to come—the conversation turned to the condition of the country.

"It's been a bad year for America," Andrew said, stirring his coffee and then sipping it. "I never admired President Harding much, but I hated that he had to be taken away at this time."

"Well, he looked like a president," Barney said. Barney

Winslow was a big man with some battle damage. He had been a prizefighter as a young man, and his years in Africa had left their mark. Still, he looked strong and virile as he sat slouched back in his chair. "I think his main trouble was he seemed to like everybody and want to do favors for everybody."

"That's right. He had a vague, fuzzy mind. I read somewhere that Harding had said once, 'I can't make a thing out of this tax problem. I listen to one side, and they seem right. And then I talk to the other side, and they seem just as right. I wish there was a book that would tell me the right and the wrong of it.'"

Dorothy listened as the two men talked, and then she asked, "Do you think it's true what they're saying about all the scandals?"

"It's true enough all right. Harding was a weak man. He couldn't distinguish between an honest man and a rascal. I suspect that his health deteriorated largely because of the Teapot Dome Scandal. There was enough bribery and corruption in those oil deals to put some big men in jail," Andrew replied. "Men that Harding had trusted."

Dorothy sat nodding at her husband's assessment of the deceased president's problems. Her thoughts turned to concerns over the loosening morals of the country. "We're so sheltered out in Africa. I'm shocked at what I see here in America. Why, the way women dress! It's a shame! Skirts are so short, and clothes are so tight. It's embarrassing to see these flappers, as the papers are calling them now."

Barney smiled grimly. "Did you hear what happened in Utah?" he asked the group.

"No," Katie said. "What was that?"

"A bill's pending there requiring fine and imprisonment for women who are on the street with skirts higher than three inches above the ankles."

"That's right," Dorothy said. "I read that the same thing is happening in Ohio. The law there says any female over fourteen can't wear a skirt that doesn't reach to the instep."

"It'll never work." Barney shook his head. "People aren't going to abide by such laws. Why, they're not paying any attention to Prohibition. There's probably as much drinking going on now as before liquor was outlawed."

"What's happening to this country, Barney?" Andrew scowled. "God has been so good to America, and we've turned away from Him."

"It's the same thing that happens everywhere when God isn't honored," Barney said, shaking his head. "Civilization goes down. I for one don't see anything good coming out of all this so-called freedom. I think we're living in an age of transition."

Katie forced a smile. "I guess that's what people always say when times get bad."

"That's right." Andrew nodded and grinned crookedly. "I'll bet Adam said one time, 'Eve, you know I don't understand the children. I think we're living in an age of transition.'"

Barney chuckled in amusement and shook his head. "You're right. We're all prophets of gloom. What a sad subject we're on for a joyful Christmas morning!"

"Uncle Barney! Aunt Katie!"

They all turned together at the sound of Amelia's voice as she entered the kitchen and greeted her aunt and uncle. After hugs all around and Christmas greetings, Amelia sat down and ate a sweet roll and had a cup of coffee.

Then, before Barney and Katie had barely heard Amelia's latest news, she jumped up from the table and grabbed Lola's mink coat off the peg by the back door. Pulling on boots, she announced, "I'm going for a walk. Anybody want to come?"

"Out in this freezing weather!" Barney exclaimed. "Not me!"

"I'll go," Andrew said quickly. "Let me get my coat and some heavier shoes."

Ten minutes later Amelia and her father were walking along the pathway underneath the enormous oaks. "When are you and Mother going back to Nairobi?" she asked.

"We haven't quite decided. Barney and Katie don't want to be gone from the mission station for too long either, but Patrick is running things in their absence, and he's a pretty mature fellow." Barney and Katie's son was, indeed, a sturdy worker at the mission field.

"I know you miss being there," Amelia said. "It's more home for you than here, isn't it?"

"You know, I really do miss it. So does your mother. Back when I was a young man, I used to think that the best time missionaries had was when they came home on furlough. But then over the years I've come to realize that home for us is the mission field. I'm a visitor here in America. I don't know this country much anymore. So many things are happening—most of them not good."

Amelia knew they were very close to talking about her own lifestyle, for she was involved in things her parents did not consider good. Her dream of a life in show business would be the last thing they would want for her. She suddenly stopped, and when her father stopped also and turned to face her with some surprise, she said, "Dad, I know you're disappointed in me and you think I'm making a terrible mistake. I'm sorry I have to put you through this."

Andrew reached out and took his daughter's hand. They were both wearing gloves, but when he squeezed her hand he felt her return his grasp. "Not too many years ago, honey, I made a very, very serious mistake. I wronged your mother, and I got as far away from the will of God as is possible."

Amelia knew some of this story, but her parents had not talked about it a great deal. Years ago, before they went to Africa, her father had been called to be the pastor of a large, powerful church and had gotten so caught up with his work there that he had ignored his wife and family. As a result of this, Dorothy had had a brief affair. Her infidelity had caused Andrew to retreat behind a hard shell of unforgiveness, and it had nearly wrecked his life. Amelia looked up into her father's face and listened as he spoke. "I made such a terrible mistake judging your mother." He looked down at the ground and avoided her eyes. "Sometimes life's like being in the middle of a bridge, and you can't find either end. All you can do is stare at the water below and ask God to get you where you're going before you destroy yourself."

"I'm sorry, Daddy."

Suddenly he put his arms around her and squeezed her. "You're my daughter no matter what happens. No matter what you do. No matter what comes into your life, Amelia. I'm your father, and you can always come to me and to your mother. Nothing you could do would make us love you any less."

Amelia leaned forward and put her head on his chest. "It's

hard to believe that," she whispered.

"Love should be unconditional." His voice was soft as he added, "It shouldn't be 'I will love you *if* . . .' It should just be 'I love you no matter what.'"

The two walked on, and Amelia felt closer to her father than she had ever felt in her life. Finally they made their way back to the house, and when they approached, they saw a young woman come running out, followed by a tall man.

"Well, if it isn't my niece Erin and her old man!" Andrew said.

Erin Winslow Merritt came running straight toward Amelia with her arms out. The last time the two had seen each other over a year ago, Amelia had been trying to steal Quaid from her. Amelia stiffened, uncertain how to respond to her cousin now. But it appeared that Erin had forgotten the whole incident, and she threw her arms around Amelia in a big hug, crying out, "It's so good to see you, Amelia!"

Relieved that Erin didn't hold anything against her for her brash behavior, Amelia hugged her back, glad to see her cousin again. They had been close friends growing up, and inwardly Amelia cringed at the shabby way she had treated Erin last year. Amelia laughed now and said, "So what's this I hear about your being married? I thought you weren't all that interested in Quaid Merritt."

Erin laughed. "Well, I guess I saw the light after all."

Erin was a fine-looking young woman of nineteen who had always been into adventures of some sort. She had learned to fly while in Africa, and after coming to America, she had gotten into show business with Quaid Merritt. He had been a flier in the Great War, shooting down many German planes. He came up now—a tall, lean man with a friendly smile. He had heard the question and said, "We sure are married, but it was awfully hard to get her to agree to it."

Erin's eyes sparkled. She had deep-set blue-green eyes, widely spaced, and she seemed very happy as she said, "Why don't you boys go on in and I'll tell my cousin all about our most recent adventures in Africa."

"I hear you've been flying missionaries around."

"That's right, and also supplies and medicine. Walk with me, and I'll fill you in on the details."

Andrew and Quaid went inside while the cousins stayed outside to be alone for a few minutes. Erin talked excitedly about their adventures in Africa and some of the lives they had touched with their emergency medical deliveries.

Amelia stared at her cousin and then shook her head. "I don't understand how you can do it."

"Do what, Amelia?"

"Give up a career in show business. Why, they wanted you to star in a picture of your own!"

"Oh, that's nothing. I never did like show business. I love flying, and I love Quaid, and God has called us to Africa to use our flying skills. And Grandfather left enough money to buy two more planes and service them for a long time. So God has made a way for us. I'm so happy, Amelia."

Amelia had been dumbfounded when she had heard that Erin was giving up a life of fame and money, all that she herself had ever dreamed of. Doubt showed in her eyes, and Erin said quietly, "It's all right. I'm giving up gravel for diamonds. I know you don't see it now, but you will someday. We'll talk later. Have you met our new visitors? I'll bet there's someone inside you haven't met."

"Who is that? I thought it was just the family."

"It is family in a way. His name is Lee Novak, and his wife's name is Sarah."

"The Novaks? That name seems to ring a bell," Amelia said.

"You must have been reading the Winslow genealogy." Erin laughed.

"You'll have to tell me who they are," Amelia said. "I don't seem to remember offhand."

"Lee's parents were Grandfather's sister Patience and her husband, Thad Novak."

"Oh, I remember the connection now! But I've never met Lee and Sarah."

"They're very nice. Quaid and I got along very well with them."

"What does he do?"

"He's in police work of some kind."

"Really? I'd like to meet him."

"Well, you will. Come on in. It's almost time for dinner."

As soon as they were in the house, Erin took Amelia over to a couple who were talking to Phil. Erin interrupted. "Excuse me, Phillip, but my cousin wants to meet the Novaks. Amelia, this is Lee Novak and his wife, Sarah."

Novak was not a large man, no more than five-ten, but he was muscular and imbued with a sense of strength. He had black hair with gray at the temples, and Amelia found out later he was fifty-five. He had a pair of steady dark eyes, and his grip was strong as he shook hands with her. His wife was a small woman with a cheerful smile. She had dark hair and alert brown eyes.

Amelia shook hands with her, then said, "I hear you're in police work, Mr. Novak."

"Law enforcement," Lee said. "I'm a special agent for the federal government."

"It's very interesting what Lee does," Phil said, excitement sparkling in his eyes. "He uses scientific investigation to track down criminals and get them convicted."

Lola came up and put her hand gently on Lee's arm. "I always loved Lee's father so much. His name was Thad. He served in the Confederacy all the way through to Appomattox." Her eyes grew fond as she said, "The old home place would have been lost if it hadn't been for Lee's father. Thad Novak took over after the war and kept the plantation going. The rest of the boys went their own way, but Thad held it all together."

"My father was very fond of you too, Aunt Lola."

"We lost him . . . hmm, about five or six years ago? And your mother earlier this year."

"Yes, the world's a lonelier place without them."

"Well, they're sitting at the Master's banquet table now. Come along. I think it's time to eat. You'll have to blame Amelia if the cooking's not done right."

Amelia shook her head. "I was just Cora's helper, and you know she never fails."

They went into the large dining room, where they found Barney and Katie, along with Andrew and Dorothy. They all took their seats with Lola at the head of the table. Spread out before them were steaming bowls of vegetables and a huge turkey in front of Barney ready for carving. The silver and fine china glittered under the lights.

"Barney, the eldest son, you ask the blessing."

Barney bowed his head, and they all grew quiet. "Our Father, we thank you for this meal. We thank you for Christmas. Not for the tinsel or the trappings that have gathered around it over the years, but for the coming of Jesus. We thank you that He did come and grew up a perfect man, and that He died as the Lamb of God, the sacrifice for our sins. We bow before Him and before you, O Father, and we beg, O Lord, that this year will be a year of sacrifice and of praise and of honor to you. And we ask it all in Jesus' name."

"Barney, start whacking that turkey," Andrew cried out. "I'm starved!"

Barney proved to be a good carver, and soon the plates were piled high with food. The talk ran around the table, and the three couples working in Africa filled everybody in on their work there. Everyone expressed great interest in Lee Novak's career and in Phil's accomplishments as well.

"I hear you've broken every record at that college, Phillip, and that you're already talking about getting through the four-year course in two," Quaid said. "I wish I were as smart as you."

Phil flushed. "Oh, it's not really that great."

"What are you going to do with all that education?" Lee Novak smiled. He was a quiet individual, but when he did speak, everybody stopped to listen.

Phil shook his head. "Things have happened so fast. I'm not at all sure."

Novak seemed to file this away, as he did everything he heard. They were finishing their desserts of pumpkin and pecan pie when Lola tapped on her glass. Everyone turned to her, and she said, "I am going to preach a sermon."

"Here, here!" Barney said. "Let's hear it for Evangelist Lola!"

A silence fell over the table, and Lola began to speak. "It was always Mark's job to speak about the family at Christmas dinner. Now here it is already the second Christmas without him. You all remember how proud he was of being a Winslow, and so am I."

Her voice was not loud, but it carried clearly. "There are so many empty places," she said somewhat sadly, "and so many did not come back from the Great War, but God brought our men back. We even have a war hero. Quaid, you're with us now. We're thankful that Logan Smith, who is a Winslow in blood, brought such honor to the family name. The Winslow name is a proud name. Our people have been judges, ministers, legislators, doctors. Some of them haven't turned out so good—as is true in every family—but many of them have. I want all of you to remember that you are Winslows, every one of you. Now I'd like to read a few lines from a book all of you know." She picked up a leather-bound volume and opened it to a place she had marked. "This is Gilbert Winslow's journal. One of my favorite passages is from the time when Gilbert and others of his family were thrown into prison at Salem. They were almost certain to be executed, but he wrote these words while standing in the very shadow of the gallows." She began to read:

"And so it seems that very soon now I must leave this earth. This is the Father's will, apparently, and I embrace it. I came to this New World to make a life, but it would have been nothing without the Lord Jesus. When He came into my heart, He took over completely and filled every part of me. Since then I have never ceased to proclaim His goodness, His riches, His mercy, His long-suffering. Now many will say, 'Well, Gilbert, there you are in a dark stinking cell about to die. What do you say now to your fine God who has let you fall into this evil?' I will say, 'Hallelujah, praise the name of God! He is the God of gods, even though I be in a cell, and if it be that I am to die tomorrow, then I will go out shouting the praise of Jesus Christ and of the Father.' The light may grow dim, but His light never does."

A silence filled the room as Lola closed the book. "I've always liked those last words of our ancestor: 'The light may grow dim, but His light never does.' " She looked around the table and said softly, "I love every one of you, and I have prayed that every one of you may find God's will for your life. I also pray for others of our family who are scattered far around the world. We are facing perilous times, and the devil is loose. He is out to destroy the homes and souls of those who call themselves believers. But I have prayed that our family, each of them, might find their way.

You all have Winslow blood. You will need all of your strength and courage to find your way through these years that seem so evil. God be with you all and keep you all."

★　★　★　★

Phil was deeply moved by his grandmother's short message. He kept thinking about it after they had left the dinner table and gathered in the drawing room to open presents. Two hours later, after all the gifts had been exchanged, he walked to the library and sat down, occupied with his thoughts. He was surprised when Lee Novak entered the room, saying, "Hello, Phil, I've been looking for you."

"Have a seat, Lee."

Novak sat down and said, "I've had you on my mind a lot since we met. I don't know why, but I think the Lord has a work for you to do."

"What do you mean, Lee?"

"I think one day you might do what I'm doing."

Phil shook his head and laughed. "Police work? Not a chance!"

"There's more to it than you think. This country's falling on hard times. Criminals are taking over."

"Yes, I've read about what's happening." Phil hesitated and then said, "Do you know Tony Morino?"

Instantly Novak's eyes narrowed. "Yes, I know him. What about him?"

"Well, I've met him. As a matter of fact, I've been in his home."

Novak stared at him and shook his head. "How did you get in there?"

He listened as Phil told him about the encounter he had had with the Morinos. He ended by saying, "I thought the girl was pretty spoiled at first, but she's turned out to be quite nice. So is her mother."

"I'm sure they are. But their family's built on wrong principles, and it can't survive."

Phil shifted uncomfortably. "Is he really that bad a man, Lee?"

"He's evil. That's all there is to it. We can't let men like that run our cities and our countries. That's the kind of man I'm out to stop. And, Phil, I hope one day you'll join the fight."

"Well, maybe I can someday . . . if I can ever afford to go to law school. That's what I'd really like to do."

Lee Novak said quietly, "We need good people in the law—both as lawyers and law-enforcement officers—to help bring justice to this land. I, for one, want to do something to make this a better world. It's gone rotten, and it's people like Big Tony who make the rottenness spread."

★　★　★　★

The day after Christmas Amelia had packed her things and was ready to go. She found Lola waiting for her and Phil carrying the things out to the car where the driver waited. Embracing her grandmother, she held her tightly, feeling the thinness of her frame. "I've had such a good time."

"I'm glad you could come, my dear, and I want you to come as often as you'd like. Here, I've got something for you."

Amelia stared at the envelope. "What is it?"

"I know you're short of money, and I wanted to help. Mark would have wanted me to do it."

"But, Grandmother, I'm planning to do something you won't approve of."

"I approve of *you*, and whatever you do, you still need to eat. Come and see me. You can tell me anything."

Amelia kissed her grandmother and turned, leaving the house. She had been moved by her grandmother's gift and even more by the trust that she knew she in no way deserved.

When she'd gotten into the car, Phil climbed in beside her and shut the door. They rode silently for a time, and finally Phil said, "Well, was it as bad as you thought?"

"I was so glad to see everybody, but I'm going to be a disappointment to them. You know what Grandmother did?" she whispered. "She gave me some money. She knows I'll use it to try to get into show business, and she hates the idea, but she said she loved me."

Phil did not answer. He simply reached over and took her hand. She turned to face him, and he saw tears in her eyes.

"I've got enough to live on for three months," she said. "If I don't get some kind of a break—"

"What will you do?"

"I'll do what I've set out to do, Phil. I'll never quit!"

CHAPTER FIVE

A BIBLICAL PRINCIPLE

★ ★ ★ ★

Amelia emerged from a small shop and looked up at the three balls hanging on the side of the building. The sign beneath them read Abe's Pawnshop. She stopped dead still, staring at the icon for a moment, then shrugged her shoulders and, smiling wryly, turned and walked down the street.

March in New York was an unpredictable month, caught in the stasis between winter and spring. February had been bitter cold, and the skies had dumped mountains of snow on the city, rendering it nearly helpless. April would no doubt bring lush grass, daisies, and robins. But here at the beginning of March, one never knew what each day would bring. A freezing blast might touch the cheeks of those making their way down Forty-second Street, while across town a mild, warming breeze might bring a moment's relief from winter's chill.

Involuntarily Amelia reached up and touched her throat. She felt strangely naked, for the necklace that had hung there almost constantly since her sixteenth birthday was absent. The beautiful gold chain with a sapphire pendant now resided inside Abe's Pawnshop. It had been the delight of her life when her parents had given it to her for her birthday, and it had wrenched her heart to march into the pawnshop and exchange it for a few bills.

Amelia felt like a traitor as she picked up her pace and hurried along the street.

The shops in this part of town were not first-class, but rather businesses serving the poorer inhabitants of the city. Pawnshops and used clothing and furniture stores alternated with liquor stores. Many of the buildings were closed, the dreams of their prior owners reduced to vacant spaces.

Amelia had managed to put several blocks between herself and Abe's Pawnshop, and as she came to an intersection, she turned and saw a poor woman leaning against a building. A child clung to her ragged skirts, and she held an infant in her arms. The woman's face was pale and her clothes thin, as were those of the children. There was a stricken quality about her and a hungry look in the faces of the children. She seemed to have no purpose in life except to stand helplessly, her eyes fixed on those who passed by. It was not the first time Amelia had seen poverty, for plenty of that existed in the city. She had been approached many times by panhandlers and beggars, but she usually ignored them. Now she paused, waiting for an opening in the traffic. Yet she could not turn away from the woman, as she might have ordinarily.

An impulse tugged at her to give the woman some money, but she well knew what was in her purse—her month's rent plus twenty dollars extra to cover the bare necessities for two weeks. For some reason her attention was caught by a bird that perched on a sign reading Sing's Laundry. He was ruffled by a blast of cold air and seemed rather tattered. He puffed his chest out, however, and began to sing as if he had not a care in the world. Amelia had no idea what kind of bird it was, but she could not help thinking of a Scripture passage she had heard her father preach on often: *Behold the fowls of the air: for they sow not, neither do they reap, nor gather into barns; yet your heavenly Father feedeth them. Are ye not much better than they?* Dropping her eyes, she was gripped by a cynical spirit. *Well, God, there's your bird, and there's your woman and her helpless babies. Are you going to come through or not?*

At that instant the woman's eyes met hers, and for a moment Amelia thought the woman would approach her for money. But nothing like that happened. The woman simply stood there. She was not young and had probably never been particularly pretty. Want and sickness and hard times had whittled her down in spirit and appearance, so that even the clothes she wore were a flag proclaiming her great need.

Unable to meet the woman's glance, Amelia turned and dashed out through a narrow gap in the traffic. She heard the blast of horns and a man's voice cursing her, but she paid no heed. Grateful to reach the other side of the street, she moved quickly away from the troubling scene and headed for the theater district. She glanced at her reflection in the plate-glass window of a clothing store and saw herself wearing a cloche hat, a pale blue woolen jacket, a pleated skirt, and a loose sweater with detachable collars and cuffs. Amelia had learned to achieve different looks with a small wardrobe by varying her accessories.

As she leaned against the biting chill of the March wind, she thought of the heat of Africa and how she had disliked it, but now she would cherish such warmth even for a few seconds. She had a moment's daydream of faces from that world—some of them dear, yet all of them now vague. She remembered standing once in the midst of the veldt, the blue sky stretching above her into the reaches of nothingness, the endless distances surrounding her, and she yearned for that. The crowded streets of New York, the hustle and bustle, the ceaseless voices that filled this world, at times hammered on her nerves. Knowing she would not go back, there were still some parts of her old life she could not abandon completely.

Her pace slowed to a walk, and a thought suddenly invaded her mind. She was so startled she stopped, turned, and looked back over her shoulder as if someone had called her name. No one had, of course, and she stood uncertainly as people passed her, throwing her irritated glances.

The thought was very clear. She had a strong impulse to return to the woman and give her the twenty dollars Amelia would need for food. Almost with disgust she shook her head, then passed her hand over her forehead. *It's the kind of thing Daddy would do, or Uncle Barney, and that's all it is. I just feel sorry for that woman, but I can't give her my food money. I'd starve to death.*

Even as she stood irresolutely between her two choices, a Scripture verse came to mind that she had heard so often from her parents: *Give, and it shall be given unto you; good measure, pressed down, and shaken together, and running over. . . .* And she also remembered a sermon her father had preached years ago. She could not recall the subject nor the location, but she remembered as clearly as if it were carved in marble the verse her father had repeated several times from the book of Proverbs: *He that hath pity upon the poor lendeth unto the Lord; and that which he hath given will he pay him again.* Amelia had long been an involuntary student of the Bible. How could she be anything else being brought up in the home of missionaries? Most of her friends had been the children of ministers, and the Bible had been a primary textbook in her education. She had a good memory—not as good as her brother's, but the verses she had soaked up in her childhood still remained alive in her. Now this verse had risen to her mind, and the more she tried to shake it off, the more she found she could not. She started to hurry away but had taken no more than a dozen steps when the impulse grew even more importunate.

"I'm not even a real believer. It can't be God," she muttered.

The woman grew ever larger in her imagination, and Amelia could no longer ignore the image. It was like a magnet drawing her back, and finally, half angrily, she whirled and said, "All right, I'll go back. She's probably not there anymore. It's just my crazy thinking and hearing too many sermons."

She retraced her steps, half hoping to find the woman gone and thus proving that it was not God speaking at all, but when she was a block away she saw the woman still standing there. Amelia considered turning and walking away, but she could not do it. The urge to help the woman was so strong she could not dismiss it. And somehow a feeling of dread held her—that perhaps one day she would be miserable and hungry and someone would turn away from her. Crossing the street, she pulled the twenty-dollar bill from her purse and extended it to the woman.

The woman stared at her in disbelief. She reached out a trembling hand and took the bill, clutching the infant tighter to her breast. The child at her side looked up at Amelia with big eyes, saying nothing.

"Why are you giving this to me?" the woman asked.

The words came out of Amelia's mouth before she could think. "God told me to do it."

Tears formed in the poor woman's eyes as she clasped the bill. "Thank you," she whispered. "May God repay you a thousand-fold."

Amelia turned away then, touched by the woman's gratitude. She made her way back across the street and had not gone a block when she began to berate herself. *That's what you get for being a preacher's kid! Now what are you going to eat? You've been a fool. That's what you've been!*

★ ★ ★ ★

Keeping a smile on one's face was part of the secret of success in the entertainment business. Amelia had learned that quickly. She was dressed well enough, and that was another part of the challenge. But being confident was the most important. People who produced Broadway shows did not want to hire failures. Amelia had learned to enter each interview with a smile on her lips and her eyes wide open as if she had not a care in the world.

As she exited from the offices of talent agent Alan Mosgrove, she allowed the smile to slip from her face, however. There was no one to see her now except strangers passing by on the street, and they could not help her. The agent said they weren't hiring people to sing or be on the stage right now. It was that simple. Mosgrove had been nice enough, nicer than most of the agents she'd seen. The diminutive man had listened to her sing one song, but at the end of the audition he'd said almost with pity, "Leave me your name and phone number. I don't have an opening right now, but who knows what will happen."

Amelia had smiled brightly as if he had just announced she had won a million dollars and left him one of her newly printed business cards. But now as she rejoined those who hurried down the streets on their ceaseless errands, the smile was nowhere to be seen, and her shoulders slumped slightly. Slowly she walked along. She had one more stop to make, but it seemed almost hopeless to her now. She was hungry and she had no money left.

A cynical smirk twisted her lips. *Go hungry if you're going to be a fool! You deserve it!*

Five minutes later she heard someone call her name, and turning, she saw Dom Costello hurrying to catch up with her. The big man was wearing a brown woolen overcoat, open at the neck, with a thick furry collar. A derby was perched on his head, and his shoes were so highly polished they gleamed in the noon sunlight. He stopped in front of her, his wide lips turning up in a smile. His battered face bore many scars, but his light gray eyes were friendly. "What are you doing in this part of town?"

"Nothing much. What about you, Dom? Do you have to break somebody's knees because they didn't pay off a loan?"

Costello's eyes almost disappeared in the folds of his face as he smiled. His one gold tooth glistened as he grinned at her. "I'm past all that. I'll admit I started out as a knee breaker, but I'm more refined now." Costello's eyes searched her face with interest. He had been taken with her audacity the night she'd pulled the pistol on him. He enjoyed telling the story now. He took in her smooth skin and the elegant clothes but could see in her eyes that Amelia Winslow was not the happiest woman in the world. Impulsively he offered, "Let's you and me go get a bite to eat. It's about lunchtime."

Amelia could not help laughing at him—a most attractive laugh, he thought—and shaking her head in disbelief. "You've got some nerve, Dom. You almost kill my brother and then want me to eat with you?"

Dom Costello was not a man of many sentiments, but now he assumed an almost meek stance, his hat off before her, and said, "You know, Miss Winslow, I'm a pretty tough nut. Not much of a conscience in me, I don't guess, but I've been thinkin' about your brother ever since the day I put him down. I don't know why." He laughed shortly. "Maybe I'm afraid you'll change your mind and come at me with that rod you're packin' in your purse. C'mon," he said. "There's Louie's place across the street. It's a nice café. I can tell you how I turned to a life of crime while you eat."

"All right, Dom," Amelia said, still shaking her head, this time in disbelief that she was actually going with the man.

She accompanied him into Louie's, where he greeted the

owner like an old friend. "Hey, Louie, give us the best you got. This is Miss Winslow. She's a right one."

Louie, a heavyset Italian with a broad smile, bobbed up and down. "I got justa the thing. Right this way, Mr. Costello."

Amelia took her seat at the table, which was covered with a red-and-white-checkered cloth, and looked around. The place was very clean, and the aroma of Italian cooking touched off acute hunger pangs. "Order something good, big guy."

Dom took over capably, and soon Louie left with the order. He returned with two cups of coffee, and as soon as Dom had dumped in four heaping spoonfuls of sugar and stirred it, he tested it and smiled. "I like a little coffee with my sugar."

Amelia, who took hers black, smiled but said nothing. The warmth of the café was almost intoxicating, and she found her stomach rumbling at the enticing smells of garlic and oregano.

"So how's the kid doin'?"

"He's doing fine, Dom. He's so *smart!* I can't believe we're related to each other." Amelia loved to talk about her brother, and she elaborated on Phil's accomplishments and how he'd never made anything but top grades all the way through school. "Now at that college," she said, "they're testing him like he's a freak or something. They throw the hardest things they've got at him, and he still comes out with the top grades every time. He's going to finish in two years instead of four. I'm so proud of him."

Dom encouraged her to talk, and finally, when a heaping plateful of spaghetti was set before each of them and a basket of wonderful-smelling garlic bread was set in the middle of the table, he said, "I guess we'd better dig in. Looks great, Louie."

"The very best in the house, Mr. Costello. I'll bring you a bottle of our best wine to go with it."

As Louie turned to leave, Dom hesitated. "I guess being the preacher's daughter, you say grace, huh?"

"I should, but I'm the black sheep of the family, Dominic. I haven't got it in me anymore."

"That's too bad," Dom said. He began winding the spaghetti with a fork and spoon and eating it expertly, all the while watching Amelia. She ate voraciously, and he knew she was hungry.

To Amelia the spaghetti was like manna from heaven, and the freshly baked Italian bread the best she had ever tasted. She savored the red wine, knowing her parents wouldn't approve, but she enjoyed it anyway.

"That was so good, Dom," she said, sitting back.

"You were pretty hungry, kid."

"Yes, I was. Not very ladylike, I'm afraid."

"What's happening with you?"

"Nothing is happening with me."

A touch of defensiveness in her voice alerted Dom, however, and he said, "Having it tough? The city's that way. People come here with big hopes and dreams, and they get shot down mighty fast—down in flames sometimes." He studied her reaction.

"I haven't had much luck," Amelia admitted.

"Tell me about it. I've eaten too much to move for a while."

And then Amelia found herself talking to Dom in a way she would never have thought possible. She had not quite blotted out of her mind the sight of Dom beating her brother so brutally, but now in the warmth of the café and filled with good food, she was off her guard. She sat there describing her struggles, how she had lost her roommate and could not find another one, and even how she had hocked her necklace and given all of her food money to a poor woman on the street.

Amelia's head jerked up, and her lips tightened. "I didn't mean to dump all that on you, Dom. Nobody wants to hear about somebody else's troubles."

"I guess not," Dom said. He dropped his eyes, and Amelia thought she had offended or at least bored him. She was about to get up, thank him, and make her exit when he said abruptly, "Wait here a minute, kid."

Amelia watched as he stood up and walked across the room. He spoke to Louie and then picked up a phone and dialed a number. She saw him wait, speak briefly, then come back and take his seat. He took a card out of his pocket, wrote something on it, and said, "Go see this guy."

Amelia took the card and read Dom's scrawl: *Mickey Riley, the Green Dragon. Thirty-second Street.*

"Who is this?"

"Riley owns a nightclub. It's not the nicest in town, but it does a good business. I go there a lot, and he told me last time I saw him, the day before yesterday, that he needed a singer."

Amelia fell silent and stared at the card for a long time. When she looked up, she saw that Dom's eyes were cautious. He shrugged his beefy shoulders. "Singing in a nightclub ain't much, but you can work nights and look for a real acting job during the days." When she still did not answer, he said, "A bad idea, I guess. A preacher's daughter wouldn't want to go into a nightclub."

Impulsively Amelia leaned over and put her hand over Dom's. It was a big hand, strong and hard, with big knuckles. "Thank you, Dom. I guess I'm past making the easy choices. I'll go see him."

"If you get the job," Dom said, very much aware of her hand on his, "you don't have to worry about guys getting funny. Riley fancies himself a ladies' man, but I told him I'd tear his head off if he or anybody else fooled with you. There'll be no funny stuff."

Amelia patted the big hand and said, "I'll go right now, and Dom . . . thanks."

Dominic Costello rose and paid the bill. When they got outside he doffed his hat and said, "Let me hear from you. My number's on the other side of that card. If you need anything, let me know."

Amelia felt so much better than she had a few hours ago. She smiled at him. "It's good to know there's one person in this town besides my family who cares about me. I'll call you, Dom, and let you know how it comes out."

★   ★   ★   ★

Mickey Riley was seated at a table in the Green Dragon and laid aside the newspaper he had been reading as Amelia approached him. Two men were busy sweeping out the club, and a piano player was competing with the clatter of dishes in the kitchen and two muted voices arguing about baseball. Amelia stated bluntly, "My name is Amelia Winslow. I'm a singer and I need a job."

Riley was a beefy-faced individual with the marks of a rough life on him. He had on a garish striped shirt and a pair of hideous green suspenders, but there was a shrewd look in his slightly bloodshot eyes. "Sit down," he said. "Dom told me to give you a try. Tell me about yourself," he said curtly as Amelia took her seat. He listened as she told her story briefly, his greenish eyes lighting up as she mentioned that she was from Africa.

"Really from Africa? You mean where the lions and the tigers are?"

"There aren't any tigers in Africa, Mr. Riley, but there are lots of lions. I shot one myself once."

"No kidding! Well, I guess you can take care of yourself." He laughed suddenly and slapped his beefy thigh. "Dom said he'd break my face if I put the moves on you. You don't have to worry about that. Can you sing?"

The question caught Amelia slightly off guard. Indeed, she did have a very fine voice, but now she said, "I can sing, but I've never been in a nightclub in my life. I don't know what kind of songs they like."

"They like loud songs. Sometimes they like sad songs. Most of the time they're so drunk they're not even listening to the singer." He turned his head. "Hey, Gus," he hollered at the thin man with the sallow face sitting at the piano. "I want to hear this lady sing. Work out something with her, eh?"

As Amelia stood and walked toward the piano she was caught by the voice of the owner behind her. "No hymns now. Just good modern stuff."

Her stomach was churning as she introduced herself to the piano player. "My name's Amelia Winslow, Gus."

"What do you want to sing?"

Amelia was baffled for a moment. She knew all the latest songs, for she had a collection of gramophone records at her apartment. She had sung along with them until she had mastered most of them. "How about 'Yes, We Have No Bananas'?"

"Sure. Let's try it."

Amelia turned as Gus's fingers flew over the keys expertly. The song was a popular hit, a novelty song that was easy enough to sing. She actually had a clear contralto voice with tremendous power when she cared to use it. But on this one she simply sang the song as she had a thousand times beside her Victrola at home.

"Hey, that's good, kid. Now try something sad. See if you can make me cry."

"Do you know 'Rose of Washington Square'?" she asked.

Gus did not answer but played the opening notes and then whispered, "There it is in your key."

"Rose of Washington Square" had also been a recent hit song. Amelia had Fanny Brice's recording of it and had imitated her and then had come up with a style of her own. One of her friends had told her once, "Every time you sing those sad songs, I want to bust out crying." Now she went through it, and when she ended and Gus's fingers were still on the keys, she heard Riley say, "Come over here, lady." She moved quickly and stood beside the table. Riley did not get to his feet. "Bring a list of songs you know tonight. Gus knows 'em all and he knows what the customers like. Come back about eight. I'll give you a tryout. If they like you, we'll talk turkey. Okay?"

"Thanks, Mr. Riley."

"Oh, I'll pay you thirty bucks for tonight."

At that instant an odd sensation came over Amelia. The face of the poor woman to whom she had given the money flashed in her mind. She saw the tears, and she heard her say, *"May the Lord repay you a thousandfold."* Somehow she knew that meeting up with Dominic Costello had not been an accident. *Is this God's doing?* she wondered.

"What should I wear, Mr. Riley?"

"Something sexy."

★　★　★　★

For just a moment Amelia hesitated. The streets were dark now except for the streetlights, but a noisy crowd was filing into the Green Dragon. Taxis continually stopped and let people out, then pulled away. All afternoon Amelia had struggled with herself. *Singing in a nightclub—that's not show business. Singing for a bunch of drunks? That can't be for me. Surely it's not what God wants!* But despite her uncertainties, she knew she was going to do it. She had chosen her outfit carefully. It was her one fancy dress she had picked up on sale at Macy's. It was a close-fitting taffeta evening gown. A décolletage was formed by wide crossed-over ribbon lapels, finishing at the waist in the front. She didn't know if it fit Riley's definition of sexy, but she had no interest in dressing provocatively. She just wanted to look her best while she sang—that was all.

She entered the nightclub with a knot in her stomach at the thought of what she was doing. A hard-faced man stopped her. "Can I help you, miss?"

"I'm the new singer. Mr. Riley told me to be here. My name's Amelia Winslow."

"Sure, Amelia, go on back. Cut to your left over there, and you'll find the dressing room. Got a good crowd tonight. Belt 'em out, eh?"

Her heart was beating rapidly as she moved through the crowd. Seeing Gus already at the piano, she went over to him and said, "Hello, Gus. I've got a list of songs for you."

Gus looked up, and his bloodhound face seemed fairly cheerful, much more so than when she had seen him earlier. He looked over the list and nodded. "These'll do. We got a little combo here—a drummer, a guitar picker, and a fellow that calls himself a horn tooter. They'll follow me, and I'll follow you."

"Thanks, Gus."

Amelia made her way to the back, where she took off her overcoat and hat. She saw a door labeled Dressing Room and knocked on it. When no one answered she stepped inside and turned the light on. It was barely large enough to turn around in, but there was a small dressing table with a mirror. A single bulb dangled from a cord overhead. She sat down and began nervously arranging her hair. Thankfully it had a natural curl and was not easily mussed up.

She was startled when a voice said, "Well, you *did* come back." She turned to find Riley grinning at her. He was wearing a tuxedo, and he said, "Stand up and let me take a look at you."

Obediently Amelia stood up and turned around self-consciously but was gratified when the owner said, "You look great. Some of those clowns out there may give you a hard time, but Dom's out front. He said he'd break anybody's neck if they got funny with you. I guess he'd do it too. Good luck, kid."

Amelia had always believed in plunging right in. She remembered the time she had tried to get up the nerve to jump off a high diving platform when she was thirteen. The only way she had achieved it was by quickly climbing the ladder to the platform, then running and flinging herself off into space. She did the same thing now.

She left the dressing room and went out into the main room. A small platform, no more than six inches high, served as the stage, and when Gus saw her, he motioned. She went over to him.

"Okay. You ready, Winslow? That your name?" Gus said.

"Just Amelia is fine."

"Okay, Amelia. We'll start out with 'Way Down Yonder in New Orleans.' That's a nice peppy thing."

Amelia moved over to the microphone, and out of the darkness of the room a light hit her right in the face. She blinked but was thankful she could not see the customers too well. She could hear them, though, and she relaxed a little at hearing Dom's voice shouting out encouragement from the front table. Suddenly Riley was there, pulling the microphone over. "Folks, we got a brand-new songbird tonight. A fine-looking lady from Africa. Her name's Amelia Winslow. Let's hear it for Amelia!"

Amelia heard the applause and instantly the music started. She had always liked the song "Way Down Yonder in New Orleans" for its snappy meter, and she forced herself to smile and sing it with all the gusto she could. Despite her bravado, she was actually trembling inside, and her knees felt weak. As she finished she was not sure whether or not the crowd would boo her. But she was relieved to hear loud applause and a few raucous voices calling, "That's great, sweetheart, do it again!"

Next she sang a song that Al Jolson had made a hit, "Toot, Toot, Tootsie." It was an easy song, usually performed by a male singer, but Amelia's voice was strong enough to fill the place. This time the applause was even stronger, and some man cried out, "That's even better than Jolson, kid!"

Amelia went from song to song for twenty minutes. She closed the first set with, "I'll Be With You in Apple Blossom Time," a plaintive melody, and here for the first time the audience grew still. Amelia threw herself into it. She had practiced singing like this and gesturing accordingly, and although she could not know it, her face caught the sorrowful quality of the song.

When the song ended she bowed, and there was dead quiet for a moment. Her heart sank—then she heard the applause. People clapped loudly and shouted out her name, and Amelia knew then she could do this job. She bowed several times, thanked the musicians, and left the small stage.

Riley intercepted her, grabbing her arm and enthusing, "Hey, kid, you done good! I never saw 'em applaud like that for a new-comer."

"I'm glad you think so, Mr. Riley."

"Go take a break. It'll be a long night. Hope your pipes hold out."

Her "pipes" did hold out, and Amelia found herself looking forward to performing the second set. Gus tried a few fancy licks with her, and she picked up on them immediately, improvising her own variations as well. Finally she sang a haunting song, "All by Myself," written by the well-loved American songwriter Irving Berlin, and again the crowd applauded lustily.

Finally Gus said in a loud whisper, "Close it out, sweetie!"

What possessed her in the next few minutes Amelia Winslow would never know. She grew still, closing her eyes in thought as an urge began to build within her, and she felt a silence fall over the nightclub. She knew there were people out there drunk, despite Prohibition, and she feared what might happen if she spoke aloud what was in her heart at that moment. Clutching her skirt in her hands to steady herself, she blurted out, "My father would hate the idea of my singing in a nightclub."

The silence became deathly. She caught a glimpse of Riley, who was in her line of vision near the stage. He had drawn him-self up absolutely still, his brows knit together.

"He's a preacher, a missionary in Africa," Amelia rushed on before she could lose her nerve. "I owe him and my mother everything, so I'm going to close with his favorite song. I hope you don't mind." Without accompaniment, she lifted her voice—quietly at first, then with growing confidence—filling the night-club with the strains of "What a Friend We Have in Jesus." She had sung only two lines when she heard the piano come in behind her and then the drums and the trumpet, muted but hinting of power. As she sang she thought of her father and mother and of her uncle Barney and her aunt Katie. She thought of her grandmother Lola and all of her family who so loved God, and it pained her that she did not. Unaware that tears were streaming down her face, she ended the song and turned blindly away, leaving the stage in a stunned hush.

Riley caught up with her and muttered, "Don't know what got into ya, kid. This sure ain't the place for that." Riley had actually enjoyed her last song but would not have admitted it. He was a hard man, always looking out for himself, and was pretty certain he'd just lost a lot of business with Amelia's surprise ending.

But even as Riley spoke, applause began. It rose and filled the place like thunder. A voice called out, "You stick with your folks, kid! They got the right idea."

Riley's dour expression did a complete turnabout. He grabbed her arm and shouted, "Hey, go back out there and take a bow, Amelia. They know a good thing when they hear it. They love you!"

Amelia returned to the stage, alone in the spotlight, and threw a kiss to the audience. "Thank you," she whispered. "Thank you all." She stepped down, and Riley led her to the dressing room, where she found a handkerchief and wiped her face. "I don't know why I sang that hymn. It just came out."

Riley shook his head over what had just happened in his nightclub. As he'd watched the face of the young woman singing her father's favorite hymn, he too had felt what the whole crowd had. Here was someone different, someone fresh and unspoiled. She had a fine voice, to be sure, but it was the sight of tears streaming down her cheeks that had grabbed them all. He reached over awkwardly and patted her shoulder. "I think it was good, kid. You do it every night."

"You mean I have a job?"

"As long as you want one, kiddo. You're the real goods!"

CHAPTER SIX

ALWAYS A FUGITIVE

★ ★ ★ ★

"I knew I couldn't keep you here long, kid, and I'm happy for you. Always like to see young folks moving up in the world."

Amelia had come to say good-bye to Mickey Riley, and now he stood there pumping her hand up and down, a regretful smile on his broad Irish face.

"You've been so good to me, Mickey. I will never forget you."

"That's good to hear, kid—real good! When do you start?"

"Opening night's tomorrow."

"Well, anybody that sings at Eddie's is on their way up."

Amelia thought for a moment of how suddenly things had changed for her in just a few days. She had been singing at the Green Dragon for three months now, performing several nights a week and always drawing a big crowd. When she sang this past Tuesday night, someone had told her that Eddie Johns, the owner of the most popular nightclub in New York City, was in the audience. She had thought little of it and had performed her act exactly as usual, but afterward he had come back to see her in her tiny dressing room. He had introduced himself, and she had immediately recognized the name. "I'm so glad to meet you, Mr. Johns."

"I caught your act tonight, Miss Winslow. I liked it a lot."

"Why, thank you."

"I'd like to hire you to sing at my place."

Amelia remembered the shock that had run through her. Eddie's Place was still a nightclub, but it was a giant step forward on making her way in show business. She knew that some very successful musical and comedic stars had gotten their start in nightclubs, and she had replied without hesitation, "I'd love to work for you, Mr. Johns."

Now as Amelia stood facing Mickey Riley, a regret came to her. "I hate to leave you like this, Mickey. It makes me seem ungrateful."

"Nothin' like that." Riley waved his thick hand in the air. "This was just an on-the-way stop for you, and so will Eddie's Place be. You'll be a hit there. The next thing you know your name will be up in lights on Broadway right along with Fanny Brice and Al Jolson." He grinned brashly and then shook his head with admiration. "You keep on singin' that church song at the end of your act, ya hear me? That always gets 'em. It's good show biz."

Amelia was not at all certain of this. She always concluded her act with a hymn. She felt like a hypocrite, since she was so far away from God, but Mickey Riley had insisted she include it. "It may do some good. Ya never know," he had said. "Guys and dolls in places like this, they need all the help they can get." Besides, it appeared to be very good for business.

"I'll be coming back to see you, Mickey."

"Not likely, but I'll be comin' to see *you*." He gave her an admiring glance and shook his head. "You remember your ol' friend Mick when you're up there with the big ones."

"I'll do that if I ever arrive."

★ ★ ★ ★

Dom intercepted Rosa as she pulled up her mare, Boadicea, and helped her down as she tossed the lines to the trainer.

"Hey, Miss Rosa, did you hear about what happened to Amelia?"

"You mean Amelia Winslow?"

"Sure."

"What about her?" Rosa asked. She was wearing her usual riding outfit: khaki jodhpurs, maroon sweater, and a black cap that matched her shiny black boots.

"Why, she's gone up to the big time. She'll be opening at Eddie's tonight."

"You mean the big nightclub?" Rosa said with interest.

"That's the one. Funny thing. After I half killed her brother, I thought she was going to shoot me. But I was able to give her a hand, and we've become pretty good friends."

Rosa had heard Dom relate the story of how he had met Amelia and had helped her get a job at the Green Dragon. Rosa had been very interested, and more than once she had asked Dom if he had seen Amelia—or Phil. Now as she walked back toward the house, an idea began to form in her mind. She said nothing to anyone, but late that afternoon she asked Dom to drive her to the stables where Phil worked. She found him exercising a horse. Getting out of the car, she said, "You wait here, Dom. I need to talk to Phil."

"Okay. I'll be right here."

Rosa waited until Phil hopped off the horse, and then she called him. "Hello, Phil!"

Turning to meet her, Phil's eyes lit up with pleasure. "Well, Rosa, what are you doing here?" He glanced over and saw Dom sitting in the car. "Got your bodyguard with you, I see."

"Phil, I just heard about Amelia." Rosa's enormous dark eyes were glowing.

To Phil she looked very young, and he smiled at her excitement. "I don't know whether to be glad or sad for her."

Rosa stared at him without comprehension. "What do you mean? Why wouldn't you be happy?"

"Well, singing in a nightclub isn't exactly my idea of a full life, Rosa."

"But some of the most famous people in the world started out singing in nightclubs. Look at Al Jolson and Eddie Cantor. That's where they started."

Knowing that arguing with Rosa was futile, Phil smiled. "Well, I try to be as glad as I can. But what are you doing here? Come to pick up another horse?"

"No, I came to ask you a favor."

"Just name it."

"I want you to take me to Amelia's opening at Eddie's."

Astonished, Phil stared at the young woman. He knew what she asked was out of the question, and he wanted to nip this idea in the bud as quickly as possible. "Well, there are about half a dozen reasons I can think of why I can't do that. The first one is that your father would have Dom take off my head if I did a thing like that. He doesn't let you date, as you well know."

"But this wouldn't be a date—not exactly anyway," Rosa said. She made an appealing figure as she stood there. She was not tall and had to look up, which made her even more attractive. She was on the brink of womanhood and did not know what a tempting figure she made as she tugged at his arm and pleaded, "You've just got to do it, Phil, you've got to! Why, you couldn't let her have her debut without your being there."

"Well, it's not just that I'm afraid your father would shoot me—or have Dom do it—but I don't have the money or the clothes."

"I can fix all that if you'll just take me."

"I don't think you need to be in a nightclub, Rosa."

"Phil, I'm almost sixteen! And if I get Dad's permission and see that the expenses are all taken care of, will you take me?"

Phil thought swiftly. *Might as well say yes. Big Tony will never let her do this anyway.* "Okay," he shrugged. "But it'll never happen."

★　★　★　★

Big Tony Morino was astute at reading men's minds. His very survival in the hard life he'd chosen testified to the fact that he was a shrewd judge of character. He could sit in a meeting with ten men and know what each one of them was planning or plotting.

But he had not yet learned how to outwit his daughter Rosa. She had figured out years earlier exactly how to get what she wanted from him, for it was no secret he wanted her to have everything. Very rarely had he given her an absolute no, and at those times Rosa had learned to simply give up. But most of the time she managed to maneuver her father into allowing her to do whatever she wanted, as long as it was not downright dangerous.

Her usual strategy was to soften him up first by fixing him one of his favorite dishes. His wife usually managed to keep his diet under control at home, but when he was out, he loved to frequent La Casa, the best Mexican restaurant in New York, and fill up on the best cheese dip in the world. Rosa had made it her business to get the secret recipe from the cook, pleading that she had to have it, and the cook had agreed to give the recipe to the daughter of one of the restaurant's best customers. Tony's doctors had forbidden him to eat it because of his heart condition, but he didn't often listen to his doctors.

Now she made up a batch of the cheese dip and brought it to him steaming hot in a small bowl with a plateful of chips for dipping.

Tony looked up, and a grin came up over his face. "Cheese dip!" He grabbed both the bowl and the plate, put them down on his desk, and began dipping the chips into the hot cheese.

"Watch out, Daddy! You'll burn your tongue!"

"I don't care. This is the best stuff I ever had in my life." Tony ate noisily, managing to get cheese dip on his tie.

Rosa leaned over with a napkin and wiped it off. "Here, Daddy, you're getting it all over. You're as messy as a baby."

"I don't care. This stuff just sets me free." Tony ate every bite, then demanded, "Is there any more?"

"Not today. You know you're not supposed to have it, and don't you dare tell Mom!"

"This will be our secret."

"You'll have to send your tie out to be cleaned or she'll see it and know what you've been eating."

Rosa climbed into Tony's lap, reached her arms around his neck, and leaned her head on his. Delighted with her attention, he said, "So what have you been doing with yourself besides making me happy with cheese dip?" He held her, listening intently as she outlined her days. He loved that his little girl still wanted to sit in his lap, and he loved listening to her talk. He dreaded the day when she would leave home. He knew it had to come eventually, but the thought made him sad.

Finally Rosa sat up and brushed back Tony's hair. "You've even got cheese dip on your eyebrows!" She laughed. "Here, let me get it off." She fished a handkerchief out of her pocket and wiped the cheese dip off, shaking her head. "You are such a glutton about cheese dip."

Defensively Tony said, "A man's got few enough pleasures in this world. He ought to take 'em all as they come."

"I think you're right."

"You do? Well, I wish you'd convince your mother."

"I think we shouldn't let anything pass us by. I mean if it's harmless, don't you think so?"

"I just said so, didn't I?" Suddenly Tony's eyes narrowed. "Uh-oh. What is it this time? A new dress? Another horse?"

"Oh no, nothing like that! You've bought me so many dresses, and Boadicea's the only horse I want."

"Well, that's a relief. I thought you were going to want Man o' War, and he's not for sale."

"He is one thing I would like, Daddy, but not right now. Do you remember Phil Winslow?"

"Sure I do. The kid Dom pounded."

"You know, he could have been nasty about that. I asked one of your lawyer friends what might have happened, and he said he could have taken you for thousands of dollars."

"But he didn't."

"That's right. He wouldn't do a thing like that."

"Why are you bringing him up?"

"It's because of his sister, Amelia."

"Yeah, I remember her. What's she got to do with it?"

"She's a singer now. She's opening tonight at Eddie's Place, and I want to go."

"You're too young to go to a nightclub."

"I'm fifteen, Daddy, and I'm not going to do anything wrong. You know that."

Tony argued valiantly, coming up with a great many reasons why it would not be suitable. But he was filled with good food, and she was sitting on his lap fussing with his hair. Finally he said, "Well, maybe it'll be all right. You'll have to ask your mother. I expect she'll say no."

"No, she'll say yes. You let me ask her, Daddy."

Tony laughed. "You can't fool her like you do me."

"I never fool you, Daddy."

"You do it all the time. You're doing it right now. Here I am promising to take you to a nightclub, which I never thought I would."

"And, Daddy, ever since Dom told me about Amelia, I've been sad about Phil."

"What's to be sad about?"

"You remember he doesn't have any money, and he's working his way through school working at the stables?"

"Sure I know that."

"Well, he wants to go see his sister at her opening, but he doesn't have any money. So could he go with us?"

Tony frowned. "I don't know if he'd want to or not, him being a preacher and all."

"It's his daddy that's the preacher, not him, and he told me he'd love to go."

Instantly Tony knew what was happening. "I see! That's what this is all about, the cheese dip and sitting on my lap."

"Oh, Daddy, I do that all the time! But I do feel sorry for Phil. Please say he can go with us."

Tony tried to talk his headstrong daughter out of this one but in the end heard himself saying, "Okay, the kid can go."

"Oh, Daddy, thank you!" Throwing her arms around his neck, Rosa kissed him firmly on the cheek and then jumped down. "I've got things to do, and Dom will have to help me."

She ran out of the room, leaving Tony half breathless. "That kid has got my number," he muttered. "But I guess it won't hurt as long as me and Dom are there to see nothing happens to her."

★　★　★　★

Standing in his small apartment, Phil looked down at the new suit he had on and could not believe it. Dom had come to the stables, picked him up, and bought him a complete outfit at one of the fanciest men's shops in New York. Now Phil looked down at the shiny shoes, ran his hand over the silk necktie, and thought, *That Rosa must be some kind of a sorceress!* He heard a car approach, and looking out the window, he saw Tony Morino's long black sedan.

He ran down the stairs, and when he reached the car, Dominic was getting out. "Just coming up to get you, Phil. Get in the front with me."

Obediently he climbed into the car, and as Dom got back in and pulled away from the curb, Phil turned around and saw Rosa sitting beside her father, looking very self-satisfied. Ignoring her, he said, "It's very generous of you to take me to see my sister, Mr. Morino. I could never have afforded it."

"Well, I'm glad to do it, Phil. There wouldn't have been any peace if I hadn't. This one here would have driven me crazy."

Rosa laughed giddily. "Oh, you look so good in your new suit, Phil!"

"Best suit I ever had on." He stroked the material of the sleeve and then laughed too. "If I drop dead, you won't have to do a thing to me. Just put me in a box and stick a lily in my hand."

"Phil! What an awful thing to say!"

Rosa may have been shocked, but both Dom and Tony guffawed at the remark.

"Tell me about your studies, kid," Tony said. "They tell me you're tearin' 'em up at that college."

"Oh, nothing like that."

"That ain't what I hear. Dominic tells me you're gonna graduate with honors in only two years."

"Well, I hope so, but there's always a chance I could flunk. If you make an enemy of one of those professors, you could be the king of Siam and still not pass."

"Must be nice to go to college. I never got beyond the fifth grade myself," Tony said with a touch of remorse.

"Hey, I beat you, Mr. Morino. I got to the sixth grade!" Dom laughed. "Not that they managed to pound anything into me that I didn't get rid of."

The friendly banter continued, and the ride passed quickly. When they pulled up in front of Eddie's, Dom said, "You folks go ahead. I'll park the car and meet you inside." The three got out, and the doorman came forward. "Mr. Morino, it's good to see you, sir. It's been a while."

"Well, I've come to hear your new singer."

"Eddie says she's a fine one, Mr. Morino. Go right on in. I'll bet Eddie will give you your favorite table."

Phil had never been in a nightclub in his life. He looked around the foyer curiously and watched as Tony checked his hat. When Rosa took off her coat, he was stunned. She was wearing a gown that accentuated her womanly figure, and he couldn't help admiring her. He did not know much about clothes, but he thought the dress might be silk—maroon and white with a snug bodice and a skirt that flared out. She turned to him and flashed a smile.

Embarrassed that she'd caught him watching her, he cleared his throat and said quickly, "You look very nice, Rosa. Is that a new dress?"

"Oh, just something I've had in my closet. Daddy always liked it."

"Well, you look absolutely beautiful!" Phil bit his lip. He hadn't meant to say so much.

Rosa beamed, and then her father turned back to her and said, "C'mon. We'll see if we can find a good table."

Finding a good table for Big Tony Morino was not difficult. The maître d' met the party with a big smile. "Does Mr. Johns know you're here, sir?"

"I don't think so."

"Well, I'll tell him you're here. In the meantime, if I remember right, you like the table over toward the back."

"That has a good view of the stage, doesn't it? We want to hear your new singer."

"Oh yes, sir. That's an excellent spot. Come along, and I'll take you."

As they followed the maître d', Dom joined them, and he and Tony walked ahead. Rosa reached out and grabbed Phil's arm. "Look over there!"

"What is it?"

"It's Al Jolson! I can't believe it! He's my favorite singer!"

Phil, of course, had heard Jolson's records. He looked with interest at the man who was the king of show business. Jolson had black hair, large eyes, and to Phil's surprise, rather pale skin without his black stage makeup. Jolson was laughing with delight at something someone in his party had said, and Rosa bubbled, "I just love to hear him sing."

She pointed out Fanny Brice at another table and added, "It makes me feel funny seeing all these famous people."

Phil noticed that many people in the crowd recognized Tony Morino, too, and whispered and gestured at him. Looking down at Rosa, he thought, *Your father's a famous person but not famous in the best ways.*

When they were all seated, Tony began asking Phil about his coursework. "What business will you get into when you get out of that college, Phil?"

"I'm not sure. Maybe accounting, bookkeeping. Something like that until I can earn enough money to go to law school."

Tony had pulled a cigar from his pocket. He unrolled it, clipped off the end with a small pair of gold scissors he kept, apparently, for that purpose, and accepted a light from Dominic. Tony puffed until blue smoke filled the air; then he turned and stared full at Phil. "Come and see me when you get out of college. I can always use a smart guy in my organization."

Phil felt Rosa's foot pressing his toe with hers, and when he looked toward her he saw she was smiling with delight. "There you are," she said. "You've got a job offer even before you graduate. I'll bet not many college students can say that."

"I guess not," Phil said. He knew for a certainty that he would not be working for Big Tony Morino, but he saw no reason for spoiling her pleasure.

They had not been seated long when suddenly a booming voice said, "Well, Tony, it's good to see you again." Everyone turned to see Jolson, who had been passing by. He stopped at their table, a big smile on his face as he shook hands with Tony. "I've been wondering why you never come to see my new show."

"Been pretty busy, Al, but everyone says it's great." He nodded toward the stage and said, "This here's Phil Winslow. His sister is singing here tonight."

Jolson reached over and shook hands with Phil. "I hope she does good. We need some fresh blood in show biz."

After a few more pleasantries, Jolson made his way back to

his table, every eye turning to follow him as he crossed the crowded room.

Phil had been nervously poring over the menu, anxious about the high prices, when finally it came time to order. Lamely, he said to the waiter, "Just bring me something good."

Rosa scolded him. "That's no way to order! Let me order for both of us."

"All right. I'll eat whatever you order."

When the meal arrived, Phil beamed with pleasure at Rosa's choice of succulent seafood in a marinara sauce on vermicelli. With delight he dug into a huge basket of fresh Italian bread spread with garlic butter and herbs, and dipped the bread in the tangy sauce as he ate.

While they were enjoying their meal, the lights dimmed, and the master of ceremonies came out onto the small stage and stepped into the spotlight. "We are delighted to have tonight, for your pleasure, Miss Amelia Winslow. I think you're going to like her, folks. Let's give her a big welcome."

Phil sat straight up and stared as Amelia came out on the stage. She was wearing a simple light blue gown that complemented her coloring, and her hair was done up stylishly. He was surprised at the poise she displayed as she came into the spotlight, smiled, and made a gracious bow. She said nothing and began singing. Phil had forgotten how good she was, and he knew she'd become even better since he'd last heard her. He took his eyes off of her from time to time to watch the audience and saw that people were pleased. She sang several Irving Berlin songs, and when they were well received, she said, "I'm going to have to ask permission to sing this next song. Mr. Al Jolson has made it his own, so no one else can really do justice to it, especially a woman, but I'd like to try 'Toot, Toot, Tootsie'—if it's all right with you, Mr. Jolson."

The lights swung around to Jolson, who waved his hand in the air, shouting, "You sing it, sweetheart! Sing it good like Jolie!"

Amelia had mastered the popular song. She sang it with gusto as she moved around the small stage, captivating the crowd. After one time through, the audience responded with thunderous applause. Then she said, "Mr. Jolson, it would be a great honor to me if you would come and we could sing your song together."

Jolson, always the ham, leaped out of his chair and was on the stage before she had finished. He put his arm around her waist and said, "Let's have the music, boys. The little lady and I are going to show you somethin' you ain't never seen before!"

Amelia had not planned to do such a thing, but seeing Jolson in the audience, the idea had just come to her. It was an exquisite bit of showmanship, and everyone there knew they were seeing something very special. The middle-aged entertainer, famous all over America, and the fresh-faced, beautiful young girl ran through the song, and then after deafening applause and cheers, Jolson said, "You ain't seen nothin' yet. Sweetheart, do you know 'California, Here I Come'?"

"I've heard your record a thousand times, Mr. Jolson." They sang that and then three other songs, and finally Jolson reached over and gave Amelia a big kiss on the cheek. "You got talent, kid," he said. "You stay in this business. Come and see me if you ever need help."

When it was time to take her break, Amelia headed toward Big Tony's table instead of going to her dressing room. The men rose as she approached, and she put her hand out to Tony. "It's good to see you, Mr. Morino."

"A little different situation from last time. Hey, Miss Winslow, you done good. That thing with Jolson, I never saw nothin' like it."

Phil moved around the table to give his sister a big hug. "You were wonderful, sis, just wonderful!"

"It's only a saloon, Phil."

"I don't care about that," he whispered in her ear. "You did fine! I wish the folks were here to hear it."

"That's not likely."

Phil released her, and Amelia turned to Dom, putting out her hand. "This is all your doing, Dom. If you hadn't gotten me my first job, I guess I'd still be cooking in a café somewhere."

Dom was pleased and shook his head. "Nah, you would have made it no matter. You done great, kid, just great."

Rosa exploded with delight. "Oh, it was so wonderful, Amelia! If I could sing like you, I'd sing all the time."

Amelia laughed. She was surprised at the young woman, who looked at least two years older than her actual age in her sophisticated evening gown. "You look beautiful, Rosa. I'm so glad you came."

Amelia sat down at the table, and Dom and Big Tony began to pepper her with questions. The band started in on a lively dance number, and Rosa seized Phil's arm. "Ask me to dance," she whispered.

"I'm not going to do that," Phil said. "Your father might not like it."

"Ask him. He won't care," Rosa begged, her dark eyes pleading.

Clearing his throat, Phil gave Tony a look. "Mr. Morino, would it be all right if Rosa danced with me?"

"Sure. Should get somethin' for them expensive dance lessons I paid for."

Phil laughed. "Well, I never had any lessons, so I'm making no promises, but come along, Rosa."

Rosa jumped up and headed to the dance floor on Phil's arm. When he put his arm around her waist and took her hand, she smiled up at him. "Isn't this the cat's pajamas?"

Phil laughed. "Where did you learn talk like that?"

"Why, that's what all the kids are saying. Don't they talk like that at college?"

"Not in accounting class."

Despite his misgivings about being in a nightclub with Rosa, Phil was enjoying himself tremendously. He spoke with excitement of Amelia and how well she had done, and finally he asked, "Are you having a good time, Rosa?"

"Oh yes, the best ever!"

Then her brow furrowed. "I wish Daddy would let me date before I turn eighteen."

"Maybe you can wheedle him down to seventeen."

"I doubt it. He loves me so much it makes him sad to think that he'll lose me one day."

Phil was startled at this revelation. It brought out a side of Big Tony Morino he had not thought of. He knew Morino was a ruthless man, but he saw a weakness here, for Rosa would not be long in finding a husband.

"But I bet you've had fellows who admired you."

"They're all afraid of Daddy."

Surprised by her blunt honesty, Phil said, "Well, that will change."

"I don't know. Daddy's very possessive of me and of Mother and of Jamie."

"I've never met your brother."

"No, he's not allowed out much. Mother and Daddy make him stay in every afternoon to work on homework. He's having a hard time with math in school."

"How old is he?"

"Thirteen."

"Well, bring him to the stable. I can take time out to help him a little bit. Math is one of my best subjects."

Suddenly Rosa's eyes glowed. "Are you good at English too? Would you help me with mine? I'm just horrible at it. I can't write a bit, and I bet you're good at it."

"It's not my best subject, but I'd like to help if I could to pay you back for this fine suit and this evening here at Eddie's. You dance very well, Rosa. Better than I do."

"No, not really."

"Oh yes, really."

When the two got back to the table, Rosa said, "Daddy, you know the trouble Jamie's having with math?"

"I guess I should know it. I get enough notes from his teacher."

"Well, I have an idea. Phil here would be a great tutor. Why, I'll bet he could help Jamie get straight A's." And then she added innocently, "And he's good at English too. He could help me with those awful themes I have to write."

"Now wait a minute, Rosa," Phil said. "Your father will think I'm asking for a job."

Big Tony laughed. "Kid, if you can help my son and daughter get through school, I'll pay through the nose."

"Oh, I wouldn't take any money."

"Sure you would," Dom said. "Always take the money, Phil. You need to learn that."

The rest of the evening passed quickly. The high point for Phil came after Amelia sang her last popular song. She stopped and waited until the room grew still; then she spoke softly. "I wish my parents were here, but they're not. They're back in Africa preaching to the people there. But my brother's here, and with your permission I'd like to sing his favorite hymn."

She began singing "The Old Rugged Cross," and for some reason, as always, after singing popular show tunes, the old hymns always touched her heart. Tonight, as on most nights, she could not keep the tears from her eyes. The room grew perfectly still as her clear contralto voice filled every corner. When she sang the last verse, the room was silent only for a moment and then the applause grew to a roar.

Phil felt his own eyes growing misty, and he looked over at Rosa. "She's great at the popular songs, but that last song was my favorite."

★ ★ ★ ★

Two weeks after her opening night at Eddie's, Amelia asked Phil to meet her for lunch at Louie's, the little Italian restaurant where she'd had her first meal with Dom before her job at the Green Dragon. She had been feeling rather lonely lately. She had met so many people, even celebrities, yet they had not filled the void in her. Now she encouraged Phil to talk about his studies and activities. She listened with interest as he told her how he had been tutoring Rosa and James Morino.

"They're good kids, sis, both of them."

"Rosa's hardly a kid. She's growing up fast."

"Well, she seems like a kid to me. Jamie is not at all like his father. I think he takes after his mother."

After the meal they sat drinking coffee for a long time. They talked about Africa, their parents, their uncle Barney, and other members of the family. Finally Amelia looked up at Phil and said, "I've got news for you that you probably won't like."

"Why wouldn't I like it?"

Shaking her head, Amelia said quietly, "Al Jolson's agent came to hear me sing. He wants me to meet with him. He wants me to sign a contract."

"Well, why wouldn't I like that, sis?"

"Because it means I'll be more tightly bound up in the kind of work I do. I'm happy for the success I've had, but I feel guilty about it. You know, being the daughter of missionaries and all." She gave Phil a teasing smile. "I guess it's because of my repressed childhood, huh?"

Phil leaned across the small table, took her hands in his, and squeezed them. He said seriously, "Mom and Dad have prayed for you every day since you were born. They told me that."

"But I've run away from all that."

"You may be a fugitive, but you're heaven's fugitive. Sooner or later Jesus is going to catch up with you."

Amelia grew very quiet, then whispered, "Heaven's fugitive. Maybe that's what I'll always be."

"No, you'll find the Lord one day. Wait and see."

"I hope so, Phil, but it seems unlikely."

PART TWO

April–October 1925

★ ★ ★

CHAPTER SEVEN

A VISIT WITH LOLA

★ ★ ★ ★

Backing quickly into a corner of her dressing room, Amelia tried desperately to shove away the big man who had forced his way in. She was terrified at the reek of whiskey on his breath and his bloodshot eyes. "Get out of my dressing room," she cried, "or I'll scream for help."

"Ah, come on, baby, don't be like that. You actresses are all alike. Let's you and me have a little lovin'."

The big man had blunt features, and a silly smile was pasted on his face. His black hair was glued flat to his skull with macadamia oil, and his odor was rank, a mixture of raw alcohol, sweat, and worse. Her eyes went over to her purse, in which she still carried the nickel-plated thirty-eight she had brought from Africa. She could not get past the big man and began to scream, "Help! Somebody help me!"

To stop her cries he fell against her and covered her mouth with his own. Furiously Amelia resisted, but he was like a huge bear. She felt herself crushed against his chest, and she was helpless to move. Disgust washed through her as she tried to release herself. Struggling futilely, she heard the door open and Phil's voice shouting, "Let her go!" and at the same time felt the drunk yanked off of her. She fell back against the wall as Phil flung the big man to the floor. "Get out of here," Phil shouted, "or I'll have you locked up!" He had placed himself between the attacker and Amelia and stood flat-footed, his eyes half closed in threat.

Cursing, the drunk staggered to his feet. He swung a round-house right that would have annihilated Phil had it landed, but Phil easily jerked his head back and then shot a crushing right-hand blow straight into the man's mouth. It drove him backward, with blood oozing from his lips. Reaching up, the man touched his bloodied mouth, blinked in confusion, and then shook his head. "You didn't have to hit me!"

"I'll do worse than that if you don't get out of here!" Then Phil grabbed the man's arm, whirled him around, and shoved him through the open door. The man windmilled out, and Phil slammed the door and locked it. He rushed over to where Amelia had slid to the floor against the wall and put his arms around her. "Are you okay, sis?"

"Yes, I'm all right. He just came barreling in here before I knew what was happening."

"You're going to have to be more careful about keeping your door locked." Phil held her away and looked directly at her, his own face showing a mixture of concern and agitation. "You're too trusting, Amelia."

Taking a deep breath, Amelia laughed shakily. "I'll be more careful, Phil. That's never happened to me before, but one time is too many."

Phil sighed and put his back against the wall next to his sister. "I don't like this kind of thing. Even if it doesn't happen often, as you say, once is enough."

"I was just getting ready to leave. Say, what are you doing here anyway?"

"I just thought I'd catch the end of your show and see if I could take my big sister out to get something to eat."

"That's a great idea! I'm starved."

Phil helped her up and waited for her to pull on a lightweight jacket, then opened the door, looking both ways before stepping out. "He's gone," he announced, then took her arm and accompanied her to the front entrance of the club. He stopped suddenly, and she turned to see what he was watching. The band was playing loudly, and the wild wailing of the saxophone was like a beast in pain.

"What is it, Phil?"

"Look at that," Phil said with disgust, nodding toward the dance floor. "That's not dancing. That's something out of the jungle!"

The floor was filled with young people dancing frenetically to the hit song "I Wish I Could Shimmy Like My Sister Kate." Some of the dancers were doing the shimmy and others the Charleston, two dances that were sweeping the country like an epidemic. Those doing the Charleston were alternately swiveling on the balls of their feet, bouncing pigeon-toed, kicking, then bending to the floor, and knocking their knees and crossing their arms. Those doing the shimmy were furiously shaking their shoulders like Gilda Gray, who would shake while she sang until her chemise straps fell from her shoulders. Phil watched the gyrations and vigorous wiggling of the dancers, then whirled and walked away with Amelia following.

When they were outside, Amelia took Phil's arm, saying, "There's a nice quiet place to eat just a couple blocks from here. Why don't we walk?"

"All right, sis. But that dancing back there took away my appetite."

Amelia did not argue, but as they walked along the sidewalk, she was grieved that he had seen this side of New York's nightlife. It was only the third time he had come to visit her, and she was ashamed.

They walked quietly, enjoying the balmy night air. Overhead, the full moon hovered between two tall buildings, shedding its pale light onto their patch of sidewalk.

Phil looked up at it without missing a step. "It reminds you of those moonlit nights on the veldt, doesn't it, Amelia?"

"Yes, it does," she murmured, glad to get Phil's mind off of the lewd dancing in the club. They were reminiscing about their home in Africa when they reached a restaurant called Burton's and went inside. The waiter showed them to a table in a far corner, and as they sat down Amelia said, "The soup here is very good, but they have excellent steak too. Your favorite." She smiled up at him.

"I'm not very hungry," Phil muttered. But when she urged him, he finally ordered a small steak and a baked potato. She ordered the soup du jour and a club sandwich, and both had coffee while they were waiting for their food to come.

"I missed you while you were gone, sis. Tell me all about your travels. Where did you go?"

Between sips of the scalding black coffee, Amelia told him about her tour. She had done well since leaving Eddie's club and signing on with Sid Menkin, Al Jolson's agent. He had scheduled her in Chicago, then had flown her out to Hollywood. She spoke lightly of these things, and he asked her, "Did you see Capone in Chicago?"

"No, but I could have. He drives around in a huge black bulletproof car. Everywhere he goes he's greeted like some kind of hero." She shook her head with disgust. "I don't understand why people put gangsters and killers on a pedestal like that."

"Neither do I. It's not what you would hope for in this country. These so-called Roaring Twenties are a lot like Babylon, I think."

Amelia smiled but said nothing. She wouldn't go quite so far as to agree with her brother on that point, though she did sometimes wonder where the world was headed. At the same time that she was drawn to the glamour of the lifestyle she had chosen, she was also bothered by the sleaziness of it. *Like a moth drawn to a flame*, she thought, then quickly switched the subject back to her tour. "I had a good time in Hollywood."

Phil brightened. "Did you meet any stars?"

"A man I met there, a friend of my agent, took me out to one of the studios, and I watched them make a movie."

"Oh yeah? Who was in it?"

"Rudolph Valentino."

"Valentino!" Phil grimaced. "I can't stand him! That fellow's hair is as greasy as a meat ax."

"I have to admit he's not my type"—Amelia laughed—"but America's sure going crazy for him."

"Women are, anyway," Phil snorted. "I don't think too many men think much of him."

The two talked more about the latest movie stars, and when the food was finally brought they started in. She noted that Phil ate eagerly, despite his insistence earlier that he was not really hungry. As he scooped up a final forkful, she said, "You've got to try their apple pie." Phil nodded, still swallowing the last bite of his steak and potato, and she signaled the waiter. "Bring us a big slice of that apple pie à la mode that's so good."

"Yes," Phil said, "and be sure you put ice cream on it." He winked at his sister.

"Oh, you crazy thing! You know better than that!"

As Phil leaned back in his seat, smiling contentedly, Amelia noticed that he had lost weight. There was a slight hollow in his cheeks and the suggestion of faint circles under his eyes. "You've been working too hard, Phil," she said, "and you're not eating right."

"I'm okay."

"How's school going?"

"It's going fine. I've got a lot of work to do in the next few weeks, but then I'll be finished."

"Finished!" Amelia exclaimed in surprise. "What do you mean finished?"

"I'm going to finish in two years like I said I would. I graduate on May twentieth."

Amelia reached over and squeezed his hand, her eyes sparkling. "I'm so proud of you!"

While they waited for the pie to come, she insisted on hearing what he was planning to do.

"Well, if I could do anything I wanted, I'd go to law school."

"Why don't you?"

"You know why, sis—I can't afford it. I've been working in a washing-machine factory since January. It pays more than the stables did, but that still isn't much, and it's as boring as anything I've ever done."

"But, Phil, I'm making lots of money now. I can help you. You must go."

Phil shook his head, a stubborn look on his face that Amelia was well familiar with. He just said, "No, I can't take help. I don't know why. I just can't."

Amelia knew how independent Phil was and how determined to make his own way in life, but she was still disappointed that he would turn down her help without a second thought. Nonetheless, she determined at that instant to see her brother go to law school. *I'll talk to Grandmother,* she thought. *We'll get him in one way or another. He's as stubborn as a blue-nosed mule!*

★   ★   ★   ★

Phil had no telephone in the small room he had moved into the previous summer. It was hard to keep up with college tuition and all the books he had to buy on his small income, so he had moved to save money on rent. On Saturday morning, his landlady handed him an envelope. "This just came for you, Phil."

"Thanks, Mrs. Harmon." He took the envelope and did not recognize the writing. He opened it quickly and scanned the note, recognizing Rosa's signature. It simply said: *Dear Phil, I need your help. Come and see me. You don't have to call. If you can come today, I'll be home.*

"This didn't come through the mail, did it?" Phil said.

"No, a big man came to the door and handed it to me."

Must've been Dom, Phil thought. The message sounded somewhat urgent, and he had the day off. He couldn't imagine what Rosa would need him for, but he immediately left the house. He had no money for a cab, but he did have a used bicycle he had picked up at a pawnshop for five dollars. It had needed some work, but he had gotten it back into operative condition. Now he pedaled off down the street, dodging traffic, and was soon out in the open country. It was a good five miles to the Morino estate, and by the time he got there, he had worked up a sweat. He pulled up in front of the gate, and a guard snapped, "What do you want?"

"Miss Rosa asked me to come." Phil knew the guard was only one part of an elaborate security system Big Tony had recently installed and kept operational twenty-four hours a day. The wall surrounding the property ended in sharp spikes and had broken glass embedded along the top. Phil also knew about an electronic alarm system that would stop anyone who managed to breach the wall. Dom had told him not even a mouse could get through every safety device on the estate.

The guard moved away, spoke over a telephone in a small guardhouse, then came back and opened the gate. "Go on up."

Phil walked his bike up toward the house, and when he was halfway there, he saw Rosa coming around the corner. She was wearing jodhpurs and a dark blue jersey, and her black hair flew behind her, bobbing up and down, as she ran to greet him.

"Phil, I'm so glad you could come!" Her eyes sparkled, and Phil thought her complexion was as smooth and creamy as anything on earth. She held out her hands, and Phil took them at once. "It's good to see you, Rosa."

"Come along. Tell me what you've been doing."

Phil accompanied the young woman, thinking how much she had matured since he'd first met her. She was sixteen-and-a-half years old now and a completely filled out and attractive young lady. He listened as she spoke of a party she had been to, and he asked, "Did you get lots of young men to dance with you?"

"Oh, I guess so. Now, what have you been doing?"

"Mostly studying. I'll graduate next month."

"Phil, how could that be? You've only been going for two years."

"I took some shortcuts."

Rosa was excited. "I'll have to get you a graduation present."

"You don't have to do that."

"Oh, but I want to." Grabbing his hand, she led him toward the stables. "I want you to look at Boadicea. I'm afraid something's wrong with her."

Phil laughed. "I'm no veterinarian."

"But you know horses." They reached the stables and went to Boadicea's stall. "Look, Phil, she won't put her foot down."

Phil watched as the young woman led the fine mare out. "She's just as haughty as ever, I see."

"But something's wrong with her foot. Please look at it, won't you, Phil?"

Guessing that Rosa was just manufacturing an excuse to be with him, Phil looked at the hoof, but as he suspected, he saw nothing. "Maybe she just strained a tendon. She'll be all right."

"Come on inside. Daddy's not home, but Mom would like to see you."

Maria Morino was indeed happy to see Phil, insisting that he

124

have some iced tea and a piece of chocolate cake she had baked. Rosa informed her that Phil would be graduating with honors next month, and Maria exclaimed with pleasure, "That's wonderful! And I must tell you, since you've been tutoring James in math, his grades have shot up."

"And my English is better too," Rosa said. "I'm about ready for another lesson. Come on and finish your cake. We'll go to the living room. All my books are in there."

Ten minutes later Phil was sitting beside Rosa on the big couch.

"I'm tired of writing themes," she griped as she tried to follow his instructions.

"You'd better get used to it. You'll be writing them in college," Phil smiled.

"This is good enough. I don't think old Mrs. Brown reads these things anyway."

"Well, I'd better go, then."

"Where you going, Phil? I thought we might go for a ride together."

"But Boadicea's crippled, you remember?" he teased her. "Besides, I can't stay. I've got to go see my grandmother."

"Where does she live?" Rosa listened as he gave the location of his grandmother's house. Then she exclaimed, "Why, you can't ride that bicycle way over there! It's too far. That must be ten miles from here."

"Good for the health. Won't hurt me a bit."

"Phil, take me with you. You've told me so much about her."

"We can't both ride a bicycle." He laughed and got up.

"Come on. I'll get Kenny to take us over. He's not doing anything anyway."

"Who's Kenny?"

"He works in the gardens and on the grounds, but he does some driving for Daddy and Mom too."

"You have to clear this with your mother."

"Oh, she'll let me go. Come on."

★   ★   ★   ★

Lola Winslow was sitting in the large den her husband had designed, looking out the windows on the south side, which provided a beautiful view of the grounds. Spring had come with a sudden intensity, so that the grass seemed greener than she had ever seen it, and the flower beds blazoned their colors flamboyantly—reds, blues, yellows, and purples.

Hearing the sound of a car, Lola got up and looked out the front windows on the other side of the room. She watched as a large black car pulled up to the door and was pleased to see her grandson Phillip step outside and then help a young woman from the car. "Who can that be?" she murmured. "She's a pretty thing. Maybe Phillip's got a budding romance. I'll have to look into this!"

She waited, knowing that Mary, the maid, would bring them into the study, and when Phil stepped back and allowed the young woman to come in, she got up and moved forward. "Phillip, it's so good to see you. Give your grandmother a kiss."

Phil kissed her on the cheek and then said, "Grandmother, this is Miss Rosa Morino."

"How do you do, Mrs. Winslow?" Rosa said almost breathlessly.

She had enormous dark eyes, Lola noticed, and hair as black as the blackest thing in nature. "Why, I'm so glad you came, my dear. I've been getting lonely, but now you can tell me all about this grandson of mine. He's so modest he never tells me any of his triumphs."

"Don't have any," Phil laughed. "Come along. Sit down, Grandmother."

Lola insisted on asking the maid to bring tea and sweet cakes. When she came back with them, Lola asked, "How are your studies going, Phillip?"

Rosa answered for him before he could get his mouth open. "He's going to graduate next month—with honors, Mrs. Winslow. It only took him two years instead of four, and he's at the top of his class. He's summa cum laude!" she finished breathlessly, looking at Phil with such pride that Lola laughed.

"I'm glad to hear of all this, but I don't know why I have to hear it from this young lady."

Phil was embarrassed. He did not like to talk about his

accomplishments and tried to change the subject. "Rosa wants to hear about your days of dealing blackjack in the saloons out west."

Lola was amused. "Everyone is shocked by that."

"Did you really do that, Mrs. Winslow?"

"Yes, I really did. Those were hard times. I was trying to find my father, and all I knew was that he was working for the Union Pacific Railroad that was being built from coast to coast."

Rosa sat forward, her eyes glued to the stately and beautiful woman as she told of her early days and her adventures when she was Lola Montez. She finally threw up her hand and said, "That's enough of my awful past."

"Oh, you've done so many things, Mrs. Winslow, and I've never done *anything!*"

Lola smiled and shook her head. "Most of the things I did in those days you wouldn't want to do."

"Yes, I would too. I want to do lots of things."

"Like what?" Lola asked curiously. She was very conscious of Rosa's frequent looks toward Phillip and knew that she had a tremendous crush on her grandson. She was also aware, however, of Rosa's father's occupation. Her husband, Mark, had spoken more than once of Big Tony Morino and what a violent, terrible man he was. The girl, of course, couldn't see that—her father showed her a different side at home. Lola saw an innocence in the young woman and felt a wave of pity for her. She listened as Rosa spoke animatedly of getting out into the world and doing exciting things.

"Maybe you could become a flier like my cousin Erin," Phil said. "And a movie star—she almost became one of those too."

"I know. I went to see her. Daddy took me to see her fly in an exhibition when she walked on the wing of that airplane. Oh, I wish I could do something like that!"

"You'd fall off," Phil teased. "Just like you fall off your horse all the time."

"I do not! I've never fallen off!"

"Not even once? I seem to remember down by the lower pasture when Boadicea gave a little sideways move, and you wound up in mud up to your—"

"Phil, don't you bring that up! It's not fair!"

Phil leaned back and laughed. He enjoyed teasing Rosa and seeing her reactions. For all her womanly beauty, she was still a little girl at heart. He was also enjoying watching the interactions between Rosa and his grandmother. He knew this was good for his grandmother. She got lonely, and he resolved that he would have to come more often. He started suddenly when he heard Rosa say, "And he wants to go to law school, but he doesn't have the money. My father would help him, but he won't take help."

Phil jumped back into the conversation. "Now, Rosa, don't be worried about my schooling. You sound like my sister! She said the same thing to me earlier."

Lola put her gaze on her grandson and smiled brightly. "You're just like your grandfather, Phillip. It was hard to give him anything, and your father is the same way." She turned back to the girl and said, "I'd like to talk about *you* for a moment, Rosa. Please don't think me forward for asking this, but do you know the Lord?"

Rosa was so startled by the sudden switch in the conversation she just stared at Lola, not able to answer for a moment. When she did reply, she stammered slightly and had none of her usual assurance. "Why, I . . . I was baptized when I was a baby. I don't remember it, of course, but Mom told me about it." She thought hard and said, "And I was confirmed, and we go to the Catholic Church."

"Well, I'm sure those are all good things, Rosa, but it's not the same thing as knowing the Lord. As a matter of fact, I'm sure there are good people in all churches who don't know the Lord—Catholics, Baptists, Methodists, you name it."

"But I go to Mass almost every Sunday."

Lola Winslow had always been outspoken in her witness. Now she said directly, "Jesus is alive, Rosa. He died for our sins and went into the grave, but He came out of the tomb and is now at the right hand of God. He wants to live in each of our hearts."

Rosa looked puzzled. "But if He's at the right hand of God, how can He live inside us?"

"I can't explain it, but I know that in my heart He's just as real, just as alive, as anything in the world to me. Why, He's more real to me than this flesh of mine."

Rosa grew quiet and cast a quick glance at Phil. She felt

humble and hardly knew what to say. Finally she said haltingly, "I . . . I've been reading the Bible that Phil gave me. I don't understand much of it."

"That's good that you're reading it. Stay in the Gospels. Read about Jesus, and the time will come that He will speak to your heart. Ask Him, and He will show you the way."

★　★　★　★

By the time Phil and Rosa returned to the Morino place, the sun had gone down. Phil got out of the car, helped Rosa out, then heard her say, "Thank you, Kenny, for taking us and for waiting so long."

"No problem at all, Miss Rosa. Anytime."

Phil turned and walked along the gravel pathway, saying, "I'm glad you went with me, Rosa. My grandmother gets lonely, I know. She was very much in love with my grandfather. I never saw anything like it."

"What was he like?"

"A fine, handsome man. Back in the early days he was pretty tough, but never with her or with any of his children or grand-children. The thing is, they were just as much in love at the end of his life as they were at the beginning. Grandmother often told me that he'd write her little poems and love letters even when he knew he would see her that day."

"I think that's so sweet," Rosa whispered. They had reached Phil's bicycle, and suddenly she put out her hands. Phil took them automatically. "Thank you for taking me, Phil."

Phil held her hands and looked into her eyes, luminous under the moonlight. The moon was low in the sky but shed its silver beams over the earth. He was aware of the firmness of her hands, the perfume she was wearing, the pleasant contours of her face. He was also uncomfortably aware of her womanliness as the moonlight touched the curve of her shoulders and the soft lines of her body.

Rosa's hands tightened on his, and she leaned toward him. "Phil, please let me help you go to law school."

"I couldn't do that, Rosa."

Her face had a pleading expression. "I want to do something for you, and you won't let me."

Phil saw that her full lower lip was trembling. He had not dated much and felt a sudden sense of awkwardness. But it was an awkwardness touched with desire, and without meaning to, he leaned forward and saw her respond, taking a step toward him so that she was almost touching him.

Quickly Phil shook his head and gave a strangled half laugh. "You've done a lot for me," he said, and he knew by the look on her face that she had expected him to kiss her.

This can't be. It just can't be, he thought, almost in a panic. "I ... I've got to go, Rosa. Thanks for going with me to my grandmother's."

Rosa Morino watched as Phil wheeled around and picked up his bicycle. She stood absolutely still as he pedaled away, turning once to wave at her. She did not return the wave, however, and even as he disappeared into the murky darkness, she felt herself trembling. *Why didn't he kiss me?* she wondered. *He wanted to. I could tell.* Giving a half sob, she turned and walked blindly toward the house.

CHAPTER EIGHT

A DOOR OPENS

★ ★ ★ ★

Phil moved slowly along the line of graduates at the outdoor ceremony, conscious of the sweet smell of honeysuckle. Glancing toward the scent, he saw the bright greenery and white blossoms of the vine climbing a wall surrounding the open area. Overhead the sky was a bright blue, and the sun poured down its heat in long yellow bars of light. The calling of the graduates' names made a loud cadence on the air, blending with the warbling of a bird on the fringes of the crowd. He heard the name "James Veasey" and took a step forward. It seemed a small step to him, but it had been a long, hard grind, compacting four years of work into the space of two.

"Eunice Wainright."

Now there were only a few people left, and Phil put his foot on the step of the platform. The dean tolled off the names, and finally Phil stood alone, watching Clarice Williams take her diploma. His name was next. "Phillip Winslow," he heard, which was followed by a pause. Then the dean said loudly, "Summa cum laude."

"Good for you, Phil!" came a cry from the audience. He grinned as he recognized Rosa's voice, and laughter spread over the crowd. The dean shook his hand and said quickly, "Fine work, Winslow. We're all very proud of you."

"Thank you, sir."

Clutching the rolled diploma in his hand, Phil strode across the platform and stepped down. He glanced up and saw Amelia sitting between his grandmother on her left and Rosa on her right. Amelia raised her hands in the traditional prizefighter clasped sign of victory, and Phil waved the diploma in the air.

Moving back to his seat, he waited until the ceremony was finished. He marched out to the sound of the band playing loudly, and all of the graduates then blended into smiling, happy, laughing groups of relatives and friends.

"Phillip, I was never so proud of anyone in my life." Lola's eyes were bright as she embraced him. She clung to him and whispered in his ear, "Your grandfather would have been so proud of you, and I know your parents are. I just wish they could have been here."

Phil felt a tug on his arm and turned, and Amelia threw herself against him, squeezing him fiercely. "I'm so happy I could scream!" she said.

"Go ahead and scream," Phil said. "I feel a little bit like hollering myself."

Amelia was wearing a subdued light gray summer dress, and her smile trembled a little as she said, "I wish the folks could have been here."

"Too far to come back for just a little thing like this."

"It's *not* a little thing!"

Phil turned to see Rosa running toward him with her arms out. He hugged her, and she clung to him, pressing against him and whispering, "You were the best, Phil. Summa cum laude. That means the very top, doesn't it?"

Phil was acutely aware of Rosa's softness as she held him close, and it stirred him in a way that was disturbing. He cleared his throat and stepped back. As she reluctantly released him, he reached out and took her hand. "It's just a piece of paper."

"No, it's not. It means you were right up there with the best in your whole class."

"I think it's time for a little ceremony," Lola said.

Phil noticed she had a peculiar smile on her face, and he looked at her closely. "A ceremony? We just had a ceremony."

"Come along, Phillip," Lola said firmly. She was wearing a pale yellow dress that shone in the sunlight, with a matching hat and veil. She seemed to be happier than Phil had seen her in a long time.

"What's this all about, Grandmother?"

"You always want to know so much. Now, come along and don't ask questions."

Lola clung to Phil's arm, and Amelia and Rosa followed them through the milling crowd. They left the field where the ceremony had been held, and Lola firmly grasped his arm, saying, "Down this way."

Mystified, Phil moved along, glancing over his shoulder to see both Rosa and Amelia smiling broadly. "What's this all about?" he said suspiciously.

Rosa laughed aloud, and her dark eyes danced with delight. "You'll see."

They made their way to the street that bordered the college, and Phil looked around for his grandmother's car and driver. He assumed they had come in the big Oldsmobile. "Are we going out to eat?"

"Yes, we are, but not right now." Lola stopped suddenly and turned to him. "You've never asked your grandfather or me for anything, Phillip, so we wanted to give you something, and we saved it until your graduation. There it is."

Puzzled, Phil turned, seeing nothing but a line of cars parked along the street. People were beginning to get in them now and leave the campus, but he shook his head. "What is it, Grandmother?"

"Oh, Phil, you're so slow!" Rosa cried. "It's that car! It's yours!"

Phil blinked with surprise, stared at Rosa, then wheeled to look at the vehicle she was pointing at.

"Why, that can't be!"

"Yes it can," Lola said. "Your grandfather always knew you'd go to college someday, and we agreed that on your graduation day you should have a beautiful car. He looked forward to that day, but when he knew he wouldn't live to see it, he put it into the will to make sure you'd get it for graduation. Do you like it?"

Phil was stunned. He moved forward like a man in a dream

and approached the vehicle. It was white and the top was down. Large balloon tires held the body of the car high off the ground. It gleamed with chrome-and-nickel plating and sported drum headlights. The chrome radiator shone like silver. Everything about it shouted speed, and he laid one hand on the front fender, then turned and said, "Grandmother, it's a Hupmobile series R!"

"I don't know what it is. Amelia and Rosa helped pick it out for you."

"We did, and I knew this would be just the one you'd want!" Rosa could restrain herself no longer. "C'mon, Phil. Take us all for a ride."

Phil was still unable to speak clearly. His throat was tight as he said, "I don't know how to thank you, Grandmother . . . and Grandfather too."

"I thought you had better manners, Phillip. You just say, 'Thank you, Grandmother,' and I say, 'You're welcome.'"

"I should do more than that."

"You can take me for a ride, then. Come along, and don't pile us up on our maiden voyage."

And then Phil Winslow spent one of the most wonderful hours of his life. First he made sure the women were safely seated, Rosa and Amelia in back and his grandmother in front. He started the engine and shook his head. "Listen to that power!"

"It sounds awfully loud to me." Lola spoke above the roar.

"It's supposed to sound loud, Mrs. Winslow." Rosa laughed. "People have to look when they hear you coming."

Phil laughed too and pulled the automobile out into the street. He had long been partial to the Hupmobile, and now he asked, "How did you know this was the one I wanted?"

"You told Rosa, and Rosa told Amelia, and Amelia told me. So here it is."

"Get out of the city where you can open it up," Amelia ordered. "Let's have some speed."

The ride was delightful. The wind blew their hair, and the women had to remove their hats to keep from losing them. Once they were out of the city on the open road, Phil grasped the wheel and leaned forward, his heart singing. He took the curves a little fast, throwing the women to one side, and when his grandmother lurched over against him, he put his arm around her and said, "You sit close to me, Miss Lola Montez. You're the Union Belle again, and I love you."

Lola had not felt well for some time, but with Phillip's arm around her holding her close, she knew a moment of perfect delight. *This is what money is for*, she thought. *It doesn't do any good stuck in an old bank or in a bond. It should be giving someone happiness and joy.* She glanced up and saw in Phil's auburn hair, green eyes, and clean-cut features her husband as he had been in his youth, strong and vigorous and daring. She prayed then, *God, give this young man your very best, for he's Mark all over again.*

Phil let Amelia drive the car and even put Rosa behind the wheel, although both girls had trouble getting out of first gear. Rosa fumed and pouted at her difficulty, but Phil said, "Your father would probably horsewhip me if he knew I was letting you drive at all."

"You treat me like a child!"

"Well, you are. A pretty child but still just an infant."

"That's what you think, Phillip Winslow," Rosa said dauntingly. She turned her dark eyes on him, a challenge in her features. "I'm not a baby, and I won't be treated like one."

Phil suddenly reached over and grabbed the wheel. "Well, baby or not, you're about to run us off the road. That's enough. Pull over, and we'll go celebrate."

They all went to a restaurant that Lola had frequented with Mark, and the maître d' greeted her warmly and spoke of their many visits. Lola smiled at him gracefully and then later, as they were eating, said, "Your grandfather and I loved to come here. It was his favorite restaurant."

Amelia looked at her grandmother as she spoke about her husband, noting her faraway gaze. There was something ethereal about the woman now—even a sense of eternity in her. Amelia could not explain it, but she somehow understood that Lola's heart and mind were in the next world far more than they were in this one.

After the meal Phil thought Lola looked tired, and he said firmly, "I'm taking you home, Grandmother. You've had enough excitement."

He drove to his grandmother's house and escorted her in. He

stopped at the door, and when she turned to him, he put his arms around her. "I can't thank you enough, Grandmother," he whispered huskily, kissing her cheek.

She held him at arm's length and said, "God bless you, dear boy. You've got your grandfather and your father in you, and a man with the blood of Mark Winslow and Andrew Winslow can't go wrong. Good night. It's been a wonderful day."

Phil went back to the car and pulled out of the driveway. He drove to Amelia's apartment, and when he started to get out to open her door, she said, "Don't bother, Phil. I'm so happy for you and so proud of you." She got out of the car, went to the driver's side, kissed him, and ruffled his hair. "Now you need another world to conquer."

"One world at a time." Phil smiled. "Thanks so much, sis. You've made it a great day for me."

Amelia moved toward the building, and Phil eased the car away from the curb. It was growing dark now, and he drove rather rapidly. "I've got to get you home, Rosa. What's your curfew?"

"Daddy's gone to Chicago on business," Rosa said. "Mom didn't tell me what time to be in. She trusts me."

"She didn't see you nearly put us in the ditch."

"You made me do that making fun of me!" Rosa said. She was sitting in the front seat now and edged over until she was touching him, her arm against his. "Come on, Phil, it's too early to go in. Let's go somewhere and get something to eat."

"You've already eaten."

"That was ages ago. I'm hungry again."

Phil argued, but she took his arm and said, "Come on, Phil, don't be such a stick-in-the-mud."

"Well, all right, but it'll have to be quick."

He drove her to a diner, where they ordered hamburgers and french fries. Rosa downed them as if she hadn't eaten all day, and he shook his head. "You know, for a baby you've got a good appetite. You've got mustard there on the side of your mouth."

Rosa's tongue darted out. "Is that it?" she said.

"No, let me get it." Phil picked up a napkin and wiped off the mustard. He leaned back, smiling and thinking about his new car. "I don't think I've ever been so surprised, Rosa."

"I knew you would be. You remember the time we saw that Hupmobile, and you remember what you said?"

"No, I don't remember."

"You said, 'I'd like to have a car like that, but I never will.' Well, I decided right then that somehow you'd have one."

Phil was touched. "Did you, Rosa? That was sweet of you. I would never have thought of asking Grandmother for anything like that."

"No, I knew you wouldn't, but I didn't mind asking *for* you."

"So you and Amelia got together and begged Grandmother out of it."

"We didn't have to beg. She told you the truth. Your grandfather had already put it in his will to give you a car, and Amelia knew about it. They just didn't know what kind to get, but I did. Oh, Phil, it's such a beautiful car! You've got to take me places in it all the time."

"I've got to make a living," he protested. "Otherwise I won't even be able to pay for the gas."

"Oh, yes you will. You'll do wonderful things, Phil. You're a summa cum laude."

"With this diploma and a nickel, I can buy a cup of coffee just about anywhere."

The two sat there making light talk, but finally Phil said, "Time to go." He paid for the food, and they left. He helped her into the car and then started the engine. The stars were already out, and he drove through the dusk with the powerful headlights searching the road before them. He was pulling up the long drive to her house when she said, "Look, Phil, turn off there!"

"What's the matter?"

"Look at the river, how pretty it is."

Phil pulled the car over to the left where a stream meandered across the property, a river of silver in the moonlight. The air was warm, and she suddenly reached over and shut off the key. "Don't be in such a hurry!" she scolded. "Life goes by too fast."

Phil leaned back in the car and ran his hand over the steering wheel. His heart was still full of gratitude at the magnificent gift, and he sighed. "She's a wonderful woman, my grandmother."

"She is and so beautiful."

They sat quietly, listening to the frogs croak out a symphony down by the stream. He said, "It reminds me of Africa. Frogs in the rivers there grow to be almost a foot across. Huge things!"

"Tell me about Africa, Phil."

Phil began to speak of the land that was so dear to him, and as he did, he grew almost lonely. "I miss it at times," he said, turning to her. She sat very still, her face outlined by the bright moonlight. In the shadows her eyes seemed even darker than usual.

She said, "Phil, I have something to tell you."

"What is it, Rosa?" he said, giving her his full attention.

"I don't want you to call me a baby anymore. I'm almost seventeen years old."

"Not for a few more months you're not," he teased. "Why are you so all-fired anxious to grow up? Enjoy your girlhood."

Suddenly she leaned over and reached her hand up to his neck. Phil was shocked at how warm and soft and vibrant the touch of her hand was, and how it stirred him. "I'm a woman, Phil, not a little girl." She pulled his head down then and pressed her lips to his. They trembled under Phil's, and an inexpressible rush pulsed through him. He put his arm around her and drew her close, lost in the softness of her lips and of her body as she leaned against him. He felt the pressure of her hands encouraging him, but it was Phil who drew back. His hands were unsteady as he placed them firmly on her shoulders. He could not think what to say, for he had not thought of her like this, or at least had tried not to.

"Phil, I think I'm falling in love with you."

Rosa's whisper struck Phil with a force he could not have described. For a moment he could neither think nor speak, and then he sat back, shaking his head. "No, Rosa, you're too young."

"But you like me too. I could tell by the way you kissed me."

"Well . . . of course I like you. I always have, you remember. You have a sweetness in you that I've always admired, but there can never be anything between us, Rosa."

"Why not?" Rosa cried. "Why not, Phil? What's wrong with me?"

Phil's stomach wrenched at the heartbroken quality in her voice. "Nothing is wrong with you, Rosa. You're a beautiful, desirable young woman—not an infant. I see that now, and I have to be more careful. But we're different. You're going one way, and I'm going another."

Rosa stiffened and turned away from him, her hands clenched into fists. "I know what it is. It's my father. That's why you won't ever love me."

Phil knew there was truth in what she was saying. "You're not your father, Rosa, but you're a member of your family. Your family and mine are very different. You must see that."

Rosa bowed her head, and he sensed that her shoulders were shaking. He put his hand on her shoulder, but she wrenched away and got out of the car.

"Rosa—" he cried out. "Don't leave!"

"Good night, Phil. I'm glad you got such a nice car."

He watched her march across the field in the moonlight toward the house, and he sat there feeling miserable, for he truly did have an affection for Rosa Morino. He had not thought of her as a woman he might love, for he knew the truth in what he had told her. Their ways were so different. He had nothing, and she was wealthy. Despite her innocence, she was tied into the Morino family, whose wealth was founded on bootlegging and violence. That could not be ignored, Phil knew, yet still he was miserable.

With a wrench he turned the car around and jammed his foot down on the accelerator. "Why do things like this have to happen?" he grunted and shook his head. The day, which had begun so beautifully, had ended in misery for him and Rosa.

★   ★   ★   ★

Phil went to his job at the washing-machine factory the Monday following graduation, but he found himself unhappy and dissatisfied. The job offered no challenge, and he knew he was merely marking time there. As soon as his shift ended he went home and fixed a meal on the hot plate his landlady allowed him to keep in his room. He had just sat down to it when he heard a knock on his door. "Yes, who is it?"

"Phil, there's a phone call for you."

"Thanks, I'll come and take it."

Phil followed his landlady downstairs, and when he picked up the phone and gave his name, he heard a voice say, "This is Lee Novak, Phil."

"Hey, Lee, good to hear from you."

"Can you come down to my office tomorrow?"

"Well, I'm working—"

"I mean after work."

"Will you still be there? I get off at six."

"I'm here all the time, Phil. Come right over as soon as you're done. I need to talk to you right away."

"All right, Lee, I can do that. I'll see you then."

Phil hung up the phone, nodded his thanks to his landlady, and then went back to his room. As he ate he thought, *Something funny about this. Why would Lee want to see me, and why is it so urgent?* He liked Novak very much, and the two had met twice since their first encounter at the Christmas dinner a year and a half ago. Novak seemed interested in him, and Phil looked forward to the meeting.

★   ★   ★   ★

"Congratulate me, Phil, I've got a new title."

Phil was seated in Novak's office. He had noticed the fresh gold paint on the door. "The sign says Director of Special Agents. What does that mean? Is it a big promotion?"

Novak sat back in his chair. He looked hard and capable and younger than his fifty-seven years. "It means I'll do more work and get precious little more money." He laughed. "I'm still risking my neck hauling in the big crime bosses, but now that I'm in charge of things, I'll not only get shot at, I'll get all the blame if anything goes wrong!"

Phil grinned. "Sounds like you needed a demotion more than a promotion."

"Nope, it's what I want. It gives me more authority to do what I must to clean up these scumbags from our fine city."

Phil listened attentively while Lee spoke, imagining himself someday helping to bring criminals to justice, and finally he said,

"Well, congratulations on your promotion, Lee."

"I didn't bring you up here to congratulate me. I want to offer you a job."

Phil blinked with surprise. "A job! You mean here in your office?"

"That's right."

"But I don't know anything about the law—not yet anyway. I want to go to law school, so I'm saving up money. One day I'll get there."

"I know all about that. Your grandmother told me." Lee leaned forward over the desk, his dark eyes intent. There was a burning intensity about the man that startled Phil. "Look, let me lay it all out on the front porch for you, Phil. I want you to come into my office. You can't actually be a full-fledged special agent yet—not without some legal training first—but for now you can be an intern, assisting me and learning about law enforcement at the same time. You'll go to law school and work for me as you can fit it in."

"But I don't have the money to go to law school."

"I've arranged for a full scholarship for you, Phil. I know a few people and have pulled some strings on your behalf."

Phil sat there stunned by this news. "I can go to law school and work here at the same time?"

"Sure, and I guarantee you, buddy, you'll learn a lot more about the law working with me in this office than you will in law school." He laughed abruptly. "You might even get to meet some of the big crime bosses. If you play your cards right, you might even have them take a shot at you."

"Lee, I don't see how I could go to law school and work for you at the same time."

"I didn't say it would be easy, but I think it'll be a good thing for you. You'll get your law degree eventually, and I'm hoping that I'll be around for a while, and I'm going to need somebody I can trust. It's going to be a rough road, and it's going to be bloody down the way. I'll put that to you right now."

Phil stared at Novak and suddenly knew that this was what he wanted to do. "All right. Let me talk to Amelia and write to my parents."

"No, I can't wait for that. I need an answer immediately. If you can't make up your mind like that, I can't use you."

Phil stared at Novak and then suddenly grinned. "All right. Yes, I'll take it!"

Novak rose from his chair and put out his hand. His grip was hard and firm, and he clapped Phil on the back. "All right. That's what I wanted to hear. Now you're playing in the big leagues, boy. The first thing we do is get you a gun."

Phil's eyes grew large. "A gun! Who am I going to shoot?"

"Anybody that's shooting at you. Come on. Call your boss and quit that job of yours, and we'll go over to the law school tomorrow."

★ ★ ★ ★

Phil Winslow's life seemed caught up in a whirlwind. He found himself running from early in the morning until midnight or even later. He enrolled in law school, and although the courses did not start till the fall, he had already bought all his books, met his advisor, and started studying for classes that would come.

As for Lee Novak, he was a whirlwind himself! Phil felt as if he'd been thrown into a swift river and was being carried along with the current. All day long Novak poured information into him, both verbally and in mountains of files. Phil had always had an excellent memory, but the long hours and the mass of materials immersed him so that he hardly knew his name.

After two weeks of this, Novak looked at his protégé, noting the red-rimmed eyes and the dark shadows. He suddenly said roughly, "Get out of here, Phil."

Phil, who was going through a stack of files, turned and blinked with surprise. "What do you mean, Lee?"

"I mean you're like a zombie. Go take two days off."

"What'll I do?"

"Go sleep beside a river. Go fishing. Get yourself a girlfriend and go do the Charleston."

Phil could scarcely credit this. "But there's so much to do, Lee."

"It'll be here when you get back. Now, that's an order. Go

relax and come back fresh Thursday morning. Then I'll wear you down again."

★   ★   ★   ★

Phil found it difficult to slow down. His mind was racing with all the facts and files Lee had poured into him. The first day of his minivacation he simply went out to the stables where he used to work. His former boss, Luke DeSalvo, was happy to see him and gladly let him borrow a horse to go riding over the hills. Back in his apartment, he wrote a long letter to his parents in Africa and slept a full eight hours that night, which was unusual for him.

The second day he got up and washed and polished his car, then set out for a drive. He explored some parts of the city he had never seen and at noon went to visit his grandmother. She was glad to see him, but he noticed that she was very weak. It saddened him, and when he saw how quickly she tired of talking, he left, saying, "I'll be back soon, Grandmother."

"Good-bye, Phillip. Thanks for coming to see me." Her voice as well as her grasp was weak, and as Phil drove away, he felt uncertain. *She looks so small and fragile. I wish Mom and Dad were here to take care of her.*

He stopped by to see Amelia late in the afternoon, but she wasn't home. So he headed to the Morino estate, where the guard told him he'd find Rosa at the stables. When he parked his Hupmobile and got out, he stopped still, for Rosa was about to mount Boadicea. He moved forward hesitantly. Their last meeting had not been happy, but he felt he needed to say more to her. He approached her and called out, "Rosa, wait a minute!"

Rosa turned and a mixture of surprise and apprehension crossed her face. "Hello, Phil," she said. Her voice was tight, and Phil knew she still felt bad about their last meeting. He was encouraged, however, that she didn't move away but sat quietly astride her horse, facing him.

"Is it all right if I get a horse and ride with you?" he asked.

"That'd be fine."

Phil chose the big bay that carried his weight well, and soon the two of them rode out across the Morino estate as the sun was going down. Only birdsong and the rustling of leaves broke the silence between them. It was a peaceful evening, but Phil found conversation hard going. He tried to get Rosa to speak about what she was doing, but she answered only in brief replies.

Finally he said, "I've got a new job, Rosa. I've been wanting to tell you about it."

She turned toward him quickly. "What kind of a job? I thought you were going to go to law school."

"Well, actually I'm going to do both. I have a distant relative named Lee Novak. He works for the justice department."

"So you'll be working for the government?" Rosa said uncertainly.

"Well, mostly for Lee. As his assistant. But the good thing is, Rosa, I get a full scholarship to law school."

Rosa suddenly brightened. "Oh, that's wonderful! I know how badly you want to go."

"Well, it just dropped into my lap, and I'm very happy about it. I'll start in the fall."

Rosa pulled Boadicea up to a halt and reached out her hand. "Congratulations, Phil. I know you'll do as well in law school as you did in college."

He took her hand and squeezed it. "I'm thankful to the Lord for it. I think He's put it in my way."

At the mention of God, Rosa released her hand. She knew God was big in this young man's life, while to her religion played a very small role.

Phil sensed her sudden reticence and said quickly, "I work pretty hard, but we could go out together once in a while, or I could come ride with you perhaps. Would you like that?"

"That would be nice. . . ." she said, a twinge of hope in her eyes. Then she lowered her gaze and went on quickly, "But I don't suppose you'll have much time for that."

Phil knew Rosa was unhappy, and he could not help thinking about their last meeting. He had thought often of her kiss, and it still stirred him to remember it. Looking at her now, he saw that her face was set, and throughout the rest of the ride she said almost nothing. Finally, when they dismounted back at the stables, she said curtly, "Good-bye, Phil."

"Well, I'll be seeing you."

"I doubt it. You'll be very busy."

Phil watched her as she led Boadicea away, and a stable hand came to take the bay. As Phil got into his car, he felt frustrated. "That wasn't very pleasant," he muttered. "I'm afraid she's still angry with me."

★ ★ ★ ★

Rosa was indeed unhappy. She had thought about Phil's kiss many times, and she was certain she was in love with him. She was also certain he did not return that love, that he still thought of her as a child. She moped around the next few days with little laughter about her.

Her father noticed this and finally said, "What's the matter with you, Rosa? You don't look happy."

"Nothing. I'm fine, Daddy."

Big Tony studied his daughter. The time he had been dreading for years was upon him; soon she would take a man and leave home. He finally said, "Are you serious about any of these young fellows that come around?"

"No, not really."

Suddenly Tony remembered that Dominic had mentioned having seen Rosa riding with Phil Winslow. "It's not Winslow, is it? You're not serious about him, are you?"

"No."

"What's he doing? Is he still in college?"

"No, he's graduated. He's working for the justice department, and next fall he's going to go to law school."

Tony Morino's eyes narrowed, and he shook his head. His voice grew tense. "So he's working for the feds, huh? I want you to stay away from him, Rosa, you hear? It can't come to any good for us. We're on opposite sides of the fence now."

"But, Daddy—"

"I've given you everything you ever wanted, but I'm telling you, stay away from Winslow."

Rosa did not answer. The tears were not far away, and she turned and fled from his study.

Tony called out, "I'm sorry, Rosa, but it has to be that way." He knew his words had hurt her, but he shook his head. "She'll get over him. She has to. We don't need a guy like that hanging around here."

CHAPTER NINE

PASSING

★   ★   ★   ★

Amelia stepped into her apartment and heaved a sigh of relief. Putting her suitcase down, she closed the door, then walked around, happy to be back. She had returned from a two-week engagement in Miami, and although it had been a triumph of sorts, she was drained of energy. She set about unpacking her suitcase, sorting out the clothes that needed washing, and then went to the phone. She called Phil's work number but only got a secretary, who informed her that Mr. Winslow was out and would not be expected back until late.

Amelia was disappointed, for she had hoped to spend the evening with Phil. It was early yet, not much past one, so she decided she would spend the afternoon and perhaps the evening with her grandmother. First she took a long, leisurely bath, filling up the tub and adding a fragrant bubble bath. As she lay there relaxing and soaking up the warmth, she went back in her mind over the events of the past two weeks. She had been so well received in Florida it had astonished her.

Of course, there were the usual lounge lizards who pursued her, but she had learned their species well and avoided them. Most of them wore their hair plastered back with oil and affected the latest fashions. All of them had a predatory gleam in their eyes no matter how smooth their speech, and as she lifted her leg and scrubbed it with a brush, she had a brief moment of distaste for those men.

But there had been others who were genuinely appreciative. She had met Mel Thompson, who was involved with the new Metro-Goldwyn-Mayer Studios in some way she did not quite understand. He had urged her to think about coming to Hollywood. She had been polite enough but had shown little interest. She had seen enough of movie making to know that all one did was film one scene at a time and not necessarily in order. The last scene of a movie might be filmed first, and something in the middle might be held over until last. That did not appeal to her as much as giving live performances on stage. She especially hoped someday to star in musicals.

Finally she finished her bath, dried off, and dressed. She had many dresses now, more than she actually needed. She slipped into her undergarments, then put on a simple straight dress with a low waistline, the skirt falling just below her knees. She put on her shoes, which had a bar-and-button fastening, then a silk cloche hat. She picked up her purse and called a cab. It was a luxury being able to use the cab service, and when the cab came within five minutes, she locked the door and left. The drive was pleasant, although warm. September had been hot in New York, but not as sultry as Amelia remembered it in Africa. She leaned back and, being rather sleepy, dozed off, awakening only when the driver said, "Here we are, miss."

With a start Amelia opened her eyes and fumbled in her purse. She paid the driver, adding a generous tip, and then got out of the cab. She walked up the steps and rang the bell. Almost at once a woman in a nurse's uniform answered, saying, "Yes, can I help you?"

"I'm Amelia Winslow, Mrs. Winslow's granddaughter."

"Come in, please. My name's Lily Stockman. I've been on duty here for three days."

Alarm ran through Amelia, and she turned quickly to the nurse, a tall woman with blond hair and very light blue eyes, obviously of Swedish extraction. "My grandmother's been ill that long?"

"I'm afraid so."

"What is it?"

Nurse Stockman hesitated. "She's had some heart problems."

"A heart attack?" Amelia demanded.

"I'd rather you talk to Dr. Locke. He can tell you much more than I can."

"Is he here?"

"No, but he'll be by this afternoon at four o'clock."

Amelia stood irresolutely, a trace of fear racing through her. "Is it serious, Nurse?"

"She's very weak. Dr. Locke is concerned and so am I."

"May I see her?"

"Oh yes. I just finished giving her a bath. Dr. Locke said to keep her very quiet, and I know you wouldn't do anything to excite her."

"Of course not."

Amelia followed the nurse upstairs and entered the bedroom, determined to let nothing show on her face. When she saw that her grandmother was awake, she said, "Grandmother, what's all this? You know I don't permit you to be sick." Approaching the bed, she leaned over and kissed the sick woman's cheek, then pulled up the chair and sat down beside her. Holding the thin hand in both of hers, she said, "I'm sorry. You should have had somebody call me."

Lola smiled faintly. "I knew you were in Florida. I didn't want to bother you."

"Bother me! I'd like to cut a switch to you." Amelia forced herself to be as cheerful as possible, but she was direly alarmed about her grandmother's condition. Lola had lost weight and seemed much more fragile than the last time Amelia had seen her. She lay very still with her eyes open, but the eyes were the only sign of life. They were still alert, and when Lola asked Amelia to tell about her trip, she spoke about it cheerfully. Finally Amelia ran out of things to say, and she simply sat there holding her grandmother's hand. The ticking of the grandfather clock to her left sounded to Amelia like a solemn incantation. The light slanted down through the tall, mullioned windows, lighting up the dusky carpet. Millions of dust motes danced in its beams and formed gossamer shapes as they swarmed in the yellow light.

Amelia felt uncomfortable and wished the doctor would

come to give her the news. She knew it would not be good—she could see that for herself—but she wanted to know what could be done.

After a period of silence, Lola turned her head on the pillow and asked, "How are things with you, my dear?"

It seemed an innocent enough question, one that could be asked under many circumstances. But somehow Amelia knew that her grandmother's question was not an idle one. She felt the power of her grandmother's gaze, as weak as the woman was, and dropped her head for a moment, thinking how she might answer. Finally she answered the question honestly, although she had not intended to. "I'm not what I ought to be, Grandmother." She lifted her eyes and saw the compassion and love in the gaze that met hers, and then it all came out. "I don't know what's wrong with me. I don't know what I want. I'm making a lot of money, and people seem to like my singing, but somehow when I'm alone at night, I know this isn't enough." She talked on, for the first time ever revealing the doubt and fear and uncertainty that had plagued her. She had learned to camouflage these feelings and even hide them from herself, but now somehow they came pouring out.

Lola Winslow did not speak for a moment, but she squeezed Amelia's hand and whispered, "You've lost your way, but you will find it again. Jesus will never let you go. You have seen too many lives invested in eternity, my dear Amelia, and you know that in the end, that's what you must do."

Hot tears stung Amelia's eyes, and she dropped her head and bit her lip. When she looked up, her grandmother's eyes were closed. Her breathing was very shallow, and Amelia silently held the frail hand for a long time.

★ ★ ★ ★

"I can't offer you much hope, Miss Winslow." Dr. Locke was a tall, powerfully built man of some fifty years, with a gray beard and salt-and-pepper hair. He had a pair of direct gray eyes, but his voice was gentle. "She's been a great favorite of mine. I've been the family doctor now for over twenty years, and God knows I would do anything I could to help her."

The words struck Amelia like a blow. "You mean," she whispered, "you can't do anything at all, Dr. Locke?"

"I'd like to say that I could, and there are miracles. I believe that God raises people up miraculously when we doctors have failed, but unless God intervenes, we will have to say good-bye to your grandmother."

Amelia could not speak for a moment. Her throat was thick, and she knew one more word would bring the tears rushing from her eyes. Finally she said, "She wants to go, doesn't she?"

"Yes, she does." Dr. Locke nodded. "She wants to be with your grandfather and with the Lord." He reached out and took her hand and held it for a moment. "You love her very much, don't you?"

"Not as much as I should have." And then in a sudden burst of honesty, she said, "I haven't been what I should, Dr. Locke. I haven't brought her much happiness."

The doctor's hand closed upon Amelia's, and he said quietly, "She loves you very much. She told me just yesterday how she believed God was going to answer her prayers. She said that she and Mark used to pray for you every day, and now she has continued by herself."

"Thank you for being honest, Doctor. How much time do you think she has? I'd like to wire my father and my uncle Barney. They'd want to be here."

"I've already done that," Dr. Locke said. "But unfortunately both of them are off on an extended journey into the interior. They're not expected back for at least two weeks, and there's no way to reach them. I think they are going to a tribe that has never heard the Gospel before." He paused then and gnawed his lower lip. "I don't want to be unduly pessimistic, but it could take them a month to get here, and it's unlikely she will last out the week."

★　★　★　★

Phil was standing at the window looking out. For the past four days he and Amelia had lived at the Winslow house. Phil had simply told his professors and Lee Novak the circumstances, and they had all been quite considerate. Dr. Franz, his favorite professor, had put his hand on Phil's shoulder, saying, "Go, my boy, be with your grandmother. I'll help you when you come back."

Lee had been even gentler and more helpful. He had come himself twice a day to check on Lola and sit beside her. He had said to Phil, "I hope when I go, I can be as close to the Lord as she is. She loves Jesus more than any woman I ever saw, except maybe my mother."

Now Phil turned from the window and began pacing the floor. Amelia, sitting in a plush chair, watched him. She was very tired, yet it had still been difficult for her to sleep. She had not realized how deep her affection for her grandmother had become. She missed her grandfather, but with her grandmother nearing death, she felt that part of her world was being taken away, and there was nothing she could do to prevent it.

The silence in the room lasted for a long time. Then Phil and Amelia heard the doorbell ring and someone opening the door.

"Who can that be?" Phil murmured.

"Maybe Dr. Locke."

It was not the doctor, however, but Lee Novak. He came into Lola's room, shook hands with Phil, then put his arm around Amelia. "How is she?"

"No better," Amelia said, a barrenness in her voice.

Novak squeezed her shoulder and then released her. They all sat down, and from time to time, one of them would speak. Finally Phil said with anguish, "I feel like I'm watching sand run out of an hourglass. We're losing Grandmother, and there's nothing we can do about it."

Lee put his hand on the young man's shoulder and squeezed it. "That's the way it is, I suppose. When I lost my own parents, I wanted to grab them and keep them from going, but that would have been cruel. They were both devout followers of the Lord Jesus, and both were ready to go home. That's the way it is with Lola. She'd be the last one to want to stay."

A half hour later Dr. Locke arrived. He spoke briefly to the family and then asked them to wait outside while he examined Lola. He came out quickly, his eyes disturbed. "You'd all better come back in. I think she's going."

Amelia felt a cold hand close around her heart. She could not rise for a moment, and then Phil reached down, took her arm, and helped her as she stood up. He held on to her as they went into the room. Nurse Stockman stood off to one side, and at Dr. Locke's nod, she left the room. "I'll just leave you here with her," the doctor murmured to the family, and then he too left.

Phil went over to one side of his grandmother's bed. Her eyes were closed, and at first he thought she was already gone. But then her eyelids fluttered, and she opened them. "Phillip?" she whispered.

"Yes, Grandmother, it's me. And here's Amelia."

Amelia went to the other side of the bed, knelt down, and kissed her grandmother on the brow. "Lee's here too, Grandmother."

"Dear Lee, how I loved your mother. She was the sweetest woman I ever knew, and your dear father—what a good man he was." Lee came forward, and as Phil stepped back he leaned over and kissed the dying woman's cheek. "Tell my parents I miss them, Lola." He stroked her hair for a moment and then stepped back.

Lola, however, smiled, and her eyes seemed to gain light. "I'll see them soon, and I'll tell Thad and Patience how well their boy turned out." She did not speak for a time, and then she looked first at Amelia and then at Phil. Amelia could not bear it, and she put her head down on the pillow beside her grandmother and began to weep. She felt her grandmother's hand touch her hair, stroking it softly, and then she heard the faint voice begin to pray for her. She wished her grandmother would find fault with her, tell her how wrong she was, but not one word of condemnation came from Lola's lips. Nothing but prayers of love and faith that this child would find her way, as had other members of her family. Phil leaned over the bed, and his grandmother turned to him. "Be faithful to Jesus, Phillip."

"I will, Grandmother. I promise."

The silence was thick in the room, and the three watched as Lola Winslow slipped away. She went so easily it was impossible to say at what exact moment she left this world and entered another. Finally Phil said huskily, "Good-bye, Grandmother, we'll miss you. But you're with the Lord now."

"And with Grandfather," Amelia sobbed.

Lee came forward and put his hand on Phil's shoulder. "I can't believe how well she endured her going forth," he whispered. "That's the way children of God ought to go. Knowing they're stepping out of an evil world into one in which all is light and goodness."

At that moment the grandfather clock tolled once on the half hour. The sound seemed to echo down the corridors of eternity as Lola Winslow stepped out of time and into life without end.

CHAPTER TEN

THE UNDERSIDE OF NEW YORK

★   ★   ★   ★

"Hey, Lee, what do you want to do with Williamson?"

The speaker was an undersized individual with large, flashing brown eyes. He seemed incapable of standing still as he waited for an answer. Snapping his fingers impatiently, he twisted his head from side to side and scooted his feet back and forth on the worn tile floor.

"Hold him over for arraignment, Billy."

"I hope they throw the book at him."

"So do I, but they probably won't. Now, get out of here and leave me alone for a while."

Lee Novak dismissed the younger agent with a wave of his hand and remained sitting at his desk with his elbows braced against the scarred walnut top, his hands supporting his chin. An enormous white cup sat before him, the hot coffee in it sending up a plume of steam like a signal, and for a while Novak stared into the cup as if it were a crystal ball. Finally he looked up and studied Phil Winslow, who was slouched on a couch flanked by stacks of paper on either side and two filing cabinets in front of him. Lee had become very fond of Phil during the time that the young man had been in the office, but now concern touched him as he noted the lines of weariness on Winslow's face and how he had to blink his eyes to keep them open.

"What are you working on now, Phil?"

"The Penelli case."

"What do you make of it?"

"I make of it he's a crook." Phil exchanged glances with his chief. "I didn't like the looks of him. He's like a cheerful embalmer—except that embalmers are respectable people. I never saw one of them get indicted like Penelli."

"I always thought he looked like a dishonest bank clerk myself, filling his pockets under the counter, but what do you think? Can we nail him?"

"Give me another day on this paper work. He's pretty good at covering his tracks."

Novak lifted the coffee cup as if it were an enormous weight. He drank half of the steaming liquid with no sign of difficulty, then stared into the black depths again. Finally he looked up and snapped, "Go home, Phil, and get some sleep!"

"I can sleep when I get old." Phil grinned at Novak, noticing that his boss never looked tired. *At his age he ought to be worn out,* Phil thought. *He's fifty-seven and I'm twenty-one, and he's about to run me to death.* Aloud he said, "I'm okay, Lee."

"I'm not so sure of that. I think this job's wearin' you down. It's a lot to take on."

"I like it, Lee."

"You don't like going down to the jail, I noticed."

"No, I don't. It's really sad. All those faces seem so hopeless when they stare out of their cells—they have lost, old faces, no matter how young they are. You know what I see in them most of the time?"

"What's that?"

"The same thing I see in the sad faces of cabdrivers and policemen and some of my professors. It seems like they're all wishing they were somewhere else—maybe even dead."

"That's because they live in a world where everything's always breaking down," Novak said mildly. "Everything always needs fixing—yet it can't be fixed. We have to deal with the same problems over and over. Only God can truly fix what ails us all." Then he laughed and said, "I had a strange dream about God the other night. I dreamed He was on His back under the world, holding it up, and I wanted to see Him, but I could only see the soles of His shoes. I woke up crying because even the soles of His shoes shone with His glory."

Phil stared at Novak in astonishment. From time to time this hard man would come out with a statement that shocked him. "You should have been a poet, Lee."

"Doesn't pay enough."

Phil laughed and shook his head. "I guess you're right."

Novak sat quietly sipping his coffee, and when he struck bottom he rose, marched over to the table where a blackened coffeepot sat on a hot plate, and put the cup down. He set the coffeepot on the table next to the hot plate, then crossed the room in spare, economical movements. Opening the door of a cabinet, he reached inside and pulled out a shoulder holster, then yanked the snub-nosed gun free of it and checked the loads. Turning, he walked over to Phil and said, "Let's get you out of those files."

Surprised, Phil looked up. "What's the gun for?"

"For you. Put it on."

Phil frowned. "What for?"

"You're not going to do files. You're going out to make an arrest with me."

Phil carefully put the papers he was holding on top of the filing cabinet and came to his feet. He took the shoulder holster, struggling for a moment to figure it out. Slipping his arm in one side and then the other, he finally fastened it. Novak handed him the pistol.

"That's a thirty-eight. Don't shoot yourself with it. It's loaded."

Taking the gun, Phil stared at it. Back in Africa he had become an expert hunter and had carried a side arm, but there the pistols had long barrels for accuracy. He looked at the small handgun and shook his head. "I wouldn't think it'd be very accurate, Lee."

"Get up close, and you don't have to be accurate." Novak suddenly shook his head. "Maybe you're not ready for this."

Phil lifted his gaze. "Why not?"

"It's one thing going over files and doing the paper work. Something else when you have to come up against what we're liable to find."

"I guess I'd better go with you, Lee. If I'm going to be of any help, I need to see all of it."

Novak stared at his young friend and shrugged. "All right. Put your coat on. It's not real cold out, but you need to cover up that rod."

Phil plucked his trench coat off the rack, slipped into it, then pulled his brown fedora from the hat rack and donned it. "Who is it we're going after?"

"Jackie Low."

"I don't know him."

"He's not one of the big fish, but he's got his finger in a lot of pies. We got a tip that he's going to be meeting with some people we've been trying to get for a long time. Jackie's a small fry, but if we can get the guys over him, I'll be satisfied. Come on."

The two left the office, and Phil was conscious of the thirty-eight and its dragging weight under his arm. It gave him an odd feeling, and he wondered if he could ever bring himself to shoot another human being. He had even had trouble at times shooting game and more than once had missed a shot on purpose simply because the animal was so beautiful. He had never confessed this to anyone, but now as the possibility rose of actually firing on a flesh-and-blood human being with a mind and heart, a peculiar feeling settled on him. He was uneasy but tried not to show it as they got into the unmarked black car.

Novak started the engine and pulled out from the curb. Phil sat silently as Novak traversed the city streets and explained what they were going to do. Looking up in the rearview mirror, Novak suddenly said, "You didn't notice those two cars right behind us."

Phil swiveled around and saw that two black sedans were indeed following very closely. "Who are they?" he asked with some alarm.

"They're our men. When we get there we'll surround the building. It's like hunting rats—you send one dog inside, but you keep more outside. The one inside chases the rats out, and the dogs outside wait for them."

Phil asked no more questions, and finally, twenty minutes later, Novak pulled over to the side of the street. Phil noted that the other cars did the same. When Novak got out, Phil got out too. He waited as six men came to join them, all of them armed. Two of them held lethal-looking shotguns.

"You know the drill," Lee said briefly. "We've been here before. Adams, you and Jacobs and Markowitz take the back. The rest of you take the sides. I don't think they'll be coming out the front."

Markowitz, a burly man with black eyebrows and a heavy shadow of a beard, spoke up at once. "Let me go in with you, Chief."

"I'll be all right. You just don't let anybody get away. And watch it. If they do come out, they'll probably be shooting. Now, get on with it."

Phil watched as the men surrounded the building. It was a little after six o'clock now, and the shadows had grown long, but there was still some daylight. He saw the men blend into the scenery, and then he heard Novak say, "You wait outside, Phil."

"Nothing doing. I'm going in with you."

Novak turned and put his hand on Phil's chest. "Not this time. You stay here."

Phil opened his mouth to speak, but Novak cut him off. "Mind what I say."

Phil knew it was useless to argue. He had discovered that a certain tone in Lee Novak's voice meant, *It's all over*. He caught this tone now, and he stayed in front of the leading car as Novak crossed the street. Lee walked as casually as if he were on his way to a ball game. He was even whistling a little, a habit he had when a situation got tense. Phil admired Novak's cool courage and wondered if he would ever achieve such confidence himself.

Novak went to the front door of the building, which appeared to be abandoned. A corrugated steel garage door was shut tight. No lights were showing from the windows on either the first or second story, but Phil tensed up, suspecting that they were being watched from the recesses of the seemingly empty building. Overhead the sky was growing darker by the minute. A slight milky area hovered in the western sky, but darkness was closing in fast. In a few moments the street itself would be a gloomy and dusky spot. Phil edged forward, staying across the street. He watched as Lee went up to the door and jimmied the lock. The door opened and Novak stepped inside, closing it behind him quickly.

Phil's heart beat faster and the blood throbbed in his ears. He remembered the same sensation from big game hunts when he'd been faced with a charging lion. Danger lurked inside that darkened building, and he wished Lee had allowed him to go inside too.

No more than two or three minutes had passed when suddenly a shot rang out. The sound penetrated Phil's brain and pulsed down his body like an electric charge. "He's in trouble!" he gasped. Even as this thought passed through his mind, a barrage of shots exploded inside the building. Some of them were obviously from weapons of heavier caliber than the thirty-eight Novak carried.

Bent over and keeping his head down, Phil pulled his gun from the holster and cautiously inched closer. He was holding the gun down at his side when suddenly he heard shots coming from somewhere other than inside. They rang sharper and clearer, as if they were coming from the back of the building. *They're trying to get away*, he thought. *The guys must have caught them.*

Phil Winslow was not always so impulsive, but now, almost without thinking, just knowing that his friend was inside and the shots were still echoing, he dashed across the street, opened the door, and stepped inside. At the same time he heard one of Novak's men shouting, "There's another one! Get him—!"

The interior was like a large warehouse, with a catwalk running around the entire area. A single light dangled from a cord, shedding a feeble gleam over the setting. Shadows blotted out almost everything, but then he heard Novak's voice. "Heads up, Phil! Up there!"

Phil looked up and saw the dim form of a man on the catwalk. A sudden burst of light hit his eyes, and he knew it was the reflection of the light bulb on the barrel of a revolver. Almost at the same instant, a shot rang out. The bullet plucked at his sleeve, and he lifted his gun. He caught the man's shadowy figure dead center in the sights, but—he could not pull the trigger!

Another shot rang out. He saw the explosion of the gun and at the same moment felt his hat fly off. "Drop your gun!" he yelled and lifted his revolver, putting a shot over the man's head.

The man bent over, and Phil saw that he had either a rifle or a shotgun in his hand, pointing directly at him. In his imagination, the muzzle of that gun was the beginning of a dark tunnel, and Phil considered himself a dead man. He fired again over the man's head, yelling and throwing himself to one side, but it was too late to get out of the way.

Suddenly three shots went off so quickly they almost sounded like one. The roar of the shotgun filled the interior, but Phil saw that the man had been driven backward and his gun had loosed its blast at the ceiling. He heard Novak shouting, "Phil, keep down! Get out of the way!"

Phil threw himself behind some large bales, still holding his gun. There were other shots, but he could see nothing. Finally he heard Novak say in a calm voice he would never forget, "That's it."

Phil eased up and saw Lee walking toward him. Novak demanded at once, "Why didn't you shoot? You had him right in your sights."

"I don't know. I just couldn't pull the trigger."

Novak stared at the younger man and shook his head. "You shouldn't have come in here. That was a mistake. And you don't need a gun if you're afraid to use it."

Phil Winslow stared down at the revolver in his hand as if he had never seen it before. He could hear men shouting outside, but he paid no attention. Looking up at Lee, he said, "I wasn't much good, was I?"

"My fault. I shouldn't have brought you here without any training."

Phil studied Novak's face, then said, "You saved my life, Lee. I'll never forget it."

Novak started to speak but changed his mind. Finally he put his hand across Phil's shoulder and said, "Come on. Let's see what we caught outside."

The rest of the night was a blur to Phil, but he knew he would never forget what had happened. It was impossible to describe his feelings, for he knew that if it had not been for Lee Novak's quick intervention, he would be lying dead in that dark building. "I'll make it up to you, Lee," he whispered as he watched Novak directing the officers who were putting cuffs on the prisoners. "I'll make it up to you. See if I don't!"

CHAPTER ELEVEN

AMELIA MEETS A MAN

★ ★ ★ ★

Amelia had just sat down before the mirror in her dressing room when she was startled by a loud knock. Turning, she moved toward the door cautiously, for her dressing room had been invaded by backstage Romeos many times. She opened the door a crack and was relieved to see the big figure of Dom Costello. She smiled and opened the door fully. "Hello, Dom."

"Hi, Amelia. You were great tonight."

"Why, thank you, Dom. Won't you come in?"

Dom shifted his feet and rubbed the back of his thick neck before answering. "Well, I've come to ask a favor."

"Ask away."

"It's Rosa's seventeenth birthday, and she asked her dad if he would bring her here to catch your act."

"How nice. I didn't see her out there. It's hard to make any-body out with those lights right in your face."

"Sure, but Mr. Morino's got a table back out of the lights. He's having them bring a cake and everything in—and what I wanted to ask was, would it be too much trouble for you to stop by and wish the kid a happy birthday? It would mean a lot to her."

Instantly Amelia agreed. "Why, of course I will, Dom. Let me change into my street clothes, and I'll be right out."

Dom's craggy face broke into a grin. "You're a good guy, Amelia Winslow."

Chuckling at Dom's comment as he left, she quickly removed her stage makeup, then changed out of her performance costume and into something less flamboyant. She had discovered that being required to wear expensive and rather gaudy dresses while performing had whetted her taste for simpler outfits. The dress she chose was a demure gray with a skirt halfway between knee and ankle. As with all the modern fashion, the belt was very low on a dropped waistline. She slipped into some high-heeled court shoes with decorative buckles and then plucked a lightweight wool jacket from a hanger. Leaving her dressing room, she went into the club. She scanned the tables and finally saw Dom stand up and wave. There was no missing his big bulk, and she made her way toward him, weaving between the tables. People greeted and congratulated her many times, and she murmured her thanks for each compliment.

Rosa did not see her approach, although Tony and Maria did. Jamie was also there, and his eyes grew big. "Gee," he said, "it's the singer lady."

Amelia noted another man at the table but paid no particular attention to him.

Rosa whirled at Jamie's comment. Her mouth open in surprise, she leaped up and came flying to meet Amelia. "Amelia, you sang so well tonight."

Amelia put her arms around the girl, took her hug, and then stepped back. "I hear you're quite an old lady now. Seventeen years. Congratulations and happy birthday."

Rosa was so excited she could hardly speak. "I begged Mom and Daddy to bring me here, and they even let Jamie come."

"Yeah, I'm fifteen. That's old enough to be in a nightclub."

"You hush, Jamie," Tony said, but he was grinning. He ruffled the boy's hair, and Amelia could see the fondness he had for the boy. For all his flaws, no one could ever find any fault with Big Tony Morino's love for his family. It was entirely genuine, and she credited him with that.

"I wish I'd known you were here, Rosa. I would have sung happy birthday to you."

"Oh, you wouldn't either!" Rosa exclaimed.

Amelia laughed. "You don't think so? Then, as Jolson says, 'You ain't seen nothin' yet.'" She turned and went back away from the far table until she reached the stage. There was no spotlight, but when she said, "Charlie, give me a spot," it came on at once. Everyone turned and people started applauding. Holding up her hand, Amelia said, "Folks, you've been such a wonderful audience tonight, and I want to ask you to do one thing for me."

"What is it, Amelia?" a male voice shouted out. "You name it, kid!"

"I have a very dear friend here tonight. It's her seventeenth birthday. Her name is Rosa Morino, and I'm going to ask you all to sing 'Happy Birthday' to Rosa. Harry, put the spotlight on our birthday girl—right over there." She started singing in a clear contralto voice, and the room was filled as every person in the place joined in.

Rosa, she saw, was blushing furiously but was enjoying the attention. When the song ended, Amelia said, "Thank you very much, all of you." She made her way amid the applause back to the table and smiled, "How was that, Rosa?"

"Oh, it was great! I didn't think you'd do that."

"I've got to do everything I can for my buddy," Amelia said affectionately.

"Hey, Miss Winslow, that was real nice of you," Tony said, his face flushed with pleasure. "I appreciate it."

"Nothing's too good for Rosa."

Her eyes went to the man she had noted earlier, and she saw that he was smiling at her. Even though he was sitting down, she could tell that he was very tall. He had flaming red hair and bright blue eyes set off by a ruddy complexion. He looked lean, trim, and fit, unlike most of the men she saw in nightclubs.

"I suppose Mr. Morino is ashamed of one of us, Miss Winslow," he said, smiling cheerfully. "I don't know whether he won't introduce me to you or you to me."

"Hey, Ryan, excuse me!" Tony was somewhat flustered. "Miss Amelia Winslow, I want you to meet Ryan Kildare."

Kildare got to his feet and nodded. "It's a pleasure to meet you. I've heard you sing before, but you were great tonight."

"Why, thank you, Mr. Kildare."

He waited until she sat down and said little else then, for

Rosa was talking excitedly about her presents. Amelia concentrated on the young woman, thinking how pretty she was and how much her brother would enjoy being here too. Out loud she said, "It's too bad Phil's not here to wish you a happy birthday, Rosa." Instantly Amelia saw Tony Morino's face harden, and she knew she had stepped into forbidden territory at the mention of Phil.

Rosa glanced at her father but said nothing, and the moment passed. But it was an awkward moment. Ryan Kildare was a tactful man and said, "They're playing the one song I know how to dance to, Miss Winslow. Could I have the pleasure?"

Anxious to get away from the tense situation, Amelia agreed. He put his hand out and led her to the floor. As they moved slowly across the floor to the hit tune "I'll Be With You in Apple Blossom Time," Amelia tilted her head back. He was very tall—six-two or so she would guess—and there was a masculine ruggedness about him. He was not handsome in a Rudolph Valentino sort of way, but Amelia found him attractive, and she liked his hair, which was not plastered down and had a rebellious curl in it. She found herself wondering about him.

"You said this is the only song you could dance to," remarked Amelia. "I don't believe that for a moment."

"Well, I can do a little black bottom when I'm in the mood."

Amelia laughed. "Not for me. I think that's the awfulest dance I've ever seen—all that jumping and slapping the backside. Why do people want to do things like that?"

"To get attention, I suppose. But you don't have to worry about that. You make a living getting attention."

He did not go into rhapsodies over her singing, for which Amelia was grateful. She had heard enough of that from too many men. "What do you do, Mr. Kildare?"

"I'm a criminal defense attorney—most of my work is done for Mr. Morino."

Amelia grew silent at this statement, and Kildare saw her reaction. "It seems like we're moving from one tense situation to another," he said.

"You mean at the table?" Amelia said. "Why do you think Tony got so upset when I mentioned my brother?"

"Why, because he's for the opposite side," Kildare said. "Tony sees everything in black and white. Us or them. Your brother works for the feds; therefore, he's a *them*. Tony doesn't want to have anything to do with them."

"I'm very proud of my brother."

"I haven't met him, but I've met Lee Novak, his boss. He's a fine fellow and as tough as they come."

Ryan saw by Amelia's eyes that she was not anxious to speak of anything having to do with Big Tony Morino's business. Even though he was accustomed to being criticized for defending Morino, he felt compelled to apologize to her. "I'm sorry that my profession bothers you. But it's what I do."

"I don't know much about it, but doesn't it bother you sometimes getting guilty people free?"

"Well, I look at it like this. Every man and woman is entitled to a good defense, so I give them the best I've got."

"Do you ask them if they're guilty?"

"Never."

The music ended, but before they left the dance floor, he said, "I'm usually not so impulsive, but I'm about to break a promise I made to my mother a long time ago."

Kildare's words caught at Amelia. "A promise to your mother? What was that?"

The corners of his mouth twitched, and he grinned broadly. "I promised her I'd never ask a girl to go out with me until I'd danced with her at least twice."

Amelia found this amusing. "Then you'd better wait. Promises to mothers should be kept."

They rejoined their party, but Amelia did not stay. She felt uncomfortable after Tony's reaction to the mention of her brother. Before she left, Kildare winked at her. "One more dance, and you'll be eligible."

He was incorrigible but not obnoxious. "I think you'd better stick with your mother. She probably loves you better than anyone else." As soon as she said this, a strange expression passed across Kildare's face. His lips tightened, and then he nodded, "You're right about that, Miss Winslow. Dead right."

★ ★ ★ ★

Every time Ryan Kildare had a meeting with Tony Morino, he grew somewhat uneasy. Morino had called a week after Rosa's birthday party and did not request but simply gave a royal commandment. "Be in my office, Ryan. We got something to talk about."

Now as Kildare sat facing the big man, he tried to analyze his feelings. He had always felt ambivalent toward Morino, for he knew there was some good in the man. On the other hand, his background and position had crafted him into a ruthless killer who could explode into violence. Kildare had seen it happen and was very careful not to trigger such a response toward him personally.

He looked around the opulent office. The massive walnut desk was empty save for a pen and a platinum ink bottle. Nothing but the best for Big Tony! The carpet underfoot was Persian and did not match the colors of the room, but that did not bother Morino. It was expensive—always his top criterion. Ryan smiled as he saw a genuine painting by Turner, which he knew would have cost thousands of dollars. Right beside it was the famous painting of "The Battle of Little Bighorn"—a copy, but a good one. It was a massive painting, perhaps four feet high and seven or eight feet across, scanning the battlefield, with dying soldiers everywhere and Custer himself dressed in yellow buckskins firing pistols in both hands, his long yellow hair flowing over his shoulders. It was a picture that had achieved immense popularity in saloons around the country. Any self-respecting saloon would have a copy of it. The idea of such a cheap, artificial work being placed next to Turner's beautifully executed painting of the sea reinforced Ryan's conviction that Tony could buy whatever he wanted, but he had no taste. But, then, how could he? He had no more than a fifth-grade education.

"What do you need to talk about, Mr. Morino?" Kildare was always careful to speak to him formally. Tony was touchy about such things. The hired hands all called him Mr. Morino to his face.

Biting off the end of a cigar and spitting it on the floor, Tony pulled a gold lighter from his vest pocket, lit the cigar, and drew on the yellow flame until he had the cigar stoked and sending up tendrils of purplish smoke. Snapping the lighter shut, he stuffed it back into his pocket, then pointed the cigar at Ryan as if it were a pistol. "This town's not big enough for me and Leo Marx both."

Ryan was accustomed to Morino's direct statements, but this one took Kildare aback. The man reminded Ryan of something he had heard said once about General Grant—*"He looks like he's about to lower his head and run it straight through a solid oak door."* There was some of this fierce tenacity and drive in Big Tony Morino.

"Leo is a pretty tough man, Mr. Morino."

Tony's eyelids narrowed until his eyes showed through a mere slit. When he spoke, his voice was low and guttural. "I want him taken out."

Murdered. Shot. Killed. Take your pick, Kildare thought. This was the side of the business he disliked intensely. He rarely experienced fear, but Big Tony's demand sent shivers through him. He held up his hands and shook his head. "Now, Mr. Morino, I don't do the rough stuff."

"I know that. I want you to take him out legally."

The words caught at Ryan, and he thought, *How do I do that?*

"You know he's the biggest crook in New York. He's bound to have left some tracks somewhere. I want you to nail him. Get him in jail."

"Are you sure you want me to handle this?" Ryan hoped desperately for a reprieve, but he was relatively sure that would not happen.

"Yes, you're the smartest guy I know. Do it."

"It'll cost a bundle. It'll mean hiring private detectives to dig up the dirt."

"I don't care what it costs. Just get him. Oh, and, Kildare—keep me out of it!"

As Tony dismissed him and Ryan Kildare left the office, he felt shaky. He himself had had a hard upbringing and had learned to be tough, but the feral savagery of the criminals who ruled New York was a frightening thing to him. He knew Tony had given him no choice. Ryan was making more money than he had ever dreamed of, and he didn't dare disappoint his boss or he could lose it all. Big Tony Morino did not tolerate failure.

"I've got to do it," he murmured. "It's either that or wind up in some dingy little office on the Lower East Side. I couldn't go back to that again!"

★ ★ ★ ★

For some reason she could not fathom, Amelia had become a baseball fan. She had started attending games at Yankee Stadium during the spring, and now as fall had come and the World Series approached, she thrilled at the rivalry between New York and Washington. The always-successful Yankees had finally been stopped the year before by one man—Walter Johnson of the Washington Senators. They lost the Series that year to the Senators, who won their first and only championship ever.

Despite their defeat that year, the Yankees still fascinated Amelia. Of course, the most colorful player on their team and in all of baseball was Babe Ruth. Ruth was bigger than life on and off the field. In 1920, his first year with the Yankees, he had hit fifty-four home runs—more than all the teams save one had managed to hit that year. America went crazy over Babe Ruth. He was everywhere advertising everything. He became America's icon, but his personal life was terrible. He caroused and spent his time with prostitutes, cheerfully endorsed cigarettes when he smoked only cigars, appeared in all-American cotton underwear ads, although he now refused to wear anything but custom-made silk undershorts. By 1925 the Babe had fallen on rough times. He had seriously neglected his own health, so by the time he got to spring training that year, he was a wreck— thirty pounds overweight and often drunk. With Ruth no longer at his best, the Yankees were falling behind.

Although Amelia was intrigued by Ruth, along with everybody else, she greatly admired another Yankee who was just starting his career. She was there in June when a broad-shouldered twenty-two-year-old newcomer was sent in to pinch-hit. The next day he went in again, and from that moment on, Lou Gehrig hit almost as many home runs as Babe Ruth. Gehrig was, however, in every way Ruth's opposite, a quiet man devoted to his mother and reluctant to be away from her.

Yankee Stadium had become a haven for Amelia, where she could unwind from the stress of her life of performing. Sometimes Phil came with her, but one day, only two weeks after Rosa's birthday party, she got up early and suddenly decided, "I'm going to watch the Yankees today."

She had received a ticket in the mail by itself with no note or return address. She often got gifts, but usually the giver wanted to be identified. This time there was simply a ticket for the game, so she thought, *Why not?*

She arrived at the stadium, fought her way in, and made her way down to seat number eighteen. The seat next to her, number seventeen, was empty. She sat down and began to study the players as they took batting practice. Babe Ruth drew most of the attention of the fans. Whatever else you might say about him, he could hit the ball! Amelia remembered an article she had read about him, in which he'd been quoted as saying, "I try to swing through it, and I hit it with everything I got. It's a home run or nothin' for me."

As the game started, Amelia entered into the spirit of it right away. She yelled and stamped her feet along with the crowd, waving her arms around when the Yankees got a hit and groaning when they made an error.

In the middle of the second inning she was aware that a man was making his way to the empty seat beside her. She did not look at him, for she had discovered this was a sure way to get an unwanted conversation going. Out of the corner of her eye she saw him sit down, and then she heard a familiar voice. "Well, this is a real surprise. I'm glad to see you again, Miss Winslow."

Amelia snapped her head around and saw Ryan Kildare smiling at her. He was wearing a white shirt, tie, and straw skimmer.

Instantly Amelia knew where the ticket had come from and felt a tinge of anger. "What about your promise to your mother?"

"I called her. She said it was all right."

Amelia's anger vanished and she laughed. She could not help it. He was so brash and cheerful she could not take offense. "You are a devious lawyer."

"I think that's redundant, isn't it? Like saying apple pie à la mode with ice cream."

She could only laugh in reply.

"Are you enjoying the game?" Kildare asked.

"Very much. You come often?"

"As often as I can," Ryan replied. "I doubt if the Yankees will win it this year. Who's your favorite player?"

"Lou Gehrig."

"Well, there's a switch. I thought you'd tell me Babe Ruth. Gehrig's just a rookie."

"I like his looks, though. He seems so steady, and I don't particularly like Ruth. He's such an immoral man."

"I don't think they check out moral credentials when they sign ball players. Just how far they can hit the ball." Ryan laughed, and once again she couldn't help joining him.

Amelia turned her attention back to the game and found she enjoyed it even more with someone to share it with. The score was one-nothing going into the eleventh inning, when Lou Gehrig slapped the ball out of the park for a homer. She rose and cheered, "That's the way, Lou! Show that Bambino how it's done!"

Aware that she was getting cold looks from several Yankee fans, she laughed and said, "Well, I must go."

"Oh, don't go yet," Ryan said. "I've got a birthday present for you."

Amelia laughed. "But it's not my birthday."

"Well, it will be sooner or later. I thought you might like to meet some of the players."

Amelia stared at him. "You mean the Yankees?"

"Yes, I've done some legal work for the team once or twice. Gotten players out of trouble really."

"Babe Ruth?"

Kildare grinned. "Yes, for one. Will you come?"

"You think it will be all right with your mother?"

"We won't tell her." Kildare winked at her and took her arm to lead her down to the field. The players had not yet gone to the locker room, and Ryan said, "Come along. I'll introduce you to Gehrig."

"Do you know him?"

"No, but we soon will." He led her up to a big broadshouldered man, slightly bowlegged, with deep dimples in each cheek and said, "Mr. Gehrig, this is a great admirer of yours.

She's the famous singer Miss Amelia Winslow."

Gehrig smiled shyly and shook hands with Amelia. Despite his size, he seemed very timid. "I'm glad to meet you, Miss Winslow."

"Congratulations on winning the game, Mr. Gehrig."

Lou Gehrig was used to taking second place to Babe Ruth, and his smile broadened, but he dropped his head humbly and muttered, "It's good for the team."

They managed to get a short conversation out of him, but he was a man of few words.

Ryan spotted Babe Ruth as Gehrig walked away. "Look, there's Ruth over there. I *do* know him."

Reluctantly Amelia followed Kildare, and they waited until the big ball player had fended off questions from several sportswriters. He saw Ryan and said, "Counselor, you come to get me out of trouble again?"

"Not this time, Babe. I want you to meet a fine lady, Miss Amelia Winslow."

Ruth's eyes fixed on Amelia. He stepped forward and without hesitation put his arm around her. "Hey, sweetheart, get rid of this guy here. You and me will go steppin'."

Amelia felt helpless in his iron grasp. He had been drinking, and his eyes were bloodshot. "I'm afraid I'll have to beg off, Mr. Ruth." She sent a pleading look toward Ryan to rescue her.

"Ah, come on, honey," Ruth said, pulling her even closer. "I'll show you somethin' you ain't seen before." The ball player winked obscenely, but then his attention turned to another woman who had come his way, heavily rouged and wearing a skin-tight dress. He dropped his arm and said to Amelia, "Well, you missed your lucky day, honey." Then he was off, embracing the other woman, who was only too delighted to receive him.

"What a horrible man!" Amelia said, brushing herself off.

"Yes, he's pretty bad," Ryan agreed, then to change the subject quickly, he took Amelia's arm and asked, "How about you and me having dinner tonight?"

"Oh, I don't think I can," Amelia said, not anxious to encourage Kildare too much. "But thanks for asking."

Kildare hesitated, then said quietly, "My mother will be there."

Despite herself, Amelia burst out laughing at his serious face. "I doubt that!"

"No, I mean it," Ryan insisted. "Come and see."

"I'm afraid of you lawyers."

"There's no need to be afraid of me. I'm just a man with the same hang-ups and problems as the next guy." He grinned. "Why don't you give me a try—if you're not too afraid, that is."

Amelia eyed him askance, then took the challenge. "All right, but if your mother's not there, you're in big trouble!"

★　★　★　★

A couple of hours later when Amelia had washed up and changed for dinner, she heard a knock on her door. She opened it to Ryan's smiling face. Smiling back at him, she said, "I wasn't sure you'd show up."

"You knew better than that. You look lovely, Amelia."

"Thanks. So do you."

Ryan laughed and shook his head. "You have a way of putting a fellow down." He did look sharp in a three-piece herringbone lounge suit with a narrow-fitted jacket, cuffed trousers, striped shirt, and black tie. "We'd better hurry. We wouldn't want to be late."

"What's the rush?" Amelia asked. "Where are we going?"

"You'll see." That's all Ryan would say as he waited for Amelia to grab her purse and wrap and follow him outside to his car, a black Oldsmobile. He helped her in, then ran around to the driver's side. No sooner had he gotten in and started to drive than he began to talk baseball to her. She sensed that he did not want to talk about his profession—and also that there was some tension in him she had not noticed at the birthday party. From time to time she looked out the window, noting that they had entered a quiet residential area. He suddenly turned to her and asked, "Do you still carry a thirty-eight?"

"How did you know about that?"

"Dom told me."

"I'm not carrying it tonight. I thought I'd be safe with an upstanding lawyer."

He smiled at her and nodded. "All right. I'm glad you feel that way."

Five minutes later he pulled the car up to the curb in front of a white frame house with dormers in the upper story. He shut the engine off, got out quickly, and opened the door for her.

"Your mother lives here alone?" Amelia asked as they walked up the front steps.

"No, one of my sisters lives with her."

He knocked on the door, and it opened almost at once. A young woman who Amelia thought must be no more than twenty smiled at them.

"Amelia, I'd like you to meet my sister, Faye Kildare. And, Faye, this is the lady I told you so much about, Miss Amelia Winslow."

Ryan's sister was also a redhead. She was not tall but had a pleasing figure and a sweet smile. "I'm so glad you could come," Faye said. "Mother's been so looking forward to it."

"I'm looking forward to meeting her too," Amelia said, stepping inside. "So we're having dinner here, huh?" she whispered to Ryan. She was relieved to learn that Ryan really had planned to bring her to dinner with his mother.

"Come along," Ryan said. Then hesitantly he added, "My mother's not in good health."

"I see." Amelia followed him down a hallway, where he knocked on a door, waited for a voice from inside, then opened it.

"I brought you a visitor, Mother."

Amelia stepped into the room and saw a woman sitting in a wheelchair. She was wearing a light brown dress, and her hair had turned silver, although Amelia suspected she was not all that old. The woman had the appearance of being very ill, but there was the same sweetness in her that Amelia had seen in Faye Kildare.

"This is my mother," Ryan said. "Mother, this is Miss Amelia Winslow."

"I'm so glad to meet you, my dear."

Mrs. Kildare lifted her hand, and Amelia went over at once to take it. She felt the smallness of the bones, although she guessed that at one time Mrs. Kildare might have been a strong, healthy woman. Amelia smiled, saying, "Your son has told me how hard you are on him."

Mrs. Kildare laughed. "I would say it's the other way around. He's hard on me."

"Mother, would you entertain Amelia while I go help Faye with dinner?"

"Of course, son."

As soon as Ryan disappeared, Mrs. Kildare said to Amelia, "You can call me Judith, dear. Do sit down."

Amelia glanced around the room. It was not opulent in the least but was pleasing. The pale yellow walls were decorated with attractive paintings. A vase of fresh flowers bloomed on the bedside table, and she exclaimed, "What beautiful flowers!"

"Ryan brings them every other day. He never misses. I used to grow a lot of flowers, but I haven't been able to do that for some time."

"I'm so sorry."

Judith Kildare studied the young woman and said, "You're a singer, I understand."

"Oh, just in nightclubs, I'm afraid."

"And you're from Africa."

"Why, yes, I am. My father and mother are missionaries there."

"How wonderful!"

Amelia soon found out more about Ryan Kildare than she ever would have from talking to him herself. She even discovered that Judith Kildare's husband had been a drunkard and had abused them all, especially Ryan, who as a child, had tried to protect his mother and sisters from his father.

"He put himself through college and law school and kept us all from starving," Mrs. Kildare explained. "He helped his two brothers get into successful businesses and has encouraged his sisters to marry well. His two older sisters are both married now to decent men who are good providers."

Amelia had known nothing of Ryan's family, and she was glad to hear that he treated them with love and generosity.

Ryan came back in, announcing that dinner was ready. He grinned at his mother as he got behind her wheelchair and began to push her out of the room. "I hope you haven't been telling

Miss Winslow what a terrible boy I was growing up."

"Of course I was. Totally rotten."

Amelia laughed. "I don't think I can believe anything you say, Judith."

The meal was delicious—a succulent lamb roast with mint sauce and roasted potatoes. Amelia complimented Ryan on his culinary skills, but he insisted the cooking was all Faye's doing. Faye stayed by her mother's side, taking care of her and helping her eat. After dinner they moved to the parlor, where they listened to two or three records, but soon Judith grew tired. Faye encouraged her mother to retire to her room, saying, "You've had enough excitement for one day, Mother."

Judith Kildare smiled at Amelia as Faye wheeled her from the room. "It was so good of you to come, dear. I hope you'll come back."

"I hope so too."

★ ★ ★ ★

Pulling up in front of her apartment building, Ryan shut off the engine. He got out of the car, opened her door, and accompanied Amelia to her apartment. She got out her key, but before unlocking the door, she turned to him. "It was a lovely evening, Ryan. Thank you."

"You made Mother very happy. I thank you for coming. She doesn't get many visitors."

"She's such a sweet lady and so is your sister."

"Faye deserves all the credit for caring for Mother. She's there on the front lines, day in and day out—all I can do is pay for it."

They were silent for a moment, then suddenly Ryan said, "I'm about to break another promise I made to my mother."

Amelia looked up at him and smiled. "I'll bet I can guess what promise you're about to break."

"I'll bet you can't."

"I'll bet you promised her you'd never kiss a girl on your first date."

He smiled and shrugged. "You should be the lawyer." He put his hands on her shoulders and saw her eyes widen. He did not pressure her, but she willingly leaned forward, her lips softening and gently parting. Ryan suddenly saw Amelia as a woman of great passion who kept her emotions bottled up inside. He pulled her close and kissed her, feeling her respond to him as they embraced for a long time. Then he felt her hand pressing lightly on his chest, and he released her.

"Good night, Ryan. I had a lovely time."

"Will you go out with me again?"

"Yes!"

CHAPTER TWELVE

SENTENCE OF DEATH

★ ★ ★ ★

"This is good, Sarah. How did you ever learn to cook Chinese food?"

Sarah Novak's face beamed with pleasure. She had just brought a steaming bowlful of fried rice and set it down when Amelia had reached out and forked herself a healthy portion. "Oh, I didn't know how to cook anything when Lee and I got married except Southern cooking. I could fry chicken, but I'd never eaten Chinese food."

Phil picked up a cabbage roll, dipped it in the sweet-and-sour sauce, and munched on it with evident pleasure. "Well, I think you ought to start a restaurant. You could call it Sarah Lee's Chinese Food. Then you could quit work, Lee, and let her support you."

Lee Novak reached across and captured his wife's hand. They were obviously a very devoted couple, and this was the third time they had invited Phil and Amelia to their home for dinner. The Novaks' children were all grown and married, so it was just the four of them. Novak looked at Sarah fondly and said, "She can cook anything—Italian, Southern, Chinese. It's a wonder I don't weigh three hundred pounds."

The talk went around the table, and Amelia found herself

liking Lee and Sarah very much. They spoke for a time about various relatives who were scattered all over the world, and then finally the talk turned to Tony Morino.

Amelia was enjoying one of the tiny pastries Sarah had set out on a tray for dessert, and she said, "I met his lawyer a few weeks ago. He seems nice enough. I've been out with him a few times."

Novak turned his eyes on Amelia and said quietly, "I know."

Startled, Amelia glanced at Phil, who shrugged his shoulders. "What do you mean you know? Did Phil tell you?"

"No, but I've been watching Tony and the men who work for him. They'll make a slip someday, and I'll put them where they belong—in prison."

"Surely you don't think Ryan Kildare is the same kind of man as Morino."

"They're all in it together. You don't see it like we do, Amelia. It's brutal. There are killings all the time, and it's Kildare who gets them off. Just last month they found one of Morino's men practically standing over a body with a smoking gun, but Kildare got him off. He's in the dirty business just as much as anybody else."

Amelia was upset, for she had grown fond of Ryan. She took a sip of tea from the small porcelain cup and then aggressively said, "Let me tell you about Ryan. He came up the hard way, Lee. . . ." She proceeded to tell the facts as she had received them from Judith Kildare. She finally ended by saying, "So he's fought his way up out of nothing and supported his family. I say that's good."

Phil was studying his sister carefully. He knew what an independent woman she was, and he hesitated to comment. He watched Lee, who also seemed reluctant to say too much. It was Sarah who finally said, "Amelia, New York City is a jungle just like Chicago and other big cities. Their gangsters aren't all as famous as Al Capone, but they're all just as ruthless."

"But Ryan's not like that," Amelia insisted. "He loves his family. I've seen it."

"The man Ryan Kildare got off is guilty as sin and will kill again," Lee said. "Now, wouldn't you say that Kildare has to take part of the responsibility for that?"

Seeing the distress on his sister's face, Phil decided to change the subject. "Let's play Mah-Jongg. I feel lucky tonight."

They all readily agreed, and soon the couples were playing the popular game. But as Phil took part, he was aware that something was troubling about Amelia's defense of Ryan Kildare. He made it a point to talk to Lee about this later, but he was fairly certain of the answer he would get.

★　★　★　★

The next day Amelia and Ryan returned to her apartment after a Yankees game, and she invited him in. It was still early, no later than four o'clock, and she fixed coffee and brought out a cake, proudly announcing, "Here, I made it myself."

Ryan pulled his chair closer to the table and dug in with his fork, closing his eyes in delight with the first bite. Licking his lips, he said, "Lady, you can make all my cakes. This is good."

Amelia had said nothing up to this point about her conversation with the Novaks the night before, but it had been on her mind all day. Now she said tentatively, "Ryan, we've talked about this before. I can't help thinking that there's something wrong in getting criminals off that are obviously guilty."

Ryan swallowed another bite of cake and put his fork down. He leaned back, his electric blue eyes fastened on her. He made a roughly handsome picture as he sat there. "Been talking to the law?" he said quietly.

Defensively, Amelia came back, "Phil and I have a meal once in a while over at the Novaks'. They are very good people."

"I'm sure they are. The word's out on the street—don't try to buy Novak. He'll bury you. He's an honest man."

Amelia did not answer, but she felt dissatisfied, and finally Ryan leaned forward and picked up her hand. "It's meant a lot to me going out with you, Amelia, and my family thinks you're wonderful. But about my job, the courts are built on the premise that every man and every woman is entitled to a defense. Would you do away with that?"

"No," Amelia said slowly, "I wouldn't do that. I don't understand these things, Ryan, but I don't like the idea of your being mixed up with Big Tony Morino. You know what he stands for. He's vicious. Oh, he puts on a good act, and he can be pleasant enough, and he loves his family, but he's no better than the men who work for him. You know what they are."

The silence built up, and finally Amelia said, "Ryan, I think we'd better not see each other for a time."

Ryan sat very still. He leaned back in his chair and studied her carefully. Finally he said, "I'm sorry you feel like that, Amelia—for I find that I've fallen in love with you."

The words frightened Amelia. She was not in love with Ryan Kildare, and she had already purposed that she would allow nothing to stand in the way of her career. She did like him very much, however, and had allowed him to kiss her several times. Still, she knew she had to break this off now. It would be too painful for both of them if she let it go on.

"I'm sorry, Ryan, but I don't want to get serious right now."

★   ★   ★   ★

Lee Novak's dark eyes were flashing, and he grabbed Phil by the shoulders and shook him. He was a powerful man, and Phil blinked with surprise. "Hey, you're going to break my neck. What's wrong with you?"

"We've got him, Phil! We've got him!"

"Got who?"

"We got Leo Marx!"

The trial of Leo Marx had been going on for nearly a week. It was almost a forgone conclusion that Marx would be found not guilty. It had happened before. He had the best legal team in the country, and the evidence was, even as Novak admitted, skimpy.

"What happened?" Phil said. "I didn't think the DA had a prayer of convicting him." He was excited, too, and watched as Novak stalked back and forth, slapping his fist into his hand with a meaty sound.

"It's not because the DA's so smart—somebody blew the whistle on him."

"Who? That'd be suicide. You know what Marx is like."

"I don't know. Probably never will. The dope came in an

unmarked brown manila envelope through the mail. It had dates, names, places—everything the prosecution needed—and I've already nailed down the witnesses who can vindicate it."

"Somebody set him up all right," Phil said abruptly.

"That's right. That's the way it is with these gangsters. They stay on top only by crushing people who get under them. Somebody is out to move Marx out of the way. He's a rat, but he's a smart rat."

As Phil and Novak talked about the case, Phil became convinced that the evidence was indeed solid. "There's no way he can beat this, and I don't care where it came from. I say it's good no matter who did the job!"

★   ★   ★   ★

The New York City jail was not particularly inviting. It had endured many years of use and abuse, and even when it was built it had not been designed for the comfort of its inmates.

Leo Marx, who was accustomed to the finest suites in the finest hotels in New York City, sat in a cell leaning over and whispering to a small man with hazel eyes and stiff blond hair. Jake Prado was the one man in the world Leo Marx trusted.

"I was set up, Jake."

"You'll beat it, Leo."

"Not this time. They've got it all. I've seen it."

Prado was a cold-blooded killer. He was smart, tough, and absolutely ruthless, and his idol was Leo Marx. He sat there shaking his head as if to deny it, but Marx reached out and grabbed him by the arm. "I'm going to be convicted. No way out of it. But there are ways of getting out if enough money goes to the right places."

"Why, sure." Prado brightened up. "Well, I bet you won't be in here a month."

"A little longer than that," Marx said dryly. He was a tall man with black hair and dark brown eyes, a thin face and a knife-edged mouth. His hands were long and graceful like those of a concert violinist, but all the grace was in his hands, for he had none in his soul.

"Jake, you'll have to hold things together until I get out. You'll be the boss."

Jake Prado was a good lieutenant, but he had no illusions about his capability. "I can't do that. I ain't up to it."

"You'll have to put a few down. They'll try to take over our territory. But you've got some good help with Abrams, Michaels, and Foy. They can do the thinking, and you do the rough stuff."

Prado nodded. He had his orders—that's all he ever wanted. "How did it happen, Leo? I can't believe it."

"I was fingered, that's what."

"Give me a name," Prado insisted.

Leaning forward, Leo Marx whispered, the sound making a sibilant hissing in the cell. "Don't tell anybody this, Jake. I've got a line right into the DA's office. They got the dope on me from an outsider."

Suddenly Jake Prado's eyes blinked. "It was Big Tony, wasn't it? I can't get in there, boss. He's too closely guarded."

"No, it wasn't him. I got it straight from my guy inside the DA's office. It was that fancy lawyer of his, Kildare. *He* ain't guarded." Marx's eyes glittered, and he whispered, "Get him, Jake, but do it like this. Let him know he's going to get it. Miss him a couple of times. I want him to be so scared he'll shake himself to pieces."

"It'd be easier just to pop a cap on him, Leo."

"I don't want that. I want him to hurt. When he's half crazy you can put him down."

★ ★ ★ ★

Tony Morino looked up and saw that his attorney was in bad shape. Ryan Kildare's clothes were rumpled, and he had circles under his eyes. Tony got up. "What is it, Kildare?" He noticed that the lawyer's hands were unsteady as he ran them through his red hair.

"They're going to get me, Tony."

"They aren't going to get you. Now calm down. What happened?"

"They got into my apartment when I was out and put a dead

cat in my bed. Here's a note they left."

Tony Morino took the note and read it. " 'You're going to die, lawyer, but slow.' " He looked up and said, "Look, you're going to have to come and live here at my place. We've got plenty of security."

"How can I do that? I've got to go to the courthouse. I've got to be out. You know what my work's like."

Morino argued for a time, but he saw that the man's nerve was completely broken.

"All right," he said. "You'll have to get out of town. Marx is behind it. I'd say Jake Prado is the triggerman. But look, Marx is going to Sing Sing. He'll lose all his power when he's there."

"Not with Prado out."

"I've got plans for him," Morino said in a deadly tone. "I wish it hadn't happened, but I'll find out who's handling the hit. If it's Prado, we'll get him. It has to be him."

Ryan Kildare shook his head. "My mother, I can't leave her."

"They won't bother your mother if you're out of the picture. I'll put two men there for a while, so don't worry. A fly wouldn't be able to get through."

Ryan Kildare was frightened. He had seen the victims of the hit men who roamed the streets of the city, and now he knew there was no mercy for him. "I'll have to do it," he whispered. "But take care of my mother."

"Sure, sure. When this thing blows over you can come back, and it'll be business as usual."

★ ★ ★ ★

Amelia had just gone to bed when the doorbell rang. It startled her, and she glanced at the clock. "After midnight. Who could that be?" At first she decided not to answer it; then she got out of bed and put on a silk robe. As she belted it she approached the door and called out, "Who's there?"

"It's me, Ryan."

"Ryan, what are you doing here?"

"I've got to talk to you for just a minute, Amelia—please."

Amelia hesitated and then turned the dead bolt. She opened

the door and was shocked at Ryan's features. Fear was etched in his face, and he was pale. "I've got to get out of town, Amelia."

"I know. Phil told me about the threats on your life."

Kildare took a deep breath, and then shook his head and grew somewhat calmer. "It's shaken me up pretty bad, Amelia."

"It would shake up anybody." She wanted to say, *Now you know what it's like to be on the receiving end of these gangsters*, but she held her tongue, feeling a great pity for him.

Ryan bit his lower lip, then met her eyes. "I don't know why I came here, but I've got a feeling I won't see you again. And a woman's got a right to know that a man loves her, even if she doesn't love him. I just came to say that."

"What about your mother?"

"Tony's taking care of her."

"I'll go see her if you'd like."

"Would you do that?" Relief washed across Ryan's face. "It would mean a lot to me and to her."

"Yes, but you'd better clear it with Big Tony."

Ryan blinked and shook his head. "Good-bye, Amelia," he said. "And thanks."

As Amelia closed the door it was as if she was closing a door on part of her life. She had had strong feelings for this man, but now she well knew that he was caught in the very machine he had helped to create. She stood there in the center of the room, and a feeling of compassion washed over her. "What will this do to his mother?" she whispered, knowing she would have to do whatever she could for Judith Kildare.

PART THREE

February–April 1927

★ ★ ★

CHAPTER THIRTEEN

A DIFFERENT ROSA

★ ★ ★ ★

The jail reeked of urine, strong cleaning chemicals, unwashed bodies, and the smell of fear. Phil had learned to adjust to it, but he had never learned to like it. Now as he sat in the small cell facing the young man who watched him with wary eyes, he wondered how he could influence the young man to save himself.

Reaching into his pocket, he pulled out a packet of chewing gum and extended it toward the prisoner. "Have a chew," he smiled.

"Don't use it."

The speaker was a wiry teenager with stiff black hair and eyes as dark as obsidian. Charlie Zlinter was seventeen years old, and Phil suspected that very few pleasant events had transpired in his life. He had read the boy's record—he had grown up in poverty, dropped out of school by the age of ten, committed many small offenses, and now was charged with a major one. The jails were filled with human debris such as Charlie Zlinter, and outside in the street they swarmed like schools of piranha feeding on whatever got in their way.

Phil stuck the chewing gum back in his pocket and said

easily, "Charlie, you probably won't believe this, but I'm here to help you."

"Why would you want to help me?"

Phil wanted to answer honestly and was fairly certain that honesty would get him nowhere. Still he decided to try. "I'm out for bigger game than you, Charlie, and that's the truth. I can put you away, but the real guys I'm after are going to be walking free."

The case was relatively simple. Lee Novak's crew had arrested Charlie as part of a bootlegging team. The big fish had gotten away, and Zlinter had been snatched up and hustled into jail with little ceremony. According to his record he had never served hard time, but he had been in the city jail three times, all on minor charges. This was not going to be minor, Phil knew, for Lee had made it plain that he intended to arrest and severely charge anybody connected with bootlegging.

"You got a family, Charlie?" Phil asked.

"No."

"Nor ever had, I suppose."

"Sure, I had a pa once. He beat me up all the time and kicked me out when I was ten."

"What about your mother?"

"She died when I was three."

It was a familiar story to Phil, and despite the antagonistic set of the young man's shoulders and his hateful stare, Phil felt that somewhere deep down under this exterior was a human being who needed a hand.

"All right, Charlie, let me explain this to you. You know what I do. We're out to put bootleggers out of business."

"You're not having much luck, are you?"

Phil grinned ruefully. He liked the boy's spirit. He knew that Zlinter was afraid, but he was doing a good job keeping it from showing. A fight broke out somewhere down the cellblock, and Phil turned, but Zlinter did not even move his eyes. He was as wary as an animal in a trap, and Phil knew the effort to get him to open up was hopeless.

"Let me tell you what's happening here, Charlie. As far as I can figure out, you were helping to load illegal liquor. That makes you guilty, but some people are guiltier than others. The big bosses upstairs—they're the ones we really want to get after."

"And you want me to give you their names."

"That's right, I do."

Zlinter cursed and glared at Phil. "I ain't no rat. I'll never squeal."

"Ah, the code of honor!" Phil had encountered it before, and it left him with a bad taste in his mouth. "Your kind will do anything—break the law, break knees, shoot each other down—but you have this one little rule that you don't squeal on anybody."

"That's right."

"No, it's not right. It's *wrong*. What's it going to get you? You're going to the penitentiary, Charlie. What about the guy who hired you? You think he'll be there? Not on your life. He'll be living in his big house with his fast women and his liquor, and if anybody ever says to him, 'Whatever happened to Charlie Zlinter?' he'll probably laugh and say, 'That poor sucker. He took the rap.'"

Zlinter's eyes faltered for a moment, but then his lips grew thin, and he shook his head without saying a word.

Phil went on. "They're using you, Charlie."

"I've had enough of this." Charlie jumped up from the table and banged on the door, but the guard outside ignored him.

Sighing heavily, Phil leaned back and studied him. He knew there was no way Charlie would ever accept his help, but he had tried, nevertheless. He reached into his pocket and pulled out a small New Testament. He extended it toward Zlinter, who still stood by the door, a suspicious light in his eyes at Phil's offer.

"Go on, take it," Phil said. "It won't bite you. It's just a Bible— a small one at that."

Zlinter stared at him and made no move to take it. "Why you giving me a Bible?"

"Because you need it just like I do, and just like everybody does. You've probably heard this before, Charlie, but we all need God. Jesus died for your sins just like He died for mine. The only difference between us is that I've called on Him and asked Him to forgive me of my sins, and He has. And just remember, that's all you have to do."

Zlinter reached out gingerly and took the Bible, and Phil knew not to press it further. "I marked a few verses in there and wrote a few notes on the inside cover." He stood up and called out, "Guard, I'm ready." As the guard came in, he turned back to Charlie and said, "My phone number's written in the back of that New Testament. If you want me to help you, Charlie, just call me."

The door clanged open, and Phil stepped outside. As the guard slammed it shut, the hollow, ringing sound had a fatal note in it. He had heard it before, and he wondered how he himself would survive if he were locked up behind steel bars with criminals, their souls abounding with every evil instinct in the world. A shiver twitched his shoulders, and he walked quickly down the corridor, his heels echoing on the concrete. The guard at the end let him out and said, "Good day to you, sir."

Phil studied the man. He was white haired, and his face was lined. "Been here a long time?" Phil asked.

"Twenty-two years."

"That would depress me watching all these men go down."

"Well, I get a chance to say a word to them every now and then about the Lord Jesus."

Instantly Phil smiled. He put out his hand and said, "My name's Winslow. I'm from the DA's office. Here's my card. If you ever need anything, give me a call."

The guard looked at the card with surprise. "Why, thanks, Mr. Winslow." He smiled slyly and said, "You're not really a lawyer, are you? You don't look old enough."

Phil laughed. "I just graduated from law school last month, so I'm pretty new at it. But I'm starting to learn the ropes."

"Well, I suppose we need lawyers, although they don't seem to do most of these fellows much good."

"We do the best we can, Sam." He had read the name tag on the white-haired man's chest. "You're doing a good work here."

The compliment caught the guard off balance. "You know, in all the years I've been here nobody's ever commended me for standing up for the Lord. I get lots of cussin' out."

"You're being faithful, and that's all any of us can do. I'll see you again, perhaps."

Phil left the cellblock and made his way toward the front gate. When he stepped outside, he breathed in an invigorating breath of the cold February air. He got into his car, and as he often did, he thought of his grandmother and how she had given him the car on his graduation from college not quite two years ago. He kept it spotless and clean, the nickel headlights and the radiator still glowing as they had the first day he had climbed into it. Starting the car, he threaded his way through the traffic until he came to the fifth precinct. He parked and went inside. Stepping over to the desk, he said, "Hello, Sarge, how you doing today?"

"Why, Counselor, it's you." The sergeant's name was Murphy, a typical Irish cop with a ruddy complexion and a pair of penetrating blue eyes. He had grown heavier since his days on the beat, but he was known as a good cop. "What can I do for you today, Mr. Winslow?"

"I just need to get one paper signed by one of your guests here, Sergeant. Tommy Bentley."

"Are you sure he can write?" Murphy grinned. "Sure. Go on back."

"Thanks, Murph." Phil turned and started toward the door that led to the interior of the building, where prisoners were held until they were either released on bail or sent to the city jail for longer terms. He had not gotten far, however, when a loud screaming suddenly brought him up short. He turned around and saw that two burly policemen were hauling in a young woman, each one holding an arm firmly. She was wearing a thin gold lamé dress with fringes. A headband held back her black hair, but as she struggled, butting her head at one of the officers, it came loose, and the hair fell down before her face. She was screaming unintelligibly, and one of the officers winked at the sergeant.

"Well, Murph, we got a live one here."

"What'd she do, Sullivan?"

"Tried to beat a girl's head in with a chair. I think the other flapper was stealing her boyfriend or something."

"Steal my boyfriend? That bleached blonde couldn't steal anything of mine!"

Phil stared at the woman with shock, for he recognized Rosa Morino. He had not seen her now in over a year and then it had been only briefly. Since her father had forbade her to see anybody connected with the law, it was almost as if the earth had swallowed her up. He had sent her a present for her eighteenth birthday, but it had been returned unopened.

Sergeant Murphy put his chin in one hand and tilted his head to one side. "Is that all she did?"

"She was drunk in a public place. That's against the law. She assaulted another woman, and she was screaming she was going to bring charges against us."

"Well, we'll have to charge you then, miss."

Rosa's eyes were dull, not the flashing bright that Phil remembered. She was obviously severely intoxicated. Her makeup was smeared, and there was a wild look about her as she struggled with the officers. She cursed them both, then the sergeant.

"You'd better call a lawyer, miss. That's my advice. What's your name?" the sergeant asked.

"None of your business."

"If you won't give me your name, you'll stay here a long time."

Phil did not move forward. He waited until Rosa had been led away, still fighting. He chewed his lip thoughtfully, and a worried expression crossed his face. He then made a quick decision, and without even bidding the sergeant good-bye, he left the precinct.

★ ★ ★ ★

"Leo's gettin' out of jail, Mr. Morino." Dom held the paper out to Tony and watched his boss scan it. "I thought they'd keep him in at least five years."

"Not with his connections and his pull. Somebody was bought off." Morino grunted.

"I think we'll have trouble with him," Dom said.

Tony Morino was sitting down behind his desk. He ran his hand through his thinning hair and shook his head. He had lost weight recently, and it had not improved his appearance. The facial muscles that had once been so tense and tight now sagged, and his eyes had sunk back in their sockets. He had been a tough young kid and then an even tougher man, but the years were beginning to creep up on him. He was sixty-three now, and for a man in his profession that was a ripe old age indeed.

Dom waited for Morino to remark and then nudged him a little bit. "We'd better put somebody on this. We've got to double our security, Mr. Morino."

"Okay, you take care of it, Dom."

More and more, Dom realized, Morino had lost the keen cutting edge that had brought him to the top of the criminal world in New York. *He's gonna get his head chopped off if he doesn't wake up*, Dom thought but merely said, "All right, I'll take care of it."

The two men spoke of a few more business matters when suddenly the door opened, and one of Morino's trusted workers, Dion Madigen, stuck his head in. "Somebody here to see you, Mr. Morino."

"What somebody? Who is it?"

Madigen chewed his lip thoughtfully as if reluctant to speak. "Well, he's from the district attorney's office. His name is Winslow. We weren't going to let him in, but he said it concerns your family."

A rich flush colored Morino's face. "Tell him to get out of here. He's not welcome here."

"I wouldn't do that, Mr. Morino," Dom said quickly. "He wouldn't have come here if it wasn't pretty important."

At one time Morino would have brushed aside his bodyguard's warning, but now he was more willing to listen. "All right," he muttered. "Tell him to come in."

Dom had kept up with Phil Winslow's career. It was his job to keep tabs on the enemy, and anybody in the district attorney's office fit that category. He studied young Winslow as he stepped inside, calculating that he must only be about twenty-three. Not many could have accomplished so much by such a young age. He remembered reading in the papers that he was the youngest law-school graduate in the history of New York, having completed his studies in only a year and a half. After his January graduation, he had immediately been offered a position with Gordon Land, the DA.

Phil was wearing a dark suit and maroon tie, and his hair was mussed from the strong breeze outside.

"What do you want, Winslow?" Morino snapped.

Phil glanced at Dom's expressionless face, then looked back at Morino. He was shocked at the deterioration of the big man, for he appeared to have aged at least ten years in only two. "You've got a problem, Tony."

"You're not my lawyer."

"No, I didn't come here as a lawyer."

"What is it, then? Tell me and get out."

"It's Rosa. She's been arrested."

Instantly Dom rose and stared at Winslow. "What are you talking about?" he demanded.

"She's at the fifth precinct. She wouldn't give them her name, so they had to book her under a Jane Doe, but if I were you, I would get your attorney down there right away. That's a rough place. I'd hate to see Rosa stay there."

"What were the charges?" Dom asked sharply.

"Drunk and disorderly conduct, maybe some kind of an assault charge. I think she broke a chair over some woman's head."

Tony could do little more than stare at Winslow, but the news hit him hard. He was breathing heavily, and he sat down again and slumped back in his chair. He did not speak for a moment, and then he put his eyes on the young lawyer. "What are you doing this for?"

Phil said quietly, "I've always liked Rosa. I wouldn't waste any time about this, Tony. That's a rough place." He turned and walked away, and the two men watched him without saying a word.

As soon as the door closed, however, Morino got up and began to pace the floor. "What's the matter with her, Dom? Has she gone crazy? Lately she's done nothing but give her mother and me trouble. I gave her everything she wanted—everything. Now look at her."

Dom listened, but he had heard it all before more than once. "We can talk about it later, Mr. Morino. You'd better let me get on it."

"That's right. Go get Reynolds. Whatever he's doing, jerk him out of there. Get her out right away and bring her home."

"I'll get right on it, Mr. Morino."

★ ★ ★ ★

J.D. Reynolds was a man of means as well as a man to be reckoned with. He had risen in his profession, not because of his astute knowledge of the law, but because of Tony Morino, who had hired him after Kildare had gone into hiding, and paid him exorbitantly. Reynolds was unbeatable in front of a jury. He was a tall man, in good shape and only forty-five years old. He had fair hair and strange green eyes that could mesmerize any jury, making them forget the facts and listen instead to their emotions.

Reynolds' home was in the most exclusive district of New York, as might be expected, and he dined with the top level of politicians and celebrities. He had defended several movie stars, and on this particular evening he was entertaining Miss Lila DeNucci, whom he had just gotten off from a serious drug-dealing charge. He had arranged the dinner with care, for Miss DeNucci was one of the current sex symbols in Hollywood. Now as he looked over at the young woman, whose figure strained at the thin fabric of her dress, Reynolds smiled in anticipation.

"Oh, Mr. Reynolds, I don't know how to thank you!" Lila was empty-headed, but that did not seem to matter in Hollywood. The fact that she was beautiful and every move she made was suggestive was more important in the making of starlets, and now as she leaned forward, she whispered, "You've been so good to me."

Reynolds laughed and reached over and put his hand on her bare shoulder. "Well, I'm always glad to help a beautiful lady in distress. Why don't we have a few drinks and then—" Reynolds did not finish his sentence, for his manservant entered, announcing, "A gentleman to see you, sir."

"Tell him to come back."

"I will tell him, sir."

Reynolds turned back to the young woman and traced her jawline with an aristocratic forefinger. He heard the muted sound of the butler's voice speaking with someone outside; then the door flew open again and before he could move, he found his arm seized by a powerful hand. "What—!"

"So sorry to interrupt, but it's time to go, Counselor."

Dom Costello enjoyed this part of his work. He had never liked Reynolds. He was a good enough lawyer, but he treated anybody below the level of a crime lord or a governor with disdain. Dom was not intimidated by the man's arrogance and now pulled him across the room simply because he could. "Better get your coat on," he said coldly.

"What are you talking about? Let go of me, Costello!"

Dom's fingers tightened, and he saw a strain come into Reynolds' eyes. As the lawyer struggled, Dom continued to increase his force. "Mr. Morino says you need to come along with me. Now, do you want me to drag you out, or do you want to walk like a real lawyer?"

Reynolds was not accustomed to taking orders—but he knew Big Tony Morino and said quickly, "Why, of course, Dominic, I was just startled."

Dom released his grip and said, "It's cold out. You'd better put your coat on."

"Where are we going?"

"I'll fill you in on the way." Dominic turned and said, "Don't go away, baby. He'll probably come back in two or three hours. If he doesn't, I'll come and keep you company." He laughed at the movie star's panicked expression, then moved inexorably outside, herding Reynolds with not-so-gentle nudges.

★　★　★　★

Rosa was considerably more sober by the time she was brought out of the cell. She had been throwing up and had not been able to clean herself properly. Now as she moved out into the station house itself, she saw one of the officers wink at the sergeant. She also saw big Dom Costello standing there and glared at him as if he had done her some harm.

Dom said nothing to her, but turned to the officer in charge. "Can she have her things back, Sergeant?"

"Sure. Just sign right here."

Dom signed the release, then collected the purse and wristwatch. He took Rosa's arm roughly and led her outside, ignoring her objections. "The car's over here," he said.

Rosa got in the car but turned her face away, staring out the window. Dom got in, started the engine, and said, "We should stop somewhere and get you cleaned up. You don't want to go home looking like that."

"What difference does it make?"

Dom Costello was accustomed to this behavior. He had watched this young woman go steadily downhill for the past year, and he thought it was a shame. She was a sweet kid, but she had sure changed. Now he shrugged, knowing all he could do was take her home.

★   ★   ★   ★

The noisy scene at the Morino estate shook Maria badly. She had tried to comfort Rosa in her gentle way, but her wayward daughter had yanked herself away and now stood with her back to her mother, her arms folded in defiance. Tony, as usual, had plowed right in and started shouting at the girl.

"I'm ashamed of you! Drunk and disorderly!"

Rosa turned to face him fiercely. "What do you think happens to that liquor you bootleg, Daddy? Do you think only the people on the street drink it? No, young girls like me drink it too."

Her words hit Tony Morino like a blow to the midsection. Looking at this girl who had the been the pride of his life only a short time ago, and now having her throw in his face that he was responsible for what she had become was more than he could take. He looked over at his wife and pleaded, "Can't you do anything with her, Maria?"

"She's not the bootlegger, Daddy. You are!" Rosa screamed.

Tony stared at his daughter, then whirled and stormed out of the room. He moved heavily, like a sick man, and the silence washed backward into the room after he closed the door.

CHAPTER FOURTEEN

OUT OF THE PAST

★   ★   ★   ★

Amelia had rather enjoyed her date with the wealthy playboy Lyle Deckerton. He was always amusing, and tonight he had seemed in particularly good spirits. Now as he opened the door and she stepped out of the car, she thought of the strangeness of their so-called affair. It was the newspapers that called it that, and of course, Lyle would have liked to put reality into the word.

Amelia had refused several of his invitations to go out but finally had agreed out of curiosity. She had never before dated a man with more money than he could possibly spend. Deckerton was rich enough to meet that description. His father had made a fortune in the stock market, then had branched out into manufacturing. Since Lyle was the only son, the odds were good that one day he would control all of the millions his father had raked together.

Deckerton had provided plenty of fodder for the nation's gossip columnists. He was handsome enough, with fair hair and mild blue eyes and a dimple on each cheek, giving him a cherubic look. There were no lines on his face, for he had not overtaxed himself with studies while at college, nor had the cares of this world been a burden. His papa had seen to it that they never bothered him.

The columnists had linked him with practically everybody, including the new acting sensations Mae West and Clara Bow. He had left behind a trail of diamond bracelets, rings, necklaces, cars, and furs. Amelia had been more amused by him than anything else. He was certainly the last man in the world she would ever want to marry.

"How about if I come in, Amelia?"

"Not tonight, Lyle. It's too late, and I'm tired."

"Just for a few minutes."

"No, I'm sorry. Afraid not. Good night."

"Wait a minute," Lyle said, wedging himself between Amelia and the door of her apartment. He had made his try at her virtue on the first date and had not been at all put off when she refused him. He never seemed to let things like that bother him. Now that Amelia's curiosity about the rich man was satisfied, however, she was ready for him to leave.

"I'm really tired, Lyle."

Deckerton reached into his inner pocket and pulled out a long plush-covered box. "Merry Christmas or happy birthday, whichever comes first."

Alarm ran lightly through Amelia. She took the box and opened it, shocked by the fiery sparkle of the diamond necklace that nestled against the black plush lining. She knew that the piece had cost thousands of dollars, judging by the size and number of diamonds in it.

"Do you like it?"

Amelia closed the lid on the box and shook her head. "Lyle, I told you before, I don't take gifts from men."

"But why not? I like to give people things."

"Because when men give 'gifts,' they are more than that. You'd be expecting something back for it."

Deckerton's eyes widened. "No, honestly, it's just a gift. That's all it is."

Amelia forced the box back into his hand. He began to protest, but Amelia said quietly, "Lyle, it would give you a hold on me, and I won't have that. Now, good night."

She slipped by him and opened the door. When she turned she saw that he was standing there like a hurt boy, his blue eyes wounded. "You'll find someone who will take it, Lyle," she assured him. "Run along now."

When she closed the door, she put her back against it and rested for a moment, reflecting on their date. Straightening up, she said to herself, "Well, that's the last of that, and it wasn't all that much fun." Remembering the look in his eyes, she laughed. "You know, if he weren't worth millions of dollars, he would actually be a very dull fellow!"

★ ★ ★ ★

A harsh ringing awakened Amelia. She had slept poorly and groped blindly for the phone with her hair down in her eyes. When she picked up the receiver, she fell back on the pillow and said, "Yes?"

"Miss Winslow?"

"Yes, who's this?"

"This is Faye Anderson."

Amelia assumed that a fan had gotten hold of her private phone number. It irritated her, for what was the point of having a private number if anyone knew it? Now she'd have to change it again. She told the caller, "I'm afraid I'm a little busy right now."

After a moment's silence the woman said, "Don't you remember me, Miss Winslow? But, of course, I forgot—you wouldn't know my married name. I'm Faye Kildare Anderson, Ryan's sister."

"Oh, Faye!" Amelia sat up in bed, and her thoughts began to come together. She had gone to see Ryan's family three times since he'd disappeared. Each time his mother and Faye had been so happy to see her. They'd been very guarded, though, about Ryan's whereabouts, and finally when she'd tried to call, the number had been disconnected.

"It's good to hear from you again, Faye. I've missed you."

"That's so kind of you to say that, Miss Winslow."

"How are you? How's your mother?"

"Well, it's Mother I'm calling about." There was an odd tightness in Faye's voice, and then after a brief silence, she said,

"Mother passed away the day before yesterday."

"Oh, I'm so sorry to hear that," Amelia said.

"It's been coming on a long time, but . . . it's still hard for me to accept. She was the sweetest person I've ever known."

"I thought a great deal of her."

"She so much appreciated the visits you made. You don't know how much they meant to her."

Amelia felt a twinge of guilt at the thought that she could have done more but didn't. Perhaps it was inevitable to think such thoughts after a death, and Amelia could say only, "I wish I'd had more time to spend with her."

Faye spoke briefly, reiterating how her mother had loved her, and then said, "The funeral is tomorrow at two o'clock."

Amelia reached over, got a pad, and wrote down the name of the funeral home. Then Faye quickly said good-bye.

As she hung up the phone, Amelia thought, *I've got to send some very nice flowers*. But even as she thought it, she knew that would not be enough. She'd have to go. She hated funerals, but then she supposed everyone did. It was too late to make anything up to Ryan's mother, but at least she could show her respect to the rest of the family.

★　★　★　★

The funeral was far better attended than Amelia had expected. She came a few minutes late and took a seat in the back. As she glanced around, she was surprised to see over a hundred people there. *They must be from Judith's church*, she thought. She saw Faye sitting with a tall man up in the front row and was somewhat startled to see Ryan seated beside her. She had thought of him many times and had understood his need to flee for his life. Certainly crime lords like Leo Marx had no scruples.

The funeral was simple, and the only thing different was that several of Mrs. Kildare's neighbors gave a brief eulogy, all very personal. They all testified to her patience, her generosity, her kindness, and her love for the Lord.

Finally the service was over, and the minister announced,

"For those who care to attend, there will be a graveside service at Lockwood Cemetery."

Amelia had not planned to attend, but she could not help thinking of Ryan. She had never been able to put him out of her mind, for there had been something between the two of them, as brief as their acquaintance had been. In her eyes, he was one of the most dynamic men she had ever met. And yet he had left a broken man, filled with fear, forced to go into hiding. She wondered how he had dared return, even for his mother's funeral. Phil had told her that Leo Marx was out of prison now and would no doubt be looking for Ryan. Marx was not a man who would have softened during his time in jail.

Instead of driving home she got into the funeral procession, which consisted of some ten cars, and went to the cemetery. The cars parked near a green pavilion set up over the open grave. She stayed back, waiting until the mourners were seated. She did not know several of the family members, including the brothers and sisters for whom Ryan had done so much.

Finally, when everyone was settled, Amelia moved into the outer circle of the gathering. She chose a place where she could watch Ryan without being observed herself. He was quite pale, she thought, but he showed no signs of nervousness. He sat between a younger woman and a man, both of whom closely resembled him. A sister and brother, she supposed.

The service was short and fitting, and after the final prayer, the minister stepped forward to shake hands with the family and whisper a word to each of them.

Amelia returned to her car, but then turned to look back on the scene before she got in. Ryan and two others were walking across the dead grass toward the cars. On impulse, she moved toward them and saw him look up. She also observed the shock that ran through him as he was caught in midstride. He stopped for a moment, then said something in a low voice to the two young men. They both gave her a curious look but left at once, headed toward one of the remaining cars parked in the drive. Ryan came forward and stood before her. He removed his hat, and she saw that his hair was still the flaming red she remembered. There was a steadiness in his eyes and a tremendous soberness in his features. "Thank you so much for coming, Amelia. It was very kind of you."

"She was a lovely woman, Ryan. I know you'll miss her very much."

"I always thought she was the kindest human being I ever knew." He dropped his head for a moment, then looked up and said, "Faye wrote me about your visits after I left. You have a good heart, Amelia."

Amelia could not think of what to say next, but finally she said, "Where are you living now, Ryan?"

"Right here in New York." He saw something flicker in her eyes, and he smiled. "I know you're thinking it's a little bit dangerous."

"Yes, I was thinking that."

"Well, I had to come back because I knew Mother was dying, and she wanted me close. She promised to keep my whereabouts a secret . . . and she did just that."

"What will you do now, Ryan?"

"I'll be around."

Amelia hesitated at his ambiguous answer. She had expected him to say he would be leaving right away. She put out her hand and said, "Take care of yourself, Ryan."

When Ryan took her hand, he did not squeeze it as some men might. Instead he held it gently and did not speak for a moment. Finally he nodded and said, "Thanks for coming. Mother thought the world of you, Amelia. Good-bye." He turned and walked away, leaving her standing there feeling dissatisfied. She had wanted to learn more of his plans, but he'd said no more.

★　★　★　★

Phil listened as Amelia told him about the funeral. He shook his head when she finished, saying, "That's bad news."

"You really think Leo Marx will try to kill him?"

"Marx is convinced Ryan was responsible for his conviction. Men like that don't forget anything. If you have any influence over Ryan, try to convince him to go far away."

"Oh, I'm sure he wouldn't listen to me."

"Why did he come back?"

"It was for his mother's sake."

The two talked for a few moments, and then Phil said, "Rosa was arrested."

As he related the circumstances, sadness filled her face. She leaned back and said, "What's happening to this country, Phil? It's going down faster than I would ever have believed."

Phil sipped his coffee and shook his head sadly. "I think a lot of it has something to do with the war. A whole generation has gotten infected by this 'eat, drink, and be merry, for tomorrow we die' sort of thing. The soldiers all had it, I understand."

"But it's not just ex-soldiers. Women, too, are doing everything they shouldn't do. What's happened to women?"

"Well, some of them are just tired of keeping house. They got a touch of freedom while the men were gone, and now this whole movement is telling them they can do anything they please. But I think a lot of it has to do with Freud."

"You mean that Austrian doctor?"

"Yes. He dresses up his teachings with a lot of fancy words, but basically he says everything we do is motivated by sex. The way to be happy is to have an uninhibited sex life. If you are going to be well and happy, obey your libido."

"And this country's fallen for it just like Sodom and Gomorrah." Amelia sighed, then suddenly chuckled to herself. "Listen to me, Phil. I sound like some kind of preacher's daughter! It's not like I can tell others how to live, now, can I?"

Phil took her hand in his and squeezed it warmly. "You're a good woman, Amelia. You're still trying to find your way, but at heart you know what's good and right."

Amelia sat there in silence for a few moments, then finally said heavily, "Phil, why don't you try to talk to Ryan? I have a feeling he needs some help."

"You got his address?"

"No, I don't."

"Well, I'd be glad to talk to him. If he calls you, get his number."

"All right, Phil. We need to help him all we can. He's had a rough blow."

CHAPTER FIFTEEN

WATER STREET

★ ★ ★ ★

"Hello, Mr. Winslow, what can I do for you?" The sergeant behind the big desk at the city jail smiled as Phil walked in.

"I'd like to talk to Charlie Zlinter."

"Hey, Zlinter must be coming up in the world," the sergeant said. "He's talking with his lawyer right now." The policeman grinned broadly. "What's Charlie done that's so important you guys from the DA's office keep coming back?"

"I just hate to see him get flushed down, Sergeant."

"Sure. Well, come on. I'll take you down. Hey, did you hear the latest definition of a lawyer? A guy who persuades two people to take off their clothes and then steals them."

Phil had heard most of the lawyer jokes, including this one, but he laughed politely anyway. He followed the policeman down the hall and watched as he opened the door without knocking. "Hey, Zlinter, I got another lawyer here to see you." He laughed, then nodded. "Go on in, Counselor."

Phil stepped inside the small room and saw Zlinter seated at a scarred table. Winslow thought the young man looked tired and older than his seventeen years. The jail had worn him down in a very short time. *That's what usually happens,* Phil thought. *I guess that's what jails are supposed to do.*

"Hello, Phil."

Phil turned quickly at the familiar voice, and a shock ran through him as he saw Ryan Kildare standing on the other side of the room. "Ryan," Phil said, "I've been trying to get in touch with you. Amelia said she saw you at your mother's funeral."

"Yes, she did. How are you, Phil? I hear great things about you."

"Oh, I'm just fine." As Phil took a chair at the table, he studied Kildare's face and tried to read the man's features. He had lost some weight, but there was a calm about him that Phil did not remember. What he did remember about Kildare was that he used to have such a ferocious drive he didn't let problems get him down but ran straight at them. Ryan Kildare seemed much calmer now, and Phil sensed that it stemmed from an inner peace rather than anything else.

Phil wanted to ask him about his plans to avoid Leo Marx, but this was not the place. He glanced at the young prisoner and spoke to him as he took a chair, too, and sat down. "Hello, Charlie."

"Hello, Mr. Winslow."

"How have you been?"

"Okay, I guess."

"Maybe I'd better tell you why I'm here, Ryan. I've been trying to get Charlie here to understand that he doesn't need to go down for this. It's his first major offense. I think I can get him a suspended sentence with a little supervision. All we want are the names of the people he worked for."

Ryan smiled. "I think Charlie's ready for that now."

Surprise swept across Phil's face. He shot a glance at Charlie and said, "Is that right?"

"Yes, sir."

"What changed your mind, Charlie?"

"Mr. Kildare here. He's been talking to me a lot."

"Well, I think you're fortunate in your lawyer, Charlie. He's telling you the straight goods. I'll do all I can for you. Can't promise anything. You never know which way a judge will jump, but I think it'll work out all right."

Phil quickly discovered that Charlie Zlinter was indeed willing to cooperate. He named names and gave dates. Phil was surprised at how much he knew about the operation.

"They didn't pay much attention to me, but I kept my eyes open," Charlie said when Phil asked him how he knew so many details.

"That's good, Charlie. You've been a great help. I'll go to bat for you. I'll wait for you outside, Ryan."

"No, I'm through. The hearing will be tomorrow."

Phil hesitated. "In a case like this I'm not even sure there has to be a trial. If you and I can agree, we can go to Judge Samuelson on Charlie's behalf. He's a reasonable man. I think we can work it all out just between the three of us."

"Fine." Ryan reached over and clapped Charlie Zlinter on the back. "You've done the right thing here, Charlie. Time to start doing things a little different."

The two lawyers left then, and as soon as they were outside, Phil said, "Got time for a cup of coffee?"

"Sure."

The two men left the jail and ten minutes later were seated in a café. After the hot coffee had come in big mugs, Phil made light conversation for a few minutes, but then said, "How long have you been back, Ryan?"

"Almost three months."

Phil hesitated, sipped his coffee, then put the cup down. He traced the squares on the red-and-white-checkered tablecloth and sought the right words. He actually had a fondness for this man, or perhaps it was more pity. He had always thought Ryan showed good sense in running for his life. Finally Phil looked up and met Kildare's eyes. "What about Leo Marx? He doesn't forget things."

"I know he doesn't." Ryan shrugged his shoulders. "But I can't live in a cave the rest of my life."

"Maybe I ought to have a talk with Leo. Let him know that if anything happens to you, something will happen to him."

"You don't have to do that."

"Actually, I don't mind it. Nothing I like better than leaning on guys like Leo Marx. I'll give it a shot."

"Thanks, Phil, it might help."

"So . . . you're practicing law again. Where's your office?"

Ryan gave the young man opposite him an odd glance, and

then he chuckled. "It's on Water Street near the mission."

Phil blinked with surprise. "The Water Street Mission? Why, that's where my uncle was converted, and that's where my father and he first ministered together before they set out for Africa!"

"Yes, I've heard all about the Winslow brothers. They left quite a legacy."

"So you've spent some time at the mission? What are you doing there?"

"It's a long story, Phil."

"Can't you give me the short version?"

"I left here running scared for my life. I stayed that way for almost a year. Got into some bad habits, but then I found the Lord. Jesus saved me and that's it."

"Why, Ryan, I think that's wonderful!" Phil said excitedly. "I want to hear all of it someday."

"Come down to the mission sometime. I'm helping with the work."

"Are you preaching there too?"

"No, not really. I guess I do a little of that, but mostly I'm just available for people who need help. Quite a few of them in that neighborhood need some legal advice."

"It's no way to get rich."

"No, probably not, but that doesn't matter to me anymore."

The two men talked for some time, and finally Ryan said, "I guess I'd better get back. When do you want to try to meet with the judge?"

"How about one o'clock tomorrow? I think I can set it up for then."

"You really think he'll go for it, Phil?"

"I'm sure he will. Especially if we agree to keep an eye on the young man."

"He doesn't have anywhere to go. I've already told him he could come and stay at the mission and help me around the place. We'll find him a job."

"That's all the judge will want. Samuelson's a good man. I'll see you tomorrow at one."

* ★ * ★

Boadicea lunged and broke into a furious run. Rosa leaned forward, the wind blowing in her face. The cold February wind cut at her and numbed her lips, but she loved to ride fast—as she loved to do almost everything else. She clung to the back of the mare, helping her with the movements of her body, but then the headache that had bothered her all morning came back, and she reined the mare in. "That's enough, Boadicea," she said rather crossly. The mare had stopped reluctantly and shook her head, trying to get rid of the bit, but Rosa held her firmly. "You behave now," she said sharply.

The late afternoon sun was sinking into the west, a huge crimson disk. Rosa had ridden for over an hour, and now she reluctantly turned back toward the stables. As she did she remembered the painful scene she'd had with her father earlier in the day. She hated scenes, especially with her father. The two of them had practically no communication now. It was obvious to Rosa that her father was going downhill physically, but emotionally he was the same. He demanded the same obedience from her that he got from Dom Costello, and Rosa was simply not constituted to live under those conditions.

As she moved along the bridle path that wound across the Morino estate, a fox trotted out in front of her, and she pulled up with surprise. The vixen turned and studied her casually without a trace of fear. Rosa held Boadicea in tightly and studied the beautiful animal. Finally the fox turned and walked away placidly, and Rosa exclaimed, "Aren't you a bold one!" She touched the mare with her heels and continued toward the stables.

She had not ridden more than fifty yards when an intersecting path revealed a rider coming from her left. Wondering who else would be riding on her father's estate, she pulled the mare over to a slow walk. As the other rider came into view, she was shocked to see Phil Winslow, mounted on the big bay.

"Good to see you, Rosa," he said casually.

Rosa flushed. The last time she had seen him, she was drunk and fighting two policemen. She hated it that he had seen her like that. It seemed worse for him than for her father, but she could not have told why.

"What are you doing here, Phil? My father will kill you if he sees you here."

"He won't see me way out here. The guard let me in so I could talk with you, and O'Connor let me saddle up the bay here to find you. I guess they know I'm not out to hurt you." He admired the mare and said, "Boadicea looks beautiful. She's a fine, fine horse."

Rosa leaned over and patted Boadicea's neck. She was at a loss for words, but even as she rode along, she thought about earlier days when she and Phil had gotten very close. She decided now that the feelings she'd had for him were only the result of an adolescent crush; still, she had never quite let go of those feelings, and for some reason this upset her.

"How is Jamie doing?" Phil asked.

"All right, I guess."

Phil glanced quickly at Rosa, his eyes questioning.

"No, actually, he's not all right." Rosa amended her statement. "Jamie's no good—just like me."

Phil pinched his brow at her comment and lifted his eyes to meet hers. She glared back at him, challenging him head-on, daring him to say something and hoping he would.

But Phil only said, "I'm sorry to hear it. He's a good kid."

Rosa felt disappointed when Phil refused to take the bait. She said nothing else but set her lips in a tight line.

Phil also remained quiet, the only sound being the clopping of the horses' hooves as they rode. The big bay suddenly moved closer, so that Phil's leg bumped against Rosa's, and he pulled the horse back. "Caesar, get back to where you belong. Sorry, Rosa, he's acting a bit rambunctious today." When she did not answer, he said, "You know, I've been thinking about Africa a lot lately. I'd like to go back there. I find myself missing it."

In the past she had always been fascinated by Phil's stories about Africa. She wanted now to hear him speak more about it but instead turned her head and stared straight ahead, stubbornly refusing to comment.

"I never thought I'd be lonesome for Africa. It's so simple there—life, I mean."

"Well, life's not simple here," she snapped.

"Most of the time it's not," he agreed.

They were in view of the stables now, and suddenly Rosa turned to him and said, "Now that I'm eighteen, I plan to do as I please."

"And just what do you please, Rosa?"

The question caught Rosa off guard. She had been so busy running at full tilt for the past two years she'd had little time for introspection. She said, "I don't know. I just want to do what I want to do."

"Well, that's simple enough. Doesn't work for most of us, though."

When they reached the Morino stables, Rosa stepped to the ground easily and slapped Boadicea on the flank as O'Connor came to take the horse away. She turned then and waited until Phil had dismounted. He was stroking the big bay's nose, and she said abruptly, "Do you ever take chances, Phil?"

"Well, I don't know. What kind of chances?"

"Are you afraid of things?"

"Certainly."

"What kind of things?"

"I'm afraid of leopards."

She laughed. "Why, there are no leopards here. That's only in Africa."

"But if there were one here, I'd be afraid of it. They can hurt you bad."

"I mean other things. Have you ever been shot at?"

"Yes, I was once."

"Were you scared?"

"Absolutely petrified."

"Did you shoot back?"

"No. Lee Novak did, though. Saved my life. But I was scared enough."

"Would you ask me out?"

"Why, Rosa—"

"You weren't afraid to come here to see me today, even though you know what my father would do if he caught you. He'd have a raging fit! So are you afraid to ask me out?"

Now it was Phil who felt at a loss for words. He looked at the young woman before him as she defiantly awaited his answer. She took off her riding cap and shook out her hair, the sunlight glistening on its silky surface and running over the gentle curve of her shoulders. Her riding outfit, a boy-figured fashion, merely accentuated her feminine appeal. He had always thought she had a beautifully fashioned face, but now there was something about her expression that troubled him. She had the same rich and self-possessed curve of her mouth, but there was an unhappiness in her lips and in the way she held her head. He could not explain it. Suddenly Phil felt the strange things a man feels when he looks on beauty and knows it will never be for him.

He finally found his voice again and smiled. "Are you daring me, Rosa?"

"Yes!"

"All right. I'll take you up on the dare. I'll pick you up tonight at six—but I get to pick the place."

"Fair enough." Rosa suddenly smiled at him, and he saw at least a trace of the young girl he remembered so fondly.

"But you'd better not tell your father." Then he turned and walked away, leaving the big bay.

"What'll I wear?" she called after him.

"Nothing fancy," he shouted back.

★ ★ ★ ★

Rosa had not known what his reply meant—"*Nothing fancy.*" She didn't dare let her father know she was going out with Phil. He had not returned from his office in any case, and she had simply told her mother she was going out. She put on a simple but expensive maroon wool dress with a hemline much lower than she was accustomed to wearing. When the doorbell rang, she grabbed the fur coat her father had given her for her eighteenth birthday and ran to open it. She saw Phil standing there smiling and said to him, "I'm ready."

"Cold tonight. It's a good thing you've got a warm coat."

He led her to the car, opened the door, and helped her in. When he got in beside her, he said, "You remember this car?"

"Of course. Your grandmother and Amelia and I picked it out. You still have it."

"Of course I still have it. Probably always will. It was the last thing my grandmother could give me . . . and my grandfather, too." He drove down the long, winding drive of the Morino estate and out the front gate, getting onto the highway leading into the city. He expertly navigated the downtown streets and finally said, "You found out I could take a dare. Now I'm going to see if you can take one."

Rosa instantly turned to him. "What are you daring me to do?"

"Don't run out on me."

Rosa was suspicious. "Where are we going?"

"A place you've never been to before."

Rosa did not answer, but she watched carefully. She knew New York City very well, and when he turned down Water Street she was curious. This was one of the toughest parts of New York, and when he pulled up in front of a sign that said Water Street Mission, she suddenly exclaimed, "You're going to make me go to a religious service?"

"Not *make* you. I'm just *daring* you." He looked at her with a challenge in his eyes, and a smile ran over his lips.

Rosa wanted to get away, but she held her ground. "All right, but after the service *I* get to pick a place to go next."

"Fair enough. Come along."

As the two went in, he explained why he had wanted to come. "My uncle Barney was converted here. My father joined him, and from this place they went out to Africa as missionaries. I've always wanted to come here, but I've got an extra reason tonight."

"What reason?"

"It's a surprise."

Rosa was curious. She felt out of place as they moved into the meeting room and among a congregation made up mostly of derelicts. The room was large and quite bare, with unmatched chairs scattered about and a platform at one end. "Come on. Let's go down closer to the front."

"The back's good enough for me," Rosa said nervously. "You know I'm a Catholic, don't you?"

"Sure, I know that. So what?"

"We're not supposed to attend Protestant services."

"You want to leave?"

Rosa stared at Phil. Actually she did want to leave, but she was too stubborn not to go through with Phil's dare. "I'll sit here—but nothing anybody says is going to change me."

"That's a good open-minded attitude. Come on." Phil led her to the front, where he found a couple of seats. They got some strange looks, for both of them were well dressed, but a few people spoke to them as they sat down.

Rosa did not know what to expect. She had been taught that it was wrong for Catholics to attend Protestant services, and in all truth, she did not even attend Catholic services anymore, except when absolutely necessary. She was, however, a curious young woman, and when the service started, she tried to follow the songs from a battered paperback hymnbook that Phil held for her. She had never heard singing like this before, being accustomed to high-church music from a trained choir. The words of the songs did filter through to her and gave her a curious feeling.

When the song service ended, a short man with an angelic face got up and said, "Now, fellas, we're gonna have a good sermon tonight, so let's hear it for Ryan Kildare."

"Surprised?" Phil whispered to Rosa as he saw her suddenly lean back and open her eyes wide.

"He's a *preacher* now? I don't believe it."

"No, he's not a preacher. He just helps down here at the mission. He's actually practicing law again."

"Doesn't he know Leo Marx is going to kill him if he stays around here?"

"He's been told. Amelia told him, and then I told him. But he feels like this is the place God wants him to be."

Rosa listened then as Ryan got up to speak. She remembered him well, especially his dashing good looks. His red hair made a vivid splash of color, and his voice, as always, was clear and powerful.

"Tonight I don't have anything new for you," Ryan began. "If I had anything new, it wouldn't be any good. I knew one preacher who once said, 'If it's new—it ain't true.' That's not exactly accurate, but basically all I want to do tonight is tell you about how I came to know Jesus Christ as my Savior."

Kildare told his story well, and Rosa listened intently while trying to appear indifferent. She was aware that Phil was watching her out of the corner of his eye. The story Kildare told was so different from anything she had ever heard, she could not relate to it. He spoke of how he had gotten in trouble with a crime lord and had fled New York in fear of his life. He went into some detail of how he had gone downhill, until finally one night at a mission, somewhat like this one, he had heard that Jesus died for sinners.

"I'd always known that, but that particular night," Ryan said clearly, "I knew it was my time to meet God. There's no magic in it, my friends. Jesus died because we were sinners. He was not a sinner, but the Scriptures say, 'For he hath made him to be sin for us, who knew no sin.' So my sin was placed on Jesus on the cross. All my life I'd thought that if I did more good things than bad, I'd make it into heaven. But at that moment I knew it wasn't true. I realized I'd been risking my eternal life on a lie. Jesus need never have died if that were true."

As he went on to relate how he had finally surrendered his heart to Jesus and God had blessed him with a new birth, Rosa was caught up with his story.

Phil was watching her cautiously and saw that her lips were slightly parted. She had feigned indifference, but now he could tell that Ryan's testimony had touched something in her.

Ryan said, "If you need a savior, if you're on the bottom, Jesus is the answer. You come forward tonight, and we'll pray for you, and you'll find Christ is the most precious thing in this world."

Several men started going down the aisle to the front to give their lives to Jesus, but Rosa was shaken. "Let's go, Phil," she said. "I've kept my part of the bargain."

Keeping his promise, Phil said quietly, "All right, Rosa."

He accompanied her out of the building, waving at Ryan, who saw them and returned his wave.

Rosa did not say a word until they were in the car, and then she turned to him and said, "I didn't understand a word he was talking about."

"Didn't you?"

"No, I think it's all crazy."

Phil was wiser than to try to talk with her in this mood. He knew she had been shaken, so he simply said, "All right, you took my dare. Now do you want something to eat?"

"Yes, I'm famished. But I get to pick the place, remember?"

She directed Phil to a small Italian restaurant, where they sat in a quiet corner and ordered her choice of entrees. During the meal she tried more than once to shock him with stories of her escapades. Unable to provoke him, however, she finally became quiet. He spoke then of Africa and of what was happening there and of his desire to go back for a vacation.

"I wish I could go there too. I'd love to see all those animals."

"It is indeed a beautiful place. Maybe someday."

CHAPTER SIXTEEN

DOM STEPS IN

★　★　★　★

Thursday evening loomed before Phil, and he was surprised to find himself with nothing to do—and rather lonely. Loneliness was not something he had been troubled with for a long time. Ever since he had come to the States, he had been pouring himself into his work and studies.

Now he sat in his apartment, fidgety and restless. He'd moved out of the small room he'd been renting after he got his job in the DA's office. Back in Africa he would have picked up a gun and gone hunting across the wide plains. But here he found himself wanting company. He had met several attractive young women and had dated a few times, but nothing serious had ever come of it. It was as if he were married to his work. His job in the DA's office was even more time-consuming than his job working as an assistant to Lee Novak in his law-enforcement activities.

Getting to his feet, he strode to the small kitchenette and poured himself a cup of coffee from the blackened pot on the stove. Amelia made fun of him for having such a relic, but it was Phil's way to grow attached to things and prefer the old, less-effective equipment, rather than new. Setting the pot back on the stove, he sipped at the black brew, and his thoughts went to the possibilities that lay before him. He could go to a theater or,

222

perhaps, the movies. He considered visiting the Novaks, then remembered that Lee was out of town on official business. He thought, without meaning to, of Rosa Morino and just for a moment toyed with the idea of calling her. Then he rejected that idea. Though he'd been drawn to her for years, he knew this was not a relationship he should pursue. He worried about the young woman, knowing she still had strong feelings for him, but he did not want to nourish those feelings.

Finally, almost in desperation, Phil changed clothes and left the apartment. He headed to the club where Amelia was singing, and when he arrived there he glanced up at the name—The Black Cat. "It's bad luck all right," Phil muttered under his breath, but he entered and gave his hat to a young woman who smiled enticingly at him. He ignored her overtures and took a seat in the back of the club, away from the main floor and far enough away from the band so that the music would not deafen him. When the waiter asked him what he wanted, he ordered ginger ale. The young waiter leaned forward and said, "I can put something in that for you, sir."

"Just ginger ale."

"Why, of course, sir."

Phil sat back and after the waiter brought his drink, he sipped at it and waited for Amelia to come on stage. He tried to shut out the raucous music the band was playing, but without success. All around him the air was filled with loud laughter, which sometimes rose above the sound of the wailing saxophones. He cared nothing for the music. Songs such as "Sheik of Araby" and "Ma, He's Making Eyes at Me" were not Phil's idea of good music. One song in particular seemed to sum up the whole decade: "Ain't We Got Fun?" The women who gyrated on the floor could all have come out of the same machine—hair bobbed, skirts fringed, stockings rolled to expose the knees. They flung themselves around wildly, galvanized by the gin that their boyfriends had brought into the club in brown paper bags. When they were not dancing, they were puffing on cigarettes. Most of them had tamed their figures into a boyish appearance, the current fad. By bunching their stockings below the knees, they blatantly announced that they wore no corsets to hold them up.

Time passed slowly as Phil waited for Amelia's performance,

and more than one woman lingered as she passed by his table. There was nothing subtle about the looks he received. He kept his head down and stared into his glass until the lights finally dimmed and the spot hit center stage.

"And here she is, our own songbird, Miss Amelia Winslow. Let's hear it, folks!"

Phil straightened up then, and when Amelia came on, he could not help thinking how disappointed their parents would be at what she was doing with her life. Yet he himself had hope that she would one day stop running from God and let Him direct her life toward more worthwhile pursuits. At heart Phil felt she was throwing away everything that was good, but he couldn't say that to Amelia directly. Nor did he think she would even listen if he tried to reason with her. She already knew what her family believed.

Despite the unappealing surroundings, Phil found himself enjoying the performance. Something about Amelia's singing was immediate and reached out to her audience. All great singers have that quality, he realized. It was not just that she sang the right notes and made no mistakes, but especially during the slow tunes, she seemed to be speaking individually to each of her listeners. Some of the songs were wild—songs like "I'm Just Wild About Harry" and "Way Down Yonder in New Orleans"—and she belted them out to satisfy the customers. She had a strong, powerful voice and could project without effort.

But the raucous beat soon slowed down, and she began to sing the slow songs she did best, starting with the poignant "My Blue Heaven." After several slow songs and ballads, she reached the end of her performance, and Phil waited in anticipation, along with the crowd, for her now well-known closing.

"I want to close with the first song I ever learned. I can't remember how old I was. I don't think more than three or four. My mother sang it to me, and then I started singing with her, and so I'll sing it for you tonight. It's the favorite hymn of China."

She sang "Jesus Loves Me," and the simplicity of the words and the haunting echoes of her voice brought a silence over the Black Cat's audience. "Jesus loves me, this I know, for the Bible tells me so. . . ."

By the time the last note had faded away, the place was

entirely quiet. She smiled and said, "God bless you all" and turned to leave. The applause came then, and Phil knew by the audience's response that there was at least something in his sister that had not completely forgotten God, something in her that touched people deeply.

Amelia immediately made her way to his table, for despite the fact that he had sat in the back, she had spotted him. "I'm so glad to see you, Phil. Why didn't you tell me you were coming?"

"I didn't know myself. I was just sitting around with the mullygrubs and decided to pay you a visit."

He stood and pulled out the chair for her. She smiled at him as she sat. "The mullygrubs—what's that?"

"What most people call the blues, I guess."

"I didn't know you ever got that way."

"Don't fool yourself, sis. Everybody gets the mullygrubs at times."

Amelia leaned forward. She was wearing a gold lamé dress that was fancier than she liked, but the club owners had requested it. Her hair was swept back, and there was something strange in her eyes as she leaned forward. "Do you suppose Dad or Mom or Uncle Barney ever get depressed?"

"I expect so. They'd never tell us, though, would they?"

"No, they wouldn't. They never do talk about their problems." She laughed shortly. "I guess they're usually too busy with *our* problems."

The two sat there talking, and when their conversation turned to where the world was headed, Amelia shrugged and sipped at her drink. "I don't have strength enough left to handle all the problems of the world, Phil. I just hide my head in the sand like the ostriches do."

Phil smiled at her. "Well, we can't carry all the world's problems—and by the way, ostriches don't hide their heads in the sand."

"They don't? I always thought they did."

"No, they don't," Phil remarked. "Ostriches need help to digest their food. They have to swallow small rocks to help their gizzard do its job."

Amelia laughed. "Phil, you know more useless stuff than anyone I've ever met!"

Phil laughed at himself. "I guess you're right. These things stick in my head, and they're absolutely worthless. For instance, do you ever wonder why military uniforms have brass buttons on the sleeves?"

"No, I never did, but I do now."

"Well, while Napoleon's troops were slogging through Russia in the dead of winter, Napoleon got tired of seeing his soldiers wipe their noses with their sleeves. So he had brass buttons pulled from the jackets of the dead and sewn onto the sleeves. Made for pretty rough nose wiping, I would guess."

Amelia was amused and more impressed than she wanted to admit. Phil did indeed know more things than anybody she had ever known. Finally she asked, "Have you seen Rosa lately?"

"No, but I'm worried about her. I think she's wasting her life."

Amelia leaned back and eyed him carefully. "And you think I'm wasting mine."

"I think you're unhappy, Amelia." When she did not respond, he said, "I find myself missing Africa. Life was simple there."

Amelia thought for a moment, then said slowly, "You know, I thought I was unhappy there, but looking back, I can see it was a good time. All of my misery was of my own making. I guess that's always the way it is." She saw Phil suddenly twist in his chair and fix his eyes on someone. "What is it?" she asked, leaning forward.

Phil had just seen Leo Marx and his henchman, Jake Prado, enter the club and take a seat. He studied the men carefully and, without taking his eyes off of them, said to Amelia, "I made a promise to Ryan Kildare."

"What kind of a promise?"

"Those two are going to kill him if something doesn't happen. I told Ryan I'd make it a little harder for them." He got to his feet, alarming Amelia.

"Phillip, those two are dangerous!"

"So are rattlesnakes, but sometimes they need to be scotched." He walked away from her, his back straight, and without pausing, approached Marx and Prado. "Hello, Leo ... Jake. Kill anybody lately, Jake?"

Caught off balance, the two gangsters turned quickly, and Prado snarled, "Get outta my sight or I'll rub *you* out, Winslow!"

"You couldn't rub your own nose unless your boss told you

to." Phil stared hard at Leo Marx. The man's time in prison had increased the pallor of his face, making his eyes appear as dark and deadly as ever. Phil held his gaze for a moment and then said, "I've got a word for you, scum."

While in prison Marx had formed the habit of speaking without moving his lips much. "Whaddya want? You got nothin' on me."

"I'll get something if I have to. Just one little word, and I'm not going to say it twice, Marx. If anything happens to Ryan Kildare, I'll be *very* upset."

"That doesn't have anything to do with me."

"Liar! You'll try to kill him one day. But if you do, you're a dead man, Leo. You don't know what a pest I can make of myself, but let me tell you this. If anything happens to him, I'll personally see to it you go down."

Marx remained silent, and Phil, seeing that he was not going to respond, turned and walked away.

Prado muttered to his boss, "Wouldn't be a bad idea to blast him, Leo."

Leo Marx was evil, but he was not stupid. "Leave him alone, Jake. We'll fix him someday, but we'll do it smart."

"What about Kildare?"

"His time will come too, but don't touch it for a while."

When Phil returned to the table and sat down, Amelia did not speak for a moment. She had watched the encounter and had seen the hatred that emanated from the two thugs. "What'd you say to them, Phil?"

"I told them to leave Ryan alone."

"Do you think they will?"

"They'd better." Phil's words were clipped, and there was a hardness in his face Amelia had not seen before. She realized what a deadly game he was involved in. No man could be soft when dealing with vermin like Leo Marx. Her voice trembled as she said, "I wish you had some other job, Phil."

Phil reached over and took her hand, smiling slightly. "I wish the same for you, Amelia."

★   ★   ★   ★

Three days after Phil had visited her at the Black Cat, Amelia heard a knock at her apartment door. She opened the door and for a moment stood there confused. She had seen this young man before but could not remember when.

"Hello, Amelia. I'm Wes Winslow."

Instantly memory came flooding back. "Why, of course, Wes, come in. I'm so glad to see you." As the young man entered, she noted his rather shy manner, his lean but strong-looking figure. She had met him at a family reunion. He was the son of Aaron and Gail Winslow. Suddenly she remembered the wonderful article she had read in the *National Geographic*, with the story written by Emily, Wes's sister, and photographs by Wes himself. The whole family was very proud of the pair.

"Well, sit down and tell me what all you've been doing, Wes. Going around taking beautiful pictures, I suppose?"

Wes smiled shyly and ran his hand through his crisp hair. "Well, not exactly, cousin. I'm doing a story on New York with Robert Alden."

"Oh, you're moving up in the world!" Alden was a prominent writer who did pieces on different cities. He had recently won a Pulitzer for his book on Los Angeles.

"How did that all happen, Wes?"

"Oh, he saw my pictures in the *Geographic* and wrote me a letter. He asked me to work with him on his new book."

"It's going to be about New York?"

"That's right. He wants to get it all. The Jazz Age, the flaming youth, and even the criminals. Say, do you know any gangsters, Amelia?"

"Well, I've met a few. Would you like me to introduce you?"

Wes said, "No, that's not necessary, but I do want to get some pictures of the Water Street Mission. Your uncle found out what I was doing, and he asked me to document the mission in my photos."

"Uncle Barney?"

"Yes."

"I can surely take you there. When would you like to go?"

"Oh, anytime you're available. I know you're busy. Your uncle told me that you're a professional singer now."

"Well, I sing in saloons. If you can call that professional, I guess I am." She smiled wryly and shook her head. "As you can imagine, Wes, none of our family is in love with the idea of my being a nightclub singer."

Wes did not answer at once but finally said, "Well, you'll find your way. All of us have to do that. Would tonight be all right?"

"We can go this morning—right now—if you'd like. I'm singing tonight."

"That would be great, Amelia."

★   ★   ★   ★

Wes was loaded down with two bulky leather bags containing his cameras and equipment as he and Amelia walked into the Water Street Mission. He'd been looking forward to meeting the director of the mission, a tall man with kindly blue eyes named Roger Helms. Helms was interested in the project that Wes was doing with Alden and said, "I hope you can get us some coverage. We need all the help we can get to let the public know what we're doing."

"Well, I'll do all I can."

Helms turned to Amelia and said, "Your brother told me you know Ryan Kildare. Did you know that he now has an office right down the street?"

"No, I hadn't heard that."

"He's doing a good job. So many people in trouble who don't have the money for a lawyer. He stays pretty busy."

"You say his office is just down the street?"

"Yes, just on the other side of the newspaper office."

Amelia saw that Wes had already started taking pictures of the mission, and she stayed in the background. Wes Winslow was a shy young man, but with his camera in hand, he became almost aggressive. He took shot after shot of the workers and the building, but mostly of the people who came in for help. Finally, after an hour, she suggested, "Why don't you come back tonight when there's a meeting?"

"All right," Wes agreed. "But I think I'll stay around now for a while longer. Just to talk to the people."

"I'll leave you, then. I'll be back a little later, Wes."

"Okay, Amelia."

Leaving the mission, Amelia walked down the street thinking about Ryan Kildare. She had ambivalent thoughts about him. The man he used to be and the man he now was did not seem to match in her mind. Nonetheless, she was curious to find out what he was up to now. When she reached the newspaper office, she saw that huddled in just beside it was a small, narrow building with a hand-printed sign reading Ryan Kildare, Attorney. She hesitated for a moment and then walked inside the door. Moving down the hallway, she found his office and stepped inside without knocking. There was no outer office. It was simply one large room. On one side a few law books leaned against each other on a homemade shelf, and behind the battered pine desk sat Ryan. A woman with bleached-blond hair sat next to the desk.

Ryan at once stood up and greeted Amelia.

"Oh, I see you're busy."

"We're just finishing up," Ryan said, then turned to the woman next to him. "Ruby, don't worry. It'll be all right."

"Thanks, Ryan." The woman was cheaply dressed and wore too much rouge. There was a bold aggressiveness about her, and she flashed a familiar smile at Kildare. "Give me a call. Maybe I'll buy you dinner for helping me out."

"Sometime. You watch yourself, Ruby."

"Don't worry. I'll stay out of trouble, Counselor."

The woman left, trailing an odor of cheap perfume, and Ryan shook his head. "Too bad," he said. "It's good to see you, Amelia. Won't you sit down?"

"Oh, I just dropped by to see your office," Amelia said. "Is that one of your clients?"

"I'm afraid so. She's headed for real trouble."

The woman was obviously a prostitute, and Amelia wondered what would be "real" trouble for a woman of her occupation. She said, "I just brought one of my relatives down to the mission. His name is Wesley Winslow. He's a photographer, and he's working with the writer Robert Alden on a book about the city."

"I read the *Geographic* all the time. I remember that article he did with his sister. It was very good." He asked, "Are you on your way home?"

"Not yet. I'm going to go back to the mission after a while to see if Wes is done taking pictures."

"Time for a bite to eat? I'm starved."

Amelia hesitated, then said, "Yes, I believe I could eat."

"They make a mean ravioli across the street. The decor's not much, but the food's great."

"I love ravioli."

Amelia followed him across the street, dodging the traffic. When they entered the small café, a young man in the kitchen spotted them and called out through the serving window into the dining room, "Hey, Mr. Kildare!"

"How are you, Charlie?"

"Doing real good. You tell me what you want. I'll fix it."

"We'd like some of that extra-special ravioli you make." Ryan guided Amelia over to the pass-through window and introduced her to the cook. "This is Phil Winslow's sister, Charlie. Amelia, this is Charlie Zlinter. Phil helped Charlie out a lot."

"He sure did." Charlie smiled broadly and reached out to shake hands through the window. "You tell him hello from me, Miss Winslow."

"I'll do that, Charlie."

They sat down, and Amelia was soon engrossed in listening to Ryan Kildare tell her about the cases he handled now for the poor. Amelia was amazed at how much Ryan had changed. He seemed to be getting real joy out of working among these people who couldn't help themselves.

The meal came quickly, Charlie bringing it out himself on two platters. She smiled up at him and said, "This smells wonderful."

"Eat all you want, Miss Winslow. There's plenty more. Tell your brother to come by here sometime. It'll be on the house."

"I got Charlie a job here after he had his trouble," Ryan explained. "He's doing real well."

"You really like what you're doing, don't you, Ryan?"

"Yes, I do."

"Quite a bit different from what you used to do with Tony Morino, huh?"

Ryan shook his head and said quietly, "Yes, it certainly is." For some time he remained silent, and the two of them enjoyed their meal without speaking. Finally Ryan said, "I wasted a lot of my life, but I'm on the right track now. As strange as it may sound, the best thing that ever happened to me was to get in trouble and have my life threatened. I would never have found the Lord if that hadn't happened. I guess a lot of people find God like that when they hit bottom."

Amelia nodded thoughtfully. "I suppose that's probably true."

"I admire your brother so much. He's doing a hard job and a dangerous one."

"I've tried to get him to find a less dangerous occupation, but he won't listen to me."

"I guess he's a little bit stubborn—like you."

Amelia laughed. "You think that, do you?"

"Yes, I do."

"What about you?"

"I'm *firm*. You're *stubborn*."

Amelia laughed, then said nothing more as they finished their meal. They left the café and crossed the street to get back to Ryan's office, only to find the doorway blocked by two men. Instantly Ryan stepped in front of Amelia. "We don't want any trouble, fellas."

"Jush give ush a bit of money, and we'll let ya go," one man slurred. The two had obviously been drinking.

"Here, I'll do it," Amelia said quickly, pulling open her purse.

"No you won't." Ryan shook his head and stopped her. "You two move along, or you'll find yourselves in trouble."

The men laughed, and one of them, the larger of the two, stepped forward and put his hand on Ryan's chest. He shoved him backward, causing Ryan to stagger. "You wanna keep your health, don't ya?"

"Do you want to keep yours?"

At the strange voice beside them, the two men whirled to see a huge man. The bigger of the two flashed a conciliatory smile. "Hey there, Dom!"

"Be on your way, Fred, and take your friend with you."

"Why, sure, Dom, anything you shay."

With cold eyes, Dominic Costello watched the drunks disappear down the street, then turned to Ryan and smiled. "You two don't need to be roaming around this neighborhood."

"I guess not," Ryan said. "Thanks a lot, Dominic."

"No charge. Fact is, I came down lookin' for you, Amelia. I went to the mission, and they said you went lookin' for the counselor here."

"What is it, Dom?"

"Well, to tell the truth, I'm lookin' for both of you. Mr. Morino would like to see you, Ryan."

"What about?"

"Can't say."

Ryan shook his head, but when Dom urged him to comply with Morino's request, he agreed. "I'll go see him, but I can't imagine why."

"Thanks. I appreciate it. Say, Miss Amelia, why don't you come along?"

"Me? What for?"

"It's Miss Rosa. She's been real sick with the flu. Going crazy in the house. If you got nothin' else goin', it would be nice if you could come and visit her."

"I wouldn't mind, but I've got my cousin with me. He's down at the mission right now taking pictures."

"Bring him along."

Amelia thought of Wes's statement that he'd like to meet a real gangster, and an impulse seized her. "All right, we'll go get him."

"He ain't a cop or nothin', is he?"

"No, he's a professional photographer."

"Hey, that's good! Tony's boy, Jamie, is crazy for cameras and takin' pictures. Maybe he could talk to the kid."

The three walked the rest of the way to the mission and discovered that Wesley was finished. After introductions, they all piled into Dom's car, and Dom began speaking to Ryan in the front seat. Amelia leaned over to Wes in the backseat and whispered, "Well, you wanted to meet a gangster. You're going to meet the biggest in New York. Big Tony Morino."

"No fooling?"

"No fooling, Wes."

CHAPTER SEVENTEEN

AN AFTERNOON WITH THE MORINOS

★   ★   ★   ★

As Dom pulled the big sedan up in front of the Morino home, he turned to face Ryan and also glanced back toward Amelia and Wes. Clearing his throat nervously, he said, "It's been a while since you've seen Mr. Morino. He's a little bit different now." He hesitated, his words coming with difficulty. "His health ain't been too good lately, and he's had some . . . well, some business reverses."

Ryan smiled wryly. "Tony was never noted for his fine manners."

"Sure, sure. I'm just telling you he's a little bit edgy. More so than usual. Come on in. He'll be expecting us."

Getting out of the car, the three visitors followed Dominic, who held the front door open. When they were inside, he said, "Let me see if he's ready for you, Ryan." He walked swiftly down the hall. Opening a pair of double doors, he found Morino sitting behind his desk. "They're here, Mr. Morino."

"Who's *they*? I just sent you to get Kildare."

"Well, that's who I went for, but it turned out a little bit different. He was with Miss Amelia Winslow. You remember her?"

"I remember, all right. Did she come too?"

"I thought it might be a good idea if she'd visit with Miss Rosa. She needs some company, I think."

"Okay, okay."

"And that's not all. She had her cousin with her. He's a photographer, a young guy. I thought he might be some company for Jamie. You know how he's always crazy about anything to do with cameras and picture taking."

"Sure, sure, okay. Well, bring Kildare in here and send the other two off to be with the kids."

"You want me to stay in with you, Mr. Morino?"

"Yes."

Hurrying back down the hall, Dom said quickly, "He's ready for you, Ryan. Miss Amelia, Miss Rosa's room is up at the head of those stairs. Second door on the right. Just go on up. She'll be glad to see you. I think she's going stir crazy." Turning to Wes, he said, "Be nice if you could teach the kid something about cameras and picture taking. Nobody around here knows anything about it, and it's all Jamie thinks about."

Wes had been hoping to meet Big Tony Morino, but he quickly agreed, "Be glad to meet the young man."

"I'll show you to his room," Dom said.

★ ★ ★ ★

Amelia mounted the stairs and knocked on the door that Dom had indicated. She heard Rosa say, "Come in!" Opening the door, she stepped inside to the sounds of ragtime music coming from the Victrola in the corner. Rosa was sitting on the bed reading a ladies' magazine, dressed in a pair of silk pajamas and matching robe. They were a light orchid and looked very good on the young woman, despite her ill appearance.

"I heard you were sick, Rosa. I came to visit."

"Who told you?"

"We ran into Dom downtown. Your dad wanted to speak to Mr. Kildare, so I thought I'd come along to visit with you, if you don't mind."

"Come on in." Rosa got up and went over to her Victrola,

lifted the arm off the record, then went back and sat on the edge of the bed. Her face was flushed and her hair somewhat awry. "I feel rotten," she announced gloomily.

"You don't look like you feel very well. How long have you been sick?"

Amelia sat down in a winged-back chair by the bed and listened as the girl spoke. Then without warning, Rosa sneezed explosively.

"God bless you," Amelia said.

Rosa found a handkerchief and blew her nose. She stared gloomily at Amelia. "Why do people always say that when you sneeze? It doesn't make any sense."

"Well, you're in luck today. As a matter of fact, I just happen to know why we say that."

Rosa stared at her suspiciously. "Why?"

"At one time it was thought that a sneeze was caused by demons either leaving the body or coming in. So when people sneezed, calling for God's blessing was theoretically protecting the sneezer from harm."

"How in the world would you know a thing like that?"

Amelia laughed and shook her head. "My brother is a walking encyclopedia. He reads all the time and never forgets anything. He told me about it."

"That must be awful to have your head so cluttered up with facts."

"Phil says it's like a closet you've stuffed full. Sometimes he gets frantic when he knows that he knows something, but he can't sort it out."

"What other kind of stuff did he tell you?"

"Oh, I don't know. Let's see. Did you know that when you squoosh a mosquito you're killing a mother?"

"A mother? You're kidding."

"No. According to Phil, only females bite, and they do it to get blood to nourish their young."

"What do the boy mosquitoes eat?"

"Just plant nectar and water. There, now you'll be able to explain that the next time the subject comes up."

Rosa finally smiled. It was good to have company after four days of being cooped up in her room. She had listened to her gramophone records until she was sick of all of them. She listened with interest as Amelia told her stories about her travels on the road and about meeting a few celebrities. She mentioned meeting Douglas Fairbanks and then added, "I had quite a crush on him when I was about twelve or so."

Rosa did not speak for a moment. "I had a crush on Phil when I was younger."

Amelia had been very much aware of this, for Rosa was not particularly adept at hiding her feelings. She could also see that her crush was still very much alive. Rosa seemed embarrassed, so Amelia quickly said, "You know, when I was a teenager, I fell madly in love with my science teacher. Oh, did I ever dream about him!" She smiled at the memory. "I was going to become a great scientist like Madame Curie. He would fall in love with me. Then we'd marry and find cures for all sorts of diseases." The memory amused her. "I know those feelings are painful when you have them, but you'll look back on them and feel differently."

"What happened to him—the science teacher, I mean? Did you fall out of love with him?"

"Oh, I found out he had false teeth!"

This delighted Rosa. "Tell me some more about when you and Phil were growing up in Africa."

Willingly, Amelia spoke for some time about her childhood and saw that Rosa was fascinated by her stories.

Rosa finally said, "I went to the mission once, the one where Ryan preaches sometimes."

"Did you? How did you like it?"

Rosa glanced down. "It scared me."

"Scared you? What's there to be afraid of?"

"He talked about things I've never heard of. I've been worried ever since."

"What sort of things did he say that bothered you?"

"Well, he talked about Jesus a lot. I'm not used to that. I don't think about Jesus much. I guess I think more about Mary."

"Mary was a wonderful woman and used by God to bring Jesus into the world. But you know the Bible says that there is only one mediator between God and man—and that's Jesus."

"Mediator? What's that?"

"It's someone who stands between two people. For instance, if I wanted you to get your father to do something, I might get you to ask him for me. And that would make you a mediator."

Rosa was quick to understand. "So if we pray to Jesus, he talks to God for us?"

"Well, yes . . . something like that. He's the one who died for our sins, so He can stand before God for us." Amelia felt uneasy trying to explain spiritual matters to the young girl. She knew all the words from her Christian upbringing, but she also knew that her life didn't reflect those words. She began to wish that Phil were here in her place. He'd know all the right things to say.

Rosa jumped up and went over to the dresser. Pulling open a drawer, she pulled out a book and came back. "This is what Phil gave me for Christmas a few years ago."

"Why, that's his old Bible!"

"Yes, he wrote everywhere in it. Look, almost every page."

"I remember this Bible. Phil was always writing in it. Have you been reading it?"

"Well, I read what he wrote more than I read the Bible. It's so interesting. Let me show you." She thumbed through the pages and read, "I killed a leopard today. He was the one that has been breaking into the compound. I was so proud of myself, but I know God helped me get him with one shot." She looked up and said, "Isn't that something?"

"I remember that day. Leopards are very dangerous in Africa." Amelia took the book and looked at the page Rosa indicated. It was in the margin next to Psalm Ninety-one, which speaks of God's protection. She read some of the verses aloud:

"He that dwelleth in the secret place of the most High shall abide under the shadow of the Almighty. I will say of the Lord, He is my refuge and my fortress: my God; in him will I trust. . . . There shall no evil befall thee. . . . Thou shalt tread upon the lion and adder. . . ."

Amelia quietly handed the Bible back to Rosa, who held it in her hands and said bluntly, "I guess I'm worried about hell. Do you ever worry about that?"

Amelia, for one instant, could not answer. Then she said carefully, "I have to be honest with you, Rosa. My parents are wonderful Christians and so is Phil, but I'm . . . well, Phil says I'm running away from God. And maybe I am."

Rosa stared at the young woman in amazement. "Are you? Why would you do that?"

Amelia thought for a minute. "Maybe because I think God wants me to do some things I don't want to do. I'm not really sure."

Rosa considered that and sighed. "I guess I don't want to do things people want me to either—mostly my parents."

Amelia was anxious to change the subject. "I'll tell you what, Rosa. As soon as you get well, why don't you and I spend some time together? There are lots of things to see in New York that I haven't seen. I'll bet you could show them to me. I've never been to the Statue of Liberty."

"Oh, I have! It's fun!" Rosa's face brightened, and she said, "Could we really do that?"

"Sure we could."

★   ★   ★   ★

While Rosa and Amelia were talking, Dom had taken Wes to Jamie's room on the first floor. Dom knocked on the door. "Hey, Jamie, I want you to meet somebody."

Wes stepped inside the door and found himself in an extremely large bedroom. It was cluttered with the things a sixteen-year-old boy would enjoy—mostly model cars and airplanes that he'd made. The boy was sitting on the bed tinkering with a model.

Wes noted that Jamie was not tall. It appeared he would probably be stocky when he grew up. He had dark eyes, dark eyebrows, and hair as black as night.

Dominic went on with his introduction. "This is Wes Winslow, Jamie. He's a famous photographer. Don't you keep all the *National Geographic*s?"

"Yeah—I've got 'em from years back."

"Well, get Mr. Winslow here to show you the pictures he took down in the jungle somewhere. He's got all kinds of cameras. Thought you two might get along."

Jamie did not move, so Wes stepped forward with a smile and put out his hand. "I'm glad to know you, Jamie. I hear you're interested in photography."

Jamie did not notice that Dominic had slipped out the door. "Yes," he said. "So you took pictures for the *National Geographic*?"

"Yes, my sister and I made a trip to the Amazon a few years ago and photographed a primitive tribe there—the Guapi."

"Wait a minute. I think I've got that issue here somewhere!"

Jamie quickly shuffled through a stack of magazines and found one with a fierce-looking tribesman holding a long spear on the cover, entitled, "The Guapi—Lost Tribe of the Amazon." He brought it over to the table. "Is this it?"

"Sure is. I've about worn out my copy. I was so proud to have one of my pictures selected for the front cover, I showed it to everyone I knew!"

The two sat down at a table, and Jamie fired question after question at Wes. Finally Wes said, "I've got some of my equipment out in the car. Maybe you'd like to see it."

"Boy, would I!"

"Well, come on down and help me bring it up."

Thirty minutes later the two were sitting in the middle of the floor with the photographic equipment all about them. Wes could hardly answer the questions as rapidly as Jamie could ask them. He finally took a deep breath and said, "Whoa, Jamie, you can ask more questions in a minute than I could answer in an hour. You really like cameras, don't you?"

"Yes, more than anything else." Jamie hesitated, then asked shyly, "You want to see some of *my* pictures?"

"I sure do."

For the next twenty minutes Wes examined the boy's photographs. Apparently he had unlimited funds for film and even had the means to develop and enlarge his own. "Why, these are great, Jamie! Look at this one. How did you get so close to that squirrel?"

"I built a blind and fed him for a long time. I was hiding there when he came to get his food, and I snapped the picture."

"Well, you've got the light just right."

Jamie's face glowed. "I want to be a photographer when I grow up. Do you think I could?"

"I don't see why not."

"What are you working on now, Mr. Winslow?"

"Why don't you just call me Wes? I'd like that." He grinned at Jamie. "Well, right now I'm working with a writer on a book about New York City." He went on to explain that he wanted to include segments on every part of New York and people of every kind.

Jamie's face sobered and he stared at Wes. "You came here because my dad's a gangster, didn't you?"

"Why, no such thing!" Wes protested. "I was with my cousin Amelia when Dom came to get Mr. Kildare. We just came along with him."

"You didn't know my dad was a gangster?"

Wes considered lying, then abandoned that idea. "I've heard of your father, of course. Almost everyone has."

Jamie dropped his head and was silent. When he finally looked up, his eyes reflected the shame he felt. "I wish he would do something else. It's wrong what he does. Everybody knows it."

"Have you ever talked to him about it?"

"No. What would I say? He wouldn't quit just because I asked him to."

Wes felt a wave of sympathy for the boy. "Maybe he will change. In the meantime, you can be your own man. You don't have to do what your father does."

"I'm not going to," Jamie said quickly.

Wes considered the boy, then said, "I'll tell you what. Tomorrow I'm going up on top of a half-finished skyscraper. Maybe you could come with me. Nothing but steel up there. To tell the truth," he said ruefully, "I'm not too fond of getting up in high places, but I want to take some pictures of the workers."

"Boy, that ought to be fun!"

"You know the workers on high steel are almost all Mohawk Indians?"

"Real Indians?"

"Real Indians. Nobody knows why, but they have a great sense of balance and no fear of heights. Almost all the steelworkers on the skyscrapers are Mohawks. Maybe you could bring your camera and get some pictures too."

"Gosh, could I really? I'd give anything to go."

"Well, you'll have to get your father's permission. I couldn't take you otherwise."

"I'll go ask him right now!"

★ ★ ★ ★

When Ryan had first shaken hands with Tony Morino, he was shocked at how the big man had aged. He knew his health had been bad, but his condition was apparently more serious than he'd thought. He let none of this show on his face but smiled and said, "Good to see you again, Mr. Morino."

Tony studied the younger man and waved him to a chair. "Sit down, Kildare. Tell me what you've been doing."

"Nothing very exciting, I'm afraid."

"I was surprised when you came back to town."

"Well, my mother was dying, and she wanted to spend what few days she had left here with me, so I really didn't have much choice."

Tony stared at him. "Is she still living?"

"No, she died a couple months ago."

"I wish I'd known," Tony said regretfully. "I could've sent flowers."

"I should have told you. My fault. How are you feeling, Tony?"

"Well, you can see. The doc says my heart's not what it ought to be. He's always trying to get me to eat less and exercise."

"Not a bad idea."

"Like I'm gonna do that!" Tony laughed and picked up a glass of amber fluid and drained it. "He also told me to avoid stress. That's a laugh, ain't it? How am I gonna avoid stress in my business?"

Ryan turned his head slightly to one side, and a small smile tweaked the corners of his lips upward. "That would be pretty hard for a man in your position, I'd say. How's your family?"

"The kids are driving me crazy, Ryan, especially Rosa. She's one of those flappers. Wears her dresses halfway up to her hips, goes out all hours of the night, and pays no attention to me."

"What about your son?"

"Well, he's a little better, but he's only sixteen. I'm afraid he'll go the same way."

"Maybe not. Did Dom tell you about Amelia's cousin?"

"Yeah, he says he's a photographer. Well, the kid's nuts about that. I've spent a pretty penny buying film and cameras for him. We even turned a bathroom upstairs into a darkroom for him."

"That's a good thing for him to be involved with, Tony."

"Yeah, but you can't get rich takin' pictures."

Ryan did not answer but sat quietly in the chair. He listened as Tony continued talking, going back once again to Rosa. "She comes in drunk and then she throws it up to me that I sell liquor. What am I going to do?"

Ryan Kildare had no answer for that, of course—at least not any that Tony Morino would have accepted. He waited, and Tony began talking about the old days when things were different. He seemed to have forgotten why he had sent for Ryan, but finally he said directly, "I want you to come back and be my lawyer again."

"I'm sorry, Mr. Morino. I thought that might be what you wanted, but I can't do it."

Morino stared at the younger man. "Why not?"

"I've got other things on the fire right now."

"Yeah, I know. Dom told me. You're not makin' any money at it, though."

"No, I'm not, but I'm doing what I want to do. I'm helping some people who maybe wouldn't get help otherwise."

"What about Leo Marx? You don't think he's forgotten you, do you?"

"I don't expect he has."

"He'll get you one day, Kildare, you can believe that. Now, if you come to work for me, I can give you some protection. Leo knows if he hits me or any of my guys, I hit him."

"Well, that's good of you to offer, but I've already got some protection."

"Oh yeah? Who's that?"

"I like to think that it's God. The Lord is my Shepherd. Though I walk through the valley of the shadow of death, I will fear no evil. I'm trusting in the Lord to take care of me."

Tony stared at Ryan, then shook his head. "I heard you got

religion, Kildare. That's okay. I ain't knockin' it, but it seems to me that we need each other—"

The door opened suddenly, and Jamie came bounding in. "Hey, Dad, Mr. Winslow says I can go with him while he takes pictures tomorrow if it's okay with you."

"What's all this?" Tony said.

"Oh, this is Wes Winslow, Amelia's cousin," Ryan said quickly. "He's a fine professional photographer. It would be a good experience for Jamie to go with him."

Tony Morino was suspicious of almost everyone. He questioned Wes for some fifteen minutes and finally got it through his head what the plans were for tomorrow. "You mean to tell me you're going up on top of one of those unfinished steel buildings? Why, I can't let my son go up there!"

"That's up to you, Mr. Morino. I don't think there'll really be any danger. There are platforms built, and believe me, I won't get within fifty feet of the edge. But he's your son."

"Please, Dad, let me go!"

Tony Morino looked at the boy and suddenly felt a longing to do something right. "All right, son, but I'll have to send Dom along, you understand."

"That's fine," Wes said quickly. "Be glad to have him."

★   ★   ★   ★

As Dom stopped the car and let the trio out, he said, "I'll bring the kid wherever you say tomorrow, Mr. Winslow. Mr. Morino says to take you anywhere you need to go. I'm really glad you're doing it for the kid. He needs somebody like you."

"It'll be fun, Dom. Do you like high places?"

"I get sick to my stomach when I step up on a curb, but I'll go."

"I'm not too crazy about getting up on those things myself, but that's where you get the best pictures."

After they got out of the car, Wes said good-bye and went to his hotel. Ryan turned to Amelia and asked about Rosa.

"She's all right. Almost over her sickness, but she's a very unhappy young woman."

"So is the boy, I understand, from what Wes says. He's ashamed of his father."

"I think the whole family is. That must hurt Tony pretty bad."

"I would think so."

Amelia had wanted to ask one question ever since leaving the Morino estate, and now she did. "I'd guess that Tony wants you to go back to work for him. Am I right?"

"Yes, that's right."

"Will you do it?"

"No."

Amelia was suddenly aware of a strength in Ryan that had not been there when they had first met. She turned to face him. "I remember the night you left. You said a woman ought to know when a man loved her."

"That's what I said."

"I assume you've gotten over it by now."

"No."

"No? Just no? Can't you say any more than one word?"

"I don't think love really changes, Amelia."

"Of course it does. People change."

"I don't agree."

"Then you're a fool."

"Quite possibly I am, but Shakespeare says, 'Love's not time's fool, though rosy lips and cheeks within his bending sickle's compass come.'"

"What does that mean?"

"It means when a man loves a woman, he doesn't love her for her outward beauty but for something else. Something inside."

Amelia glanced at him skeptically. "You wouldn't believe how many lines I've heard since I came to New York. Men have tried everything to get to me."

"This is no line, Amelia." He stepped forward, and before she could move away, he put his arms around her and pulled her close. "I kissed you once," he said, "and I'm about to do it again."

Amelia should have protested, but she was curious. She remained still in his arms and let his lips meet hers. She felt a rush of pleasure at his embrace as he held her tighter, his own feelings for her obvious in the warmth of his touch. He stepped back and looked deeply into her eyes, not speaking but asking in his expression if she did not indeed return his love.

She was quick to respond to his unspoken question, pushing him away and turning from his gaze. "This means nothing, Ryan."

"I'll tell you something, Amelia," he said, cupping her face in his hands and turning her to look at him again. "I still love you. I love the woman that's in you potentially . . . who you can be . . . and *will* be someday."

"It'll never happen, Ryan," she said, pulling out of his grasp. "Leave me alone." She turned quickly and walked away, not looking back. His kiss had disturbed her terribly, and she knew she would not forget it anytime soon. She remembered the time they had been together before—before he had disappeared and returned a changed man. Back then he'd had the power to stir her, and now, to her dismay, she found that he still did. She hated it!

CHAPTER EIGHTEEN

THE TRAP

★ ★ ★ ★

The year 1927 was a mixture of the sublime and the ridiculous in America. Charles Lindbergh became the first person to cross the Atlantic alone by airplane. His audacious endeavor grabbed the world's attention as no event had done since the signing of the Armistice in 1918. The twenty-five-year-old had found a company to build a plane to his own specifications. The Spirit of St. Louis was built in a hurry, and Lindbergh became an international hero upon completion of his thirty-six-hundred-mile trip.

At the other end of the celebrity spectrum, Mae West, the burlesque entertainer with the overblown figure, became the antithesis of the chic, boyish flapper of the twenties. She wrote and starred in a play blatantly entitled *Sex* and was imprisoned for ten days for indecency, but only after giving three hundred seventy-five performances.

The silent motion picture met an abrupt end in 1927 as the words uttered by Al Jolson in the film *The Jazz Singer* changed the motion-picture industry forever. Every producer rushed at once into the production of movies that had sound.

In sports it was the year of the famous "long count" bout in which Gene Tunny was flattened by a vicious blow from Jack

Dempsey. Then the match was decided on a mere technicality. Dempsey failed to retreat to a neutral corner, giving Tunny time to recover and win the battle.

Stan Laurel and Oliver Hardy first appeared on the silver screen, as did Clara Bow, the famous "It" girl. This movie star appeared in the 1927 movie entitled *It*, meaning sex appeal. She embodied the flapper ideal: bobbed and tousled hair, slim hips, bee-stung mouth, long beaded necklaces, and a voracious appetite for scandal.

In the world of industry, Henry Ford finally admitted that the Model T was outdated and closed his plant to retool for the Model A, which would prove to do even better. In technology, X rays were used for the first time, and the iron lung was invented, which for a time was a polio victim's only hope of survival. In communications, the first transatlantic telephone call was made in January 1927.

On the political scene, President Coolidge announced he would not run for president in 1928. Massachusetts became the first state to require automobile insurance. And the Supreme Court ruled illegal income as taxable, allowing them to demand payment from the likes of Al Capone, whose yearly income was $105 million, the largest gross private income to date for an American citizen.

And so, with the world ever changing, the year 1927 moved forward, filled with the excitement of the times. Yet no one realized what a dark and ominous future lay ahead. In the final year of the decade a stock market crash would shake America to its foundation. Very few, however, in the year 1927 ever dreamed that such a reversal of America's fortune was looming on the horizon.

★　★　★　★

Cigar smoke filled the air, and the raw smell of alcohol laced the room. Five men were seated around a table, all of them a part of Leo Marx's organization. He had divided his territory in New York and assigned a lieutenant to each section. All of these men had come up through the ranks of organized crime until they were now at the very pinnacle of their success.

Marx looked around briefly, sipped from his whiskey glass, then began to lay out his plans.

"All right, here's the way it'll play out. We're going to take Big Tony and his whole organization out."

Jake Prado, always right beside Marx, looked up. His eyes usually looked cold and almost dead, but now there appeared a slight glitter in them. "That'll suit me. He needs to be taken down."

Sitting across from Marx, a short, stocky man with a bullish face and a crop of slick black hair shook his head. "I don't know, Leo. That's a big chunk to bite off."

"What's the matter, Frank, you haven't got the stomach for it?"

Frank Delano controlled the Lower East Side. He had killed men often, and no one ever accused him of being afraid. He put his strange light-gray eyes on Prado and whispered, "You want to find out if I'm afraid, Jake?"

"All right, we can't be fightin' among ourselves, Frank. I know it's going to be tough, but Morino's not what he was. We're gonna start pushing. I want you all to start taking bigger bites out of his territory. Let's hit some of his deliveries too. We take what we can and ruin the rest of it."

A small, dapper man wearing an immaculate striped suit smoothed his mustache down and murmured in a voice soft as a summer breeze, "That may bring on a war, Leo."

"It's a war we'll win," Leo said. "He's got nobody in the number two spot."

"What about Dominic?"

"He's just an errand boy. Don't worry about him. When Tony goes down"—Leo exposed his teeth in a meaningless grin—"we'll take it all."

★ ★ ★ ★

Almost at the exact moment that Leo was instructing his men to open what amounted to a gang war throughout the city, Lee Novak was meeting with his crew of agents to lay out special plans from top government officials to turn up the heat on New York's criminal gangs. He'd been given almost unlimited authority to do whatever was necessary to bring them down.

War had been declared on all sides.

★　★　★　★

Jamie Morino was talking as fast as he possibly could. He was showing Rosa the new camera Wes Winslow had helped him buy, and his eyes shone like stars. "He's going to teach me how to use it. I'm going to meet him over at City Hall right now to take pictures. Why don't you come along, sis?" Jamie said. "I can get some pictures of you next to some big shots."

Rosa laughed. "All right, I think I will."

Dom Costello drove the two to City Hall, and on the way the big man listened indulgently as James rattled on about the camera. Dom winked at Rosa, who was sitting in the front seat beside him, and she winked back. "Maybe you'll get a chance to see your old boyfriend," he teased her.

Rosa instantly glared at him. "What boyfriend?"

"Oh, come on, you were pretty sweet on Phil Winslow at one time."

"That was a long time ago. I'm over that now."

Dom saw the defensiveness in the young woman and shrugged his shoulders, saying no more.

When they arrived at City Hall, Jamie shouted, "Look, there's Wes over there! Stop the car, Dom!"

"Wait a minute! Don't go jumping out. You'll kill yourself."

Jamie, however, ignored the bodyguard's instructions, hopping out as soon as the car stopped and running across the street to greet Wes.

"Jamie's found a good friend there," Dom said to Rosa.

"Yes, I guess it's been good for him," Rosa agreed. "He didn't have anybody to talk with."

"Well, I'll park the car. Don't know how long this will take. I s'pose he'll want to take a picture of everybody in the building."

Despite Rosa's denial of her feelings for Phil Winslow, she had actually come along to City Hall in the hope of seeing him.

Now that he worked for the DA, she knew he frequented the courtrooms at City Hall. She moved quickly to where her brother and Wes were talking, and when Wes greeted her, she smiled at him.

"Come along, Rosa," Wes said. "I'm going to take some pictures of the mayor first. Maybe I can take one of you shaking his hand."

"He'd never shake hands with anybody named Morino," Rosa said bitterly.

Wes blinked with surprise and then saw a look of embarrassment on Jamie's face. Quickly he covered by saying, "Well, there's lots of things to take pictures of. Come on, we'll find some of them."

Rosa enjoyed her trip out after her bout with the flu had kept her in for so long. April had brought refreshingly warm weather and spring flowers. The courthouse was warm inside but not overly so. She followed Wes and Jamie around from room to room, when suddenly her breath caught at seeing Phil step out of an office and start down the hall.

"Phil!" she called out and headed toward him. She saw Phil turn, and at that moment a young woman came out of the same room he had appeared from. She reached up and took Phil's arm and smiled at him in a familiar way. Rosa recognized her at once. It was Mary Emmets, the debutante of the year. Her father was a wealthy speculator with a seat on the stock market, and the society papers considered her the catch of the moment. She was not a tall woman but well shaped, and she held on to Phil with a proprietary air.

Phil spotted Rosa just then as she approached the pair. "Oh, Miss Emmets," he said, "I'd like you to meet Miss Rosa Morino."

Mary Emmets stared at Rosa and did not speak for a moment. "I'm glad to meet you," she said coldly.

Rosa knew that look. She was certain the woman had recognized the name and was disgusted. She saw Mary's hand tighten on Phil's arm, then heard her saying, "We'd better hurry, Phil, or we'll be late."

Phil lingered for a moment, although the young woman was tugging at his arm. "Will you be around later, Rosa? I'd like to talk to you."

"No, I'm leaving now."

Rosa had not intended to leave just then, but the frigid look in the socialite's eyes infuriated her. She and Jamie were both hurt by what their father was, but rarely did she meet such blatant rejection. She turned and left the building at once.

Dom was leaning against the car talking with two other men when Rosa walked up to him. "Hey, where's Jamie?" he asked.

"He's staying awhile. I'm leaving, Dom."

"You can't do that!"

"Oh yeah? Watch me!"

Rosa leaned into the street to wave down a passing cab. The driver pulled right over, and she climbed in, saying, "Take me to Twenty-second Street."

Twenty minutes later she was sitting in a speakeasy, already tipsy from too many drinks. She had come here before but never alone, and it was only a few moments before a man came over to her and leered at her. "You all alone?"

"Yes," she said.

"Maybe you'd like a little company."

"Maybe I would. . . ."

★   ★   ★   ★

Leo Marx was unhappy. His plan had not worked, for although his lieutenants had followed his orders to put the pressure on Big Tony Morino's operation, Morino's men were tough. As a matter of fact, they had hurt Marx worse than he had hurt them!

Marx had withdrawn for two days after the latest sharp battle between the two forces. He had drunk more than usual and had become obsessed with his losses. Morino wasn't his only problem. Lee Novak's federal agents had hit them hard. Several of his key men were in jail, and he knew that more would follow unless something was done. Marx was not a heavy drinker, so the liquor affected him more than it would another man. After mulling over the situation, he finally sent for Jake Prado.

"Jake, it's not Tony that's hurtin' us. We can take care of him. It's that agent Lee Novak."

"Yeah, I know. It's always been Novak."

"We're just not safe with guys like that around. We got to set 'im back, Jake."

Prado was as tough as a man could be and as unfeeling. He was shrewd, however, and shook his head doubtfully. "I don't know about that. Takin' out anybody that even looks like a cop is dangerous. You know how it stirs 'em up."

"That's right. We hit 'im, but it's got to look like somebody else did it. As a matter of fact, it's got to look like it's some of Big Tony's guys."

Prado stared at his boss. "How would you do that? You tell me."

"All right. Here's the way it'll play out. We can find out about the next big delivery that Morino's going to make. As soon as we find out, we set him up with Novak."

"We blow the whistle on him?"

"That's right. And when Novak's men close in, they'll think they've got a lead pipe cinch, but they won't because you'll be there, Jake, and every man we got. When Novak's men move in to make the arrest, you blast 'em. Everybody will think it's Morino because that's who they're gonna nail. With Novak and his crew out of the way," he grinned, "we can easily take care of Morino before the feds have a chance to train and send in fresh recruits. Set it up, Jake. If we do this right, we're home free. We'll hurt Big Tony, and we'll take the feds out at the same time. Don't spare the ammunition."

"Right, boss, I'll take care of it."

The trap set by Leo Marx took place exactly a week after Prado's conversation with Marx. Prado had arranged for an informant to leak the information to Lee Novak that the biggest shipment of illegal alcohol ever moved in the city would be coming in. Then Prado had hired enough gunmen to wipe out both Morino's men and Lee Novak's crew of special agents.

★　★　★　★

Lee Novak was elated. Phil had never seen him so excited. "Are you sure this information's right, Lee? It sounds too easy."

Lee had contacted Phil to alert him as to what was going down shortly. He wanted the DA's office to be prepared to handle all the indictments that would be pouring in after his special agents captured the city's biggest warlords.

"We've got it straight, and we've checked on it. It's coming in all right. Five big trucks. We'll pin them down, and that'll be the end of that. This'll put Morino out of business for good."

Phil was naturally cautious and concerned for the safety of Lee and his men. He shook his head. "I don't know, Lee. I hope it works."

"It'll work all right," Lee said confidently. "I have the utmost trust in my men."

★   ★   ★   ★

Dom Costello was accustomed to organizing the shipments of bootleg alcohol, but this was the biggest haul yet. He had worked hard on it to be sure nothing went wrong, and now he felt fairly comfortable. He was just getting ready to leave to receive the shipment when he got a call from a friend of his, a saloonkeeper. "Hey, Dom, this is Chick."

"What do you want, Chick? I'm busy."

"You'd better look into this. You know your boss's daughter, Rosa? She's down here, and she's drunk, and there's a guy here that means her no good."

"She's at your place?"

"Yeah. I tried to get her to go home, Dom, but she wouldn't do it. I'd feel better if you came for her."

"Okay, I'll pick her up." Dom slammed the receiver down and shook his head angrily. He was upset with Rosa. But he still cared for the girl a great deal and knew he had to do something.

Dom ran outside, got into his car, and drove as fast he dared to Chick's place. It took him fifteen minutes, and when he got inside he saw Rosa seated at a table. Across from her was a smooth-looking middle-aged man whose hand was on her knee. Dom walked over, reached down and grabbed the man by the neck, then jerked him to his feet. "Beat it," he said, "or I'll kill you."

Rosa's admirer did not argue. He turned pale, swallowed hard, and made an almost magical exit.

"Come on, Rosa. You need to go home."

"I'm having a good time," Rosa said drunkenly.

Dom wasn't about to argue. Reaching down, he grabbed her arm and lifted her up. "You're going home," he said harshly. "Deal with it!"

Rosa resisted him, but it was useless. Dom's strength was proverbial, and when he put her in the car, she slumped down.

Getting back into the driver's seat, Dom threaded his way through the traffic. It was late now, almost midnight. He thought about taking Rosa home but decided there wasn't time. The shipment was due at an old warehouse any minute, and he needed to be there. He parked the car a block away and said to Rosa, "You wait here. And don't you dare think about getting out of this car!"

"Where you going?"

"A little business. You stay put."

Dom walked quickly down the street. He saw that the trucks were already pulling into the warehouse. He hurried forward, and just as he reached the entrance, he heard light footsteps behind him. Turning quickly, Dom saw that Rosa had followed him. She was unsteady on her feet, and he furiously shook his head. "Rosa—" he started, but then there was a sudden shout and a shot rang out.

Instantly Dom ran toward Rosa and pulled her toward the shelter of the doorway.

From everywhere, it seemed then, shots were ringing out. Dom gasped, "We've been set up!" He jumped behind the doorframe for protection and set Rosa down behind him. Then he pulled his gun, knowing full well it was Leo Marx's men. He shot at a shadowy figure and drew fire in return. The ferocity of the gun battle was terrible, worse than anything he had ever experienced.

Rosa, terrified, jumped up and began running away.

"Rosa, get back here! Get down!"

But Rosa never heard Dom's voice in the chaos that filled her ears.

★ ★ ★ ★

Phil had insisted on going along with Lee on this raid. Though it was not standard protocol for someone from the DA's office to attend a raid, in this case he couldn't stay away. Lee Novak was a close friend as well as a collaborator in the law's pursuit of New York's worst thugs. The two men had different jobs in the process now—Lee on the streets making arrests and Phil prosecuting the criminals in court—but their jobs were two sides of the same coin. They shared the common goal of cleaning up the city to make it safe for its law-abiding citizens. This one raid could be the turning point they'd all been waiting for.

Lee had not wanted Phil to come, but since he was there anyway, he ordered him to stay out of sight at a safe distance and keep down. So Phil hunkered down behind a car across the street, watching as Novak and his men closed in. So far it had gone according to plan, but now as they moved toward the building, attempting to surround it, rifle fire erupted.

"Behind us!" Lee shouted at his men. "Over there on the roof!"

Phil turned to see the blinking fire of rifles, and then he yelled, "Lee, take cover!"

Lee shouted orders to his agents. "Get everybody out of here! Pull the men back!" He hobbled across the street with blood streaming from his legs. He was within a few feet of the car where Phil was hiding when he was driven to his knees.

"Lee, are you hurt bad?"

Novak ignored Phil and continued shouting orders to his agents. Phil kept his head down as Lee dragged himself behind the car and fired at every target he saw.

Phil heard the dying groans of men fallen in the street in the midst of the gun battle, and he kept his head down. But at a slight lull in the shooting, he could not resist the urge to peek over the top of the car. His eyes met a gruesome sight—bodies strewn in the street in dark pools of blood. He thought he saw Dom Costello's big body slumped in the doorway of the warehouse, but he couldn't be sure. Then in an instant a shock ran through him. Rosa was standing in the middle of the street in the direct line of fire!

"Rosa!" he cried, leaping to his feet without thought and running toward her. Even as Phil rushed forward, a bullet struck Rosa full in the chest. She made a slight cry and was driven backward.

"Rosa!"

Oblivious to the bullets that filled the air, he reached down and scooped her up. The front of her dress was stained with blood, and as Phil's heart wrenched at the sight, he knew that this war had claimed a casualty he could not spare.

PART FOUR

April–July 1927

★ ★ ★

CHAPTER NINETEEN

CASUALTIES

★ ★ ★ ★

The darkness was cold and silent . . . frightening. More than simply a lack of sound, the silence was tangible. Her first conscious thought was, *I'm dead*.

She heard a tiny sound, unrecognizable. Yet a sense of relief washed through her at the knowledge that something existed other than the silence. She seemed to be at the bottom of a deep pit—lifeless, airless—cut off from everything alive and warm. She tried to cry out for help but had no voice.

The sound she had heard intensified. Then pain like a white-hot knife plunged into her chest. It stunned her. She could do no more than remain still until the intensity of it passed, dulled to a throbbing ache instead of the terrifying agony she feared must be her death.

The darkness thinned, and a milky whiteness filled her vision. A wonderful relief swept through her as the light grew brighter and the sound she was hearing grew louder. It was ticking, she realized, like the ticking of a clock.

Consciousness came to her; the confusion, darkness, and silence passed away. Opening her eyes to slits, letting in a gray wash of antiseptic light, she realized she was lying in a bed. The touch of cool, soft sheets against her body became a reality. The ticking was to her left, and turning her head slightly, which brought a hot twinge to her chest, she saw a clock sitting on a dark table. She stared at it until the hands came into focus—eight minutes after four. She had no idea whether it was morning or afternoon, but a sense of gratitude rushed through her that she was no longer in that pit of stygian darkness.

"Rosa?"

The voice startled her and she stiffened. She turned in the direction of the voice and saw a face. At first she could not make out the features, for the light was behind whoever stood there. She tried to speak, but her lips were dry, her throat constricted.

"Rosa, can you hear me?"

Then Rosa knew that voice—it was Phil! As he leaned closer the light struck against his face, outlining his features. She saw lines of strain around his eyes, and his lips were drawn tightly together. He laid his hand on her forehead. His light touch felt cool, and she was grateful. She tried to speak again but could only whisper huskily, "Phil . . ." and could only choke, "water . . . please . . ."

Phil's face disappeared, and she heard the tinkling of water as it passed from one container to another. She felt his hand on the back of her head. "See if you can sip through this straw, Rosa."

The straw touched Rosa's lips. She opened them and began to pull at it frantically. The water touched her parched tissues, and she drank until she heard Phil say, "I think you'd better take a break. Just take a mouthful and hold it until it soaks up."

Rosa obeyed and lay still, savoring the moisture that brought life to her lips and the dry tissues of her mouth. She watched Phil standing over her with the glass in his hand. "How do you feel?" he asked.

Rosa tried to respond, then tried to move, but the pain prevented her from doing either.

"Take it easy. Don't stir."

"What . . . happened?"

Phil reached out and brushed a lock of hair from Rosa's face. After a moment he said quietly, "You were injured, Rosa. There was some shooting, and you got hit."

Rosa's fear returned. She searched his face, saw the grief, and whispered, "Am I going to die, Phil?"

"No—no, nothing like that!" Phil assured her. "You took a bullet up high in the chest, but it missed the lung and it missed the bone. I know it's painful now, but you'll be all right. Here, take another sip."

He held her head again, and Rosa obediently sipped at the water, relief washing through her. He let her have several mouthfuls, then withdrew the straw and gently replaced her head on the pillow.

"How long . . . have I been here?"

"Just since yesterday. You had me worried, Rosa—all of us, as a matter of fact. But you're going to be all right. The Lord took care of you."

His words were like a balm to the wounded young woman, and she closed her eyes and lay quietly. Other anxious thoughts troubled her mind, and she opened her eyes. Memory slowly returned. She thought back to the scene, but she had been drinking, and it was all like a kaleidoscope of flashing memories, with no clear order or meaning. She did remember hearing the gunfire, and she remembered running. She also remembered Dom dragging her to safety . . . then running again and Phil's voice . . .

"Where's Dom, Phil?" she asked, looking up at him.

Phil's expression disturbed her. He did not answer for a moment, but his lips tightened, and she demanded, "Is he all right?"

"He's pretty badly hurt, Rosa."

Rosa felt a stab of fear. Dom Costello was a rough man, but he'd watched over her and kept her safe since she was a child, and now the harsh reality of his condition touched her with dread. She tried to see some hope in Phil's face, but he said no more.

For several minutes Rosa lay quietly, then demanded, "What happened? What was the shooting about?"

"You don't want to talk about that now, Rosa."

"Yes I do. What was it?"

Phil shifted uneasily and ran his hand across his hair. He thought he should go get the doctor and let Rosa's family know she was awake. They had been at the hospital all night and had finally gone home to get a little rest. It was almost time for them to return, and Phil wished they would.

Rosa saw Phil's hesitation, and then the truth came to her. "It was a gang war, wasn't it?"

"It was connected with that. There was a raid, and a number of men were killed."

"Who?"

"Two of them were special agents from the justice department—from Lee Novak's team. That's who I used to work for before I became a lawyer. Lee himself was hit twice."

"Did he . . . did he die?"

"No, he's all right, thank God! Just badly hurt, but he'll make it. But two of his men didn't."

Rosa turned her face away and lifted her hand to cover the side of her face as if to cut off his gaze. Phil was startled. "What's the matter, Rosa?"

Rosa did not answer. She shook her head and felt hot tears coming down her cheeks. She then felt Phil's hand touching hers. He leaned over and looked directly into her face. "Are you in pain?"

"It's not that."

"What is it, then?"

She would not answer, and Phil remained silent too. He stood beside her, gently brushing back her silky black hair. "You're going to be all right. Don't worry."

"No, I'm not." Rosa removed her hand, and when she turned her face to his, he saw the tortured light in her eyes. "It's never going to be all right!"

Baffled by her words and thinking her disturbance stemmed from the drugs they had given her to ease the pain, Phil shook his head and smiled. "It'll be all right," he said. "You'll see."

"My father's a gangster. All our money comes from crime. Everybody knows it, Phil. I'm so ashamed, and it'll never change."

Phil tried to protest, but Rosa put her hand back over her face. He leaned forward and tried to whisper something to console her, but he heard her say faintly, "My family . . . my family . . . who would ever want me?"

Phil was stunned by the words. He knew that Rosa, Jamie, and Mrs. Morino all hated the life they led, but he had not known before how deeply these feelings touched Rosa's heart.

★　★　★　★

Rosa said nothing more and Phil waited patiently by her side. Ten minutes later Tony and his wife came in. Phil was shocked at Morino's condition. His hands were trembling, and he was pale as paste. When he spoke his voice was unsteady. "How is she?"

"She's doing fine. She woke up about twenty minutes ago. I'm glad you've come." Actually Phil was apprehensive. If Rosa were to tell her father what was on her heart, he knew that would destroy Tony Morino. Somehow, sometime, that was going to come, but he hoped that such a confrontation would not happen until Rosa was completely out of danger. "I've got to go down and see Lee," Phil said.

Morino had been looking at Rosa, but he turned and licked his lips nervously. "I hope he's okay."

"Do you, Tony?"

"Why . . . sure I do."

"Two of Lee's men won't be okay." Phil could not help saying this. He knew it was neither the time nor place, and he was aware that Mrs. Morino had turned her face away to avoid looking at him. Quickly Phil said, "I'm glad Rosa's all right. I'll tell the doctor she's awake."

Phil left the room and went down to the nurses' station. A bright-eyed young woman with flaming red hair turned to him as he said, "Miss Morino is awake."

"Oh, that's good! She's going to be all right, then. Now don't you worry."

Phil smiled at her optimism. "Thanks. Her parents are with her now, but maybe you'd want to note it down for the doctor that she woke up about twenty minutes ago."

"Thank you, Mr. Winslow." She leaned forward over the desk and said, "You were lucky you didn't get shot."

"Not luck. The Lord took care of me."

The nurse blinked with surprise. "Well, yes, of course, that's true."

"Has the doctor been in to see Mr. Novak yet?"

"Not since you were here last."

"I'd like to go sit with him awhile."

"Oh, that'll be fine. His wife has left to go get some rest. She's worn out, poor thing."

"Thanks, Nurse."

Phil turned and walked down the corridor thinking of the casualties that had resulted from the shoot-out. Rosa would be all right and so would Lee, but Dom Costello was not likely to live. The doctor had offered little hope, and the two special agents who had died had been good men. Phil had known both of them, and a slow, cold anger burned in him as he thought of the loss to their families and the grief they now suffered. Two of Morino's men had died instantly, and two more were badly wounded but would probably live. Of course, Morino himself could not be held, for as usual, his men refused to implicate him. It infuriated Phil that such things could happen, but he knew it was the story of the war against crime all over America. He turned into Lee Novak's room and found his friend lying with his eyes open, staring at the ceiling. "How are you, Lee?"

"It hurts."

"I would think so. Can I get you anything?"

"No, just sit down a minute. I want to talk."

"Sure, but let me stand up. You can't see me if I sit down."

"All right. I wish I could stand up myself." He tried to move, but pain washed across his face, and he gritted his teeth.

"Pretty bad?" Phil asked quickly.

"Could have been worse." Novak had taken two slugs, one in the knee and the other in the side. The bullet in the side had been painful but had missed all the vital organs. He had lost a great deal of blood, which had left him weak. It was the bullet in the knee that troubled him the most, having done considerable damage.

"What does the doctor say about your knee?"

"He says I'll walk, but I'll limp the rest of my life."

"Maybe it'll heal better than that."

Lee Novak did not answer for a time. Finally he sighed and

said, "You know we all could have bought the farm the way bullets were flying around."

Phil stood over Novak, thankful that they were both alive. He knew their fight with the criminal gangs of New York was far from over. Perhaps they'd suffered only the first skirmish in a war that would not be easy to win. He'd been shaken by what he'd seen and experienced, and a part of him wanted to flee, to find another more comfortable job. But even as he knew his friend Lee would recover and go back to fighting the warlords, he also knew that he played a vital role, too, in getting these dangerous criminals off the streets and behind bars.

Lee reached up and took Phil's hand and squeezed it. His hands were as hard as if he had done manual labor all his life. He had a crushing grip, and now Phil felt the power of the man. "Don't be discouraged by this minor setback, Phil. We've got them on the run now. Just a little more time, and we'll be able to break up the kingpins. You've gotta stay in this fight too, Phil—help put every last one of them behind bars. Can you do that?"

Phil Winslow felt inadequate to the task, but he knew the power of the law was on their side. The dark intensity of Lee Novak's gaze held him. He took a deep breath and then nodded. "I'll do the best I can, Lee."

★　★　★　★

Jamie had looked at every magazine in the waiting room and was bored. He wished he had brought his new book on photography with him. His parents were sitting with Rosa in her room, but he had chosen to sit out in the waiting room. It was not crowded, occupied only by an older couple sitting at the end of the room. They were poorly dressed and held hands. Their faces were lined, and they seemed very worried. Jamie wondered whom they were waiting for and hoped that whoever it was would come out all right.

Restlessly Jamie paced around the room, then went out into the hallway to get a drink of water he didn't really want. He watched the nurses as they patrolled the corridors. They appeared pretty cheerful for people in such a grim occupation.

One of them stopped and asked, "How are you today, Jamie?"

"All right, Miss Madigen."

"Your sister is doing very well. I think she'll be going home soon."

"Yes, maybe day after tomorrow, the doctor said."

The brunette nurse winked at him. "You've been missing seeing your girlfriend, spending so much time here, haven't you? What's her name?"

"Penelope."

The nurse blinked and then laughed. "You're putting me on, Jamie. You wouldn't date a girl named Penelope."

Jamie said earnestly, "Oh yes, she's a very nice girl. Not very pretty, but she's earnest and means well."

The nurse laughed and shook her head. "You shouldn't tease like that. I'll bet she's beautiful."

Jamie watched the nurse as she went down the hall. Then he started back toward the waiting room. He had almost reached it when the elevator stopped, the door opened, and Wes Winslow got out. Instantly Jamie brightened up. "Hello, Wes," he said, walking over to meet him.

"Hi, Jamie, how's Rosa?"

"She's doing fine. She might get to go home day after tomorrow."

"Hey, that's great!"

"Did you come to see her?"

"Yes, but I'm also meeting Amelia here. She's going to help me meet some show business people and get some shots of them."

"You mean movie stars?"

"I don't think so. There are plenty of pictures of the stars. I want to get some of the less successful people. Come on, let's go down to the cafeteria."

Jamie accompanied him, and Wes bought some pie and coffee while Jamie got a soft drink. "Why would you want to take pictures of unsuccessful people?" Jamie asked.

"Well, they interest me," Wes said. "You know, after a prize-fight they always interview the winner. That's what everybody expects, but I went to one last night, and I went to the loser's room. He was beat up pretty bad, and I got a terrific shot." He fumbled through the leather bag he carried and pulled out an envelope. Taking out a group of photographs, he selected one and said, "Look at that."

"Boy, he is beat up, isn't he? Look at his eyes. He can hardly see out of them."

"I thought the picture was pretty good. It caught the whole essence of defeat, and all of us have to learn how to handle that, don't we, Jamie?"

"I guess so," Jamie said quietly.

Wes had gotten to know Jamie rather well. He had taken him out on two assignments and had quickly learned that the boy was very intelligent. He was good with his hands too, and Wes had told him once, "I wish I'd had good equipment like yours when I was your age. I'd be famous by now."

The two sat talking for some time, and finally Wes looked up to see Amelia walk into the cafeteria. He jumped up and hurried over to her. "Amelia!"

Amelia turned and looked at him with surprise. "I thought you'd be up visiting with Rosa."

"I will. I was just spending a little time with Jamie first. They probably don't want her to have too many visitors at once anyway."

Jamie walked over to join the two. "Rosa will be glad to see you, Amelia," he said.

She laid her hand on his arm. "I hope you're doing okay, too, Jamie. Why don't you two go visit with her while I grab a sandwich? I haven't eaten anything yet today."

"All right," Jamie said, and he and Wes headed for the elevator.

Amelia was just getting in line to pick out a sandwich when she saw Ryan Kildare come in. He caught her eye and headed in her direction.

"Hello, Amelia," Ryan said. "Have you been to see Rosa?"

"No, I was just going to have a sandwich first."

Amelia felt very uncomfortable, and she saw that Ryan was feeling much the same. "Do you want something to eat, Ryan?"

"No, but I'll have some coffee."

Five minutes later the two were seated, with Amelia eating a chicken salad sandwich and Ryan sipping a cup of black coffee.

He looked curiously at her and said, "How's your career?"

"It's all right."

Something about her answer or her attitude, perhaps, caught at Ryan. He knew she had been troubled by the shootings, and now he turned the cup around in his hands and stared down into the coffee. "I'm worried about James and Rosa."

"Rosa's going to be all right."

"Oh yes, from the shooting, but you know those two hate what their father does. So does Mrs. Morino. I see some trouble ahead for them."

They sat there for some time and then went up to visit Rosa. Jamie met them in the hallway and informed them that Rosa was asleep.

"Well, I'll go down and see Dom, then."

"I'll go with you, Ryan."

The two went down the hall and turned into Dom's room. The big man's face was ashen, but his eyes were open.

Amelia did not like sickrooms. Forcing herself to go in, she went over to Dom's bed. When he lifted his eyes, she made herself smile. "Hello, Dom. A couple visitors for you."

Ryan came to stand beside her and said, "How are you feeling?"

Dom did not answer for a while. Indeed, he didn't look good. His face was strained when he finally spoke in a hoarse whisper, "Not . . . too good."

Amelia reached down and took his hand. "You're going to make it, Dom," she said.

But Dom Costello had been around death enough to know better. "No," he whispered, "not this time. It's all up with me."

Amelia could not say a word. She knew he was speaking the truth. The doctors had said as much. A death pallor was on the face of the big man who lay so helplessly before her. She remembered his former vitality and strength, and now all that was gone.

Ryan touched Amelia. She looked at him, startled, then moved aside. Ryan reached down and took Dom's hand. "Dom, I want to talk to you about Jesus."

Dom Costello stared at Kildare. He said nothing but lay there, his eyes fixed on the face of the other who spoke slowly, never taking his eyes off of the man in the bed.

"We all have to face God. We're all going to die. I'll go some-day. Amelia will go. Tony will go. We all have to face the Lord, but we don't have to face Him unprepared."

Dom blinked his eyes and shook his head almost impercep-tibly. "You don't know the bad stuff I've done, Ryan."

"It doesn't matter. Jesus died for sinners. That's what I am, a sinner, so He died for me. If you see yourself as a sinner, then He died for you."

Amelia listened as Ryan spoke gently but insistently of the death of Jesus Christ. She knew this was the sort of thing her father could do, or her uncle Barney or her mother, but she her-self could not. Something about it frightened her because she was well aware that this was Dom Costello's last chance.

Dom listened intently, then said, "I heard a preacher once on the street. He said . . . that when Jesus died, there was a crook right by him who asked for mercy."

"That's right. Let me read it to you, Dom." Reaching into his pocket, Ryan pulled out a New Testament. He thumbed through a few pages and then said, "Jesus had just been crucified, and the Bible gives us a record of it." He read slowly: " 'And one of the malefactors which were hanged railed on him, saying, If thou be Christ, save thyself and us. But the other answering rebuked him, saying, Dost not thou fear God, seeing thou art in the same condemnation? And we indeed justly; for we receive the due reward of our deeds: but this man hath done nothing amiss. And he said unto Jesus, Lord, remember me when thou comest into thy kingdom. And Jesus said unto him, Verily I say unto thee, To day shalt thou be with me in paradise.' "

Dom Costello listened intently. His injuries had drained the strength out of him, and now he appeared barely conscious. "That's all he done? Just asked?"

"That's all any of us have to do, Dom. All of us are sinners, and all God asks is that we admit it . . . and ask for forgiveness."

"I ain't nothin' but a crook. That's all I've ever been."

"Jesus loves crooks."

The statement startled Dom. His eyes opened wider, and he stared at the man beside him. Slowly he closed his eyes, and Amelia was shocked and yet gladdened to see two tears form and run down his cheeks. She stood there as Ryan continued to speak, quoting Scriptures, and found herself praying that Dom Costello would not go out to meet God unprepared. It shocked her that her heart seemed to be breaking for the dying man, and she was startled when she heard Ryan say, "He's asleep. Come along, Amelia."

As they turned away she was silent, but outside the room she said, "Do you think there's a chance for him?"

"Yes, I think there is. You're fond of him, aren't you, Amelia?"

"Yes, I am. He's had so little chance, and now he's going out to meet God in judgment if something doesn't happen."

Ryan took both her hands in his. "God is love, Amelia." He saw the tears run down her cheeks and knew that the same God who was pursuing Dom Costello was touching this woman. "He'll reach Dom . . . and He'll reach you, Amelia!"

CHAPTER TWENTY

FATHER AND SON

★　★　★　★

Victor Caruso stared across the desk at Tony Morino. Caruso had worked for Tony for years, always as the number three man immediately behind Dominic Costello. After the shooting, Caruso had immediately, at Tony's orders, moved into the number two slot. He was a tall man with cold black eyes and black hair to match. He dressed immaculately and looked more like an extra in a movie than he did a professional criminal. He had grown up on New York's Lower East Side, a hard school, and had absorbed the brutality of that world into his soul. Caruso was extremely intelligent and shrewd, and now as he fixed his eyes on Morino, he said with great forcefulness, "We've got to hit Marx, Tony."

Morino was taken aback by the intensity of Caruso's stare and by the boldness of the statement. "Sure, sooner or later—but not now."

"No, it's got to be *now*, Tony. He's stronger, and we're getting weaker. With Dom out of the picture, he'll see that as a weakness. They took out our guys with that setup, and we're going to get blamed for killing those two feds."

"They'll never prove that."

"They might. You should know that this isn't going to slow

Novak down. He'll regroup and train new men in no time. He's comin' after us, I tell you, and if we don't tighten our holes, we're going to lose out. It's Leo's time, and he's comin' to get us."

There had been a time when Tony Morino was the driving force behind the organization, but his health had deteriorated and some of his will had gone with it as well. He felt lost without Dom, who had been his shadow for years, and now he stared almost helplessly at Vic Caruso. "I'll think about it."

"You'd better do more than think about it," Vic insisted. "You've come to a fork in the road, Tony. You've been asleep. You'd better wake up, boss. It's wake-up time."

★   ★   ★   ★

Tony had been restless ever since Caruso had pushed him about Leo Marx. He felt uneasy, which was a new experience for him. He had come up a fighter, and his enemies had found him always ready to meet them head-on. Now, however, he could not seem to pull himself together. He sat at his desk for a while fidgeting with papers, trying to put things together in his mind, but found he could not concentrate.

A thought came to him, and he rose and left the study. He went upstairs and paused outside Jamie's door. At one time he would have simply gone in, but it seemed the boy had been more inaccessible lately. So now he knocked, asking, "James, are you there?"

A long silence followed and then the door slowly opened. Jamie stood looking at him and finally said, "What is it, Dad?"

"I thought you might show me what you're doing with those cameras I been spendin' so much money for."

"Okay." Jamie stepped back, and for the next ten minutes he displayed the newest camera his father had bought him. He also showed him a great many prints, and the name Wes Winslow came up often.

"This guy Wes—he's a good one, is he?"

"Yes, he was just like I am when he was my age. Always taking pictures, and now he's doing great."

The thought crossed Morino's mind, *This is the first conversa-*

tion I've had with Jamie in a long time. I've got to get closer to him.

However, as soon as the conversation about photography ended, Jamie fell silent. Tony struggled to find something else to talk about, but more and more Jamie withdrew. Finally Tony asked, "Are you worrying about Rosa? You don't have to. She's going to be all right."

Jamie Morino was on the verge of young manhood. He had always been a rather quiet boy, which sometimes troubled his father. Now, however, something in his eyes was different. Tony could not make it out, and finally he said, "What's wrong? Rosa will be all right."

"Dom's going to die, Dad. *He's* not going to be all right."

Tony blinked with surprise at the mature quality in Jamie's voice. This was no child standing here, but one coming out of boyhood into manhood. Somehow the years had passed by, and at that moment he knew he'd missed a large part of his son's life. "Maybe Dom will make it," he offered weakly.

"The doctors say he's going to die," Jamie said flatly, accusation coloring his voice. "He's not going to be all right—and neither are those two men who worked for the government. They're dead, and they left families."

Tony could not meet Jamie's gaze. It was the first time in his life he had ever been overwhelmed by the boy, and now he cleared his throat and tried to justify what had happened.

"Look, Jamie, you just don't understand these things. It's . . . it's a business."

"It's *not* a business, Dad." Jamie's face was pale, and strain was etched on his youthful features. Something had been building up in him for years. He had never said it aloud, and perhaps he would not now, but he was very attached to Dom Costello, and Rosa's brush with death had frightened him. Now he stood straight as a ramrod and said, "Everybody knows what you do, Dad, everybody in New York City."

"I'm just a businessman, son."

"Al Capone, is he just a businessman? Everybody knows he's a criminal."

Anger flashed through Tony. "Are you calling me a criminal?"

"That's what you are, Dad. You break the law. It's against the law to sell alcohol, and that's what you do." Jamie's face changed. It was a look Tony had never seen before. "But I won't be what you are. I'd be ashamed."

Tony could not speak. He had learned over the years to explain his activities in a language that made it more respectable. Like Capone, he called himself simply a businessman. He had the usual excuses that if he didn't sell liquor, somebody else would. That rich men could buy and drink in their own clubs safe from the law, so poor people should have the same right. But as he stood facing his son, he suddenly could not bear it. He turned and left the room, his throat tight.

He left the house and walked around the grounds for a long time. The beauty of the spring meant nothing to him. He could only hear the voice of his son saying, *"I won't be what you are. I'd be ashamed."* He knew those words would echo in his mind and in his heart . . . perhaps forever.

When he returned to the house, he found Maria waiting for him. He stood before her and related brokenly what had happened.

Maria Morino did not speak for a time, but she knew that now she had to. She faced him and said, "He's right, Anthony. Don't you know that Rosa and Jamie hate what you do?"

"I never . . . I never realized it."

And then with a heartbroken tone, she said, "And so do I hate it. I've always hated it."

Tony stared at his wife, whom he loved dearly, but could not meet her gaze. Blindly, he turned and fled from her.

★ ★ ★ ★

Rosa improved dramatically. Each day home from the hospital brought more strength. Her parents rejoiced and so did Jamie, but after she had been home only a few days, Rosa became aware of the rift between her father and her brother. She could not speak to Tony, but she asked Jamie about it. He simply related the scene that had passed between them. When he finished, Rosa bit her lip. "I'm sorry you had to say those things to Daddy."

"But you feel the same way, Rosa," Jamie insisted. "I know you do."

"Yes, I do. I think about it all the time," Rosa whispered. "I love my father, but I don't want to see you getting into what he does. I wish we could just move away and go where people don't know us!"

★ ★ ★ ★

On her first outing, Rosa insisted on going to the hospital to visit Dom. He was still on the very edge of death, and when Tony said, "You're too weak to go out, Rosa," she had stood before him, pale but determined.

"I've got to go see Dom. He's going to die, Daddy. I think you ought to go too."

Tony swallowed hard. "All right. I'll take you myself."

The two went, and when they reached Dom's room they found, to Rosa's surprise, that Phil was there. He was standing beside the bed, and Rosa swallowed hard. "Hello, Phil," she said.

"Hello, Rosa. How are you, Mr. Morino?"

Tony stared down at the pale face of Dom Costello. "How . . . how is he?"

Phil shook his head. "The doctors say he can't last much longer."

Tony was startled that he would speak of death in front of Dom, and he whispered, "You shouldn't talk like that. He'll hear you."

"Dom knows he's dying, Tony."

At that moment Dom opened his eyes. "Hello, Tony," he whispered.

"Hey, how are you, fella?" Tony turned to Dom, forcing a smile. He held his hand out, but Dom was too weak even to lift his own.

"I'm glad . . . you came. Wanted to tell you good-bye."

"Don't talk like that, Dom," Tony said nervously, his voice rising. "Don't ever talk like that."

"It's . . . my time."

Fear gripped Rosa at his words. She had known that Dom

could not live, but now that the moment was near, she felt light-headed and wanted to run from the room. She was standing beside Phil and now reached out and grasped his arm. She turned to face him and whispered, "I'm so afraid, Phil."

Phil put his arm around her. "It's all right, Rosa. Dom knows where he's going now."

Rosa felt the warmth of his body as his arm went around her. She was unaware that her father was staring at them, but she heard Phil speaking warmly to Dom.

"Dom, you're going to be in the presence of God soon. When we prayed together last night, you asked Jesus into your heart, and I believe He came in."

Dom Costello's eyes were glazed, but life shone from them. "Yes, something happened. As soon as I called on Jesus, I knew . . . something had changed."

Rosa could not believe what she was hearing. Dom continued to speak, and despite his pallor, his eyes brightened. He reached over to Rosa and said, "It's the real thing, Rosa. Jesus is real. He came and took away everything that was bad in me. I feel so clean, washed. . . ."

Dom could not speak anymore, but Rosa reached out and took his hand. He held it firmly, and when she said, "I love you, Dom," he whispered, "I love you too, kid." His eyes went to Tony, and he said, "Tony . . . don't leave God out. Trust in Jesus."

Those were the last words big Dom Costello spoke. His eyes closed, and the three stood around the bed watching his breath grow shallower. Phil sent for the doctor, but it was too late. Dom never spoke again, but he did open his eyes once and half lifted his hand. Rosa saw something in Dom's eyes she had never seen before—and then he sighed and closed his eyes.

"He's gone!" Tony gasped. "He's gone!"

"He's gone to be with the Lord, Tony," Phil said. He turned to Rosa. "Don't worry about him now. He went out to meet God trusting in Jesus."

Rosa could not answer. The death of the big man had shaken her as nothing ever had before, not even her own gunshot wound. She was in the presence of eternity, and she was frightened, but something about the going forth of Dom Costello made an impact on her she knew she would never forget.

CHAPTER TWENTY-ONE

ALL FOR LOVE

★ ★ ★ ★

Sid Menkin stared at Amelia with disbelief written across his face. Something akin to shock rested on the short, round man who now stood in the middle of the room, and Amelia thought for a moment he was about to have a heart attack. Sid was always red-faced, and his eyes bulged out from his face, but now as she stood watching him, she became concerned. "Sid, what's the matter with you? Here, sit down. You're going to have a stroke."

"Sit down! I *can't* sit down! I'm telling you it hit me like a ton of bricks, Amelia. I wasn't expecting anything this great."

Amelia studied her rotund agent. He wore his thinning black hair combed over to one side, trying unsuccessfully to hide a bald spot. "Well, if it's that great, don't make it worse by dying of a seizure. What is it, Sid?"

Sid took a deep breath and ran his hand over his hair, trying to calm himself. He pulled out a handkerchief, pausing to wipe it across his forehead. He finally smiled apologetically. "I let myself get too carried away, Amelia, but I've wanted this for a long time for you."

"You got me a good engagement, Sid?"

"Engagement nothing! You've got a shot at working in Saul

Meyer's hit, the biggest thing on Broadway—*All for Love.*"

"But Myrna Stockman's got that role nailed down."

"Not anymore she hasn't. She's going to have a baby, and she's leaving the show. Ain't it great?"

"Having the baby or her leaving the show?"

Sid began to pace the floor of Amelia's apartment. He had appeared without calling and had simply burst through the door, unable to contain his excitement. His bulging eyes flashed as he paced. He windmilled his arms around and continued to talk breathlessly in his high-pitched voice. "It's the best break you could have had, Amelia. I don't mean just *good.* I mean it's terrific! The very best. It's the top. You're going straight up. You just needed one break like this, and now you've got it." He came over and grabbed Amelia's hands, squeezing them and pumping them up and down. "But what do you say, kid? What do you say?"

Amelia endured Sid's enthusiasm and smiled. "Well, it sounds great, but I've never done a musical comedy. All I've ever done is sing in nightclubs. Saul Meyer can have anybody he wants for that role. You know that."

Sid released her hands and once again patted his thinning strands into place. "Well, of course, you'll have to audition, but there ain't nobody that can sing like you, baby."

"But there are some who can act a lot better. What about Mabel Ramsey? Didn't I read that she wanted to work for Saul Meyer?"

"Yeah, but she's too old. She's over thirty. Over the hill."

Amelia smiled. "Well, I'm twenty-five. That's practically getting around on crutches, isn't it?"

"Nah, you don't look it. That lead's a young role, and you can do it. Listen," he said, "I've got an appointment for you to try out this afternoon at three o'clock down at the Crystal Theater. It's a special audition. You're right. They're trying out two or three singers, but none of them's got what you got."

"Who are they?"

"Well, I don't know exactly," Sid grinned, "but they're not as good as you, sweetheart."

"I'm not going to let myself get excited, Sid, and you shouldn't either. I'll go down and try out, but you'd better hold on to yourself. It won't do you any good to put yourself in the hospital with a heart attack."

Amelia eased Sid out the door, promising him she would be at the audition. He left her a list of the songs from the show, and she found she already knew two of them fairly well. They had become hit records and were not particularly difficult.

As soon as Sid was gone, Amelia turned and walked back to the window of her apartment and stared outside. It was early June, and the sun was beating down on the streets below her window. She did not particularly notice the traffic on the street or the people walking along the sidewalk. She was thinking of what a long road she had traveled to get this far. Ever since she had left Africa, and even before, she had dreamed of being on stage and entertaining people, and now possibly that door was swinging open. She closed her eyes and tried to imagine herself acting on stage, but for some reason it was hard. Then she laughed and turned away. "I probably won't get the part anyway, so why get all worked up?"

★ ★ ★ ★

Amelia finished dressing and paused to look at herself in the mirror. She had chosen an afternoon dress with a low décolletage and a chiffon fill-in. The hemline had a stylish uneven cut, and over the dress she wore a lightweight three-quarter-length jacket with lace trim. She carefully donned her decorated turban-style hat and fluffed her now shoulder-length hair. She had allowed the bob she used to wear to grow out and was glad for it now. She had never seen a woman she thought looked pretty with hair cut like a boy's and wondered if her rather old-fashioned hairstyle would count against her.

"If they're going to choose stars for the way they cut their hair, I'll never make it," she said. "But who knows what they want?" She slipped on her shoes, which were open-toed with three button fastenings, and then left the apartment.

On the cab ride there she became more and more nervous, but by the time she had reached the Crystal Theater she had calmed herself. She paid her cab, got out, and walked up to the entrance. There was no afternoon performance, and the door was open, so she walked in. The lobby was empty also, but she could hear a band tuning up as she stepped inside. The lights were up over the stage, and people were moving around talking loudly. She hesitated for a moment, then started down the aisle. She had not reached the front before she saw a tall, burly man arguing vehemently with a long, lean individual wearing a sweater and a pair of baggy pants.

She stopped in the aisle until the burly man finally turned and caught her eye. His eyes lit up, and he came at once to say, "Well, it's you, Amelia. Glad you could come." He put out his hands, which swallowed up Amelia's. "I'm Saul Meyer, and this is Dave Baxter. I suppose you know him."

"No, I don't think so." Amelia smiled.

"You don't? Well, he's the director. We're having a little discussion right now. The trouble is both of us always think we're right."

Amelia hardly knew what to say. She was startled that the famous producer Saul Meyer looked more like a stevedore than a wealthy producer of Broadway plays. Her agent had told her that he had made his fortune in shipping, but a lifelong affair with the theater had lured him to Broadway. She felt completely out of place.

Saul Meyer took her arm and said, "Tell you what, you come and sit down. We can talk a little bit. They're going to do a couple of the numbers, and then you can do your stuff."

Amelia was practically pulled back to the seats in the third row. She sat down next to Meyer and answered his questions as accurately as she could, but there was little time. "Here's a number you'll like," Meyer said eagerly.

Amelia sat up and gave her attention to the stage. A line of women came out, and Amelia gasped. She was shocked by their costumes. They all wore sheer, scanty dresses that left practically nothing to the imagination. Their movements also were suggestive, and the lyrics to the song were, to her mind, crude.

"Ain't that great?" Meyer said happily. "It knocks 'em dead every night. What d'ya think of it?"

Amelia could not possibly find an answer to that, but she had no need.

Meyer went on without a breath. "Tell you what, you go back and find Doris. You'll need some time to get changed."

"You want me to get in costume?"

"Oh, just to make you fit in and show us that pretty figure of yours. We already know it's okay. Go on, sweetheart, you'll knock us all dead."

Amelia went back with as much reservation as she had ever felt about anything. Backstage she found a matronly woman with a hard face and said, "I'm looking for Doris."

"That's me. You Miss Winslow?"

"Yes."

"Mr. Meyer told me you'd be trying out. Come on, we'll get you fitted. I think I got just what you need in your size."

When Mabel brought her "just what you need," Amelia gasped. The dress looked even more sheer and abbreviated than those she had seen on the dancers. She almost blurted out, *Why, I can't wear a thing like this in public*, but Doris gave her no chance.

"Just slip into it. I'll find you some slippers."

Amelia stared with dismay at the dress. Her heart sank, and she thought of the numbers she had just seen with their blatantly sexual gyrations and lyrics. She had heard that *All for Love* was somewhat raw, but she had never imagined anything like this. For just one instant she was tempted to throw the dress down and leave—but she had come too far. Resolutely she stripped off her clothes and donned the costume. By the time she had it on, Doris was back with a pair of shoes. "Hey, you look great, Miss Winslow! Here, take a look at yourself."

Amelia turned to the mirror Doris indicated and stared at her image. Her heart sank, and she once again wondered how in the world she could wear a thing like this in public. She had no chance to think much, for Doris said urgently, "Look, they're playing the song they want you to do. You'd better get out there, Miss Winslow."

Amelia put her mind as far as possible into neutral. *I'll sing this, and if I get the part, surely I'll have something to say about my clothes*. She went onstage, and Dave, the director, looked her up and down. "Hey, you look great, Miss Winslow. You know the song 'All for Love'?"

"Yes, I do."

"Well, we won't do the whole number. You just sing it and let the dancers do a little dance around you, and Charlie here will come in for the final kiss. This is the closing number, the finale. You'll have to learn to do a few steps, but it'll be no problem for you, I'm sure."

Amelia had always liked the song. It had simple lyrics, saying that lovers ought to give everything to their love. But as she sang it and the chorus danced around her in their scanty costumes, she realized that to the audience the song was saying, *Don't stop at anything with your lover.* After singing the first two verses, there was a flurry of dancing in which she was picked up and moved around by one of the male dancers. Then one of the men, apparently a stand-in for the star, stood with her and they sang the last verse. At the very end, he put his arms around her and kissed her for a long time. His hands roved all over her body, and she resisted his kiss. But when it was over, he merely laughed and said, "Might as well enjoy it, kid. It's one of the benefits of this work."

Amelia had no time to think, for Saul Meyer was instantly on the stage. His face glowed with pleasure, and he came over and put his arms around her, kissing her on the cheek. "You did great, baby, great! Didn't she do good, Dave?"

"Very good," the director said. "I think she can handle it."

"Why don't you change your costume and we'll see a few other numbers," Saul urged.

"I really need to get dressed. I have to work tonight, Mr. Meyer."

"Oh, sure. Well, I'll get in touch with Sid. As far as I'm concerned, you're in."

"Thank you, Mr. Meyer."

Amelia left the stage as quickly as she could and whipped off the skimpy dress. When she was fully dressed in her own clothing, she looked at the miserable excuse for a costume and shook her head. "If I do this, I won't wear that thing," she muttered. She left the theater at once, and as soon as she stepped outside, she felt in need of a bath. Taking a cab, she went straight home, greatly disturbed and wondering how she would handle this situation.

★　★　★　★

At the club that night Amelia performed mechanically and was sure that people noticed the difference. Audiences were sensitive, and she felt she had done very poorly.

After changing, she left her dressing room to head for home but was intercepted by Ryan Kildare, who greeted her cheerfully. "Hello, Amelia."

"Hello, Ryan. What are you doing here?"

"Why, I came to hear my favorite singer and maybe get her to go out and have a late supper. I'm starved. I've been running all day."

"I'm not very hungry, Ryan."

"Well, come along," he smiled, "and you can listen to me eat."

She laughed and said, "Your manners aren't that bad."

She almost refused, but the experience at the Crystal Theater had depressed her. She had gotten an excited phone call from her agent, Sid, who said that everything was going very well. It looked like she had the part. The news had not encouraged Amelia greatly. Now she said to Ryan impulsively, "I . . . I might eat a sandwich."

"Fine. Come on, we'll go to Luigi's."

They went to the Italian restaurant and found a table in the back. Ryan had spaghetti, as he nearly always did, but Amelia ate only a salad with her coffee.

Ryan was aware that something was troubling her and finally asked, "Amelia, what's wrong? Problems?"

"Oh, not really."

Ryan said nothing more about her depressed manner, but later on as the two left the restaurant, he said, "It's not far to your place. Do you want to walk or take a cab?"

"Let's walk."

As they walked along, Amelia found herself telling Ryan about her tryout at the Crystal. She had not intended to tell anyone her reservations, but Ryan Kildare was a good person to confide in. He was quiet and listened attentively, and before she knew it, she had laid the whole thing out in front of him.

"I thought I'd be so happy to get a break like this, but Ryan, it was humiliating. The costumes were almost nonexistent. It would be like being in burlesque. I don't like it."

Ryan had listened quietly. Now he asked a few penetrating questions and then finally said, "I haven't seen the show *All for Love*, but I've seen pictures of the advertisements. It looks pretty low, Amelia."

"It is low. Lower than you can imagine. It's not just the scanty costumes and those vulgar dances they do—they make a mockery out of real love. It's nothing but sex."

"It sounds like you're going to have trouble fitting in if you do get the part."

"But, Ryan, it would be so good for my career."

Ryan did not answer, and Amelia felt his displeasure. "I know you don't like it. I don't either, but look at it this way. If I do the show and I'm good at it, I can get better parts. Why, I might even be able to talk them into letting me wear a more . . . well . . . a more decent costume."

"You really think that, Amelia?"

Amelia knew she had been fantasizing. "No," she said flatly. "I'd have to be what they want me to be. It goes with the part."

Ryan said abruptly, "You know, I read a story about trapping beavers out west in the early part of our history."

"What do beavers have to do with what I'm telling you?"

"Well, sometimes the trappers would come and instead of finding a beaver they'd find just a leg. The beaver would gnaw off his own leg in order to escape."

"What a horrible thought!"

"I thought about those beavers," Ryan said quietly. The traffic was light, and the stars overhead illuminated the dark canopy like tiny flashing candles. "Those beavers got away, but they had to limp around on three legs the rest of their lives. I've known so many people who have had to do something like that. They got into something unpleasant. They got out of it, but they had to, in effect, injure themselves just like those beavers. They left something of themselves behind. I'd hate to see that happen to you, Amelia."

Amelia was accustomed to this sort of advice from Ryan Kildare. He had a poetic mind and a quick imagination. The little parable he had told her expressed her own fears. She was afraid she would lose part of herself if she signed the contract with Saul Meyer.

When they reached the door of her apartment, she turned to him and smiled. "You wouldn't like my being in that musical, would you?"

"No, I wouldn't, Amelia."

"I wouldn't like it either, but it's what I've worked for. I don't want to miss my big chance."

"If you're unhappy about it now," Ryan said quietly, "you'll be much more unhappy later."

Amelia knew he was right. She tried to summon up an argument, some way to answer his questioning, but she could not. "Good night, Ryan."

"Just a minute, Amelia." Ryan suddenly stepped forward and put his hands on her shoulders. She stopped with surprise and saw a look in his eyes that held her still.

"I want you to marry me, Amelia."

Amelia could not answer. She had been expecting this moment to come for a long time, and now it was here. She thought she had her answer prepared in case he ever asked the question, but now she found herself unable to speak. She studied the cleanness of his features and felt the power of his eyes. She had never had such strong feelings for a man before and wondered if she ever would for another man. She had always tried to control her feelings for him, had built a wall she thought he could not get through. He stood for things now she could not afford if she were to be a success on the stage. But, despite her effort to resist him, her wall seemed to be breaking down. He put his arms around her, and his lips came down on hers. She no longer resisted, aware of his strength and goodness. She felt the pressure of his body against hers and felt herself responding as she had never allowed herself to before.

Finally he drew back, releasing her, and said, "I don't have anything to offer you but my love. I'll never be rich, but I love you, Amelia, and I always will."

Amelia felt weak, not just in her limbs, which were trembling, but in her spirit as well. She knew it had something to do with the way a woman needs a man. She was physically attracted to Ryan Kildare and always had been. There were other men who were, perhaps, more handsome and certainly many who were more witty and charming, but Ryan had always had the power to touch her. And she felt that now more powerfully than she ever had. She longed to respond, to let herself go, but the struggle she had known for so many years to make something of her life was still there. She still desired fame, money, her name in lights. She knew if she said yes to whatever drove her into the arms of Ryan Kildare, she would be giving up those things.

Painfully, she whispered, "I can't do it, Ryan." She put her hand on his chest and pushed him back, turning away almost forcefully. She fumbled with the key and did not look back. When she stepped inside her apartment, she heard him say, "God wants you, Amelia, and so do I."

Amelia could not bear it. She shut the door without answering and ran into the bedroom. She threw herself across the bed and, without understanding her reaction, began to weep. She was not a crying woman, but something had broken within her, and she knew she would not forget this moment for a long time.

$$\star \quad \star \quad \star \quad \star$$

Rosa did not know why she had agreed to go with Phil to one of his speaking engagements. Lately, he had been accepting invitations to share his testimony and the Gospel at churches and other Christian organizations around the city. His reputation as a fine speaker had grown in the past few months and was enhanced by his status as a public prosecutor and his skill in the courtroom. But something about his Christian talks frightened Rosa. However, when he had called her and asked her out to dinner, she did not know that Phil had received a call from her brother. Jamie had begged Phil to see his sister. "Something's wrong with her, Mr. Winslow. She's well physically, so I don't know what it is. Please try to talk to her. She's scared, and I'm afraid for her."

Phil had said none of this to Rosa, but he himself had been concerned about her. Now as he sat across from her in the car on the way to his speaking engagement, he tried to keep the conversation as light as he could, but he sensed that she was depressed. Finally he asked, "Is that wound still troubling you, Rosa?"

"Oh no." Involuntarily Rosa reached up and touched her chest. "It's all healed up. Dr. Clarkson said it would never give me any problem, but I have nightmares about everything that happened."

"It was a tough time."

"Do you think about things like that after they're over?"

"Why, sure. I can't help it."

Phil noted that Rosa had lost weight and that her face was drawn. "You need to take good care of yourself. Get lots of fresh air and exercise."

Rosa did not answer. She was turned in upon herself, and she spoke only when he asked her a question. Finally, when they reached the church where he was speaking, she said, "I feel funny going into Protestant churches."

"Don't think about that. I don't. I don't care what's on the sign outside. It's what Jesus thinks that counts."

Rosa could not understand talk like this. It frightened her. She said no more but went inside with him. He found her a seat and then went to speak with the pastor.

Rosa was stirred by the song service. They sang a song called "Amazing Grace." She found it very different from the music sung in the church she had grown up in. The people here sang with enthusiasm, and she listened carefully to the words.

> "Amazing grace, how sweet the sound
> That saved a wretch like me.
> I once was lost but now am found,
> Was blind but now I see."

Rosa could make little of the words. *Lost? A wretch like me? What does that mean?*

Finally the song service ended, and Phil got up to preach after an introduction by the pastor.

Rosa sat uncomfortably in her seat. She was accustomed to great ceremonial correctness in church. Everyone knew what was going to happen next in her church, but here she looked around furtively and saw anticipation on many faces. She understood that they had come expecting God, but how did they find

Him? What did they have in their hearts that brought such joy to their expressions?

When Phil began to speak, she felt a surge of pride in him—he was so handsome and strong—and again she thought, *I could never feel about any other man as I do about him. Why can't he feel that way about me?*

Phil had a fine voice and started with, "I have come at the invitation of your pastor to bring you good tidings. Everywhere I speak I have only one message, and that message is that Jesus Christ is the answer to every need. If you are here tonight and you are sick, He is the healer. If you are sad, He can bring joy into your life. If you are bound by some terrible sin, He can bring you out of that bondage. Whatever your need, Jesus is the answer."

It was this sort of thing that disturbed Rosa. How could Jesus do all these things? She had no clear idea in her mind about Jesus. She really had more ideas about Mary, for she had learned from childhood to pray to her. But when Phil even pronounced the name Jesus, he said it as if it were a good name, a strong name. She unconsciously leaned forward, listening with all her might as he spoke.

"In the gospel of Luke, the eighth chapter, there is a very wonderful and a very powerful story. It concerns a woman who had been ill for twelve years. The Scriptures say in the forty-third verse that she had an issue of blood, that she was hemorrhaging. The Scripture also says in that verse that she had spent every penny she had on doctors, and none of them had been able to help her."

Phil looked up then and ran his eyes over the congregation. "I don't know most of you, but I would say to any of you who are in this building, if you have a great need, you've come to the right place. Jesus is present right now, as He always is in every place, to meet that need. I ask you to bow your heads with me, and we will pray that Jesus Christ will walk these aisles, that He will lay His hands on those who need His help, and that we will see those who are helpless made strong in the power of Jesus Christ."

The challenge frightened Rosa. She had never prayed like this, but ever since the shooting, she had felt her weakness and how close she had been—as was everyone—to death. Without thinking, she prayed, *Oh, Jesus, you know I need help. I don't understand any of this, but if you can help me, I ask you to do it.*

After the prayer, Phil continued the story of the woman with the issue of blood. She was a woman without hope. He drew a picture of her life and the fear that was in her, how no one on earth could do anything for her, and then he spoke of Jesus. "This woman had heard of Jesus," he said, "and when she heard He was coming to her town, she went and determined that she would get help for her exhausted, sick body. The streets were probably crowded, for Jesus was a popular man. I imagine she was pushed and shoved around, weak as she was with no man to help her. As far as we know, she had no sons or brothers, but she made her way down the street and finally heard the crowd shouting, 'Jesus is coming! Jesus is coming!' "

Phil looked out, and his eyes caught Rosa's. He held her gaze and smiled gently. "I would like to have been there that day when that poor woman did all she could. She simply reached out as Jesus passed and touched His garment. That's not much to do, is it? It wouldn't do her any good to touch *my* coat, but when she touched the garment of Jesus, the Bible says, 'Immediately her issue of blood stanched.' She was healed in that moment!

"And then a very wonderful thing happened. Jesus said, 'Who touched me?' And the woman came trembling and fell down before him. And there before all those people, she cried out, with tears of joy, I imagine, how by just touching His garment, she had been healed."

Rosa felt tears beginning to form in her eyes. She bowed her head, for she could not face anyone's gaze.

"And Jesus said, 'Daughter, be of good comfort: thy faith hath made thee whole; go in peace.' " Phil's voice seemed very close, and as he continued to speak of Jesus, Rosa knew that God was in this place. She felt a presence she had never felt in all of her life, and she simply sat there, her heart crying out. Finally she heard Phil say, "Jesus is standing beside some of you right now. He wants you to reach out and touch His garment, not His literal garment, of course, but you need to reach out just as that poor, sick woman reached out as best she knew how. Jesus responded to her and He'll respond to you. I want you to reach out with your heart and simply tell Jesus that you are a sinner. I want you to ask Him to cleanse your heart the way He cleansed the body of this woman. I promise you He will do it. That's why He came to this earth. That's why He died on the cross. That's why He's here tonight—and that's why you're here tonight. Will you touch Jesus right now as I pray?"

Rosa was now sobbing uncontrollably. She knew that something outside herself was surrounding her, holding her, and she wept so hard her shoulders shook.

Suddenly she felt a stir and then an arm fell across her shoulders. She looked up and saw Phil through the tears, and his face was filled with compassion. "Tonight is for you, Rosa. Reach out and touch Jesus. It's so easy. He longs to cleanse you and make you His daughter."

And so Rosa bowed her head, and Phil prayed, and she prayed.

And as she prayed, she felt something deep inside that had not been there before. A peace came, and she looked up to Phil and whispered brokenly, "Phil, what is it? What is it inside me that's so different?"

"It's the presence of Jesus Christ, Rosa. You've given yourself to Him, and now you're a child of the King!"

CHAPTER TWENTY-TWO

"I'VE ALWAYS WANTED THE WRONG THINGS"

★ ★ ★ ★

Jamie had turned from the camera he had been cleaning, surprised at Rosa's entrance. Ever since the shooting she had been mostly keeping to herself, but for the past few days he had noticed that a change had come over her. Now as he took in her expression and saw her dark eyes glowing, he felt a gush of relief.

"Hi, sis," he said. "What's up?"

Rosa reached out and ruffled Jamie's hair, a fondness for him coming out as it had not done for some time. "I'm just feeling so wonderfully good, Jamie, and I want everybody else to feel the same way."

"Well, that's good news. I was getting real worried about you, sis."

"I know you were, and you *should* have been worried—I was in terrible shape."

"Do you still have bad dreams about the shooting?"

"No, they're all gone." She smiled then and hugged herself. "I have much better dreams now."

"Well, I'm glad. It was the roughest time any of us ever went through."

"Something good did come out of it, Jamie, and that's what I want to tell you about." Rosa sat down in the chair across from Jamie's desk and paused for a moment. She had put this off for several days and now was apprehensive, but she knew she could not contain what had happened to her. This was her first attempt at trying to explain it.

"I have to tell you something, Jamie," she began carefully. "After I was shot, my whole life seemed to be going from bad to worse. Even before I got hurt, I was unhappy—for such a long time—and I didn't know what the problem was. I had everything money could buy, but I was still restless and dissatisfied."

Jamie listened as Rosa spoke and could not imagine what secret she had come to reveal. Obviously she was tense, and as she paused, he said, "Look, sis, just tell me what it is. No matter what, I can handle it."

"You can, can't you?" Rosa flashed a smile and took a deep breath. "Well, I've become a Christian."

"A Christian? But you've always been a Christian."

"No, I haven't."

"But you were baptized when you were a baby just like me, and you go to Mass now almost every Sunday."

"That's right, Jamie, I've done all those things, but I've just found out that that's not enough. I've always been afraid of those people who talked about Jesus as if He were real to them. It always made me nervous, and I thought they were putting me on and making it up. But they're not, Jamie." As Rosa ran a hand over her glossy black hair, Jamie saw a beauty in her that could not stem from her features or her hair. Jamie was looking into her eyes, and it was like peering into windows where something warm and beautiful was happening on the other side. He could see that her spirit was entirely different, and he listened intently without interrupting as she related how she had cried out to God in the church where Phil had spoken.

Finally she concluded, saying, "It's been so different ever since that moment. As different as night and day, Jamie. I wake up every day full of joy, and I know Jesus is with me until I go to sleep at night. I don't know how to explain it, but it's like nothing I've ever known before. But I know Jesus is real, and I'm learning how to be obedient to Him. The Bible that Phil gave me so long ago didn't mean much to me except for his notes, but now as I read it, it's just like God is speaking out of that book directly to my heart."

Jamie was transfixed and at the same time troubled. "Does this mean you won't be going to Mass anymore? That you're not going to be a Catholic?"

"I'm going to be whatever God tells me to be. If He wants me to stay in the Catholic Church, I'll do it. If He wants me to leave, I'll do that."

"Have you thought about what the folks would say?"

"Sure, I've thought about it a lot, but it's something I have to do." She rose and stood close to her brother. "You're still my friend, aren't you, Jamie, just like always?"

Jamie was not a demonstrative young man, but he suddenly put his arms around Rosa and hugged her tightly. "Sure," he said huskily. "I can see you're happy, and that's all I ever wanted. The folks will just have to understand."

★ ★ ★ ★

As soon as Rosa walked into the family room, both Tony and Maria knew something was on her mind and gave her their full attention. They had been reading, and now they laid their books down as Rosa announced, "I have to talk to you, Mom and Dad."

"Why, what is it?" Tony asked. "Something wrong?"

Rosa drew a chair up closer in front of the two and said, "Please, I want you to do me one favor."

Maria saw the intensity in her daughter and said, "Why, of course. What is it, Rosa?"

"I want you to listen to everything I have to say. It may take a while, and I know you're going to be shocked by it, but please let me say everything, and then I promise to listen to you as long as you want to talk to me."

Tony Morino was apprehensive. "What is it? Are you in some kind of trouble, Rosa?"

"Please, Daddy, just promise me you'll listen."

Tony glanced at Maria and saw the baffled look in her eyes. "Well, sure, Rosa, go ahead. I'll keep still."

Rosa began to speak, talking about her life from way back. She had never completely revealed to her father how unhappy she was, and as well as she could, she kept references to his criminal ties out of it. She spoke of how grateful she was for everything they had done for her, but she also let them know that all the expensive gifts and fancy living had not brought peace to her.

She had to get to the heart of the matter, and as soon as she mentioned Phil Winslow, she saw Tony stiffen. He started to speak, but then blinked his eyes and clamped his lips shut. She could see the resistance in his body, but she went on anyway. She related what had happened to her and how ever since she had cried out to God, a peace had come over her along with a happiness she had never known.

"I know both of you are going to be upset by this. We've always been Catholic, but I have to tell you that it was all just something on the outside for me. It didn't change me. I guess you've seen in the last few years with all my craziness—my drinking, smoking, and running with a wild crowd—that God hadn't done anything in my life. And all that time I was going to confession and Mass, but it didn't change me. Not in my heart. But ever since I called upon Jesus it's been so different."

Maria Morino was transfixed. She could not deny the joy and the reality that seemed to flow out of her daughter. *Why, she's like a new girl*, she thought. *I've never seen her so happy.*

Rosa went on. "I've told Jamie, and I'll tell you, I believe God speaks to people. If He tells me to stay in the Catholic Church, then I will. But if He tells me to leave, then I'll have to obey Him. Now," she said, "it's your turn. Please say anything you'd like to. I love you both and always will."

Tony breathed a sigh of relief. He had been expecting something far worse, although he didn't know what. Now he simply stared at Rosa. To him religion had been merely a matter of form, and when she had spoken of how little it had affected her, her words had gone straight to his heart. His reaction was, *It's never done anything for me either. It hasn't changed me a bit. My religion has all been on the outside, just like Rosa's.*

Maria stood. Of all the family, she was the most faithful to her church, but as she came toward her daughter and Rosa stood up, she embraced her. "I don't understand what it is that's happened to you, but I know it's good. I can see it, and I'm so glad you've found peace with God. Whatever He tells you to do, I want you to obey Him."

Rosa's eyes swam with tears, and she clutched her mother fiercely. "Thanks, Mom," she whispered huskily. "Thanks for always being there to support me."

Tony Morino remained seated, and when Rosa turned to him, waiting for his reply, it was clear he was having a difficult time responding. He looked down at his hands, twisting them and fidgeting in his seat. When he looked up again, he did not say what had first jumped into his mind. He saw the same thing in his daughter his wife saw—a joy and a peace and a contentment that had never been there before. He knew she was different now, and he sat there wondering many things.

"Well, Rosa," he said quietly, "I guess I've got something to tell you, but first I agree with your mother. I don't know about this thing that's happened to you, but I can see it's good. And anything that makes you happy, you know I'm for it, no matter what."

Rosa ran over and threw her arms around Tony. She sat down in his lap, as she had done ever since she was a little girl. Tony enjoyed the embrace and thought, *I wouldn't trade this for anything.*

When Rosa stood up, Tony said, "I've been talking to Doc Clarkson. He sent me to see a specialist."

"Daddy, what's wrong?"

"My heart's not doing too good," Tony said quietly. "I've known it for a long time. Clarkson's been getting me to eat right and exercise, and most of all," he smiled rather grimly, "he said I needed to avoid stress. Well, you know how impossible that is for a man like me doing what I do."

Rosa stood very still, feeling fearful, for she loved her father. She had known he was not well and that he had never taken care of himself, and now she feared worse news was to come.

Tony said abruptly, "I'm getting out of everything, Rosa. I'm stepping down. From now on I'll pursue some of my legitimate business interests, but mostly I'm going to stop and take a look at the world." He got up and walked over to Maria and hugged her. "I'm going to pay attention to this woman here and do all I can," he said simply, "to help my kids. Maybe," he went on with a smile, "you can teach me to ride, and maybe Jamie can teach me to take a picture."

At that moment Rosa Morino felt a wave of pure joy. She threw her arms around him again and then felt her mother hugging her. The three stood there, and finally Rosa said, "Dad, go tell Jamie what you've just told me. He needs to hear it."

★ ★ ★ ★

Amelia had accepted Rosa's invitation to meet her for lunch, but the food they'd ordered had not been touched. Amelia had sat transfixed as Rosa, with her eyes glowing and words tumbling over her lips, poured out the story of her conversion and how things had changed so drastically in her family. Finally Rosa took a deep breath and gave a half laugh. "Well, that's what has happened to me, Amelia, and I'm so happy."

Amelia was touched. She had always liked Rosa, and now she reached over and covered the girl's hand with her own. "I'm glad for you, Rosa. I can see that there's something in you that wasn't there before."

Rosa smiled, then asked quietly, "Amelia, can I ask you something?"

"Why, of course, what is it?"

"Why didn't you ever tell me about salvation—the new birth, as Phil called it. I didn't know anything about it. I was lost and on my way to hell, and you never said a word to me. Why is that?"

"Isn't it obvious?"

"No, not to me."

Amelia became agitated. She put her fork down and then placed both hands on the table, pressing them hard against the cloth. She did not answer for a moment. Then she looked up and said, "I didn't tell you about it because I don't have it."

"You're not a Christian?"

"No."

"But I thought—" Rosa broke off in confusion. "You were raised by missionaries."

"Being in a Christian home doesn't make you a Christian— any more than being in a garage makes you an automobile."

Rosa stared at Amelia. "I don't understand. How could you live with people like Phil and like your parents must be and not give your heart to Jesus?"

"I don't know, Rosa." Amelia sat there, and many things passed through her mind. Memories from her past came floating before her. She remembered when she was just a little girl listening to her uncle Barney preaching—how the words he had spoken about Jesus had broken her heart. She had gone forward and given her heart to Him—or so she thought. But as she grew older, she had resisted God at every turn and decided He wasn't for her. Maybe her commitment as a child wasn't real, or maybe she had willingly turned away. She was never sure, but she knew now that her life might have been very different indeed if she had continued to live her life for Him. Now she felt it was too late. She had blown any chance she had of making things right with God.

"I've always wanted the wrong things, Rosa," she whispered. "The world's got a hold on me, and I can't break away. All my life I've run from God. Phil calls me heaven's fugitive, and . . ." Here Amelia's lips trembled, and she had to pause for a moment. Finally she shook her head and rose. "I guess I always will be. I'm happy for you, Rosa, but I'm a lost cause."

★ ★ ★ ★

Leo Marx stared out the window but really saw nothing. His mind, always quick and impulsive, leaped from point to point. He ignored Jake Prado, who stood behind him like a shadow, and when he turned, his eyes glared with rage.

"Jake, they got me. That DA and his assistant!"

"You mean Winslow?"

"Sure. He's been in my hair for too long, and he's sharper than anybody I've ever been up against."

"What's he got?"

"He's got evidence is what he's got. I got a call from him thirty minutes ago. He's got it on paper, black and white, enough to put me away."

"What did he want?"

"He wants me to turn state's evidence. He says he'll get me a lighter sentence if I'll do that."

Jake Prado stared at his boss. "You'd never do a thing like that. You ain't no stoolie, Leo."

Leo Marx gripped his hands together. He stared at them as if they did not belong to him, and then flung them apart in a wild gesture. He was usually a careful, guarded man, but now facing a long sentence, he cast all caution aside.

"Okay, there's one way out of this, and we're going to take it."

"What's that, Leo?"

"We're going to get that evidence back. If I can get it, he can do all he wants to, but he's got no case. Black marks on paper is all it is, but it's life or death to me, so we've got to get it."

"Do you want me to bust into his office? I can get Sammy. He can open any safe ever made."

"No, he wouldn't be fool enough to leave it where we could find it. He's got to give it to us."

"Give it to us!" Prado stared at Marx. "Why would he do that?"

"He'd do it," Marx said slowly, "to get something from us that he wants more than he wants me in jail."

Jake Prado was shrewd, but he could not understand this. "What do you mean? What have we got that he wants?"

"Nothing now, but we're *going* to." Marx lifted his eyes and held Prado's gaze. "We're gonna snatch his sister, that nightclub singer."

"Kidnap her?"

"That's right."

Jake Prado was a tough individual. He had killed before, but this plan shook his confidence. "You know what they do to kidnappers? It's the death penalty, Leo."

"It's the death penalty for me if I get twenty years in the pen or even more, and don't think you'll get off, Jake. They've got the goods on all of us. You included. It's the only way. We grab his sister, he gives us the papers, and that's it."

"What if he won't?"

"He will. I had some people looking at these two. They're real close, Jake. His own flesh and blood. Don't worry. Once we get her, he'll do anything to save her."

Jake nodded slowly. "You're the boss, Leo. How do you want to do it?"

"It won't be any problem, Jake. Her name is Amelia Winslow, and she's working every night at the Orchid Club. Stake her out, and you can either take her there or in her apartment. Probably coming out of the club would be better, but I'll leave that to you."

"Where do you want to hold her?"

"We'll take her out to the farm. No one knows about that place."

Jake Prado was a simple-minded man who attacked one problem at a time. He nodded. "I'll do it, Leo."

"Call me when you've got her out there, Jake."

★ ★ ★ ★

As Amelia emerged from the Orchid Club, the doorman smiled and said, "Good night, Miss Winslow."

"Good night, Kenny."

Kenny walked to the curb and opened the door of the cab that had pulled up. He waited until Amelia stepped inside, then shut it firmly and stepped back. The cab pulled away, and Kenny walked back to take his position.

Amelia gave her address to the cabdriver and said, "You're new, aren't you? Usually Kelly takes me home."

"His night off, miss."

"Oh, I see."

The cab moved down the street, and Amelia slumped back against the seat with her eyes closed. She was tired, and she had struggled with her decision about *All for Love* until she was weary of it. Sid, her agent, thought she was crazy. His hair practically stood on end when she had told him she was having trouble deciding.

"Having trouble!" he had shouted. "What's trouble? You'll make tons of dough and be the brightest star on Broadway. You call that trouble? Come on, wake up, Amelia!"

Amelia tried to put the thoughts out of her mind, but they would not leave. Suddenly the cab swerved, and she was thrown to one side. Looking out the window, she saw they had pulled into an alley. "What are you doing?" she cried out. She hardly had time to think as the door opened and she was roughly seized by her wrists and dragged out of the car. Panicking now, she opened her lips and screamed, "Help!" But she only had time for that one cry before a blunt object struck her in the temple, and a thousand brilliant, dancing lights exploded across her vision. Then she knew nothing.

CHAPTER TWENTY-THREE

AMELIA'S CHOICE

★ ★ ★ ★

The sun dropped slowly behind the low-lying hills in the west, and for one moment shadow and light seemed to stand still. Rosa held Boadicea's reins firmly, looking out on the rolling countryside and admiring the pearl-colored air that surrounded them.

"It's been a fine day, Phil," she said, turning to meet her companion's eyes.

Rosa had invited Phil to go riding with her at the Morino estate, and he had gladly accepted the invitation. The two of them had ridden hard until both horses were now ready to move more slowly. They slowed their mounts to a walk, and he turned and smiled at her. As the years had passed, thoughts of Rosa had never left Phil's mind and heart, and now as he studied her face, he knew with a certainty that his life would never be complete without this woman in it. He met her glance and was struck anew by her physical beauty. She had a teasing expression in her eyes and a youthful air. She also presented a provocative challenge, which for all her youth made her a complex and unfathomable woman. Color ran freshly across her cheeks as she studied him. She drew away the curtain of reserve, and at that moment her face graphically registered the light and shadows of her feelings. Phil saw the wonder and fullness of heart that flowed in her. He was aware that her search for love had come to an end, and he knew that he loved her.

The thought stirred him, but it was not new. It had been coming on for some time. He said nothing until they reached the stables and let O'Connor take the horses, and then as they walked slowly back toward his car, he paused and turned toward her. She turned to him quickly, her eyes beautiful and dark in the deepening twilight.

Rosa, too, was lost in her own strange and humble thoughts. As he drew her close she saw the scar on his temple and noted the breadth and regularity of his face. She lifted her face and met his lips with hers, clinging to him with a fierce, quick, and loving spirit. She was not quite crying when she kissed him, but an emotion so strong filled her she could not explain it. She only knew that this was right and that she had found a harbor for her love. When he pulled back and searched her face, she smiled at him with tears glistening in her eyes, knowing that her girlhood and all the things that belonged to it were gone, and she came now as a mature woman ready for love.

"I've loved you since I was fifteen years old, Phil," she whispered.

Her words caught at Phil, and he held her lightly in his arms. "I don't know when I started loving you. You were just a child to me then, but you're not a child any longer, Rosa. You're a woman."

"Do you love me, Phil?"

The question was simple, childlike. Rosa indeed had a childlike spirit, which had increased since she had found God. Phil tightened his arms. "Yes," he said. "I love you, and I'll never love anyone else."

"Then that's enough. Whatever happens, we'll have each other." She lifted her lips, and he kissed her again, more gently this time, and the two turned and walked into the gathering darkness.

★ ★ ★ ★

After Phil reached home, he found he could not stop thinking about Rosa. His life had changed, and he knew he would never again be alone. As he started to undress and get ready for bed, he marveled at how things had worked out. A sheer stream of pleasure ran through him as he recalled their evening together, and even more as he thought of the love that shone in her dark, eloquent eyes.

He sat down on the bed to remove his shoes but paused when the phone rang. Reaching over, he picked it up. "Hello?"

"Winslow?"

"This is Phil Winslow. Who's this?"

"This is Leo Marx."

Instantly Phil grew wary and concentrated on the voice. "What do you want, Marx?"

"I want the papers you've got that can send me to the pen."

"You're not likely to get them."

"Oh, I don't know. I think I might."

"If that's all you wanted to talk about—"

"Wait a minute. Don't hang up. There's one more thing. I've got somebody here that wants to talk to you."

"I'm not interested."

"I think you will be. It's your sister."

A cold rush of adrenaline shot through Phil Winslow. It was like the time on a hunt in Africa when he had looked down to see a black mamba rearing up at his feet ready to strike. He had been momentarily paralyzed then, and now was much the same. "Marx, you'd better—"

"I get the papers, you get your sister. It's that's simple. Here, I'll let her talk to you to show you we mean business."

Phil grasped the phone harder as he heard Amelia's voice. "Phil, don't give it to them!"

"Are you all right, Amelia?"

"Never mind me. Don't let them make you do this!"

And then there were sounds of a scuffle, and Marx's voice came back. "I'm not fooling, Winslow. If you don't give us the papers, I'll send your sister back to you one finger at a time. I'll call later to tell you where to bring them."

The phone slammed down, jarring Phil. He sat there blankly, his mind still momentarily paralyzed by what he had heard.

"I'll send her back to you one finger at a time."

One thing Phil had learned about Leo Marx and others of his kind—they were men who were missing normal human compassion. It would not give Leo Marx any sleepless nights to murder one more person. Phil knew, without a doubt, that Marx would do it.

He slowly put the receiver back on the hook, then sat for a few moments. Finally he knelt beside his bed and began to pray, silently at first and then aloud, his voice choked with fear.

★   ★   ★   ★

"You think he'll come through? Winslow, I mean?" Jake Prado poured himself a drink out of a dark bottle and downed it. He flinched as the liquor hit his stomach; then he poured another. "He's a pretty straight arrow, this Winslow guy."

Above their heads, Amelia peered down at the two men through a crack in the pine-board ceiling. She had regained consciousness before reaching this apparently abandoned farm and had been hauled inside and shoved into this room. She had heard the hasp and the lock on the outside and had quickly discovered that the one window in the room was barred. It had evidently been used to imprison someone before.

She had been stunned by the rapidity of all that had happened, and she had sat down on the single chair and gazed hopelessly around the room, which was illuminated by an oil lamp.

She had heard voices below her, then noticed light coming from the crack in the floor. She had knelt down and peered through the crack at the two men, listening carefully to their conversation.

She heard one man call the other one Leo. Leo answered roughly, "We gotta have those documents, and this is the only way to get 'em."

Amelia knew of Leo Marx from what she had read in the papers and what she had learned from Phil. She assumed this was the same man. He was as evil as Al Capone—not as famous but just as vicious. Now as she listened it became clear from the men's conversation that there was no hope of mercy from these two.

The men fell silent as they drank, and then the one called Jake said, "Leo, even if you get the stuff from her brother, this woman's a problem."

"I know that, Jake."

"What I mean is she's seen us. She knows who we are. I can just see us in a courtroom and her pointing her finger at us saying, 'These are the men that kidnapped me.' You know what that means, Leo."

"Yeah, but she can't testify if she's dead."

The coldness of Leo Marx's voice ran through Amelia. She knelt there paralyzed as Marx said calmly, "We make Winslow bring us the papers, and then, Jake, we feed both of them to the fish."

Amelia quietly got to her feet and stood there in the amber corona of the lamp. The light twisted her shadow into a tortured shape on the floor and painted odd yellow shapes on the walls. Amelia was a strong young woman, but now all of her strength seemed to have evaporated. There was no hope at all. Even if Phil brought what Marx wanted, he would still kill her and Phil too. Somehow the thought of Phil's death seemed worse than her own.

Her knees were suddenly weak as she thought of death. She had always avoided thinking about her own demise, but now it was here, and she could not escape it. She started to pace the floor, but soon the fear became greater than her physical strength. She slumped down on the bed and buried her face in the musty pillow, rank with various odors, but she hardly noticed. Finally she fell into a fitful sleep.

She must have slept for at least a couple of hours, for she remembered parts of several upsetting dreams, but Amelia had no watch to know for sure what time it was. All she knew was that the darkness outside was no deeper than the darkness in her own soul.

As time crept by, hope fled, and for once in her life Amelia Winslow was alone with herself—and with God.

She had always scorned deathbed confessions. She thought they were phony and had always vowed she would never do such a thing herself. But as time passed, and she knew that within a matter of hours she would be dead, something changed within her. She began thinking of words her father had spoken in a sermon on the text "Come unto me, all ye that labour and are heavy laden, and I will give you rest."

Somehow those words came alive, and she slowly rolled off the bed and fell on her knees. Words would not come, and her thoughts ran like quicksilver, wondering wildly.

Finally she gasped, "Oh, God, I can't bring you anything. I've run from you all of my life, and I've never loved you, but I'm going to die. I've always thought it was only cowards who would pray when death faced them, and that means I'm just a coward, but I do need you, O God. . . ."

★ ★ ★ ★

Johnny Pesky was a small man, his movements quick. His eyes darted around Ryan Kildare's office. He had once been a jockey, until his weight and lack of skill caught up with him. From there he had turned to crime, as had most of the young men he had grown up with.

Ryan smiled at Pesky and said, "Sit down, Johnny. What's on your mind?"

"I can't sit. I can't sit down," Pesky said nervously. He even talked faster than most people. He walked over to the window and peered out, snapping his fingers and shaking his head. "I shouldn't have come here. I shouldn't have come." He had a habit of repeating his sentences, especially when he was nervous, as he appeared to be now.

"What's the trouble, Johnny?"

"It ain't my trouble. It's yours. It's all your trouble."

Ryan turned his head to one side. "What does that mean?" he said.

"You gotta promise me something, Kildare. Promise that whatever I tell you, it don't get outta this room—not ever, you hear me? Not outta this room!"

"Sure. Privileged communication. What kind of trouble are you talking about?"

"I got your word, then? You gonna keep all this to yourself? Especially about me."

"All right. You know my word's good."

"Yeah, I know it is. I wouldn't be here except—well, when you pulled my brother out of that spot he was in last month, I felt grateful. I still do. He's a good kid. I don't want him to go the way I'm going."

Ryan had been able to help Johnny's brother Timothy out of a rather difficult legal situation. The boy had been involved in one of Johnny's deals. It wasn't Johnny's intention for his brother to get in trouble, but he was caught and charged. Kildare got him free with no sentence, and Johnny was indeed grateful.

Suddenly Pesky shook his shoulders rapidly, like a dog shaking off after a swim, stepped closer, and whispered furtively, though there was no possibility of any hearer except Kildare. "I'll tell you what," he said. "That friend of yours, Winslow?"

"You mean Phil Winslow?"

"Yeah, yeah, yeah, the DA's assistant."

"What about him?"

"Look, I work for Leo Marx, you know that. I ain't proud of it, but that's what I do. Well, here's what's comin' down, Kildare. Leo's snatched Winslow's sister."

"You mean Amelia?"

"Yeah, that's the one. The canary that sings in the nightclubs. That's her. That's her."

"Leo's kidnapped her?"

"That's right. Winslow's got something he wants, and he's holding the dame until he gets it from him."

"How do you know all this?"

"I was in on it, but I didn't know what they was up to. I just drove the car was all I done. Then they grabbed her and put her in the car. Knocked her out cold. All I done was drive 'em. That's all I done. You gotta believe me."

"I believe you, Johnny, but it's a bad spot for you. Anybody involved in a kidnapping is in big trouble."

"I know that. I'm gettin' out. Goin' to Chicago. I got friends there. Just leave me out of it."

Ryan Kildare's mind worked rapidly. "Tell me everything you

know about it, Johnny, and I'll keep you out of it. I'll even help you get away."

"All right. Here's the deal. There's an old farmhouse twenty miles out of the city. . . ."

★ ★ ★ ★

Ryan stared across the desk at Phil. He had called Winslow, and the two had met in Phil's office at the courthouse. Ryan had poured out the story he'd heard from Johnny Pesky, without revealing his source. "It'll take a miracle to get her back. According to what my informant told me, that farmhouse is out in the middle of nowhere in the middle of a big empty field. The first sign they see of police moving in, they'll kill her. You know they will."

"Where is it? Where are they keeping her?" Phil said tersely.

Ryan shook his head. "I can't tell you unless you promise me something."

"Promise what? This is no time for games, Ryan."

"I know that. I'm going with you. That's all. Give me your word on that, and we can do something."

Phil nodded quickly. "Sure. It'll be you and me."

"It'll have to be that way. According to my informant's story"—Ryan pulled out a map and laid it on the desk—"this big farmhouse is right here just north of Tarrytown. Look, I've drawn a plan according to what he told me about the house. It's out in the middle of this big field. There's a barn out here, you see, about fifty yards from the house, but she's on the second floor of the house, and the door is barred and there are bars on the window."

Phil studied Ryan's rough sketch of the farmhouse and its environs and finally asked, "How many men have they got?"

"My informant says it changes. They use this big barn out here to store liquor before moving it into the city in smaller loads. There's always two men on guard outside, but they always go into the house at noon to eat."

"The guard will be closer at night."

"I think so."

"It looks like you and I will have to go in at high noon, Ryan."

The two men stared at each other, and Ryan said, "If I ever wanted to pray about anything, this is it."

"All right, let's pray now."

The two men got on their knees and laid the matter before God, and when they got up, Phil asked Ryan, "Why are you doing this?"

"I think you know. I love Amelia. Have for a long time. Does that bother you?"

Phil clapped the other man on the shoulder. "Not a bit. Come on, brother, let's do it."

CHAPTER TWENTY-FOUR

A HEAVENLY FUGITIVE NO MORE!

★ ★ ★ ★

Dawn brought sunlight, fresh and sharp, through the windows of Amelia's prison room. It flashed against the panes, cutting long, sharp shadows against the dusty patch of carpet. Amelia stood at the window looking out on the farm field surrounded by groves of trees. A breeze came through the barred window, stirring the musty, pungent odors of the room.

A queer twinge stirred in her as she closed her eyes and thought about the events of the night. Something had changed in her—an inexpressible peace had filled her. She knew it was the same peace she had seen in Rosa when they had last talked. Now as she thought back on her own life, there was regret and some grief and sorrow, but it was all as if it had happened to someone else. She no longer felt the pain.

She turned from the window and stood beside the bed where she had knelt for so long in the darkness. She had cried out to God, had shed tears on the faded, threadbare sheets. She could not remember everything she had said to God, but did remember crying out, *"Please, God, help me!"* And she also remembered calling out for Jesus. At His name she had suddenly felt the fear dissipate and had slumped to the floor sobbing quietly, not from fear but from an incredible release that had swept over her.

For a long time she stood quietly, and her thoughts went to her parents. "I would like them to know that I finally made it into God's family," she murmured. "They'll be so happy to know that—if I can only get out of this alive."

The man called Jake came up with a plate of badly cooked eggs, burned bacon, and half a pot of coffee. He stared at her and said nothing for a moment, then muttered, "Your brother is coming to deliver the stuff sometime late this afternoon."

Amelia said nothing to him. She suspected this man would be the one to execute both her and her brother. He left the food and went back downstairs. She ate half of it, then sat on the bed and waited.

The morning passed slowly, and she spent much of that time praying. She had no Bible, but she was soaked in the Word of God, having heard it all of her life. It amazed her how much of it came back to her memory now at her hour of desperate need. She prayed simply, "God, keep Phil safe. Don't let anything happen to him." Almost as an afterthought, she also prayed, "And, Lord, help me. I don't deserve any help, but I want to serve you if it's your will for me to live."

When the sun was directly overhead and the shadows had disappeared, she knew it was midday. She heard one of the men—not the one who had brought her breakfast but another— call from outside. "Hey, Ed, you and Sammy come on in. The grub's ready." Looking out the window toward the barn, she saw the two men, both armed with pistols in their belts and rifles in the crooks of their arms, turn and walk toward the house. They had been there all morning and, she suspected, all night. But now they disappeared under the roof that sheltered the front porch. Their feet clumped across the wooden floor below, and she could clearly hear dishes rattling and someone humming.

A few minutes after the men had entered, Amelia heard a sound outside the window and turned to look. She thought it might be a bird, but instead she saw a man's cap rising just outside the window, and her heart leaped into her throat. She could not imagine what one of Marx's men would be doing, and she watched with trepidation.

And then suddenly a face appeared, and Amelia gasped, "Ryan!"

It was Kildare on a ladder. He was wearing a soft cap pulled down firmly over his head and dark clothing. He pressed his finger to his lips, urgently indicating for her to keep silent. She moved toward the window and whispered, "Ryan, what are you doing here?"

"Getting you out. Phil's waiting out there. We've got to hurry. We've only got until those men finish eating."

"But how will I get out?"

"Look." Reaching behind him, he pulled up a pair of heavy red-handled bolt cutters. Quickly he put the jaws over the bottom of one bar and strained to pull them together. At first he seemed to make no impression, and then there was a distinct *twang* and the bar was free. He quickly snapped the two remaining bars and moved upward until he had cut all three of them. "Come on," he said, hooking the cutters on his belt.

"How did you get here, Ryan?"

"We hid in the barn last night. We knew the guards would go in at noon. Come on, there's no time to explain."

Amelia awkwardly climbed out of the window. Ryan was already halfway down, reaching up to steady her. Clinging to the edge of the long ladder he had placed against the house, she started creeping down. She had taken no more than five or six steps on the rungs when a noise came from overhead. She looked up startled and saw Jake leaning out of the window.

"Hey, you, stop right there!" he shouted.

Amelia froze and Jake laughed. "I don't know who that is, but he's gonna wish he hadn't found his way here."

Amelia looked down and saw Ryan reach under his coat and pull out a gun. Jake saw it also, and as she glanced up, she saw him take aim at Ryan. Jake was pulling the trigger when the flat crack of a rifle broke the silence. The bullet caught Jake in the chest and drove him backward out of sight. Amelia heard his body crash to the floor, and then she heard Phil yelling, "Come on, get down from there!"

Amelia scrambled down the ladder, and Ryan grasped her as she reached the bottom. "This way," he said.

Shots began to ring out, and Ryan pulled her down to the ground. "We've got to get to the barn," he said. "They're firing out that window. Phil will keep them busy. Come on."

Amelia got up and ran awkwardly, following Ryan around the corner of the house. She took one glance at Phil, who was behind a walnut tree. Bullets were chipping off the bark, and he was returning the fire furiously.

The barn was at least fifty yards away, and Amelia had difficulty running in her high heels. Once she looked around and saw Phil running toward her, bent over. A bullet whistled over her head, and then Ryan said, "Here, get inside." Amelia stumbled into the gloomy interior of the barn while Ryan returned fire with his handgun. "Come on, Phil!" he yelled, and seconds later Phil stumbled in, falling flat.

"Phil, are you hurt?"

"No, I'm okay," Phil said. "Come on, get behind that beam over there. They're going to be rushing us."

"We can't hold them off for long," Ryan said.

"No, that's why I got this." Reaching into the deep pocket of his coat, Phil pulled out a strange-looking weapon. "It's a flare gun," he told Amelia. "The police are waiting until they're sure you're clear." He ran quickly to the other end of the barn, stepped outside, lifted the flare gun, and pulled the trigger. As the flare hissed into the sky he ducked back inside. "Now we just have to hold out for a few minutes."

Amelia stared at Phil, who was peering out the door. "Phil, how did you know where to find me?"

"You can thank Ryan for that."

There was no time for explanations, for Leo Marx's henchmen were pouring slugs into the barn.

"No more rifle bullets," Phil said, throwing the rifle down and pulling out his handgun. "The police better get here fast."

Only a few seconds later they heard a shout from outside. "Look out, here come the cops!"

"They're here!" Ryan yelled. He ran to the door and looked out. "Marx's men are running."

"They won't get far," Phil said grimly. "We've got fifty men surrounding this place. They'll all be coming in now that they've seen the flare."

He walked over to Amelia and halted. His face was grim, and lines of strain marred his cheeks. "Are you all right, sis?"

"Yes."

"They didn't hurt you, did they?"

"I just have a lump on my head—but worse than that is they were going to kill me, and you too." She turned to Ryan, who was standing to one side saying nothing. She walked over to him and said, "You found me, Ryan?"

"I think God must have had something to do with it." He explained how he had located her and then said, "I think it's the end for Leo Marx and his bunch. Was he inside?"

"Yes, he and Jake—the man you shot at—but he might be dead."

"Leo might be better off if he were," Ryan said slowly.

Amelia reached out and took his hand. "You came for me."

"Yes, I did."

"I've got something to tell you. Something you'll like."

"Tell me now."

"All right. You know I've been a fugitive from God for years. That's what Phil always called me, but last night when I thought I was going to die, I cried out to God. I've always thought that was a poor way to treat God, to run from Him until you got into trouble. But I cried anyway and something happened, Ryan. I've always heard my father's and my uncle's stories about how people were changed. I saw Rosa get changed, and last night it happened to me. Jesus Christ came into my heart. I'm afraid I've got a long way to go, but I'm on my way."

Ryan stepped forward and took her in his arms. She clung to him almost desperately, and he whispered, "We'll go together, Amelia."

★ ★ ★ ★

Leo Marx's gang was annihilated in the gunfight with the police. Prado and the other lieutenants who had been in the house were all killed, and Marx was captured. The charge of kidnapping would lead him to the electric chair.

Now that his sister was safe, Phil's concerns shifted to Rosa and their life together. He took time off work to go to her house. She met him at the door but closed it behind her, saying, "Let's walk outside for a time."

"All right."

The two walked along the shaded drive of the Morino estate, and finally Phil said, "I want to marry you, Rosa, but it's going to be hard because of your father."

Rosa turned and put her hands on his chest. Her eyes were bright with hope as she said, "He's getting out of the rackets, Phil. He's worried about Jamie, and he's sick. He may not have much time left, and he wants to spend it with his family."

Phil listened, and a load seemed to come off his shoulders. "That makes things a lot easier. Someday I'd like to run for district attorney. It'll be a hard fight, and if I win, it'll be even harder. Do you think you could be a politician's wife?"

Rosa reached up, put her hands on the back of his neck, and pulled his head down. "I can be *your* wife," she whispered, and then she kissed him.

★ ★ ★ ★

Amelia's agent, Sid Menkin, had done everything but get down on his knees to get her to accept the lead role in *All for Love*. He had met with her three times, and the last time, Ryan Kildare was with her. "Talk some sense into her, Mr. Kildare," Sid pleaded. "She's throwing away a fortune!"

"I can't do a thing with her." Ryan smiled. "You have no idea how stubborn this woman is."

"You might as well give up, Sid," Amelia said. "I'm not going to be in that play."

The short, round man stared at her, sighed, then drew his shoulders together in a gesture of defeat. "You're crazy," he muttered. "You're totally, completely crazy." He left, moaning to himself, and Ryan studied Amelia.

"Are you sure this is what you want to do?"

"It's what you want me to do, isn't it?" Amelia smiled.

"Yes."

He came over, took her hand, and held it. "I don't have anything to offer you, Amelia. I've devoted my life to working for the poor, which means I'll never again be a rich lawyer."

"That doesn't matter to me, Ryan." Amelia put her hand on

his cheek. "All that matters is having you beside me. I'm so happy!" She thought about her life fleetingly and then smiled. "I'm not a heavenly fugitive anymore. God has found me . . . and so have you."

COURAGEOUS WOMEN OVERCOME DIFFICULT STRUGGLES

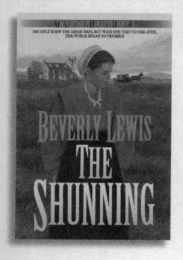

THE HERITAGE OF LANCASTER COUNTY: Her World's Turned Upside-Down!

In the quaint Amish community of Hickory Hollow, time stands still while cherished traditions and heartfelt beliefs continue to flourish. When Katie Lapp uncovers a satin baby gown, buried deep in her mamma's attic trunk, the tranquility of her life is shattered. Will the community of the People bring her to redemption, or will her world unravel, leaving in its wake a hopeless furrow of pain?

The Shunning by Beverly Lewis

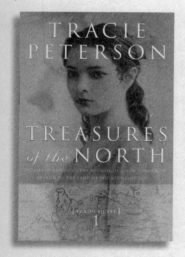

YUKON QUEST: A Series of Renewed Hope

Torn between her desire to obey her parents and her terror of the man they've arranged for her to marry, young Grace decides to escape to Alaska. With "gold fever" and the call of the wild drawing a host of characters to the frozen north, she encounters others who believe they can build a future of hope and peace with the growing opportunities Alaska offers. Will they ever truly escape the pasts that threaten them?

Treasures of the North by Tracie Peterson

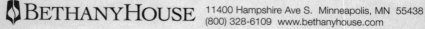